WISH YOU WERE MINE

ALEXA RIVERS

Wish You Were Mine.

Copyright © 2024 by Alexa Rivers

All rights reserved.

No part of this book may be reproduced in any form or by any electronic or mechanical means, including information storage and retrieval systems, without written permission from the author, except for the use of brief quotations in a book review.

This book is a work of fiction. All people, places, events and organizations within it are fictional or are used fictitiously. Any resemblance to real people, places, events and organizations is entirely coincidental.

Cover design by Shannon Passmore.

Cover photography by Lindee Robinson.

Editing and proofreading by Paper Poppy Editorial and Proof It Write.

*To every girl
who's had to wait
for an oblivious man
to see what's right
in front of him.*

PROLOGUE — NINE YEARS AGO

SUMMER

"Are you sure you want to do this?" Bailey asked as we wove between people, making our way to the makeshift dance floor at Drunken Destiny. Bodies writhed as our graduating class let loose, celebrating the end of our school career and the beginning of whatever came next.

"I'm certain." Despite the nerves that rioted in my gut. "I've waited long enough. It's time."

I was officially no longer a high school student. I was old enough to vote, drink, and have sex. I was a woman now, not a girl, and it was about time Asher Heaton realized it.

Bailey sipped her juice. "How are you going to ask him?"

"I'm going to get straight to the point. I've been practicing in the mirror."

She rolled her eyes, her mouth curling in a smile. "Of course you have."

I drank a few mouthfuls of raspberry vodka, my eyes finding Asher in the semi-dark. After years of seeing him at nearly every family gathering, recognizing his profile was easy. He stood beside my older brother, Liam.

His best friend.

I couldn't see Asher's face, but I knew it was gorgeous. Square, but with a pointed chin. Dark eyes and rich chocolatey colored hair. Then there were those broad shoulders. I'd spent so much time staring at his back that I could practically draw them blindfolded.

"So...are you going to do it?" Bailey asked, perhaps concerned by the fact I hadn't moved an inch. "If you don't want to, that's fine. There's no rush."

I brushed my hair away from my face. I'd left it loose because Bailey said it made me look older.

"I'm just preparing myself," I said.

After all, it wasn't easy to tell a man you'd loved him since the dawn of time. Or for the past few years, at least. Although I'd decided not to use the word "love", in case that scared him off. But that didn't make the prospect of spilling my guts to him any less intimidating.

"You've got this." Bailey hugged me. "You're stunning. You're smart. You're kind. He'd be lucky to have you."

Aww.

"I love you," I told her.

"Love you too, beautiful. Go and get him."

I straightened my back and clasped the bottle more tightly. I took one step, and then another. Out of the corner of my eye, I saw Sam from school ask Bailey to dance. She set her glass aside and took his arms as they began to move.

Another step.

I made my way slowly around the people watching the action. Neither Liam nor Asher were on the dance floor. In fact, they were hardly paying the dancers any attention at all.

A guy tripped in front of me, and I darted out of the way

as he caught himself in a drunken stumble and managed not to fall. I waited for him to get out of the way before continuing. Finally, I stood before Liam and Asher, my heart beating a mile a minute.

"Um, hey." I cleared my throat, and they both turned to me.

A smile creased Liam's face. He was my third oldest brother, after the twins—Max and Nate—and he fell solidly in the midzone as far as brotherly protectiveness went. Nate and Connor were the most protective, while Max and Toby tended to think I could take care of myself. Liam sat somewhere in between.

"Hey, Summer," he said. "You're officially done with school. How's it feel?"

"Pretty good," I admitted. "Although I'm still going to be a student."

He shrugged. "It's a bit different though, isn't it?"

"Yeah." I glanced at Asher, and he sent me his charming, toothy smile. "Liam, can I talk to Ash alone for a minute?"

"Sure." Liam looked surprised but didn't argue.

"Thanks." Before Asher could protest or Liam could change his mind, I took his hand and pulled him toward the corner. Actually, this would probably be best done outside. There would be less risk of being interrupted or overheard.

"Do you mind going outside with me?" I asked.

"That's fine."

He disentangled his fingers from mine but followed close behind. A shiver of awareness rippled up my spine. He was so much bigger than me. Wider through the shoulders, with strong arms I'd dreamed of having wrap around me. He always smelled of the woods, and I longed to bury my face in his chest and breathe him in.

We left through the main entrance, and I slipped around the side of the pub, into an alley between Drunken Destiny and the neighboring building. I shivered again, this time with anticipation.

Asher shrugged off his jacket and offered it to me. "You're cold."

I bit my lip. Of all the times I'd imagined myself wearing his clothes, it had never been out of practicality. More of a silly fantasy where he instructed me to walk around naked except for his T-shirt.

Still, this was romantic because it was real. Even if I wasn't actually cold. I took the jacket and slipped my arms into the sleeves, inhaling his scent.

"What's up?" he asked, putting his hands in his pockets.

"I...' I gathered all my courage and took a breath. "I like you."

His mouth quirked. "I'm glad to hear it."

I rolled my eyes. Men are so dense. "No, I mean I like you. I think you're really handsome, and maybe we could date."

The last words ran together in a nearly incomprehensible stream.

His eyebrows knitted together. "Summer—"

"I'm eighteen now," I blurted out, cutting him off. I couldn't read his expression, and since he hadn't swept me into his arms, I was scared of what he might say. "I'm not at school anymore. I'm an adult."

He winced and tugged his hand through his hair. "You know I care about you."

My stomach sank. Somehow, that didn't sound good. "I do."

"I know you used to have a crush on me," he said.

I fought the urge to bury my face in my hands as humiliation swamped me. He knew?

"I thought you'd gotten over it," he continued. "I'm sorry, Summer, but I don't see you that way."

I looked down. There was absolutely no way I could gaze into his eyes as he crushed my heart. To my mortification, tears welled in my eyes. I blinked rapidly, and tried to swallow but there was an enormous lump in my throat.

"Have you tried?" I asked quietly. "Maybe you've just never tried to look at me that way, but if you do, you'll see how good we can be together."

He put his hand on my shoulder, and I immediately shook it off. "I'm really sorry, but it's not going to happen. To me, you're Liam's little sister. That's just the way it is."

Then, I couldn't stop the tears. They streaked down my face, and I felt every inch a girl and not at all a woman.

He reached for me. "Don't cry, Summer."

"Don't touch me," I sniffed, pulling away from him.

For five years, I'd had a crush on him.

I always pictured us sharing a happily ever after in Destiny Falls once I was old enough.

What a joke.

1

———

SUMMER

As I listened to my date, Ben, explain his job—something for an accountancy firm that wasn't actually accounting—the door at the Destiny Peak Resort's onsite restaurant swung inward and a pretty brunette stepped through.

I took a moment to appreciate her dress, which was a classy black number, and started to turn back to my date. But then the man behind the brunette caught my attention and my stomach flipped over.

Asher goddamn Heaton.

Could I not go on a first date without the object of my unrequited affection showing up to torment me?

I sighed. Suddenly, it didn't matter that the restaurant was warm and cozy with lovely music playing in the background and the scent of gourmet food permeating the air. Nor did it matter that Ben was good-looking in a generic kind of way, and that he'd treated me with kindness and respect.

Because if Asher was here, our date wouldn't go anywhere. I simply didn't have it in me to focus on another man when he was present.

I could at least try not to be rude though, so I aimed my face toward Ben and curved my lips, hoping to give the impression I was still interested. There was no reason to offend him just because I was hopelessly hung up on someone who didn't want me.

I tuned in just in time to hear, "...and you?"

Shit. What had he been saying? Something about his job. Perhaps he'd asked about mine.

"Do you like being a vet?" he repeated, and I thanked my lucky stars he hadn't caught me out.

"I love it," I said truthfully. "I've always known what I wanted to do, and I never went through that phase some people have where they become disillusioned with their dream job. It has its downsides—I hate seeing animals in pain—but that just makes it more special when I'm able to help."

I glanced at Asher and his companion out of the corner of my eye. Was she his date? Were they seeing each other? I hadn't heard anything about him dating, but he wasn't one to gossip about the women in his life as much as my twin, Toby, did.

Maybe she was just a fling. But she'd clearly gone to a lot of effort to look nice, which implied there was more to it than that.

"Do you have any pets of your own?" Ben asked.

"No. Living alone, and with my busy work schedule, it doesn't seem practical. But hopefully when I settle down with someone, we can get one together."

He smiled, his eyes twinkling. "Cat or dog?"

"No preference."

The server brought Asher and his maybe-date to the

table beside ours. I made eye contact with Asher, careful not to cringe. This was awkward. Especially because now all I could think about was how Ben might be handsome, but his face wasn't nearly as interesting as Asher's, and he didn't have any tattoos like Asher did.

I loved those tattoos.

"I like dogs best," Ben said.

If he noticed my distraction, he was polite enough not to mention it.

"Excuse me," I heard Asher say to the server. "Could we sit somewhere else?"

My cheeks heated, and I wished I could disappear in a puff of smoke. The awkwardness was one thing when we were ignoring it. Making a request like that would only bring everyone's attention to the problem.

The server wrung her hands. "I'm afraid not. There aren't any other available tables."

He gestured to one across the room. "What about over there?"

"It's reserved for a group who should be arriving in ten minutes."

"It's fine," I said.

Ben frowned and it took him a moment to realize I wasn't addressing him.

"Honestly, sit down, Ash." I forced myself to smile. "It isn't a problem."

"Are you sure?"

"Yes." I refused to meet his eyes. My gut rolled nauseatingly. I didn't want to hear him flirting with another woman, but there was no other choice, and the longer he dragged it out, the more awkward this would become.

He pulled out a chair for his date, and then sat. I tried very hard not to listen as the server took their drink order.

Ben leaned across the table toward me. "What was that about?"

I grimaced. "He's my brother's best friend. We don't get along very well."

"Oh." He glanced around, and then said, "We could go somewhere else if you prefer. Or see if we can take our meals to go?"

"It's fine." If I said it enough times, maybe it would become true. "Thank you, though. That was a kind offer."

He seemed like a good person, and he deserved better than a half-hearted date. Unfortunately, I felt nothing for him but gratitude and a general sense of liking. Nothing on the same level as the belly flips and heart flutters I experienced when Asher was around.

I'd come to hate those intensely.

Our meals arrived nine minutes later. I knew this because every second that passed with Asher next to me, on a date with another woman, was downright excruciating. I plastered a smile on my face and told Ben about my big, chaotic family while he did his best to entertain me with stories from his accountancy firm, but my heart wasn't in it.

All I could think of was whether Asher intended to kiss his date after dinner...or take her home with him.

When she reached across the table and touched his hand, my teeth gritted, and I nearly growled at her. I wanted to shout that Asher was mine and that if she had a problem with that, she could wrestle me. Winner takes all. Growing up with five brothers had honed my wrestling skills.

But I wasn't feral, so I settled for ignoring her.

My chicken was perfectly cooked, as was Ben's steak, but I barely noticed as I ate on autopilot. I managed to maintain a conversation about university, and another about my favorite places to hike—apparently, he was an indoor guy, so maybe he wasn't perfect after all.

Once we'd finished the meal, I excused myself to the bathroom and returned just in time to hear Asher's date let out a peal of laughter as pretty as she was.

"Can we go?" I asked Ben quietly. "I don't feel well."

"Sure."

We paid the bill fifty-fifty and I donned my coat before we exited the building. It was June, and we were coming into winter, so the sky was dark, and a chill had already descended over the mountainside. We walked to Ben's car, and he opened the passenger door for me like a gentleman.

I felt nothing other than guilt.

"Could we have a do-over?" I asked when he settled into the driver's seat. "Perhaps in Queenstown?"

That was where he lived, and we were far less likely to run into anyone I knew there, than here.

He glanced at me as he started the engine. "I don't think there's any point seeing each other again when you're clearly not emotionally available."

My shoulders slumped and the guilt sunk its teeth in harder. "I'm so sorry."

If he'd picked up on it, I must have been obvious. How mortifying.

He smiled, and to my surprise, it was gentle rather than annoyed. "I know how it feels. I've been there. But there's still no point wasting each other's time."

"I know," I whispered, staring out the window so he wouldn't see the tears trying to come to the surface. Why did he have to be so understanding? And why did my heart insist on beating for Asher and no one else? I wished I could be something other than a mess who ruined any chance of having a real relationship.

We didn't talk much while Ben drove me home, but the silence wasn't awkward. It was resigned. We'd both accepted that nothing else would happen between us, and fortunately, neither of us was too hurt by that.

He took the mountain road slowly and drove to my cottage on the far side of Destiny Falls. I thanked him, said goodnight, and made my way to the front door. My heart ached with how much I wished there was someone inside, waiting for me to come home.

Nights like tonight, loneliness pressed in on me, and I could no longer pretend not to feel it.

I entered, locked the door behind myself, and checked my phone. There was a message from Asher. I opened it.

Asher: *Are you okay?*

"Far from it," I muttered, and plugged the phone into the charger without replying.

Of course he would be thoughtful via text. Any time I saw him in real life these days, all we did was snap at each other or say the wrong thing. But perhaps that was for the best. After all, the last time he'd been nice to me, he'd been drunk off his ass.

He'd hit on me at a party, and I'd been ecstatic for a few seconds, until I realized that he'd never go anywhere near me sober, and that if anything were to happen between us while he was drunk, he'd regret it. I'd let him down gently, hoping he'd come back in the morning and tell me he'd meant every word.

Of course, he never did. Because Asher Heaton didn't really want me. He'd made that painfully clear.

2

———

ASHER

I SURREPTITIOUSLY TOOK MY PHONE FROM MY POCKET BENEATH the table and glanced at the screen. Still no reply from Summer.

Worry knitted in my gut. Was she okay? She'd seemed upset when they left, and as much as I enjoy winding her up on occasion, this was different. I'd never want to see her truly hurt.

"What's wrong?" Kylie asked.

"Nothing." I returned my phone to my pocket. I obviously needed to work on my stealth skills.

Kylie sipped from her glass of wine, set it down, and cocked her head. "So, who was the girl?"

I frowned. "Huh?"

She arched her eyebrow, looking at me as if I was an idiot. "The one who was sitting beside us earlier. You could hardly take your eyes off her."

Ugh. Awkward.

"It's not what you think," I said weakly.

She popped the last piece of fish into her mouth and held my gaze while she chewed and swallowed. "And what do I think?"

Yeah, no way in hell was I stupid enough to try to answer that. No man could ever know exactly what a woman was thinking.

"She's my best friend's little sister," I explained. "She used to have a bit of a crush on me, and I was worried she might be upset by seeing me on a date."

"Hmm." She narrowed her eyes. "I believe you."

I had no idea why that was such a relief. I'd told her the truth, after all.

"I don't think she's the only one who was bothered by someone else's date though," she added.

I stiffened. "I don't know what you mean."

That was a big fat lie.

Kylie pushed her plate away and positioned her wine glass in front of herself. "Are you sure you don't feel something for her too?"

Damn. She had to go and say it.

"It's not like that." Another lie. Or, at least, a partial one.

When Summer had returned from university, properly grown up, she'd blindsided me. I honestly hadn't expected to ever see her as anything other than Liam's baby sister, but I'd barely run into her at all for years because her avoidance game was top notch, so by the time I did, she'd transitioned from a pretty girl into a knockout woman.

Not that I'd ever been able to tell her as much. I'd tried once, and she'd sassed and snarked until I gave up and snarked right back. Now, that was pretty much all we did with each other.

"Whatever you say," Kylie replied, then muttered something about men that I couldn't quite hear.

Fortunately, she didn't want to stay for dessert, because I

was in no mood to linger. I'd liked Kylie when I'd met her during a callout to the adventure company where she worked, but something about having Summer nearby had put a dampener on any potential chemistry between us.

We headed to our cars. We'd driven separately, since we'd come from different directions. As we emerged into the cool night air, the stars sparkling overhead, Kylie turned to me.

"Can I give you some advice?" she asked.

I bit my tongue so I wouldn't say no. I owed her enough to listen after a dud of a night.

"Ask your friend's sister on a date before you take another girl out. Work through whatever you need to work through. It's not fair to future partners if you have that kind of emotional connection with someone else."

I pursed my lips. "It isn't that simple."

There were years of history between Summer and me. I'd been like a brother to her when we were growing up, and if I got involved with her and messed it up, I'd lose my oldest and most important friendship.

Liam had made no bones about the kind of man he thought Summer needed. Someone stable, well-balanced, and uncomplicated. That wasn't me. Not only was my work-life balance practically non-existent, but my job was unpredictable and occasionally dangerous. She deserved better.

Besides, it was jumping the gun to even assume she returned my interest. Given how she'd shot me down a while ago, there was every chance she'd moved on from her teenage crush.

It was for the best, but I still couldn't help feeling disappointed.

"It doesn't have to be complicated," Kylie said, dragging me back to the present. "You're the one making it like that."

"I'll consider what you've said." I wouldn't really, but I could hardly be rude to her after that shitshow of a date.

"Good." She patted my arm and backed away. "Maybe I'll see you around."

Frustration simmered in my gut as I got into my car and drove home. As soon as I was inside, I shed my clothes, pulled on a pair of cycle shorts, and headed for my exercise bike. I put my earbuds in, turned on a rock soundtrack, and cycled until sweat coated my skin and my breath came in harsh pants.

My thighs burned, but I pushed harder. Cycling like this —whether inside or on one of the many mountain bike trails that cut through the forest around Destiny Falls—was the only thing that could quiet my thoughts.

Meditation didn't work. My mind whirred too quickly for that. Nor did journaling or tai chi or fucking yoga. I'd tried them all. Drinking might take the edge off, but I'd never given it a real go. I didn't need another problem. At least working out my restlessness on a bike was a reasonably healthy coping mechanism.

Eventually, Cookie decided I'd had enough. She parked her fluffy bum on the ground in front of the cycle and meowed over and over until I dismounted on shaky legs and scooped her into my arms.

"You are such a little demon," I told her, burying my face against her belly and nuzzling her.

She grabbed my head playfully, without digging her sharp claws in. I carried her to the kitchen and set her on the floor. She immediately ran to her food bowl, her tail swishing.

"Fine." I grabbed her treats from the cupboard and poured a few into the bowl.

My phone vibrated on the kitchen counter. I checked,

hoping it was Summer, but found a message from Liam instead.

Liam: *How was your date?*

Sighing, I dragged my hand down my face. I could hardly tell him that I was too distracted by his gorgeous sister and my impossible feelings for her to make a real connection with Kylie.

Asher: *There was no chemistry.*

I tamped down a flare of guilt and put the phone aside while I showered. As I dried, I stretched my legs, realizing that I should have done it sooner. Summer was messing with my mind.

By the time I checked my phone again, I'd received another two messages from Liam.

Liam: *Too bad. Sorry, man.*

Liam: *Off to bed. Talk tomorrow.*

I sent him a quick goodnight, hoping it wouldn't wake him, and went to my own bed. Cookie must have finished her treats because she was curled on the spare pillow. I climbed in and switched off the light.

As soon as I lay on my back, she crawled onto my chest and started purring. If I wasn't used to it, the pressure and noise would probably keep me awake, but this had become our routine ever since I'd adopted her two years ago.

I stroked her and closed my eyes. An image of Summer flashed through my mind. Not as she'd been tonight, wholesomely pretty in dark jeans and a blouse, but as she'd been the night of her graduation. The evening I'd done my best to let her down gently but firmly.

In the end, it hadn't mattered how gentle I'd been. She'd looked devastated, with unshed tears in her eyes and her mouth twisted with the effort not to cry.

If only I'd known how much I'd come to regret my words to her that day.

3

———————

SUMMER

I PARKED OUTSIDE MY PARENTS' HOUSE AND GROANED AT THE sight of Asher's silver sedan pulling up on the opposite side of the road.

After my disastrous date last night, I wanted to avoid him for as long as possible, so I threw open the car door and hurried around the car to grab the platter of cheeses, crackers, and dried fruit that I'd brought for brunch.

The cold air nipped at my skin as I shut the door, clicked the button on my key fob to lock it, and made a beeline for the house.

Too slow. Asher cut me off part way there.

"Hey," he said, his expression serious. "Are you okay—"

"Fine," I interrupted, relief thrumming through my veins as Liam and Kennedy's vehicle turned onto the street and parked beside Asher's. I raced toward their car, knowing he wouldn't mention anything where Liam could overhear.

I opened one of the back doors and Daisy spilled out. The golden labrador mix-breed bounced around me excitedly, and I balanced the platter on one hand so I could give her some love.

"Hey, Summer," Kennedy said as she got out of the passenger side.

"Hi, Kenz." I circled around and hugged her, then dared to glance at Asher, who was watching me with an eyebrow raised.

Liam got out and locked the car. He had a container tucked under his arm. My best guess was that Kennedy had made brownies. Baking wasn't her forte, but she could manage brownies and a few other staples safely enough.

"Good date last night?" Kennedy asked, a little too loudly.

I shot her a look. "Not great. Details later."

Liam seemed to be having the same conversation with Asher, so I took advantage of the opportunity to slip past them both and into the house. Inside, I made my way to the kitchen, where I set my platter down on the island. My mother, Heather, stood in front of the stove, scrambling eggs, frying bacon, and sautéing mushrooms.

"Good morning!" I greeted her and went over to kiss her cheek.

She hugged me with one arm and tended to the eggs with the other hand. "Morning, honey."

"Do you need help with anything?" I asked.

"There are fresh rolls in the oven that need to be checked," she said. "And we should start laying out the cold food. Yogurt, cereal, juice—you know the drill."

"I'm on it." I washed my hands and got busy, grateful that Asher wasn't the sort of person to offer assistance in the kitchen. If there was a grill outside, he'd be eager to help, but from what I understood, he was a terrible cook otherwise.

I carried everything out to the long table in the living

room. During the warmer months, we ate outside, but it was too cold for that in winter. Mum finished cooking and dished the eggs, mushrooms, and bacon onto separate plates. We were preparing to take them to the table when Bailey breezed into the kitchen.

"Good morning, Heather," she said, her perfectly straight teeth flashing between bright red lips. "Hey, Summer."

"Hi, beautiful," I replied.

She held a glass bowl of salad in her hands. "Superfood salad. Are we about to eat?"

Mum nodded. "Grab the salad tongs. You know where they are."

Mum took the eggs and mushrooms out of the room, leaving me and Bailey alone.

"How was the date?" she asked quietly, her eyes darting around to check that no one could overhear us.

Years of being around my brothers had taught her the importance of secrecy when it came to dating. If they learned anything, they'd either tease me mercilessly or get insanely overprotective. There didn't seem to be any middle ground. It didn't even matter to them that I was a grown woman now. I was still their baby sister.

I grimaced. "Asher was there."

I quickly explained what had happened.

"Ugh, I'm sorry." She put the bowl of salad down and hugged me.

I buried my face in her silky black hair and breathed in the familiar scent of her favorite herbal shampoo.

"It's fine," I said, pulling back. "Ben wasn't the right guy for me anyway."

"He's out there somewhere," she said with forced cheer.

We both knew the only man I wanted was Asher. Just like the only man she wanted was Max, who always treated her kindly but still seemed to think she was twelve years old.

Mutual pining wasn't the only thing that bonded us, but it certainly helped.

We took the bacon and salad out to the table, where the rest of the family were already seated. Since we'd been expanding, we'd had to get a second table, which was positioned end-to-end with the other to fit us all.

Mum and Dad sat at the end closest to the glass sliding doors that opened onto the deck. Nate, his daughter Tess, and Grace were nearby. Grace's hands rested on her swollen belly. She looked about ready to pop, but there were still a few weeks before the baby was due.

Kennedy and Liam were beside them, with Asher, Toby, Connor, and Max on the other table. Two seats remained free for us. While neither Asher nor Bailey were technically members of the family, they came almost every time my parents hosted a brunch, so Mum made sure there was always room for them.

With a sigh, I sat on the chair closest to Asher, with only Connor between us, allowing Bailey to take the seat beside Max. She beamed and bounced over, practically giddy at the prospect of being close to him.

While I resented my feelings for Asher because he'd rejected me, Bailey had never made a move on Max and seemed reasonably content to enjoy his nearness however she could—although sometimes I caught her watching him wistfully.

As soon as we were seated, people began to reach for the food. I helped myself to some of Grace's homemade granola, along with a dollop of yogurt and a little honey. I wasn't much for heavy breakfasts.

"How was your date?" Toby asked Asher across the table.

I stared down at my meal, determined not to look at him. I wouldn't give away how interested I was in his answer.

"Disappointing," he said.

My heart lightened, even though I'd deny it until my dying breath.

"Bummer." Toby pulled a face. "What didn't you like about her?"

I crammed granola in my mouth, torn between listening and distracting myself.

"There was just no connection."

I felt Asher's gaze on the side of my head and continued to ignore him.

"How was your date, Summer?" he asked.

Damn the man.

Slowly, I turned to face him. "He was nice."

"Nice?" Asher winced. "Ouch. Poor guy."

Toby snickered. "The kiss of death, right?"

I glared at them both. "Like Asher said, there was no connection, but he was a good guy."

I was hardly going to admit that I'd been willing to try again but he'd turned me down. After all, it wasn't like I was upset about it, and I'd never hear the end of it from Toby if he found out I'd been rejected by a guy I'd called "nice."

"Sometimes it's like that," Max said sympathetically.

"What would you know about it?" Toby teased. "Have you even dated this millennium?"

"Leave him alone." I could see Bailey's cheeks growing red. If anyone picked on Max too much, she'd have a meltdown, and surely then even my most oblivious brother would see what had been right under his nose for years.

"You'll find someone when you're ready." Liam said, smiling down the table at me. "You're still young. There's no rush."

"At least you've grown up enough to start dating the "nice" ones," Nate muttered, not looking up from his plate. "Some of the guys you've brought around..."

I scowled and narrowed my eyes. Okay, so perhaps I'd intentionally brought home a couple of guys I knew were losers purely to wind up my brothers. It wasn't like I'd been serious about them. I'd just wanted my family to realize how bad it could be, so they'd stop giving me a hard time when I brought home men I really did see the possibility of a future with.

My plan had backfired. They'd just seen it as more proof that I wasn't capable of making good decisions on my own.

"So, who's ready for the ski season to begin?" Toby asked, thankfully changing the subject. I shot him a grateful look.

"I'm looking forward to it," Max said, serving himself some of Bailey's superfood salad. My friend met my eyes, her smile adoring.

"Calm down," I mouthed when no one else was looking.

How the hell Max hadn't noticed her infatuation was beyond me.

"I'm excited to be on the slopes again," Toby continued, his gaze becoming distant. "Nothing but me, snow, and pretty girls."

"Pig," I muttered.

He pretended not to hear me. "I've got a good feeling about this year. I think I'll find The One."

We all exchanged looks. Toby had met 'The One' several times over the course of his seasonal career as a ski instructor at Destiny Peak Ski Field. Year after year, he fell madly in love with tourists only for them to up and leave at the end of the season. He took it well every time, but I had to believe he'd eventually tire of the cycle.

"Of course you will," Bailey assured him with a gentle smile.

Connor changed the subject to when we could expect our first snowfall, and we finished brunch with lighthearted chatter. When we were done, I helped Mom, Kennedy, and Liam clear the dirty dishes away. Tess and Nate had gone outside and were playing fetch with Daisy and their dog, Duke.

A hand landed on my arm as I passed Asher at one point, but I shook it off.

"Summer," he said softly.

I chose not to hear him.

Instead, I looped my arm through Bailey's and made a point to ask her loudly about a hike we had planned for the afternoon. When he followed, I decided it was time to leave.

4

ASHER

MY MUSCLES BURNED AS I PUSHED THE BARBELL ABOVE MY head and slowly lowered it back to my shoulders. I repeated the motion, grunting with the effort. Technically, para- medics didn't have to keep in shape the same way fire- fighters did, but what else was I supposed to do between callouts?

An alarm sounded through the intercom, and Captain Parks's voice instructed all ambulance and engine personnel to report to their vehicles. Apparently there had been a car accident on the road up Destiny Peak.

I quickly wiped the sweat off my face, grabbed my go bag, and headed for the ambulance. My partner, Maia, met me there. I got behind the wheel and she took the passenger seat and plugged the coordinates into our GPS system. She glanced at me, her dark eyes bright despite the early hour.

"What do you think? One car or two?" she asked.

"Could be either. My money is on two though." The mountain road was dangerous, but most people could navigate it safely unless something happened to mess with them.

The garage door rolled up and we took off, sirens wailing. It wasn't even 8 a.m. yet, so Destiny Falls was quiet and sleepy as we sped down Centennial Street and onto the highway out of town. We turned onto the mountain road, and I checked the mirror to make sure the engine was still behind us.

"Black ice," Maia exclaimed, pointing at a shimmer where the headlights fell on the road up ahead.

I swerved around the icy patch and checked for more.

"Want to bet that's what caused the crash?" I asked.

She snorted. "I'm not taking you up on that one."

I kept my foot on the accelerator, flying up the mountain as fast as I safely could. We weren't far from the scene of the accident now. Maybe a kilometer or so.

We rounded a bend, and then another. Finally, I spotted them. One car had rolled off the road and was upside down on the side of the slope. We'd have to be careful, or it might slip further. A woman lay on the ground, part way through the shattered windscreen. A man was still in the car, suspended from the seat by his seatbelt.

My stomach dropped as I pulled to the side of the road and parked. The fact the woman wasn't moving gave me a bad feeling.

The second vehicle had been sideswiped, and the driver's side was crumpled in. The driver was conscious, but he seemed to be stuck, and his shirt was crimson with blood.

"I've got the one that's gone off-road," I told Maia.

"I'm on the other one then."

I threw the door open, grabbed a medical kit, and carefully picked my way down the hillside to the overturned car.

I'd like to move faster, but if I rushed, I could end up causing more problems than I solved.

When I reached them, I knelt beside the woman, but even before I touched her neck to check her pulse, I knew she was gone. A pane of glass had impaled her, and her face and upper torso were dotted with dozens of thin red cuts. Blood was pooled around her, no longer flowing. Her eyes were glassy, and her skin was already cooling off.

This crash must have happened well before the call came in, or her temperature wouldn't have changed yet. Perhaps all involved had been unconscious and unable to call for help until recently.

I checked inside the cab. The man was dangling, blood dried on his face, and his eyes were closed. His chest rose and fell on ragged gasps. He probably had a broken nose from the airbag deploying, and perhaps a couple of broken ribs from the impact. We'd just have to hope none of them had pierced anything vital.

Voices sounded behind me, and I turned as Liam and Zane edged down the slope toward me.

"You need to get him out of here," I said.

I stood back as they scanned our surroundings for hazards and then levered the door open. Darcy joined us a moment later, bringing a stretcher, and between the three of them, they maneuvered the guy out of the car and onto the stretcher.

He stirred, shaking his head and opening blurry eyes. I bent over him and began to examine him for injuries. His breathing was still shallow, and it rattled in and out, but as long as it was steady, I wasn't too concerned.

He murmured something.

"What's that buddy?" I asked, shining a light in his eyes to see if his pupils would react. They didn't.

Likely concussion.

Broken nose.

Possible fractured ribs.

Possible spinal injury.

"Save Susan," he croaked.

I exchanged a glance with Liam. "Susan?"

"My wife." He tried to sit up, growing agitated. "She's hurt. Help her."

"Whoa." I pressed him back against the stretcher. "Don't move. We don't know how badly you're injured yet."

"I don't care." His eyes were wild, and he began to buck. Clearly his back wasn't broken, although from the way he cried out with pain, something else might be.

"Susan!" he yelled hoarsely. "Susan! Where are you?"

"Was Susan with you?" I asked, sick in the pit of my gut as I recalled the battered body of the woman through the windshield. I hated having to break bad news.

"Yes," he panted, his face white.

I sighed as I skimmed my hands up his sides, cataloging any damage. "I'm really sorry, but Susan is gone. It was too late to save her."

His entire body stiffened. "No. She can't be."

"I'm sorry," I repeated.

"No." He knocked my hands aside and tried to push me, but then wheezed and curled in on himself. "You can save her. Even when people are dead, you can bring them back. Do CPR. Use the electric paddle things. Do fucking something!"

"She's past that." God, I wished I didn't have to do this.

"Save her," he growled, struggling to get to his feet.

When I tried to stop him, he kicked me—thankfully not hard enough to do any damage. He didn't stop there though. He threw a punch at Darcy, catching him off guard, and a spray of scarlet erupted from his nose. Then the guy tried to lunge past Liam to get to his wife.

"Maia!" I shouted. "I could use some help!"

Between the four of us, we managed to pin him down.

"You're going to injure yourself," I told him, but I couldn't help feeling sorry for him.

He was hurting, and he'd lost someone he'd clearly loved—while he'd been driving. I doubted his brain was even able to process everything yet. He was acting purely on instinct.

Maia appeared in front of me, her dark ponytail swinging as she tapped a syringe and carefully inserted it into the man's thigh.

A moment later, the fight drained out of him, but guilt weighed heavily on my shoulders.

I'm sorry. It's for the best.

5

———

SUMMER

Warm air greeted me as I pushed open the door to Drunken Destiny and stepped inside. My eyes immediately went to the table where Asher sat with his colleagues, but I forced myself to focus on the bar instead. Bailey was working tonight, and we'd agreed to meet since it was usually one of her quieter midweek shifts.

She was busy serving drinks, so I scanned the patrons, noting the usual locals, tourists, and then in the corner nearest the bar were the guys from the fire station. Asher, Liam, Darcy, Igor, and Zane. Asher's partner, Maia, was nowhere to be seen, but she'd probably opted to go home to her husband and daughter rather than join the men.

Liam glanced over, and I lifted my hand to acknowledge him. He tipped his head, but I couldn't help noticing that there was no spark in his eyes. They looked dull. He must have had a tough call today.

I made my way to the bar, where Bailey had finished

serving a cluster of twenty-something backpackers—more than one of whom couldn't take their eyes off her.

"How's your night?" I asked, sitting my bum on a bar stool. She poured me a glass of the house white wine and passed it to me. "Thanks."

"It's been steady, but the mood isn't great," she said. "How was work?"

"Good. I de-balled a couple of farm dogs, delivered a litter of kittens, and treated Mrs. Hawkins's bichon again."

She laughed. "What was it this time?"

"Supposedly, a rash, but I couldn't see anything. I gave her a steroid that should help if there's really anything there."

"Poor Dolores," Bailey said.

I chuckled. "Doomed from birth."

Mrs. Hawkins was not only a hypochondriac, but also obsessed with Harry Potter. She'd named her beloved pet after the evil Dolores Umbridge.

"I recorded another gymnastics tutorial today," Bailey said, changing the subject. "I'm surprised by how popular those are, but as long as they keep getting views, I'll keep posting them."

I grinned. "Of course they're doing well. You're amazing."

Bailey had started a health and beauty blog years ago, which had escalated into a multi-platform, influencing mini-empire where she also shared gymnastics tips and advice for girls who were interested in experiencing the great outdoors but weren't stereotypically "outdoorsy."

"Thanks, babe." She blew me a kiss, then smiled at someone over my shoulder.

I turned. Asher was hovering behind me, an empty glass clasped in each hand.

"God, you look like crap." I clapped my hand to my

mouth, horrified. Based on the somber mood at their table, it had been a hard day, and I had to go and let that pop out?

It was true. He did look terrible, but it wasn't as if he needed to hear it.

He put the glasses on the bar. "Don't start, Summer. Not tonight. Refills all around please, Bailey."

"Sure thing, Ash." Her sweet smile didn't budge as she got to work, and for once, I wished I was a little more like her. Perhaps then I wouldn't put my foot in my mouth so often. Maybe my family were right to worry about my impulsiveness getting the better of me.

"What's wrong?" I asked.

He sighed and rubbed his temples. "We lost someone today."

My heart dropped. "I'm so sorry."

Perhaps in big cities, the emergency crew would be used to losing people, but fatal accidents—or any fatalities—were rare out here. I couldn't begin to imagine how it felt. I was shattered enough when I was unable to save someone's pet. For it to be a human...

Yeah, rough.

I resisted the urge to hug him. He wouldn't appreciate the gesture. "Want to talk about it?"

He shrugged. "Not much to talk about. It was a car accident."

I waited, hoping he might go on. Eventually, he did.

"Fuck, it was awful. The guy kept yelling at us to save his wife, but she was long gone." He shook his head. "There was no way... We couldn't do anything, but he was desperate. I felt so bad for him."

My stomach clenched. This time, I didn't hesitate to put my hand on his arm. "I'm sorry. That must have been horrible."

"Yeah." His expression was bleak. "We had to sedate him

so we could transport him to the hospital safely. Once he woke up, he just kept crying, and there was nothing we could do to help."

Emotion clogged my throat. "I can't even imagine how difficult that was for you."

Or for that poor man. Having his wife stolen from him so suddenly and cruelly. He would never be the same.

"Not as hard as it was for him," he said, as if he'd heard my thoughts. Something dark tainted his voice, and I studied him closely. What was that flicker in his eyes? Guilt, or something else?

I bit my lip, praying that I wasn't about to overstep. "I hope you know it wasn't your fault. If she was already dead before you got there, then you couldn't save her, right?"

He nodded, but his face was twisted. Conflicted. "Logically, I know that, but it's hard to remember sometimes. Especially when people are hurting so badly."

Bailey finished pouring his table's drinks and loaded them onto a metal tray.

Asher slid the tray off the bar. "Have a good night, Summer."

He walked away, his footsteps dragging and his dark head hanging low. He reminded me of a kicked puppy, and I wanted to hold him and tell him it would all be okay. But after the day he'd had, nothing I could say would take away his pain.

"He won't sleep well tonight," Bailey murmured.

"I know."

We probably weren't supposed to be aware of Asher's issues with insomnia when he got stressed, but my brothers could be dreadful gossips.

"Do you think there's anything I can do to help them?" I asked, glancing over at the table. "They're all miserable."

6

———

ASHER

I placed the tray of beers on the center of the table and grabbed the darkest one for myself. The others each reached for theirs and we all drank. Some days just called for fucking beer.

"What was up with Summer?" Darcy asked as he licked his lips and hummed in appreciation.

I pinched the bridge of my nose. "She wanted to make sure I knew how shit I looked."

Although I didn't really think she'd meant to say it. She'd looked horrified when she'd realized what had come out of her mouth. But it was a nice shitty cherry on top of my shitty day.

Yeah, she was definitely over her crush on me.

Across the table, Liam winced. "Sorry, man."

"Not your fault." No. It was mine for hurting her all those years ago, so now her default was to spout snark like a prickly little hedgehog, as if she needed to defend herself against me when, in reality, the opposite was true. Our situation had somehow reversed itself.

"It looked like more than that," Darcy said. "You were talking for a while."

I grunted. I didn't care to repeat our entire conversation for his entertainment. Especially not when it felt oddly private.

Liam shook his head. "I don't know what it is with her. She never used to be so hard on you."

No, because she'd been infatuated with me. But it was best not to say that to my closest friend. She was his baby sister, after all.

I did sometimes wonder if I'd done her a disservice to dismiss her feelings back then as a teenage crush. The fact she kept me at a distance year after year spoke of a deeper wound. Or perhaps I only wanted to believe that because it might mean there was a chance she still cared for me.

Not that I could ever do anything about it. Days like today only emphasized how quickly things could change. Even if Summer still wanted me and her family were willing to overlook the fact I wasn't good enough for her, my job was dangerous. It could all too easily be me bleeding out on the ground one day, leaving my partner to cry alone.

I wouldn't do that to her.

"I heard she's been dating again," Darcy said, looking livelier than he had all evening. "Do you know if it's true?"

"She's been on a couple of dates," Liam confirmed.

I fought the urge to cringe even thinking of that excruciating evening when we'd ended up beside each other, both on dates. How unlikely was that? But it was just my luck.

"Do you think she'd give me a chance?" Darcy asked.

Zane stopped drawing in the condensation on the side of his glass and looked at him. "Are you interested in her?"

Darcy rolled his eyes. "Who wouldn't be? She's gorgeous, smart, and she owns half a freaking business. She's a total boss babe." He glanced at Liam. "No disrespect intended."

Liam grimaced. "Not words I ever thought I'd hear you say about my sister."

He shrugged. "What? She is. So, do you think she'd go for me?"

"Keep me out of this." Liam crossed his arms. "If you want to date her, then ask her out, but I don't want to hear any of the drama if it goes wrong."

"Got you." Darcy straightened. "Should I do it now?"

"Go," Zane urged. "You've got this."

I could already see the hearts in Zane's eyes. God, he was such a hopeless romantic.

But Darcy hesitated. "What's her type, Liam?"

Liam looked like he'd rather be anywhere else. "I have no idea. As far as I can tell based on the guys she's brought around, 'asshole' is her type."

I huffed. I was pretty sure she wasn't actually interested in any of the douchebags she'd flaunted in front of Liam and me. She just wanted to make me squirm.

She'd succeeded.

"I can be an asshole," Darcy said eagerly. "Hang on. Is that actually what I want? Or should I be my usual self and hope all the assholes mean that the bar is set low?"

"Just be yourself," Igor said, breaking his sullen silence for the first time. "But stop talking and do it already. You're giving me a headache."

Darcy started to stand.

"Don't." The words left my mouth before I could think them through. Everyone turned to stare at me. I hunched inward. "You're too young for her."

It was the only thing I could think of, but it should be

blatantly obvious. Darcy was an exuberant golden retriever, and some people liked that, but Summer had her shit together and she deserved a guy who was the same.

Darcy frowned. "I'm only a few years younger than her, and age is just a number anyway."

"It's too much," I insisted. "You're...what? Twenty-one?"

"Twenty-two," he said firmly.

"Well, Summer is twenty-seven and, as you pointed out, a business owner. She needs someone older. Someone stable and reliable." Just as Liam often said. Why wasn't he speaking up now?

Darcy crossed his arms and pouted. "I can be reliable. Why are you being weird about this?"

My heart skipped as I realized he didn't seem to be the only one looking at me strangely. "I'm not. I'm just saying what I've heard from her family. Summer deserves someone who'll be there for her when they say they will, and with our jobs, we can't make that promise."

Darcy looked hurt. "Maybe not, but I'd treat her well in other ways."

I groaned. This was getting out of hand. "Sorry, Darce. If you want to ask her out, then do it."

If she accepted—which she might do just to piss me off—I'd find a way to live with it. Even if I really didn't want to see them together. Honestly, I didn't want to see her with anyone who wasn't me, but I also wasn't prepared to pursue her myself, which put me in a difficult position.

"You might need something stronger than beer. You're clearly in a mood," Darcy said, but he stopped pouting and relaxed a little. Still, he didn't approach Summer, so I must have put him off. I should feel worse about that than I actually did.

After we finished the round, we all walked home. I had a

faint buzz going, but I was far from drunk. I hadn't had nearly enough alcohol to quiet my mind.

As Liam and I parted, he leaned close and murmured, "Don't worry. Summer would never be interested in him anyway."

Ah. So that's why he hadn't said anything to put Darcy off. He didn't think it was necessary.

"If you say so," I muttered back. I was less certain than him. Summer liked to be contrary.

I let myself into my house, stooping to greet Cookie at the door. I patted the top of her fluffy head and watched her tail swish as she trotted along ahead of me into the kitchen.

I fed her, then changed into shorts and a tank top and racked up ten kilometers on the indoor cycle. I showered and got into bed, but even Cookie's familiar weight on my chest didn't comfort me.

Every time I closed my eyes, Susan's broken body appeared on the inside of my eyelids, and Robert's pleas echoed in my ears.

You couldn't save her, I reminded myself.

It didn't stop the haunting memories though. Instead, a highlight reel began to play in the dark recesses of my mind.

A pale old man, dead from a heart attack.

A ten year old girl who'd been hit by a drunk driver, her vacant eyes begging for help that would arrive too late.

A pensioner who'd fallen and cracked her head against the hearth.

And on and on they went. All the faces of the people I hadn't been able to save.

Eventually, my eyes gritty and my pulse pounding way too fast, I lifted Cookie off my chest and got out of bed. I dressed in the dark, put my headphones on, and climbed back onto the cycle, turning up my music to drown out the endless chorus of the dead.

If I couldn't sleep, the only thing left to do was try to outrun them.

7

SUMMER

I moved to the front of the line in Taste of Destiny and greeted Eden, the young woman behind the counter, with a smile. Hopefully, she could help me make up for putting my foot in my mouth last night.

"What can I get you?" she asked.

"A box of assorted bakery items, please," I said. "Perhaps some slices, some donuts, and cookies."

"Sure thing," she replied. "How many, and what's the occasion?"

"Let's say ten." I wasn't certain how many people would be at the station. Most likely, at least four in the fire crew, plus two paramedics, and the captain, but there might be a few others hanging around too. "It's for the fire station."

Eden winced. "I heard about the accident yesterday. Let me give you the local hero discount."

"There's no need for that," I protested. I could afford to pay the full cost. The veterinary practice did well, and I was entitled to fifty percent of our profits in addition to my salary, so while I wasn't rich, I was never short of cash when I needed it.

"I insist." Eden took my payment, grabbed a box from beneath the counter and filled it with treats. When it was full, she closed the lid and passed it to me. "Tell them thank you for what they do, from all of us here."

"I will." I took the box and carried it down a couple of blocks to the turn off to the fire station. The morning was still dim, and as I left the sidewalk and moved onto the grass, it crunched beneath my feet, stiff with frost.

The doors into the fire station were all closed, but the main entrance opened when I pushed it. I made my way along the corridor and into the staff room. The bitter scent of coffee permeated the air, and several empty cups showed that many of the people on duty had already enjoyed their first coffee of the day.

"Morning, Summer," Liam called from a sofa in the corner.

Darcy, who was sprawled beside him, tipped his chin at me. "Hey."

Asher and Maia, who were both in the connected kitchen area, nodded in greeting.

I put the box on the center of the table. "I come with goodies."

Darcy immediately perked up. "What have you got?"

"A selection from Taste of Destiny." I opened the box. "For you guys from me and Eden. I know you lost someone yesterday, and we wanted to remind you that the community appreciates everything you do."

Liam rose from the sofa, walked straight over and hugged me. "Thanks for being sweet."

"No problem." I hugged him back and pulled away.

Maia, a tall, lean Māori woman, squeezed my shoulder. "Thanks, Summer. Those callouts are always hard."

"I can't even imagine." I moved aside so they could help themselves.

Liam chose a muffin while Maia grabbed a chocolate caramel slice. I watched her delicately break off a piece from the end and nibble on it. Back when she'd started working with Asher, I'd been jealous of her, but I'd quickly realized there was nothing between them. Now, she was married with a kid, and I found myself jealous of her in a whole other way.

I wanted that. But I wanted it with Asher, and he'd made his position clear.

I checked the time. "I'd better get to work. I have patients arriving soon."

"Let me walk you out," Asher said.

I hesitated, but he hadn't tried to raise the subject of our dates last night, so hopefully he wouldn't now.

"Okay, thanks."

He grabbed a chocolate chip cookie and brought it with him as he followed me out of the staff room. I glanced at him while we walked down the corridor. His eyes were bloodshot and red-rimmed. Dark circles marred the skin beneath them, and the lines on his forehead were more pronounced than usual.

He looked tired.

No, more than that: He seemed weary on a bone-deep level.

But after telling him he looked like crap last night, I could hardly double down on that this morning.

"Thanks for the treats from Taste of Destiny," Asher said as we exited the building. "It means a lot to the guys. Calls like the one yesterday are never easy."

I shrugged. "I don't know how to help in a more meaningful way, so it seemed like the least I could do."

He smiled tightly. "You've always got to help, don't you?"

Why did he make that sound like a bad thing?

"I try."

He shook his head, then dragged his fingers through his hair. "Anyway, thanks. And, uh, about the other night... I'm sorry if my being there made your date un—"

"It's fine," I interrupted, my cheeks burning with embarrassment. Apparently, I hadn't escaped the awkward conversation after all. "You're allowed to date whomever and whenever you like."

If I had to listen to him reference my feelings for him, I might go up in flames.

"But if—"

"Seriously, Ash."

"I just don't want to make you uncomfortable." He looked so adorably uncertain that I didn't point out how he was doing exactly that, right this instant.

Instead, I forced a laugh. "I had an adolescent crush on you almost ten years ago. I'm over it. The other night was just too weird for my liking."

His lips formed a thin line. "Right. I guess if you're sure?"

"I am. I moved on from that stupid crush on you ages ago."

And I was a lying liar who lied.

8

————

ASHER

I RUBBED AT MY GRITTY EYES AFTER A LONG AND UNEVENTFUL night shift spent lying on my bunk at the fire station, staring at the underside of the bed above me.

"Parks wants to see me now?" I asked.

"Yeah." Paul, who'd just arrived for the day shift, had shaken me awake a few minutes earlier with instructions to report to Parks's office.

"Fuck. Okay."

I hauled myself out of bed and glanced over, went to the bathroom and splashed cold water on my face. I ran into Maia in the corridor outside.

"Any idea what this is about?" I asked.

I hated being summoned by the boss. It reminded me of being called to the principal's office at school. I'd been a naughty kid, and that had happened far too often.

"Nothing to worry about." She didn't seem concerned, but then I was the one who'd been called in, not her.

I reached his office door, but it was shut. I knocked, and

a moment later, he called me in. Two chairs sat in front of his desk, and he gestured for me to take one of them.

"Morning, Asher." He moved aside a stack of papers to see me better and steepled his hands in front of him. His craggy countenance gave nothing away. "You look like you've been ridden hard and put away wet."

I stiffened. Why did people keep telling me I looked like crap? "Thanks, sir. Glad to hear it."

He rolled his eyes. "Don't be a smartass. I just wanted to make sure you're doing all right. Is there anything you'd like to talk about?"

I cringed. Talking about my feelings was the last thing I wanted to do. Especially with my boss. "I'm fine. Just not sleeping well."

He pursed his lips. "Do I need to worry about your ability to perform your job?"

My heart dropped. "No! Absolutely not. I'm a little tired, but it won't interfere with my work."

He nodded and searched my eyes. "If you ever do need to talk, or if you need some personal time, you know where to find me."

"Got it. Is that all?" I really wanted to escape this conversation.

"The woman you lost. Susan Warner. You seemed to take that hard."

I sighed. "Difficult not to when her husband, Robert, was so upset."

"You did the best you could." His tone was firm. "We can't save them all."

"I know." I just didn't like it. I always felt like I'd failed both the people we lost and the loved ones they left behind.

He gestured toward the door. "Go on. Head home. Get a proper night's sleep. That's an order."

I rose to my feet and strode out. As I left, Parks reached

for a stack of files on his desk. Despite my mixed up emotions over that shitshow of a conversation, I experienced a pang of relief that I didn't have to deal with the same paperwork he did. It seemed never-ending.

"All good?" Maia asked as we gathered our things from our lockers.

"Parks is worried I'm going to let the team down," I replied, pulling my jacket over my uniform.

"He's just watching out for you." Her expression was sympathetic, which only made me feel worse. "Want to get a coffee on the way home?"

I almost dismissed the offer, but maybe a little time to decompress with a friend was what I needed. "Yeah. Actually, that'd be nice."

We walked to Taste of Destiny together. The tables were full, and the line stretched almost all the way to the door. The morning rush was in full swing. We joined the end of the line, and I checked out the contents of the food cabinet, debating internally whether I should treat myself to a pastry as a distraction from the shitty morning.

Maia reached the front of the line first, and she ordered an espresso and a triple chocolate chunk muffin.

She turned to me. "What do you want?"

I waved my wallet. "I can get my own."

She tapped her foot impatiently. "Are we gonna play this game, Ash?"

Rolling my eyes, I asked Eden for a double shot long black and let Maia pay.

"I heard about the accident earlier in the week," Eden said. "I'm sorry."

"Thanks." Maia smiled more genuinely than she had all morning. "The junk food helped."

Eden smiled back. "I'm glad to hear it."

"You people are too damn soft," a gruff voice cut in from the other side of Maia.

My expression froze in place as I slowly raised my eyes to where Lionel Lowry was waiting for his morning coffee. He scowled at me, and my gaze dipped to the cane he had to use to help him get around since the farm accident he'd been in a few months earlier.

"Trying to make these useless losers feel okay about themselves." He shook his head at Eden. "You'd do better for them if you told them to get their fucking act together. Maybe if they had, that woman would still be alive."

I forced myself to make eye contact with him. His deep-set eyes burned with loathing.

"Maybe," Lionel gritted out, "if good old Asher was more concerned with doing his job than being everyone's favorite town hero, I'd still have full use of my goddamn leg."

To my right, I was vaguely aware of Maia staring him down.

"I'm very sorry for what happened to Susan Warner, but we aren't doctors," she said. "We have limited tools, and if someone is dead, unless it happened in the past couple of minutes and all their parts are in reasonable working order, then they're dead. It doesn't matter how hard we try. We aren't miracle workers."

"Aaand here's your coffee, Mr. Lowry," Eden chirped brightly, holding out a takeout cup to the grizzled former farmer. "Have a lovely day."

With a grunt, he snatched the coffee from her and limped out. My shoulders slumped as the door swung shut behind him.

"What was that?" Maia asked, digging her elbow into my ribs. "Why didn't you say something to defend us?"

I shrugged, my heart heavy. "Honestly, some days I feel like he might be right that we should try to do more."

A sharp pain throbbed on my forearm.

"You pinched me," I exclaimed, stunned.

"Because you need to snap out of it," she hissed, glancing around as if to make sure we weren't being eavesdropped on—which we definitely were. "Lionel Lowry is a sour old coot. He was one before the accident, and he's even worse now. There was no saving his leg, just like there was no saving Susan Warner. Have you—?"

I arched an eyebrow. "Have I what?"

She bit her lip, her eyes darting around again. "Have you seen a therapist lately?"

"No." I shifted uncomfortably, hoping that, despite their interest, no one could hear our whispered conversation.

"Maybe you should. If you're internalizing all the awful things people say, you need to find a healthy way to work through it."

I shook my head. "I'm fine. I have coping mechanisms."

Like cycling, loud music, and cuddling with my cat.

"You can ignore me if you like," she said as Eden passed our drinks over. "Just think about it."

I didn't reply, and together, we left the cafe. As soon as we were outside, her phone rang.

She raised it to her ear. "What's up? Oh, no. Sure. Of course. I'll be there soon." She hung up and pocketed her phone. "Aroha has a fever. I need to get home. Are you going to be okay?"

"I always am."

For some reason, that didn't seem to reassure her, but worry for her daughter outweighed her worry for me, and she gave me a little wave and left.

I finally allowed every trace of a smile to fall from my face.

Christ. What a mess.

I definitely wasn't in any shape to be at home by myself. I

needed a distraction. I racked my mind, and as Summer's Ute crawled past, driving toward the veterinary clinic, I got an idea.

I pulled my phone from my pocket and sent a message.

Asher: *Want to go sky diving with me?*

Toby: *Fuck, yeah. When and where?*

Asher: *I'll be at your place in ten.*

Hopefully the adrenaline rush would be enough to get me out of my head.

9

———

SUMMER

"Dᴅ Lɪᴏɴᴇʟ Lᴏᴡʀʏ ʀᴇᴀʟʟʏ ʜᴀᴠᴇ ᴀ ɢᴏ ᴀᴛ Asʜᴇʀ ᴀɴᴅ Mᴀɪᴀ for not saving a woman who was already dead?" Bailey asked as she set up her phone on a stand and aimed it at a pair of chairs facing each other.

"He did." I sat on one of the chairs and Bailey adjusted the phone's position slightly. "I heard it from Liam, and then again from Toby, who was roped into a last minute skydiving trip with Asher yesterday."

As the expert in all things Asher Heaton, I'd noticed long ago that in addition to insomnia, he tended to become an adrenaline junkie when he was stressed or upset. I just hoped it wouldn't get him into trouble one day.

"Even Max couldn't save someone who was already dead," Bailey said, gathering her array of makeup and placing it beside my feet.

"And we all know Max is practically a saint," I teased, just to watch her blush.

Honestly, it was sweet how she seemed to think my most

50

sensible, levelheaded brother was capable of anything. In her mind, he wore a super suit beneath his button down shirt and slacks.

"He's pretty incredible," Bailey agreed. "By the way, thanks for doing this with me. It's nice to have company while I work."

"No problem." I grinned. "Happy to do it."

Bailey had already done her own makeup, and now she turned to face the camera and briefly introduced me and explained what she was going to do. Then she picked up her brushes and got to work.

An hour later, the two of us made our way to the track behind Destiny Fibers that led up to Destiny Falls. We parked near the start of the track and got out of the car. Bailey passed me her camera phone and I turned on the video and aimed it at her, keeping my hands as steady as I could while we started to walk.

As we moved slowly up the track, Bailey spoke to the camera, explaining where the track was, its difficulty level, and then going on to explain the significance of the falls.

Grace had unearthed some of the falls' history, which had become more myth than fact, and Bailey certainly dramatized it as she retold the star-crossed love story of Rocky and his Jewel.

Jewel—real name Pearl—and Rocky—real name Charles—had tied the knot at the base of the falls the night before she was due to marry someone else and had skipped town afterward. Sure, it was romantic, but I felt a little bad for them. They'd lived out their days away from their families and the place they'd once called home.

When the waterfall came into view, I panned the camera away from Bailey to capture the full beauty of the mossy backdrop and the rush of water cascading over the tiered rock structure.

I stopped and zoomed in as two figures appeared to the right of the falls.

Liam and Kennedy.

I jerked my head toward them so Bailey would see, and then stopped recording. These days, Kennedy lived a quiet life in Destiny Falls, but she used to be a Hollywood A-lister, and I refused to record one of her private moments. She'd been hounded by the press enough.

I passed Bailey the phone and walked up the trail toward them. They met us halfway. Liam had one of his arms around Kennedy and they were both beaming.

"You two look like it's been a good morning," I said, hoping we hadn't caught them in the aftermath of a little outdoors lovemaking. It should be too cold for that craziness, but Liam and Kennedy could never stop touching each other, so I couldn't rule it out.

"It has," Kennedy said, gazing up at Liam with adoration painted all over her pretty face.

He smiled down at her and kissed her softly.

"Aww," Bailey murmured. "They're so cute."

They really were.

"Can I tell them?" Liam asked.

"Go on," Kennedy replied.

"Tell us what?" I asked eagerly. I had a nose for gossip, and I could smell something juicy.

They exchanged another look.

"We're having a baby," Liam said.

My jaw dropped. "Congratulations! That's the greatest news I've heard all year." I bounded across the space between us and wrapped my arms around them both. "You're going to be incredible parents. I'm so happy for you."

They really would. But even as I said it, envy gnawed at my insides. I wanted what they had. I wanted someone to get freaky with in the middle of the forest simply because we couldn't keep our hands off each other. I ached for a man to love and to create a family with. But as long as I was hung up on Asher, I doubted it would happen.

I released them and Bailey took my place, hugging first Kennedy and then Liam.

"That's so wonderful," she said. "When are you due?"

"I'm about ten weeks along," Kennedy said, "so I'm due in mid-December."

Bailey's grin grew. "How sweet would it be to have a Christmas baby?"

"Probably not as sweet as you'd think. Their birthday would always get lumped in with Christmas," I said, already able to imagine how it would go.

She frowned. "Then we'll just have to make sure that doesn't happen."

"Thanks." Kennedy sounded amused. "Are you up here recording footage for your channel?"

"Yeah, but don't worry, we'll cut out anything with you in it," Bailey assured her.

Kennedy was visibly relieved. "I'd appreciate that. We're going to walk back now and break the news to the rest of the family. See you later?"

"Definitely." I kissed her cheek. "Congratulations, again."

Liam looked nervous, but I knew he'd be a great dad. He'd be the sort to get outside and play with his kids, and then snuggle on the sofa and watch a movie with them when they wanted to be indoors.

We shuffled around each other, steering clear of the creek, and then Bailey and I resumed filming. When we finished, we perched on either side of a rock near to the water and simply watched it fall.

The forest around us was alive with sound. Birds chirped, animals rustled in the undergrowth, and every now and then, I caught snippets of conversations as people passed by on one of the other trails. I breathed in the scent of earth and greenery and rubbed my hands together to warm them. Despite the sunny weather, it was cool.

"Do you want a family one day?" I asked Bailey, made braver by the fact I couldn't see her face in our current position.

"Yes." She didn't hesitate for a second.

I rubbed my lips together. "What will you do if Max never notices you?"

I didn't want to hurt her, but I needed to know. Our situations were so similar, and I was lost as to what to do myself. I was young enough to still have time, but I didn't want to throw away some of my best years waiting for something that would never happen. I also didn't want to do anything impulsive that I might come to regret.

Bailey sighed. "I honestly don't know."

"Yeah." My shoulders slumped. "Me neither. I've been wondering if I should move away, but I don't want to leave my family."

"Or me." She swiveled around and dragged me into a hug. "You're not allowed to leave me behind either."

"I don't want to." I just sometimes wondered if it might be my best option.

10

———

ASHER

MY BEER GLASS WAS TO MY LIPS, MY MOUTH FULL OF bittersweet ale, when Summer strolled into Drunken Destiny looking like a goddamn wet dream. I sputtered and choked as my drink caught in the back of my throat, and it was only by a miracle that I didn't spit ale all over Connor, who was seated opposite me at our table.

Toby clapped me on the back, harder than necessary. "You okay there, Ash?"

"Fine," I muttered, coughing into my elbow to clear the last dregs of liquid from my windpipe. "Went down the wrong tube."

"You're supposed to swallow it, not inhale it," he teased.

"Yeah, yeah."

My eyes found Summer again. Grace and Nate were with her, but I barely noticed either of them, my attention consumed by the tight gold dress wrapped around her stunning little body.

The neckline rode low over her breasts, exposing

55

cleavage and collarbones, and the skirt only fell to mid-thigh, revealing tanned legs that seemed to go on forever thanks to the high-heeled black boots she wore.

Holy fucking shit.

I blinked a few times, but the gorgeous mirage didn't disappear.

"Wow," Darcy breathed.

Liam shoved his shoulder. "Don't undress my baby sister with your eyes."

Guilt soured in my stomach, and I snapped my gaze away from Summer.

That's right. There were reasons I hadn't already claimed her. Firstly, she might not even want me. Secondly, she was my best friend's sister. And thirdly, I wasn't the stable, predictable Mr. Right she deserved. The fact she'd opted for a dress more suited to clubbing than the jeans or sundresses she usually preferred didn't give me any excuse to ogle her.

"I'm not," Darcy protested. "She's pretty, that's all I'm saying."

"Too old for you," I reminded him.

Not too old for me, though.

I ignored the rogue thought. It didn't matter that I was more than happy—and ready—to settle down. She was Liam's baby sister—a sassy, impulsive woman who would be better off with a steady man who could balance her out. She and I were like a fire and gasoline.

A bad idea.

Nate joined us, and when I glanced over, I saw that Grace and Summer were chatting with Heather and Kennedy at the bar. We were officially here to celebrate the pregnancy, although it wasn't a baby shower. That would come later. This was just an excuse for Eugene to throw a party.

"I'm glad we've already done all the baby parties," Nate

said, gesturing for Bailey to bring him a beer. "I'm more than happy for it to be someone else's turn."

Liam chuckled. "You think you're through it all? Just wait until the birth."

"Nope." Nate held up one of his fingers. "I made Mum promise. No parties, and no massive family gatherings until they're at least a month old. "There's no need to put either Grace or our child through that."

Liam laughed. "Good luck with that."

"What do you mean? I—"

The music suddenly got louder, and Nate stopped talking midstream. I looked around to see that a few people had started dancing in the area of the pub that Eugene had cleared to serve as a dance floor.

Bailey brought Nate's beer over and I watched her return to the bar, snag Summer's hand, and pull her onto the dance floor. They bounced and spun together, both laughing.

Damn, Summer's smile was gorgeous.

Kennedy joined them, and they all held hands and swayed to the beat.

"Are you going to dance with them?" I asked Liam, who was gazing at Kennedy fondly.

"Maybe later, but I have two left feet. No one needs to see that until they're a few drinks in."

I shot him a look. "Kennedy isn't drinking, is she?"

He snorted. "Hardly. She's having those virgin cocktails that Bailey has been making for Grace the past few months. All fruit juice and sugar, so I don't need to worry about her getting drunk, just sugar high."

Bailey disconnected from the group and went to the bar, where Eugene had been inundated with orders.

Darcy stood and wiped his hands on the front of his dark jeans. "Well, even if none of you are dancing, I am."

He made his way around the tables to the dance floor,

where he headed straight for Summer. I narrowed my eyes as he spoke to her, and gritted my teeth as he touched her arm.

"You seriously don't have a problem with that?" I asked Liam.

He shrugged. "Is he what I want for her? No. But like I said before, I don't think there's any reason to worry. He isn't what Summer wants for herself either. Haven't you ever noticed that the men she brings home are usually older than her, not younger?"

Huh. I'd never picked up on that. I filed it away to think about later.

"What about you?" I asked Connor.

His lips twitched. "I trust that Summer knows exactly what she's doing."

"Since when?" I demanded. After Nate, Connor was the most overprotective of her brothers. But the bastard just gave me his signature Mona Lisa smirk.

"I have a problem with it," Nate said, swigging his beer. "But I also like to keep all my parts in working order, and if I interfere right now, there's every chance that Summer will break something. It's easier to let it go until later. I have a good view from here, so I can see whether she's making good choices or not."

I side-eyed him. Being married to Grace had mellowed him, which was usually a good thing, but right now, I wouldn't have minded the old, hot-tempered Nate showing his face.

A new song started, and on the dance floor, Darcy took Summer's hands and whisked her into his embrace. My scowl deepened as I realized that, to my annoyance, Darcy was a decent dancer. He had light feet and spun Summer with ease.

Perhaps once, I might have thought they were a good fit

for each other, but now, I knew better. Darcy couldn't give Summer what she needed, just like I couldn't. Unfortunately, that didn't seem to be holding him back the same way it did me.

My jaw clenched as he checked out her legs when she twirled away from him.

"Calm down before you break something," Toby said cheerfully.

I settled back sullenly and did my best not to pay any attention to Summer and Darcy. However, a few songs later, when Summer broke off from him to go to the bar, my feet carried me right to her side.

I shoved through the cluster of people around the bar until I was beside her. "You look cozy with Darcy."

I cursed myself as soon as the words were out of my mouth. The last thing I needed was for her to guess I was jealous. Especially considering our history.

She glanced over her shoulder at me, but fortunately, the wicked temper she so often displayed around me was nowhere to be seen.

"He's a great dancer," she said.

I scoffed, even though yeah, he was.

"What?" One of her eyebrows arched up. "If you think you can do better, I'd be happy to see you try."

I was tempted.

Damn, I was so tempted.

I longed to take her hand, sweep her onto the floor, and show her exactly how good we could be together. But I wouldn't. If I did that now, her brothers would know exactly why I'd been so sour about her dancing with Darcy, and then I'd be in trouble.

I shook my head. "I just didn't think you'd want to be seen as a cougar."

Her mouth fell open, and warning alarms blared in my head.

Fuck, I'd gone too far.

Oh, shit.

Fury blazed in her eyes, and for a moment, I thought she might hit me. But then she snatched up a glass of wine from the bar and tossed it in my face. I closed my eyes and sputtered, my nose burning as I inhaled. I wiped my eyes on the back of my sleeve and blinked at her.

She went onto her tiptoes, her nose an inch from mine. "At least Darcy knows what he wants and isn't afraid to go for it."

Then she spun around and sashayed away. Right back to Darcy.

Fuck my life.

"Asher."

I glanced up. Bailey was holding a towel out to me.

I took it and dried my face, then passed the towel back to her. "Thanks."

"It's fine," she said, tossing it aside.

I flinched. Coming from Bailey, the queen of enthusiasm, a simple "fine" was definitely the cold shoulder.

Fair enough. I'd insulted her best friend.

My head down, I returned to our table, beer-less and reeking of wine.

"What was that about?" Liam asked.

Toby looked like he was about to bust himself trying to hold in his laughter.

"Let it out," I snapped. "Go on."

He burst out laughing. Nate joined him. To their credit, both Liam and Connor resisted.

"Seriously," Toby gasped between laughs. "What did you do to her?"

I didn't reply, but I felt my face turning red as shame

heated my insides. I'd been an ass. I looked over at Summer, who was once again spinning in Darcy's arms. I wanted to stride over there and tear them apart, but after how poorly I'd behaved, I deserved to have to sit here and watch her with someone else.

Karma at its finest.

11

———————

SUMMER

"WHAT DID ASHER SAY TO END UP WEARING YOUR DRINK?" Darcy asked as I rejoined him.

"It wasn't my drink." I didn't know whose it was, but I trusted that Bailey would replace it. "He was acting like an ass, as usual."

Darcy grimaced. "I don't know what's gotten into him lately. He's being weird."

I kept quiet because I hadn't noticed whether he was behaving differently. We were always at odds, so it was difficult to tell.

"Let's just dance," I said, taking his hand.

A grin crept across his face. "Sure."

We danced until my feet ached. Through pop music, country songs, and ballads. I laughed and smiled nearly enough to wipe the sting of Asher's comment from my mind —but not quite.

Darcy was good company. I wasn't interested in him romantically—he reminded me too much of a younger version of my brothers for that—but I liked spending time with him. Eventually, he pulled me off the dance floor, dropped my hand, and let his head flop back.

"I need a breather," he said. "I haven't done this much cardio in ages."

I laughed. "You'd never know. You've been keeping up well."

He winked. "Thanks, beautiful. I'd better bow out now though."

He turned and made his way toward the bar. I lingered for a moment, debating whether to sit down or find another partner. If I stopped dancing, I'd have time to mull over Asher's cruel words, and I'd rather not do that.

"May I have this dance?" a raspy American-accented voice said from behind me.

I spun around and squealed. "Blair!"

"Hey, Summer." He opened his arms and caught me as I lunged into them, his shaggy hair flopping around his face. "It's good to see you."

I embraced him fiercely. "I didn't know you were coming."

"I wouldn't miss it." He released me and stepped back. "Mina and the twins weren't able to get away, but it was easier for me."

Blair was a musician. His band was reasonably successful, but he wasn't famous enough that every second of his time was scheduled weeks into the future.

"How long are you here for?" I asked.

"Just a week, maybe two." He scowled at me when my face fell. "Don't go getting mopey on me. I get enough of that from Kennedy."

I laughed. "Just wait until the pregnancy hormones kick in properly."

His eyes widened. "You mean, they haven't already?"

I touched the tip of my finger to my nose. "Didn't you promise me a dance?"

"Too right." He took one of my hands. "You ever learned any Latin dancing?"

"Uh...no," I admitted.

His teeth flashed between his lips as he smiled. "Don't worry. Just go where I guide you and spin when I turn you."

"Easy."

To my absolute shock, he placed one of his hands on my hip and pulled me closer. He was a good head taller than me, and much broader, so being close to him made me feel petite in comparison.

He lowered his head, and his breath gusted across my ear as he spoke. If there had been any chemistry between us whatsoever, I'd have swooned. Unfortunately, once again, he was too much like a brother.

"Want to make Asher jealous?" he whispered.

My gaze snapped to his. "What?"

He smirked. "Don't worry. Our secret."

I stared at him. "H-how did you know?"

His green eyes locked onto mine. "I've been taking courses on body language and microexpressions. I don't want to be caught off guard again like I was with Tyler."

I felt a pang of sympathy for him. "I get it."

Tyler had been a friend of his, until he'd knocked Blair out and kidnapped Kennedy.

"So," he prompted, "what do you say?"

The first thrums of a new song played over the speakers, and I let him draw me deeper onto the dance floor.

"I say yes."

Assuming it was possible to make Asher jealous at all. But at this point, I was willing to try.

His feet moved quickly as the song kicked up a notch. The singer was crooning in Spanish, and I took a moment to wonder if he'd requested the song with whoever was in charge of the playlist.

I did my best to follow along, admiring his flourishes and how easily he showed me where I needed to be. His hands wandered up my body, but there was nothing sexual about it. I suspected it was just how he'd been taught the dance. Either that, or he was putting on a show for Asher's benefit.

When the song ended, he gripped my hand and tugged me off the dance floor and across the pub. I followed him, my heart light. I'd liked Blair since the day I'd met him. He was gruff, but he had a way of making people feel good.

He led me out the exit and around the corner of the building, into the same alley where I'd once had the most excruciating conversation of my life with Asher.

"What are we doing out here?" I asked.

He raised his finger to his lips. "Wait for it."

I cocked my head, listening carefully. A few seconds later, heavy footfalls pounded around the side of the building, approaching rapidly.

Asher appeared out of the dark, a scowl plastered across his face. "Blair, your sister is looking for you."

Blair grinned, his eyes twinkling mischievously in the dim light. "I'll be in soon."

Asher's scowl deepened. "She wants you now."

Blair rested his hand on my hip. Asher's eyes followed the motion.

"Five minutes won't make a difference," Blair said.

I shifted from one foot to the other as the two men stared each other down, not one hundred percent sure what was going on except that it was a giant pissing contest with me in the center.

Asher shifted his attention to me. "Do you really want to do this? He's just going to leave in another week or two."

My instincts screamed at me to push Blair away and reassure Asher, but where did he get off questioning my choices when he'd told me both through his words and actions that he didn't want me himself?

"It's my choice what I do and with whom," I said firmly.

The corners of his mouth turned downward. "I just don't want to see you hurt, and neither do your brothers."

I softened toward him a smidge. "That's sweet—although it has nothing to do with any of you, and again, it's my choice. If you're really bothered by the decisions I make, perhaps you should ask yourself why."

His breath caught, and he looked stricken. He backed up a step. "I can't." He shook his head, as if reinforcing that fact. "I just can't."

With that, he turned and stalked away.

"Wait!" I called after him.

I hadn't meant to upset him. Just to make him question why he cared so much about what I did. But he didn't stop, and he didn't return to the pub. Instead, he took off down the darkened street.

I was about to turn away when movement in the corner of my eye stopped me. I stared hard at the alcove where I'd seen the movement. I could have sworn there was someone there. But I couldn't see anything.

I took a few steps toward the alcove, but halted when Blair touched my shoulder.

"Did you see that?" I asked, glancing back at him.

He frowned. "See what?"

12

———————

ASHER

My head throbbed and my eyes were gritty as I dragged myself out of bed on Saturday morning. I couldn't even blame it on a hangover. I'd made a monumental ass of myself last night, and then I'd run instead of facing up to the consequences of my actions when Summer called me on my bullshit.

Hopefully no one had noticed that I'd left just after Summer and Blair and never returned. The last thing I needed was for Liam to put two and two together and realize I was lusting after his little sister, or for some other good Samaritan to break the news to him. I already knew nothing could happen, so all that would do was create a ton of awkwardness.

Blair had definitely clocked my interest. His smug expression when I'd followed them out told me that. But I didn't think he'd say anything. I suspected it was more a case of him using this opportunity to get back at me for being rude to his sister when she first moved back to Destiny Falls.

Cookie wound around my legs as I made my way to the bathroom, and she waited at the door as I finished up, washed my hands, and went to the kitchen. I poured cat food into her bowl, refilled her water, and switched the kettle on to boil. I needed coffee.

Coffee, and then exercise. Very little could distract me like hurtling down the mountainside on my bike.

I made toast for breakfast, along with a mug of black coffee, and ate quickly, then dressed and loaded my cycle onto the back of my car. I double checked my first aid kit was under the front seat, filled a bottle with water, and grabbed a sweater and my helmet on the way out the door.

The morning air was brisk, with a hint of frost on the grass, but the sky was clear and once the sun was high, it would get warmer.

I drove to the parking area just outside of town, on the side closest to Destiny Peak, where a bunch of mountain biking trails began. Once there, I unloaded my bike, clipped my helmet into place, slotted my water bottle into its compartment, set my exercise watch to go, and started up a trail.

I cycled toward a lookout point, my legs burning with every rotation, but no matter how hard I pushed myself, I couldn't get Summer out of my head. I kept picturing her laughing with Darcy or standing in a dark corner with Blair. The images were messing with my mind.

What the hell was going on?

I gritted my teeth, straightened my legs slightly, and lifted my ass off the bike seat, trying to get a bit more leverage so I could go a little faster. Breathe a little harder. Sweat a little more.

Summer continued to consume my goddamn thoughts.

I didn't get it. I'd accepted a while ago that I was attracted to her, however much I might not want to be, but this was something more, and I didn't know what to make of it.

When I reached the lookout, I dismounted and gazed out over the forest, panting heavily. I grabbed my water bottle and chugged a third of it, then turned around, ready for the return journey. Perhaps once I reached the bottom, I'd cycle another of the trails. One that was less well-maintained and would require more concentration.

I navigated downhill, taking the sharp corners less and less carefully each time. I picked up speed along a straight section, flying faster and faster until, all of a sudden, a figure appeared on the trail in front of me.

My heart leapt into my throat, and I squeezed the brakes, the tires skidding beneath me, spraying dirt in all directions.

The figure grew larger. I wasn't slowing quickly enough. I was going to hit them.

They turned, and their eyes widened. Recognition flared. It was Connor, clad in his ranger's uniform.

At that second, my front tire hit a stone, and I veered sideways, off the trail. I landed on my side in a pile of damp leaves and fallen branches. The air whooshed out of my lungs, and my hip throbbed from the impact.

"Ah, fuck," I groaned. Pinpricks of pain danced along my shins and forearms. The scent of rotting organic matter filled my nose, and slowly, I pushed myself upright. Blinking rapidly, I waited for my vision to stop wavering, and then scanned my forearms. They were scratched to shit but didn't seem to be bleeding much.

"Here." Connor leaned over and extended his hand toward me.

I clasped his hand and let him pull me to my feet. I

brushed myself down, sweeping away twigs and leaves, and reached down for my bike to haul it back onto the trail.

I bent to check my shins. My hip protested the movement, and I flinched. Like my forearms, my shins were scratched, but only one scratch was bleeding much. I touched it and hissed.

"Ouch."

Straightening, I tested each of my muscles. Everything seemed to be in working order, if a bit achy.

When I turned to Connor, he was watching my every move with that intense focus of his.

He met my gaze and scowled. "What were you thinking? You came speeding down there like a bat out of hell."

I grimaced. "I wasn't expecting to see anyone else out here this early."

It hadn't occurred to me that Connor's cabin was nearby, or that he might be up and about.

"You still have to be careful," he growled. "What if some tourist had wandered in front of you?"

Guilt churned in my gut. He was right. I needed to behave more responsibly. As a paramedic, I knew exactly what could happen when things went wrong. My preoccupation with Summer was making me careless—and worse, proving I was exactly the sort of reckless man she didn't need in her life.

"Sorry. I'll be more careful," I promised.

Connor crossed his arms and frowned. "What's with the Speed Racer act anyway? You trying to outrun something?"

My quick intake of breath seemed to echo in the space between us. Damn, I'd forgotten how perceptive Connor could be. He didn't say much, so it was easy to underestimate him, but he saw more than he let on.

"Is it something to do with Summer?" he persisted. "I noticed the tension between you two yesterday."

I snorted. "She tossed a drink in my face. I think everyone noticed."

He continued to stare at me. "There's more to it than that. All the arguing you two do is a weird type of foreplay, but it's been different lately. Something is changing."

"It's not like that. There's nothing between us. I'd never..."

My breath started to come in rough pants. If Connor had noticed my attraction to Summer, did that mean others had too?

I'd hoped to have more time to get my head around whatever was happening, and to remind myself of why I needed to keep my distance. But if everyone in town was talking about us, I was screwed. I wouldn't have any time to figure out my own feelings.

"Hey, calm down." Connor clapped his hand on my shoulder. "I don't think anyone else noticed."

"Other than Blair," I muttered.

He inclined his head. "Maybe. But it would be easier for him to see since he's been out of town. You know how it is, it's harder to perceive change when it's gradual."

"Then how come you did?" I asked. "And why aren't you angry?"

He shrugged. "I'm around you less than the others too, and I'm not angry because you can't help the way you feel. As far as I know, you haven't done anything I need to be angry about, right?"

"No," I said quickly. "I haven't."

"Good." He pursed his lips. "You might want to be more careful, unless you want people asking questions."

I sighed, slowly regaining control of my breathing. "You're right. Again."

He smirked. "I know. That said, there's another option too."

I frowned. "What?"

"You could get your shit together and do something about whatever you feel for my sister."

My heart almost stopped. "I'm not the right kind of guy for her."

He shrugged. "If you say so."

"Everyone always says so." Or at least, that's how it felt. Surely, Connor had said something along those lines at some point too, even if I couldn't quite recall it now.

He studied me. "I never realized you were such a rule follower. Do whatever you think is best. You okay to keep biking?"

"Yeah."

"Great." He shoved his hands into his pockets and backed away. "Remember what I said. Either do something, or don't, but don't let other people's opinions be what stops you."

He strode away, whistling to himself, leaving me to wonder what the hell I was supposed to do now.

13

SUMMER

"Is she going to be all right?" Helena Smith asked, wringing her hands nervously.

"I believe so." I finished palpating her spaniel's abdomen and glanced at the clock on the wall. The Saturday morning clinic was almost over. Helena and Rose were my last clients. "I need to run a test, but I'm pretty sure that Rose is going to be a mother."

Helena's face creased into a brilliant smile. "Really?"

"Mmhmm. I'll let you know in just a few minutes."

Sure enough, with a quick test, I was able to confirm that Helena and Rose were soon to welcome a litter of puppies into their home.

Helena gathered Rose in her arms and smothered her furry belly with kisses. The placid dog just accepted this display of love and gazed back at her owner with soulful brown eyes.

"I'm so excited," Helena exclaimed. "When will the puppies come?"

"About six weeks would be my guess," I replied. "But don't rely on that too heavily. You'll want to be ready within a month, just in case."

"I will." She petted Rose's fluffy ears. "I wonder who the father is. We intended to breed her, but we haven't arranged anything yet, so I have no idea who the culprit could be."

I laughed. "Maybe you'll be able to work it out when the puppies are born."

She grinned. "I'll certainly try. I'm not upset, of course. Just curious."

I peeled off my gloves and tossed them in the bin. "Fair enough. But all you can do for now is take Rose home and make sure you keep her fed and comfortable until the puppies arrive."

"She's going to be smothered with affection. The kids will be thrilled."

"I'm sure they will be." I'd have been ecstatic if our dog had puppies while we were growing up. Mum and Dad were never interested in caring for newborns though, so they'd always been careful to spay or neuter our animals as soon as they were brought into the house.

"Thanks, Summer. I'll see you next time." She waved and carried Rose out of the examination room.

I shook my head and laughed to myself. Someone had been getting up to no good at the dog park.

I cleaned the examination table and finished entering my consultation notes into the computer. I'd just shut it down when Beverley, our receptionist, stuck her head around the door.

"You have a visitor," she said, her lips curled in an odd little smile.

I groaned. "Did someone come in last minute?"

"Not for a consult." Her smile stretched. "It's Asher."

"Ah."

I bit my lip, debating what to do. He'd been rude enough to me last night that I didn't want to see him, but he'd also seemed vulnerable when he'd left, and I couldn't push him away if he needed me.

"Send him in," I said.

She winked and bustled out. I rolled my eyes. Both Beverley and Cal, the other veterinarian, were aware of my unrequited feelings for Asher. They'd caught me poring over his social media on my work computer one day and I'd been forced to confess. Cal was polite enough not to mention it, but Beverley had no such qualms.

Asher entered, his hair damp and his cheeks flushed, bringing with him the spicy scent of whatever masculine soap or shampoo he must have used in the shower. At first glance, he looked healthy and gorgeous as ever, but as my gaze lingered, I noticed the redness around his eyes and the scratches up his arms.

"What happened?" I asked, gesturing at the scratches.

He rubbed at them self-consciously. "Came off my bike."

"Ouch." I crossed my arms and leaned against the examination table. "Why are you here?"

I couldn't afford to be distracted by the desire to kiss his boo-boos, or by the fact I wanted to burrow my face in his chest and breathe him in.

He grimaced and moved his weight from one foot to the other, wincing slightly. "I came to apologize for last night," he said, the flush on his cheeks darkening. "My behavior toward you was way out of line and it won't happen again."

"Hmm." I appreciated the apology, obviously, but I wasn't satisfied with how this left things between us. "Why did it happen?"

He looked down at his feet. "I don't know. I was feeling irrationally angry yesterday, and it burst out of me in the worst possible way."

My heart twinged for him. He'd been having a difficult time lately. His job wasn't easy, especially when they lost people. He wasn't superman, no matter how much he might like to think otherwise.

"I can understand why you'd be upset after the week you've had," I conceded, wondering whether to push. I decided to go for it. "I think there's more to it than that though."

"Oh, yeah?" He raised his eyebrows. "Like what?"

I hesitated, a faint alarm jangling in the back of my mind, warning me that I might not like what would happen if I pushed too far.

"I think you're attracted to me but don't want to admit it," I told him. Screw my internal warning system. We'd been tiptoeing around this for long enough.

He gaped, completely taken aback. "What?"

I shrugged one shoulder. "Am I wrong?"

"Fuck. Summer." He yanked his hand through his hair and turned away from me for a moment. His back expanded as he drew in a deep breath, and then he faced me again. "You can't just say shit like that. Yeah, I think you're pretty, but you're my best friend's sister. Practically my extended family. Anything else between us would be too strange."

I put my hand on my hip. "Grace was basically part of the family before she and Nate got together, and no one thinks it's strange."

A muscle in his jaw ticked. "That's different."

"How?" I didn't understand his logic.

"It just is." He huffed, and fisted his hands at his sides, as if he needed to do something with them but wasn't sure what. "Besides, I'm wrong for you in so many other ways."

"How so?"

He ignored my question. "Look, I came to apologize, and I did. From now on, you can flirt with, dance with, and date whomever you want, and I'll butt out. It's none of my business."

I straightened and stepped toward him. "Maybe I don't want you to butt out. Maybe I want my love life to be your business."

"It can't be," he rasped. "It won't happen."

My heart sank. For a moment, I'd thought maybe he would finally admit there was something between us, but it seemed I'd been mistaken.

"Can you really look me in the eye and tell me you don't feel anything for me?" I asked, willing him to be honest with both of us for a change.

He met my eyes. "I care about you as a person, but I have no feelings for you beyond that. I can't."

My chest felt like it was splitting in two. I nodded mutely and waved him out of the examination room. To my relief, he went. If he'd stayed for a second longer, I might have cried at him.

I didn't think he'd be able to do it. I'd thought for sure that he'd have to own up to his feelings for once.

I'd been wrong.

Again.

14

ASHER

"Hey, Ash," Zane called as I inhaled the mouthwatering scent of chili as I served myself a generous portion and added a dollop of mashed potato. "I've got a question for you."

I made my way to the table in the center of the fire station's staff room and sat beside him. "What?"

"How do you feel about going on a blind date?" he asked, grinning.

I stiffened. "Excuse me?"

He shoved a spoonful of chili in his mouth, making me wait until he'd finished to explain. "My cousin, Tiff, is in town. She's thirty, single, and has a thing for men in uniform. You interested?"

I stared at him, stumped. I didn't know how to reply. I should say yes. Seeing someone else might help get my mind off Summer, but then I recalled Kylie's words, and I couldn't bring myself to open my mouth and agree.

Fortunately, at that moment, an alarm blared through

the station and Parks's voice came over the intercom, instructing both fire and ambulance teams to report to a house a few blocks over.

I leapt to my feet, eager for an excuse to avoid replying. Maia and I hurried to the ambulance, checked everything was in order, and I got behind the wheel and pulled out of the garage behind the fire engine.

We followed them around several corners to an unassuming single story house. Flames issued from one of the front windows, but it appeared the fire hadn't spread yet. The acrid scent of smoke filled the air.

While the fire crew got started with the house, Maia and I went straight to the couple standing beside the road. I frowned, recognizing the male as James, a guy I'd gone to school with. He wore only boxers, his slightly flabby belly on display to the world, and pale, red burn marks dotted his forearms.

I had no idea who the woman with him was, but one of James's sweaters covered her torso and hung to the tops of her thighs. She certainly wasn't his girlfriend, Tia, who worked with Heather Braddock at the local information center.

I scowled at James as I approached. I liked Tia. She was a nice person. And the fact James and this woman were half-dressed didn't fill me with confidence that they'd been respecting the boundaries of his relationship.

"Is anyone else inside?" I asked.

"No." James shook his head. "It's just us."

I raised my eyebrow. "Tia isn't here?"

He flushed and glanced at the ground. "She's working."

"Right."

Maia elbowed me and shot me a look, silently warning me to mind my own business. "What happened?" she asked. "Where are you hurt?"

Behind us, water was now being pumped through the broken front window, and the flames were already receding.

"Um, we had some candles lit," the woman said, huddling against James's side. Her face was pale, and I felt a pang of unwanted sympathy. Despite my disapproval of her choice to be with a man who was dating someone else, she'd had a shock, and it showed.

"We'd been using massage oil earlier, and some of it had spilled on the floor," she continued. "We were, um, you know, and I accidentally knocked over a candle. It landed on the massage oil and caught on fire."

"The oil was all over the bed too," James added. "It went up so fast we barely had time to react."

"Do you have any injuries other than burns?" I asked, doing my best to ignore my disdain and get into a professional mindset.

"I'm fine," the woman said. "No burns or anything. Just scared."

"That's good." I turned to James. "Show me the worst of it."

He angled his right forearm to show me a darker mark on the inside of his wrist. "I tried to put the fire out, but it got too big too quickly."

I inspected each of his burns. "The good news is that you don't need to go to the hospital, or see a doctor. We can patch you up and after that, you'll just need to change the dressings regularly and keep an eye on them for signs of infection."

I treated his burns while Maia kept the woman company. By the time I'd finished, the fire had been put out. Liam walked toward us, his blue gaze flicking from James to the woman and back again.

"We'll station someone here for a while longer, just to make sure there are no signs of the fire restarting," he told

James. "You should be safe to enter in a few hours though. If I were you, I'd get on the phone to your insurance company as soon as you can. We tried to limit the damage, but there's only so much we can do."

James nodded. "Thanks. I'll call them as soon as we're done here. I guess we'll need to find some clothes."

"Yeah." My voice had no inflection. "You might want to get in touch with Tia too. You know, since her house is partly burned down and all."

He grimaced and picked at the edge of one of his dressings. "I'll do that. Just got to think of a good story first."

"So you—" I stopped when Maia elbowed me again. I glared right back at her but shut my mouth.

"She doesn't need to know what really happened," James said. "It will only upset her more. I'll figure something out, and it will be fine as long as no one contradicts me. But that's all right. You guys have taken some kind of privacy oath, right?"

"Something like that," Maia replied.

I strode away, anger burning in my chest. Tia deserved better. It was guys like James who made the rest of us look bad. Fuck him, and fuck the fact he'd been able to settle down with a lovely woman and yet was so willing to throw it away.

If I had the woman I wanted, you can bet your ass I wouldn't make a mistake like that.

I packed away our gear and waited in the driver's seat until Maia joined me.

"You have to rein your temper in, Ash," she warned. "You can't lose your shit at people just because you disapprove of their choices."

"Come on." I turned the key in the ignition. "You can't say you don't want to hit his smug face."

She huffed. "No, but that's not the point. I didn't let my

emotions get the better of me. We're professionals. We have to act like it."

"I know." But that didn't make me like it any better.

I drove back to the station and parked in the garage. Maia and I did a quick inventory and replenished the burn kit. As we were closing up the bus, the fire engine crawled into the garage beside us. It came to a halt and the crew spilled out of the passenger door.

Liam and I walked down the corridor to the staff room together.

"That was bullshit, right?" I said to him, quiet enough that Maia hopefully wouldn't overhear. "Someone should tell Tia that James is cheating on her."

"I agree." He glanced over at me. "But you know we can't."

I grumbled. Yes, the nature of our callouts was supposed to be kept confidential, but there were ways around that.

"I'm going to do it," I said. "Somehow."

"Be careful, and don't do anything stupid. You know how this town works. She's bound to learn the truth soon anyway."

As we entered the staff room, Zane slung an arm around each of our shoulders.

"So, what do you want me to tell my cousin?" he asked. "Does she have a date with a hot paramedic?"

Damn. I hadn't avoided that after all. "Sorry, but no."

He released me and circled around to look at my face. "Why not? She's a great girl."

"I just..." Am hopelessly hung up on someone else. "Don't feel like dating at the moment."

"But you're always on the lookout for your forever girl," he protested. "It's one of the things I like most about you."

"Not right now." I turned away and busied myself making coffee.

"No," Liam protested, snatching the coffee away from me. "Please, spare us."

I rolled my eyes. "Coffee snob."

He didn't like the way I made coffee. I didn't get what the big deal was. Coffee was coffee.

"Is everything okay?" Zane asked me, his expression uncharacteristically serious. "It really isn't like you to turn down a date."

I didn't know how to answer. I wasn't sure if I was all right. Not with Summer Braddock consuming my thoughts.

15

SUMMER

As the birthday song crescendoed, my friends and family all lending their voices, I leaned over and blew out the candles on my cake. Closing my eyes, I made a wish.

I want a birthday kiss from Asher.

Opening my eyes again, I smiled at everyone gathered around me as they cheered. Beside me, Toby began to clap, counting off the years of my age. I narrowed my eyes at him, but he'd timed this well. He'd already blown out his candles, so it was too late for me to retaliate in kind.

"Happy birthday, sweetheart," Mum said, giving me a squeeze and kissing my cheek. She handed me a knife. "Cut the cake."

I set the blade to the chocolate frosting and glanced up, my eyes locking with Asher's. He stared back with an intensity that made me shiver. Toby yanked me into an embrace, his feet thudding against the wood of the deck outside Mom and Dad's house.

"I could have stabbed you," I squeaked as he knocked the air from me.

He scoffed. "You handle sharp tools all the time. You wouldn't make an amateur mistake like that."

I rolled my eyes and pushed him away. "Usually, I handle them around animals that are already unconscious and, you know, not moving."

"Psh. Details." He waved his hand like it didn't matter.

I sliced into the cake and cut several segments, then took a portion for myself and stepped aside. If there were fewer people here, I'd serve everyone individually, but there were too many—it seemed like half of Destiny Falls had turned up for our birthday party—so I'd just let them take what they wanted.

Bailey appeared beside me. "What did you wish for?"

I raised my eyebrow at her. "You know I can't tell you or it might not come true."

I glanced at Asher again, but he was no longer looking my way. Instead, he was smiling at Liam, his sexy mouth hooked up at the corner. How would it feel to kiss him there?

"Someone's superstitious," Bailey said. "I bet I can guess what it is, but it's more fun to leave it as a secret."

Gratitude surged through me. I suspected Bailey could, indeed, guess exactly what I'd wished for, and I appreciated her for not pushing the matter.

"I heard that Zane offered to set Asher up with his cousin, but he refused," Bailey murmured, low enough for only me to hear.

My eyes found Asher again, inextricably drawn to him. We hadn't spoken since he'd told me he wasn't interested in me, and the wound was still fresh. It didn't stop me from wanting him, but it stung nonetheless.

"That's surprising," I replied.

Asher didn't seem to have any qualms about dating as many women as possible. Not that he was a playboy. I doubted many of the dates progressed beyond a kiss on the cheek, but he certainly wasn't choosy about whom he took out.

Other than me.

"Maybe he's already interested in someone else," Bailey said, bouncing her eyebrows meaningfully.

Hope zapped through me, but I ruthlessly stomped it down.

"If he is, it isn't me," I said.

She looked disappointed. "Why do you assume the worst? You never know. Maybe he's finally come around."

I sighed. "Or maybe he's in his thirties and has less energy to date all the time."

A group of Toby's friends rushed past, heading for the empty fire pit. The sun had dipped beneath the horizon and apparently they'd decided it was time to light the fire. Toby was in the thick of it, tossing wood and beer boxes into the pit while one of his friends messed around with a box of matches.

"Sometimes I wonder if they're still twelve," I said.

Bailey rested the side of her head against mine. "It's nice that they still get excited about things."

"I guess."

The fire flickered to life. One of the guys opened a massive bag of marshmallows and they were all sticking them onto skewers to hold over the fire.

"Want to toast some marshmallows?" I asked.

"Definitely." She flashed me a dazzling grin. "Cook off?"

"You're on."

We strolled over, making our way through the cluster of people around the marshmallow bag. A cooler of beer stood nearby, although I doubted there was much point in using it.

The air was already crisp. Hopefully the fire would take the edge off the cold.

I grabbed a skewer and poked it through a marshmallow, then held it just above the fire, rotating the marshmallow slowly to achieve an even spread of golden brown. Bailey's marshmallow joined mine, but she dipped it too close to the flame and it caught on fire and fell into the pit.

"I win!" I cried, pulling mine out.

"Here you go, Bailey," a younger guy said, shyly offering her his perfectly toasted marshmallow.

She beamed at him and plucked it off the skewer. "Thank you, Tim."

I opened my mouth, then shut it again. "That doesn't count."

She smiled smugly. "Doesn't it?" She popped the marshmallow into her mouth. "It tastes like it counts."

I bit into my own marshmallow, humming as the warm, gooey interior burst onto my tongue, coating it with sweet goodness, then licked my fingers clean.

"Call it a draw?" I suggested.

"Sure."

A clang behind me caught my attention, and I looked around. Kennedy and Grace were lifting the lid from the spa pool and had dropped it a little too heavily.

"I'm surprised Nate and Liam let their pregnant wives lift anything," Bailey observed.

"I doubt they know." I laughed as Nate ran onto the deck from inside the house, waving his arms at Grace. "I might join them in the spa. Want to come?"

She considered for a moment, then shook her head. "No, I'll stay here. Maybe there will be some dancing soon."

"Okay. Have fun." I kissed her cheek and left her, scooting past Kennedy and Grace, who were engaged in a heated discussion about what they should and shouldn't do with their husbands, before entering the house.

I went to my old bedroom, where Mum still kept some of my clothes, and changed into a black bikini. I slung a towel over my shoulder and stopped at the refreshments table to pour myself a mimosa, then I took the glass out to the spa pool.

By now, Liam and Nate were nowhere to be seen, and Grace and Kennedy were lounging in the pool. Kennedy wore a pink bikini while Grace was in a one-piece that must have been a maternity design or else I had no idea how she'd fit her massively pregnant belly into it.

Music started playing through the speakers positioned around the edge of the deck, and I set my glass on the side of the spa pool and climbed in. Warmth engulfed me, and my muscles instantly relaxed, although the water didn't seem as hot as usual.

"I think you girls have the right idea," I said, sliding into a seat in one corner and grabbing my glass again. I sipped the mimosa and closed my eyes. "It's so nice in here."

Kennedy laughed. "I know. It would be lovely if we could have it hotter, but we set it to a lower temperature so it would be safe for the babies. Anything above body temperature can be dangerous to them."

"Huh." I drank again. "I didn't know that."

"Are you enjoying your birthday?" Grace asked, crossing her legs, which were extended along one side of the pool.

"I am. It's been a while since Tobes and I had a big party, so we're probably overdue for this."

"Hopefully Toby doesn't get too crazy," Grace said.

I shook my head, not worried about that. "The others will keep an eye on him."

By unspoken agreement, keeping Toby out of trouble

was not my responsibility on our birthday. The rest of the time, I couldn't say the same, but this was my break.

My chance to let loose.

Kennedy, Grace, and I chatted for a while. Bailey dropped by and replaced my drink, and Mum did the same a little later. I was pleasantly tipsy by the time I got out. The cold sobered me a little, and I dried myself and pulled on a pair of thick tights beneath my dress to combat the falling temperature.

Several couples, and a group of women, were dancing now. I made my way over to the fire pit and spotted Blair hovering near the dancers.

"Would you like to join them?" I asked him, a faint buzz still thrumming through my veins.

He took my hand. "Are you up for learning another Latin dance?"

I grinned. "Absolutely."

He let me go and jogged over to one of Toby's friends, who was controlling the music. A new song began to play with a distinctly Latin beat. Blair returned and tugged me toward the other dancers. He demonstrated the first few steps and then repeated them with me.

"You're really good at this," I said.

He looked bashful. "It's a musician thing. We have to have a good sense of rhythm."

"That doesn't make it less impressive."

He pivoted me around and I caught sight of Toby, near the fire pit, mooning over a pretty blonde woman in a short, tight dress. I had to admire her strength. I'd be frozen if I were wearing that outfit.

"Have you seen Toby?" I asked Blair. "He seems to be smitten."

He pivoted me around again and made a sound of agreement. "New winter fling?"

"I think so." I sighed. "It seems like he falls in and out of love every other week."

Blair's hand grazed my lower back as he prompted me to turn. "Meanwhile you've been hung up on the same guy for...how long exactly?"

"Most of my life," I admitted.

I sought out Asher. He was sitting near the fire pit, with Liam on one side and Zane on the other, but his dark eyes were locked on me. I tore my gaze away, my cheeks blazing.

I noticed Blair looking the same way, and at first, I thought he was studying Asher too, but then he asked, "Does Zane still have a boyfriend."

I threw my head back and laughed. "You sly guy. No, he's single. This song is about to end, and Zane loves to dance. Why don't you ask him for the next one?"

He hesitated for a fraction of a second, but then nodded. "You'll be fine on your own?"

I swatted his arm. "I'm not helpless. I'll find Bailey, and we can dance together."

"Okay, then."

As the music tapered out, Blair and I separated, and he headed toward the fire pit. I scanned my surroundings, looking for the best place to sit for a few minutes until I could locate Bailey. I started moving forward but stopped abruptly when the most gorgeous man alive appeared like a vision in front of me.

Asher's expression was unreadable, but he held his hand toward me. "Dance with me?"

16

———————

ASHER

MY MOUTH TURNED DRY AS I WAITED FOR SUMMER'S response. A muscle in my abdomen quivered and I smoothed my hands down the front of my tidy, black jeans.

Summer tilted her head, her mossy green gaze sharp, and I wondered briefly if she might shoot me down—again. At least this time I wasn't drunk. But then she placed her delicate hand in mine.

"I'd love to dance with you," she said softly.

Her eyes searched mine, presumably as she tried to figure out why I was doing this. She wouldn't find an answer because I didn't know myself. I'd seen her dancing, looking sexy and sinful in a gold dress that molded to her curves, and before I'd been able to think anything through, I'd found myself by her side, asking for a dance.

I couldn't look away from her as I drew her closer and began to sway. My free hand skimmed down her back and curved around to rest on the slight swell of her hips.

I wasn't a bad dancer. I may not know the fancy moves

that Blair did, but I could hold my own. As we moved together, all I could think was how much I loved having Summer in my arms. Contentment warmed my insides. She belonged here, and there was no denying I wanted her.

Still, that didn't mean I could have her.

I was a mess. Overly tired most days, and barely functioning some of the time. Riddled with anxiety—not that I let anybody see it—and driven to cycle myself into exhaustion for the sake of a decent sleep. Completely the opposite of the calm, collected, and responsible man she deserved.

"What brought this on?" Summer asked as the song changed to a slower one.

"I don't know," I admitted. "You looked beautiful tonight, and I couldn't stay away."

Her nostrils flared and she growled. "I'm getting some seriously mixed messages from you, and I don't know what you want me to do about it."

I bit the inside of my cheek as conflicted emotions roiled in my gut. She was right. It wasn't fair of me to be hot and cold.

"I'm sorry." I squeezed her hand gently. "I'm still figuring that out myself, but I'll try to be less confusing."

"I'd appreciate that."

Someone bumped Summer from behind, and she caught herself on my chest. Instinctively, my arms tightened around her, my hands coming to rest on the small of her back. I could feel each inhalation and exhalation as her wide eyes held mine.

I buried my face against the side of her neck and skimmed my lips along her silky skin. She smelled faintly of chlorine, with a sweeter underlying scent that was all her own. I breathed her in, and noticed her chest expand as if she were doing the same to me.

I pulled back just enough to see her face. Her pupils

nearly swallowed her irises, and her pouty lower lip was caught between her teeth. Those beautiful emerald eyes of hers sparkled in the firelight.

She stole my breath. For all I cared, she could have it.

Her teeth released her lip, and her tongue darted out to wet it. I couldn't look away. I wanted to taste her. To trace the same path her tongue had, and to discover whether those lips were as plush as they looked.

I wanted to learn whether she'd gasp when I kissed her, or if she'd be silent. Would she take whatever I gave her or make her own demands?

I suspected the latter. Summer Braddock wasn't a submissive kind of girl. I loved that about her, even when it meant listening to her chew me out for something idiotic I'd said or done.

"Ash," she whispered.

My head lowered. Inch by inch, the distance between our mouths vanished. But just before they made contact, a body slammed into me from the side. I jerked in shock and automatically shifted to shield Summer from the impact. Once I was sure she was fine, I spun to glare at whichever asshole had interrupted us.

Toby beamed at me, his arm around the waist of a tall, athletic blonde woman.

"Ash!" he exclaimed. "This is Winita. She's my new girl-friend. Isn't that right, baby?"

Winita, clearly every bit as drunk as Toby, swayed on her feet. "Nice to meet you."

She spoke with a European accent, which suggested she was a tourist who'd come to town for the skiing. How on earth she'd found her way to the party, I had no idea.

I sighed and forced myself to smile at her. "I'm Asher. This is Summer, Toby's sister."

Winita stumbled forward and tried to hug Summer. "Happy birthday!"

"Uh, thanks." She steadied the other woman and patted her shoulder.

"Summer, you have to come and talk to Wini," Toby said. "You're going to love her so much."

"But I—"

He grabbed her arm and tugged her away. With a reluctant glance back at me, she followed him.

I watched her go, and I couldn't help but feel like I'd just lost something special. But maybe it was for the best. If I'd kissed her right here, where anyone could see, everyone would assume we were an item. Best not to open that can of worms.

Dragging my feet, I returned to the chair beside Liam and grabbed the drink I'd left there earlier. I flopped onto the seat and drained the beer, grimacing at the unpleasant aftertaste. Smoke and something bitter. Ash from the fire must have landed in it at some point while I'd been gone.

"I'm going to get another drink," I told Liam, and began to make my way across the yard, toward the cooler. Part way there, the world seemed to shift around me. I couldn't focus on where I was going, and my thoughts became as blurry as my vision.

Damn, I must have had more to drink earlier than I'd thought. Perhaps I'd been so distracted by Summer and irritated seeing her whirl in Blair's arms that I hadn't noticed. Hopefully, she wouldn't realize. After how she'd shut me down the last time I'd drunkenly hit on her, I couldn't imagine she'd be pleased if she did.

I changed direction and ambled toward the house, slowly making my way up the stairs and across the deck. My heart was racing, and my head spun. If I lay down for a while, hopefully I'd feel better.

I entered through the open double doors. The lights were off, and I'd seen Heather and Eugene dancing earlier, so I doubted anyone was inside—unless they, like me, needed a rest.

I crossed the living room and patted the wall until my fingers brushed the edge of the light switch. I flicked it and rushed to shield my eyes as the hall was suddenly illuminated.

I blinked, my eyes adjusting slowly, and made my way down the hall to the first bedroom. I didn't know whose it was—or had once been—but it had a bed, and that was all that mattered.

I collapsed onto the bed, closed my eyes, and everything went dark.

17

———

SUMMER

FRUSTRATION SIMMERED IN MY GUT AS I TRIED TO MAKE polite small talk with my drunk brother and his even drunker date. I'd been so close to kissing Asher.

So. Close.

Our mouths had literally been inches apart. But Toby had to interrupt. It wasn't even as if he'd done it maliciously. He'd never done an ill-intentioned thing in his life. He was a freaking golden retriever of a person. But that didn't make me want to shout at him any less.

For years, I'd been pining for Asher, and this was the closest I'd ever gotten to kissing him. Why couldn't the universe let me have what I wanted for once? Instead, I got to chat with Toby and Winita until they decided they'd rather make out on the chair beside me.

Sighing, I got up and went to find Asher. I doubted I could re-initiate the kiss, but maybe I could salvage something. After all, the chemistry between us earlier had been intense. I couldn't have been the only one who'd felt it.

Unfortunately, there was no sign of Asher anywhere. He wasn't dancing, and the seat he'd occupied earlier, beside Liam, was empty. My heart skipped. Surely he wouldn't have left.

I walked over and dropped onto Asher's empty chair.

"Where's Ash?" I asked Liam. "Did he go home already?"

Liam shook his head. "He went to get a drink a while ago and then went inside. Maybe he needed to use the bathroom."

"Thanks."

I got up again and picked my way across the yard to the house, around partygoers and discarded beer bottles. I waved to Grace and Kennedy as I passed them by and stepped over the threshold into the house.

The living area was dark, but light from the hall provided enough illumination for me to cross the room unhindered. For a moment, I wondered what I was doing. I shouldn't bother Asher on the toilet. What was wrong with me?

Perhaps I'd just make sure that's where he was. Otherwise, I'd worry that I'd frightened him away from the party. I hated the thought of that.

The music from outside grew fainter as I paced down the hall to the bathroom door. It stood open, and no one was inside. So much for that theory. I took the stairs to my old bedroom, where I'd left my phone when I got changed. I quickly typed a message.

Summer: *Where are you?*

I sat on the edge of the bed and waited for a reply. When none came after several minutes, I hit the "Call" button. A muted melody came from somewhere below me. I jolted to my feet and rushed down the stairs again. I followed the sound along the hall and into the first bedroom—Max's old room.

Hesitantly, I pushed the door open and peered inside. The call stopped, but I'd already spotted Asher. He lay sprawled face down on the bed, his feet hanging off the end. My gut clenched. The fact his phone hadn't woken him concerned me.

I tiptoed over to him and shook his shoulder gently. "Ash? Are you okay?"

His face tilted toward me, and his eyelashes fluttered but didn't open.

"Come on." I shook him more firmly. "Look at me."

"Sum-ma?" he slurred, his eyes forming slits for all of a second before they closed again. "Is 'at you?"

I sat beside him. "How much did you have to drink?"

He didn't reply. I frowned. It hadn't been that long since we'd been dancing, and he'd been reasonably sober then— or at least, he'd seemed that way.

"Ash." I jostled him again. "What did you drink?"

"Jus' some beer." With a grunt of effort, he pushed himself into a semi-upright position. His eyes opened, but didn't seem able to focus, and every few seconds, they closed again, and he struggled to reopen them.

"You're pretty, Sum-ma. Can I..." He trailed off, his eyes shutting, but then jolted awake again. "Wanna kiss?"

My heart flipped over. I stared at him, unsure how to feel. On the one hand, I'd been waiting forever for him to tell me I was pretty and ask for a kiss, but on the other, he was clearly drunk, and that cheapened the moment.

Anger flashed through me, hot and sharp, that he'd ruin such a special memory, but it quickly dissipated. He was in no shape to be held accountable for anything.

"Kiss?" he repeated.

"No." I guided him back into a horizontal position and adjusted the pillow to make sure he could breathe properly. "I want you, but only when you're fully conscious."

"I know wha' I..." He drifted off into sleep.

Worry knotted my insides. I stood and hurried outside, back across the deck and the yard until I reached Max, who was sitting with Liam.

"Asher is passed out in your old bedroom. I think he's just drunk, but would you check him for me?"

"Sure. No problem." He pushed off from the chair and followed me inside. Liam came too, but fortunately, our parents didn't notice us or else the entire Braddock family would be hovering over Asher the next time he woke.

In the bedroom, Max turned the overhead light on and knelt beside the bed. He roused Asher and tried to ask a few basic questions with little success. He peeled Asher's eyelids back and checked his eyes, then sniffed and scanned our surroundings.

"Has he been sick?" he asked.

"Not that I'm aware of. It's possible he was sick in the bathroom earlier but there's no sign of vomit in there."

"Liam?" he asked.

"He wasn't sick outside either," Liam confirmed.

Max sat back on his heels. "I don't think there's any reason to worry. Most likely he just had a few too many. As long as he doesn't get feverish or choke on his vomit, he should be fine."

"I'll sit with him," I said.

Both of my brothers turned toward me.

"It's your birthday," Liam said. "Surely you'd rather be outside with your friends. I can stay here."

"No." My heart thumped erratically. I didn't want to leave Asher. Not until I knew he was okay. "I'll stay."

18

———

ASHER

My head throbbed. I tried to move, and my mind screamed internally. Fuck, it felt like my brain had been wrung out and left to dry. What had happened?

I tried to open my eyes but realized I was face down. Excruciatingly slowly, I rolled onto my side. Somehow, despite my closed eyes, the world seemed to spin. I clutched my stomach and rode out a wave of nausea.

My lips were glued together, and when I forced them apart, my tongue was thick and fuzzy, sticking to the insides of my cheek each time I moved.

I opened my eyes and blinked in the dim light. I was in a bedroom, but not one I recognized. Had I gone home with someone?

I reached behind myself, but the bed was empty. Thank God. The last thing I needed was to have to deal with a woman I didn't remember. I strained my ears in case she was in another room, but the house remained silent.

I sat up, groaning when my head protested. I squeezed my eyes shut and rubbed my temples until the pounding receded. When I opened my eyes again, my jaw dropped. So much for being alone. A woman lay on a foam mattress on the floor beside the bed. Her hair was over her face, a blanket pulled up around her shoulders, and she was completely out of it.

Cautiously, I leaned closer. Relief lightened my heart as I realized she was wearing pajamas. And was that...?

"Summer?" I rasped, my voice barely audible.

Summer bolted upright, blinking sleepily. "I'm awake, I'm awake. What's going on?" Her gaze landed on me and her eyes widened. "You're up. How do you feel?"

"My head hurts like hell." The words husked out of me from my painfully dry throat.

"Hold on," she said, and reached past the far end of the mattress, grabbing for something. She lifted a glass of water and passed it to me. "Here. I also have painkillers, if you'd like them."

I nodded, and swiftly regretted it as the throbbing worsened. She retrieved a pack of acetaminophen and popped two out of their cases, then offered them to me. I took them, swallowed enough water to wet my mouth, and then gulped down the painkillers along with the rest of the glass of water.

I set the glass on the nightstand. "What am I doing here?"

She frowned. "Don't you remember?"

I wracked my mind but came up empty. I remembered singing, eating a slice of cake, and then...nothing.

"No." Panic clawed at my chest. What if I'd done something bad? Would anyone even tell me if I'd made an ass of myself? "What happened?"

She nibbled her lower lip. "You passed out last night. I

was worried about you, so I stayed here to make sure you'd be okay."

Shame coursed through me, hot and unpleasant. We'd been celebrating her birthday. She shouldn't have had to babysit me.

I hung my head. "I'm so sorry."

She shrugged. "Don't worry about it. If I'd stayed at the party, all I'd have done is danced, and nothing could top *our* dance, so what would have been the point?"

My chest tightened. We'd danced? And it had been good? Had I done anything? Touched her in ways I shouldn't because my inhibitions were lowered?

Fuck, I wished I knew.

"I hope I didn't do anything to make you uncomfortable while I was drunk," I said.

"You didn't." For some reason, she looked sad, her expressive eyes without their usual sparkle.

"How much do you remember from last night?"

I grimaced. "Nothing after the cake."

"Right. I guess that's that, then." She sighed. "I'll get you some more water."

I closed my eyes as she left and tried once again, to recall the previous evening. I could remember the sweet chocolatey taste of the cake on my tongue and then it was like my memory ran up against a brick wall. Damn. I couldn't help feeling like something significant had happened after that and I'd forgotten.

I gazed around the room, noting that it was Max's former bedroom. Some of his fantasy novels still lined the bookshelves against one wall. He'd been a Dungeons and Dragons nerd, but he got away with it because he was a Braddock, and they were practically Destiny Falls royalty. Everyone loved the Braddocks.

Summer appeared in the doorway, silhouetted against

the light emanating from the hallway. "Do you feel up to having breakfast? Dad has been cooking."

My mouth watered. "Is there bacon?"

She grinned. "Yes. Eggs too. Hashbrowns, and all the greasy stuff."

"Then I'll manage."

With effort, I clambered off the bed and righted myself. She gave me the glass and I drank it down. The ache in my head was already fading, although I doubted it would disappear completely.

I followed Summer out to the dining room, where plates loaded with bacon, eggs, hash browns, and toast occupied the center of the table. Toby sat at one end, his head in his hands, his complexion waxy and white.

"You look as terrible as I feel," I told him.

He raised his eyes and groaned. "Everything hurts. I wouldn't mind, but Winita snuck out on me in the middle of the night, so now I'm miserable."

"Winita?"

"Yeah." He squinted at me. "I introduced you at the party."

"I hardly remember last night," I told him, slumping on a chair a few over from his and dragging an empty plate toward myself.

"Bummer. At least I have the memories."

"Hey, boys," Eugene called from the doorway.

Was it just me, or had he spoken a little too loudly? And did he need to look so perky? It was ass o'clock, and some of us felt like an unwashed ball sack.

"I have pancakes," he announced, and I forgave him for everything. He raised the bottle in his other hand. "And maple syrup."

As soon as he placed the pancakes on the table, I

pounced. I loaded two onto my plate, then stacked bacon on top and drizzled maple syrup over everything.

Eugene sat opposite, and Heather joined us, carrying a tray of radioactively green drinks.

Toby's eyes bugged out. "God, no. Don't do this to us."

Heather laughed. "Sorry, boys. If you drink half a bar's worth of alcohol, you have to deal with the consequences."

"Uh...I'm not actually feeling that bad," I lied.

Everyone knew Heather's homemade hangover cure was worse than the affliction itself.

Summer bounced in behind her, smiling evilly. "Bottoms up."

Toby snatched one of the glasses and chugged it, wrinkling his face up as he did so. Summer raised her phone and snapped a photo. Toby shoved the glass away from himself and tore a bite from his pancake, using his hands and teeth. He chewed furiously and swallowed, then rinsed his mouth out with water.

"Delete that photo," he panted, glaring at Summer.

"Hmm." She tapped her chin thoughtfully. "Nope."

He slumped. "Come on, do me a favor. I already had to accept that my new girlfriend doesn't love me after all."

Summer rolled her eyes. "Maybe if you came off a little less intense..." She shook her head. "No. On second thought, don't change a thing. Anyone who can't handle you as you are doesn't deserve you."

"Aww. Does that mean—"

"Still not deleting it." She pushed one of Heather's concoctions toward me.

I drank it, knowing there would be no escape, and I pulled a face at Summer's phone camera when she aimed it at me. I shoveled bacon into my mouth to erase the nasty taste and slimy sensation of it on my tongue.

Summer and Heather joined us at the table, and

Summer smugly sipped from a mug of coffee that neither looked nor smelled green and revolting. Show off.

Halfway through the meal, I shot to my feet. "I forgot to feed Cookie."

Summer wiped her mouth on a napkin. "Kennedy has taken care of it."

I lowered myself back down. "Thank you."

"You're welcome." She narrowed her eyes at me. "Are you sure you're doing all right?"

"As well as I can be."

It was true, but also not the full story.

I hated having no memory of last night. I hadn't been blackout drunk since my early twenties, and I couldn't shake the feeling that I was missing something important. The trouble was, if I didn't remember, and no one else felt inclined to tell me, how could I know what it was?

19

———

SUMMER

"I CAN DROP YOU BOTH AT HOME," I VOLUNTEERED AS TOBY and Asher were discussing the best way to get back to their respective houses. Neither of them felt up to driving.

"Yes, please." Toby had no trouble accepting, but Asher hesitated. I wondered if he could sense that I wanted to get him alone. I needed him to confirm that he really didn't remember anything from last night—both so I wouldn't make a fool of myself and because it seemed suspicious that he'd conveniently forgotten our dance and near-kiss.

"Uh." He glanced out the window, looking a little lost. I felt for him. Either he was trying really hard to pretend nothing had happened between us, or he'd gotten himself completely hammered.

"Ash." Toby elbowed him. "Pay attention. You want a ride?"

Asher winced. "Yeah. Okay. Thanks, Summer."

He clearly didn't want to accept, but unless he asked

Mum or Dad to take him home—or was willing to walk several kilometers back to town—he was out of luck.

We helped Mum and Dad clean up and then headed out to my Ute, which was parked on the road frontage. I smiled at the Destiny Falls Veterinary Clinic logo on the side and pressed the button on the key fob to unlock the doors. Having my own business would never get old.

Toby got in the front, and Asher in the back. I drove Toby home first, both because his place was closer and so I'd have the opportunity to talk to Asher without anyone over-hearing.

Toby leaned across the center console and hugged me with one arm when we arrived. "See you later."

I hugged him back, then pushed him toward the door. "Go nurse your broken heart."

He clutched his chest and pouted as he got out. I laughed. He liked to be dramatic, but I had every faith he'd be head over heels for another girl by the end of the week. He shut the door and dragged his feet up the path to his front porch. I watched as he withdrew a key from his pocket and let himself in. Only then did I back out of the driveway.

The silence between Asher and I wasn't as easy as it had been previously. My gut tightened as I turned a corner. I just had to ask. There was no point in delaying.

I glanced at him. "You really remember nothing from last night?"

"Nothing." He seemed bothered by this. "Apparently, I can't handle my alcohol like I used to. I'm embarrassed, honestly, and a bit ashamed too. You deserve more than to have to look after me on your birthday."

"I didn't *have to*," I reminded him. "I chose to. Don't worry about it."

He huffed. "Still."

We'd reached his house sooner than I'd hoped, but I

pulled over to let him out, nonetheless. I could hardly keep him captive in my car just because I was upset I'd finally made progress with him only to lose it again.

He opened the door and turned toward me. "Thanks for the ride, and for keeping an eye on me overnight."

My stupid heart flip-flopped. "It wasn't a big deal."

His mouth quirked. "I know we don't always get along, but I appreciate you taking care of me."

"No problem." He needed to get out of my car before I mauled him with my mouth.

He climbed out of the Ute, then stopped. "Huh."

"What?" I asked, following his gaze. Cookie was trotting across the small lawn toward him, her fluffy black tail in the air. She meowed and twitched the patch of fur beneath her nose shaped like a white bowtie.

"She should be inside," he said. "I lock the cat door overnight. Kennedy must have let her out."

"Must have," I agreed, but unease stirred in the pit of my gut. I got out of the car. "Let's check your cat door."

He forced a nonchalance it was obvious he didn't feel. "Sure."

We walked to his front door together, and he unlocked it and entered. I followed him through the house to the back door, where the cat flap was set low to the ground. He knelt and pushed the flap. It didn't move.

"It's still locked," he said, rotating the dial so Cookie could come and go as she wished.

"Perhaps Kennedy let her out when she left," I suggested.

Asher pointed at the cat bowl to the side of the door. The meat was untouched. "Why would she let Cookie out if she hadn't eaten yet?"

"Maybe the cat slipped past her by mistake." Even as I said it, I knew it was unlikely. If that had happened,

Kennedy would have either put Cookie back inside, unlocked the cat flap so she could return to her meal if she wanted, or let Asher or me know.

"Mm." He didn't believe that version of events either.

I bit my lip. "Ash...I've got a weird feeling about this."

He crossed his arms over his broad chest. "How so?"

Put on the spot, I shrugged. "I don't know. It just makes me nervous."

For a few seconds, he looked thoughtful, but then his expression shut down.

"I'm sure it's random," he said. "Kennedy doesn't have a cat. She probably didn't think to keep an eye out to make sure Cookie didn't slip outside."

"Maybe you're right." I hoped he was, but something about the situation just didn't sit well with me.

20

____

ASHER

I STRODE THROUGH THE HOUSE, RATTLING THE CAT FOOD TIN.

"Cookie," I called. "Here kitty kitty kitty."

There was no response. I paused and listened carefully for the sound of running feet, or a plaintive meow, but everything was silent. She hadn't been on my chest when I'd woken, and I hadn't seen or heard her since.

I took the tin to the bedroom, shaking it while I circled the bed, double checking that she wasn't pushed up against the side. Sometimes she liked to curl up in the strangest places. Dropping to my knees, I looked under the bed, but she wasn't there either.

"Cookie." I clucked my tongue, which usually brought her out of hiding because she knew it meant I had either treats or cuddles for her. "Come here you silly cat. I need to go to work."

I couldn't leave without seeing her first or I'd spend all day worrying. I backtracked to the kitchen and took her catnip treats from the pantry. With them in hand, I retraced my steps through the house, stopping in the bedroom, the spare room, and the gym.

I stuck my head into the bathroom and froze. Cookie's shivering form was huddled in the dirty laundry basket. Her eyes were closed, and she didn't seem to notice me.

"Cookie," I said, racing to the basket.

I set the food on the ground and stroked her. She didn't react, and her entire body continued to tremble. I lifted her up, and she was limp in my arms.

Fuck. Something was wrong with her.

"It's okay," I crooned, turning her over in my arms to check her underside in case she'd been hurt. Her black belly was furry and unharmed, but she still hadn't opened her eyes, and usually she'd at least be making a fuss about me manhandling her.

I maneuvered her around so I could check the time on my watch. Damn, the veterinary clinic wouldn't be open yet.

I carried Cookie out to the living room and gently set her down on the sofa, then I took my phone from my pocket and called Summer. The phone nearly rang out before she answered.

"Hello?" Her tone was laced with sleep, and desire lanced through me.

Inappropriate.

"Hey, Summer. It's Ash. There's something wrong with Cookie." I stroked my fluffy baby, looking for signs of change, but she was still shivering and unaware of me.

"What are her symptoms?" She sounded more alert now, and rustling noises came through the line, as if she were getting out of bed. I mentally ordered myself not to dwell on that image.

"She's shivering and unconscious. Even when I picked her up, she didn't respond."

My gut tightened. Nothing could happen to Cookie. She was literally my substitute child. I'd adopted her when Mum started harassing me about giving her grandchildren a couple of years ago. In the absence of a wife or girlfriend, it had seemed the best I could do.

"Bring her to the clinic." Summer spoke briskly, her brain fully awake now. "I'll be there as soon as I can."

Relief flooded through me. Whatever tension there had been between Summer and I lately, she was a damn good vet, and I knew she'd help Cookie.

"Thank you."

I grabbed Cookie's pet carrier from the spare bedroom, shoved a blanket inside, and carefully placed her on top. I probably didn't need it to keep her contained since she was already unconscious, but the carrier would make it easier to move her.

I slung my work bag over my shoulder, grabbed the pet carrier with the other hand, and strode out through the front door, making sure to lock it behind myself. At the car, I dumped my bag on the ground and loaded Cookie onto the passenger seat, then chucked my bag into the back.

The drive to the veterinary clinic seemed to take forever, despite there being no traffic, and I sped the whole way. I beat Summer there, so I waited outside for her to arrive.

She pulled up only a few minutes later, jumped out of her Ute and jogged to the front entrance. Despite the fact that I'd woken her, she looked ready to go, with blue-green scrubs on her lower half and her hair pulled into a neat ponytail.

She swiped a card beside the lock and the glass door slid open. She motioned for me to stay where I was while she entered a code into the alarm keypad.

"All right, come in," she said, hurrying to the nearest examination room without looking back. "Through here."

I followed her and placed the pet carrier on the examination table. She undid the front, reached inside, and pulled Cookie out. My fluffy baby was whimpering now with every shudder, but her eyes remained closed.

Summer conducted a quick physical examination, checking for injuries the same way I had, and feeling along each of Cookie's limbs and her torso. Then she listened to her breathing. My insides felt tight as I awaited a verdict. I had to believe this was something serious. I'd never seen any cat like this, let alone Cookie.

She opened Cookie's mouth and looked inside, then checked her eyes. Her movements were brisk and efficient. It was strange seeing her in this setting. So competent. Very much a medical professional and not at all Liam's baby sister. If this was the first time I'd met her, would I want to ask her out?

Probably.

Although there must be something wrong with me if I could wonder about that while poor Cookie was in such discomfort.

"Do you know whether she could have ingested any toxins?" Summer asked as she continued to assess her.

"Like what?" I asked, feeling useless. I inhaled slowly, breathing in the scents of antiseptic and wet fur. Cookie wasn't wet, so it must be a lingering odor from all the animals who'd passed through this room.

"Chocolate, alcohol, acetaminophen, or any pesticides or herbicides you might use in the garden?"

I racked my mind. "I don't think so. At least, not at my place. It's possible one of the neighbors was spraying and she got into it. Why?"

She stopped moving and met my eyes. "I think Cookie has been poisoned. I'm going to pump her stomach and treat her for some of the more common toxins since we can't be certain what it is."

I clenched my hands. "Will she be okay?"

She pursed her lips. "She should be, but the sooner I can begin treatment, the better. I'm going to call one of the nurses to help, and while she's on her way, I'll get everything prepared. You can wait in the front if you'd like, but you can't stay in the room with us."

I nodded. However much I might not want to leave Cookie's side, I got it. When I was treating someone in the ambulance, the last thing I needed was one of their worried relatives underfoot.

"I'll be out there," I told her, and bent to kiss Cookie's head before leaving the room.

I sat on one of those padded vinyl benches that seems to be a staple in veterinary clinics and called Parks to let him know I was running late. He called me back five minutes later and told me to stay where I was. He'd found a replacement to work my shift for the day.

I thanked him effusively and watched as a car rumbled into the park. Sarah, a vet nurse a little younger than Summer, hurried out of the car and through the front entrance. She smiled at me but didn't stop to talk. The door shut behind her. I checked my watch. Time seemed to be crawling by.

I waited.

And waited.

Eventually, Beverley arrived. She seemed surprised to see me, and paused to chat and assure me that Cookie was in good hands. I knew that, but it didn't make the wait any less excruciating.

Cal turned up soon after, but he left again almost immediately, citing an appointment with a farmer out of town. A few customers passed through, purchasing treats, toys, and in one case, an eight foot tall cat palace.

Finally, Summer emerged from the back. Strain lines bracketed her mouth, but when her gaze landed on me, she smiled.

"She's out of the woods," she said.

My muscles went limp. "Oh, thank God."

I leapt to my feet and opened my arms, ready to hug her tightly—in need of comfort—but then I remembered where we were, and the fact she was wearing her work gear and didn't want my germs all over her, so I stopped short.

"Seriously, thank you," I said. "How is she doing?"

She grabbed my forearm and squeezed, as if sensing my need for human contact. "She's still unconscious, but she's breathing easily. We've cleared as much of the toxin out of her system as we can, and she's responding well to treatment. We're giving her fluids, and she'll need to stay for a while longer."

She hesitated.

"What is it?" I asked.

She tugged on the sleeve of her lab coat. "I'd like to take some blood samples so we can test to determine which toxin she ingested. It would be good to know what it was so you can make sure she doesn't have access to it again."

"That would be great." I didn't know why she'd hesitated. "I hate seeing her like that. I'll do whatever I can to avoid it happening again."

"Good." She clasped her hands together and looked down at them. "I'll have Sarah draw up a form for you to sign, giving us permission to take the samples. Once you sign that, there's no point in continuing to hang around here."

"When can I pick her up?" I asked.

"This afternoon should be fine. Perhaps just before closing, so we can make sure she's in the best possible condition."

I nodded. "I'll come back for her then."

Impulsively, I took her hand. Her gaze jumped to mine, surprise and awareness flaring in their mossy depths. I held onto her for just a beat too long, and she pulled her hand away.

"Before you come back, you should make sure you've checked the inside of your house and that you have a way to keep Cookie contained until we know what caused the damage. You'll want to replace her food too, in case it's contaminated."

My stomach sank. It hadn't even occurred to me that her food could be the problem. "Of course."

I really hoped she could tell me what had poisoned Cookie. If I didn't know, then how could I possibly keep her safe?

21

———

SUMMER

I FINISHED DRAWING BLOOD FROM COOKIE, DISCARDED THE used syringe, and sealed the labeled sample tube. I hoped we could get the answers we needed from them quickly.

"Here." I passed the three small tubes to Sarah. "These need to be couriered to the lab as soon as possible. Can you make sure they get there?"

"I'll do that right now." She took the samples and left the room.

I petted Cookie, ruffling the fur on top of her head. She was beginning to come around but wasn't fully conscious yet. Fortunately, she was a placid cat, or else I might have had to sedate her for longer to make sure she wouldn't tear out the IV.

"You're going to be fine," I told her, although I couldn't shake the unsettled feeling I'd had since Asher woke me up this morning. Something was off here, but considering how easily Asher had dismissed my concerns last night, I was reluctant to raise them again.

I left Cookie, stripped off my gloves, cleaned my hands, and returned to the examination room to check who my first patient was. Sarah had already sterilized the examination table, and the scent of antibacterial spray was even more pungent than usual.

I opened a tab on my computer and laughed. Mrs. Hawkins and Dolores. According to the notes Beverley had taken, Dolores was off her food, which probably just meant that she hadn't eaten one of the dozens of treats Mrs. Hawkins plied her with.

I rolled up my sleeves and opened the door. "Mrs. Hawkins, I'm ready to see Dolores now."

Two hours later, I managed to take a quick break before my scheduled appointment with Duke for his annual vaccination booster.

Grace arrived right on time, as always, and greeted me with a smile. "Good morning, Summer. We're here for our jab."

I crouched in front of Duke, who nuzzled my hand, searching for a treat. I slipped one out of my pocket and offered it to him.

"Half now, and half after."

He snuffled it up, and I straightened.

"Come on through."

In the examination room, I checked Duke's weight, his heart rate, his temperature, and performed a physical checkup.

"Everything seems to be in good working order," I told Grace.

"Good." She sounded relieved. Probably because Duke had gotten caught up in a dangerous situation last year and been injured as a result. No matter how often we assured her that he'd recovered completely, she always worried about him. I'd be glad for any way I could ease her mind considering she was only a little more than a week away from giving birth.

"I'll just prepare the vaccination," I said.

I left the room and took the vaccination from the fridge, then opened a fresh syringe and drew the liquid into it. I carried the syringe back to the examination room, where Grace was now awkwardly bending over to pet Duke, one hand on the small of her back as she stroked the dog with the other.

"Hold still," I said as I pinched some of the loose skin at the back of Duke's neck between my thumb and forefinger. "What a good boy."

The needle pricked his skin, and I pushed the plunger down and withdrew the whole thing before he had time to flinch, then I offered him the second half of his treat. He wolfed it down, his tail wagging.

Grace ruffled his fur and told him how well behaved he was. The professional part of our visit was complete, but I didn't want her to go yet. She had first-hand experience that could be useful to me.

"Asher brought Cookie in this morning. She'd been exposed to some kind of poison."

Her forehead creased. "Is she okay?"

I nodded. "Thankfully."

"Good." She hesitated, then asked, "How did it happen?"

"He doesn't know, and until I know what the toxin was, I can't really guess either." The uncertainty bothered me more than it should.

Grace cocked her head. "You don't think someone did it on purpose, do you?"

I pursed my lips. "I don't know what to think. Surely not. Who would hurt a cat?"

Grace continued to stroke Duke's back. "It might be nothing, but if your instincts tell you there's something up, then you should trust them." She gave me a sad smile. "I didn't, and it got me into trouble."

I let out a ragged breath. Until now, I hadn't realized how badly I needed someone to tell me that my gut might not be completely wrong. "Thanks, Grace."

She straightened and Duke slumped against her long legs. "I can quietly ask Nate to keep an eye on Asher and Cookie if you like."

I raised an eyebrow. "Can he do that without making it obvious?"

Nate didn't exactly do "subtle."

She just smiles a little too smugly. "If I ask, he will."

"Thanks." A shard of envy lodged in my chest. I longed to have a relationship like the one she shared with my brother, but I couldn't begrudge her for it when she'd had to wait so long for him to get his head out of his ass and realize what was right in front of him.

She'd wanted him for even longer than I'd craved Asher, and if anyone deserved happiness, it was Grace. She was the kindest, gentlest soul I'd ever met.

Grace swept her hair over her shoulder. "Speaking of Asher, I saw you two dancing. It seems like things might be changing between you."

She didn't say it in a prying way, but my cheeks heated nonetheless. I liked to think that not too many people were aware of my hopelessly unrequited love, but at least five were in the know: Bailey, Beverley, Cal, Blair, and now Grace. I just had to thank my lucky stars that none of them were likely to spread rumors.

"It could be," I said slowly. "I really don't know. After this long with nothing happening, I doubt it."

Grace dropped her hand to scratch the top of Duke's head. "If things can change for Nate and me after fifteen years, they can change for you too."

"God, I hope so." But I was afraid to believe it. "Anyway, it was good to see you. I'd better check whether the next patient is ready."

I guided Grace out and, sure enough, another patient was waiting to take Duke's place.

My feet ached by the time evening rolled around. I'd been seeing clients all day, but at least tomorrow would be spent in the operating theater so I wouldn't have to interact with so many people. I loved catching up with everyone, but it could be exhausting.

I'd cleaned up and was waving Beverley off when Asher drove into the parking lot and parked near the main entrance. I met him at the doors.

"Cookie is doing well," I said as he approached. "She's looking forward to going home."

He smiled, but his lips wobbled. "She's really okay?"

"Yes." I wished I could hug him. He looked like he needed it.

I led him through a door labeled Staff Only to the rear room where we kept inpatients who were ready to be discharged. Cookie was curled in the cubicle nearest the door, and she stretched and butted her head against the bars when she saw Asher. He reached in and rubbed the underside of her chin.

My insides melted into a puddle of goo. They were so adorable together. I opened the cubicle, and he scooped her out and cradled her against his chest. My ovaries broke into song. Somehow, I knew he'd look just as sweet cuddling a baby.

Ugh, I had it so bad.

But for once, my hopeless crush didn't feel quite so hopeless. Whether or not he remembered it, he had almost kissed me the other night. If it had happened once, it could happen again, and I was an expert at exercising patience.

Asher shifted Cookie into her pet carrier, which I'd stored against the wall, and followed me out.

"What do I owe you?" he asked once we reached the reception area.

I waved my hand dismissively. "We can sort it out later. I'm not as good with the billing software as Beverley is."

"Summer." His tone was stern. "I am paying."

"I know." I grabbed my bag from where I'd left it behind the counter and slung it over my shoulder. I withdrew my keycard and headed for the exit.

"I'm serious," Asher said.

"I know," I repeated, turning to face him. "I said we'll sort it out, and I meant it."

But I also knew that he wouldn't get paid until next week —he was on the same pay schedule as Liam—and that paramedics weren't necessarily paid what they deserved. I could afford to wait and give him a grace period.

He nodded, and the tightness eased from his jaw. Good. We wouldn't have to fight about this. He carried Cookie across to the door. It slid open and I entered the code to set the alarm while he left the building, then I hurried out and waited until the door automatically closed.

I checked to make sure it was locked and glanced over at my Ute. "Blair!"

Kennedy's brother was leaning against the passenger door, holding a takeout cup and a brown paper bag from Taste of Destiny.

"What's he doing here?" Asher grumbled.

"No idea." I smiled at Blair and waved. "But I'm going to find out. Let me know if you run into any trouble with Cookie."

"I will." He narrowed his eyes at Blair, huffed, and then marched to his car.

I frowned, wondering what his mood was about, but I shook it off. He was probably still upset about Cookie.

As I closed the distance between me and Blair, he called, "I heard you can sing."

I cocked my head, curious where this was going. "I'm no Taylor Swift but I can hold my own."

He extended the takeout cup toward me. "That's a chai latte, which I have on good authority is your favorite."

I wrapped my hand around the cup. Heat radiated through the cardboard. Still hot. Excellent. "Why does this feel like a bribe?"

He smirked. "It's not a bribe. I'm just making sure you're in a good frame of mind before I ask for a favor." He offered me the paper bag. "Cinnamon roll."

I opened the bag, balancing the coffee as I reached in and pulled out the cinnamon roll, inhaling its mouthwateringly sweet scent. I bit into it and closed my eyes, savoring the deliciousness, then I sipped the coffee.

"Okay, hit me with it."

He studied my face, any trace of humor gone from his expression. "I promised Eugene that I'd play a set on guitar at Drunken Destiny this Saturday. I don't have my band or backing vocalists obviously, so I'd really love it if you'd join me. We could do a duet."

I hesitated. "It's a big risk on your part to ask without listening to me sing. How do you know I'm actually any good?"

His smirk returned. "Heather showed me a video of you performing in one of your school's musicals."

I grimaced. "She would do that, wouldn't she?"

I'd gone through a period when I'd thought that theater might be my calling, but it turned out that I both hated acting and was terrible at it.

"I'm out of practice," I warned him.

He shrugged. "So, we'll get together sometime this week and clear the rust off your vocal cords." He held out his hand. "Let me see your calendar and I'll find a time that suits."

I passed my phone over. "What makes you think I use a calendar app?"

"You seem like the type." He scrolled through my phone and tapped on something. "Uh-huh. I thought so. How about after work on Wednesday?"

Asher's car crawled past us. I glanced through the window and blinked in surprise. He was glaring a hole through Blair.

"Um, sure," I said distractedly. "That should be fine."

He entered the time into my calendar, and I watched Asher pull out onto the road. What the hell was up with him?

22

———

ASHER

JEERS RANG OUT AS I STRODE INTO THE STAFF ROOM AT WORK. Darcy whistled from the table where he, Liam, and Zane were playing cards. Someone catcalled.

"You're getting all the excitement lately," Zane said, grinning broadly.

"We thought we could have cucumber salad for lunch tomorrow," Igor added from where he lay stretched out on the sofa.

I groaned and turned to Maia. "You told them?"

She snickered. "Wouldn't you? Come on."

I threw up my hands. "Yes. I did have to rescue a cucumber from someone's ass. It happens, okay?"

"Yeah, you did," Darcy hooted.

Zane laughed. "People need to remember that butt plugs have a thicker base for a reason. Ass safety is very important."

I flopped onto one of the chairs at the table. Maia joined Igor, shifting his legs out of the way so she could sit.

"Can you deal me in for the next round?" I asked Darcy, who was shuffling the pack of cards.

"It's euchre," he said. "You'll have to wait until we finish this game, but it shouldn't be too long. Zane only needs two more points."

"Speaking of sex accidents," Liam said, picking up the cards Darcy dealt him. "Did Tia ever find out what really happened to her house?"

I glanced at the door to check that Parks wasn't hovering nearby, then over at Maia, who thankfully wasn't listening. "Someone may have sent an anonymous note that suggested she might want to ask a few questions about particular details of his story."

"Good." His tone was blunt. "Think she'll end it?"

"I hope so." She deserved better, but I also knew it could be tempting to stay with someone you'd been with for years. People got used to each other, and change was scary. I just hoped Tia had enough self-respect to kick him to the curb.

I waited out the rest of their game and joined in the next hand. Half an hour later, our shift ended, and Liam and I changed out of our uniforms and headed outside together. A brisk wind was blowing, and I shivered, wishing I'd packed a jacket when I'd left home this morning.

"You should come over to our place for a while," Liam said as we walked to our vehicles. "Summer and Blair are practicing for Saturday."

I frowned. "Practicing what?"

His eyebrows jumped up. "They're performing together at Drunken Destiny. I thought you would have heard."

"Nope."

Perhaps that's what they'd been discussing in the veterinary clinic parking lot the other day. I'd seen him with a drink and food, and then messing around with her phone, and my mind had instantly leapt to them dating. They were the same age, and much as I hated to admit it, Blair was a good looking guy. That said, he was even less stable and reliable than I was.

"Do you think there's something happening between Blair and Summer?" I asked Liam, hoping he wouldn't see how badly I wanted to hear a negative reply.

He shook his head. "I doubt it. They get on well, but there's no chemistry there." He dropped his voice. "Besides, I think Blair is interested in Zane."

The knots in my gut loosened. I scowled, looking the other way so Liam wouldn't notice. I hated how relieved I was that another man wouldn't be sweeping Summer off her feet before I had a chance to decide whether I wanted to act on the attraction simmering between us.

"I'll meet you at your place," I told him, using the key fob to unlock my car. "See you again soon."

We drove to his place, and as soon as I parked on the streetside, the soft notes of an acoustic guitar melody sounded from inside the house. I paused and listened, but no voices accompanied the music, and a moment later, it stopped.

I got out of the car, waited for Liam to join me, and together, we walked up the path and let ourselves inside. Warm air rushed out the open door, and Liam closed it quickly behind us.

"Kennedy must have lit the fire," he said. "The heat pump doesn't get that hot."

"Great. It was too cold at the station."

We found the others in the living area. Kennedy was reclined on a cushy chair, her feet up, while Blair and Summer sat at each end of the sofa. Both women were watching as Blair strummed the guitar.

"You're too late for the main event," Kennedy said. "Blair is just playing us some of their new music."

My heart sank. I hadn't realized how much I'd wanted to hear Summer sing, but I'd been anticipating it the whole way here and couldn't help being disappointed.

"Won't you give us a little sample?" I asked, sinking onto another chair and eyeballing the space between Summer and Blair. A good two feet separated them, which made me more inclined to believe Liam's assessment of their relationship.

Summer's lips quirked into a teasing smile. "You'll just have to come and listen on Saturday."

Satisfaction bubbled through me because that made it sound like she wanted me there. I kept my expression neutral though. The last thing I needed was for anyone to pay close attention to my behavior around Summer.

"I guess I can manage that." It wasn't as if there was anything else to do in Destiny Falls on a Saturday night. Usually, I'd be at Drunken Destiny anyway. Either that or at home on my cycle or cuddled with Cookie while we watched science fiction movies.

"You'd better." Her gaze caressed me, and I fought the urge to shiver.

"So, Grace must be due soon." I addressed the statement to Kennedy, in a bid to divert attention away from my exchange with Summer.

"She could go into labor any day now," Kennedy replied. "She's officially due next Wednesday, but you know babies aren't always punctual."

I nodded. My sister, Frannie, had given birth almost two weeks after their due date. If it had taken much longer, the doctors would have induced her.

"Do you know how she's feeling about it?" Summer asked.

Kennedy smiled and rubbed her still-flat belly. "You

know, I don't actually think she's nervous at all. Just excited to meet their little one."

Summer laughed. "If anyone can stay serene throughout childbirth, it's Grace. She's so calm. I'm sure that's the only reason she's able to put up with Nate."

"You might be onto something," Liam said. "But let's not tell him that."

Kennedy rolled her eyes. "She adores Nate."

Summer sighed. "She really does. It's sweet."

Was that a hint of wistfulness in her voice? If so, why?

"You guys are sweet too," she said, gesturing at Kennedy and Liam. "But not as much as them."

Neither Kennedy nor Liam seemed to know how to respond.

"You'll have your turn for the sickening happy ever after," Blair told Summer, but he wasn't looking at her. Instead, he narrowed his eyes at me, a little too meaningfully for my liking.

"Thanks, B." Summer glanced at me. "Oh, Ash, I meant to say: I heard from the lab today. We should have Cookie's blood test results back by this time next week."

23

———

DRUNKEN DESTINY WAS CROWDED ON SATURDAY EVENING before Blair and Summer's performance. As Liam, Kennedy, and I entered, we had to squeeze around people in order to reach the table Nate had saved for us up front.

I shucked my jacket and hung it over the back of a chair, eager to get it off before I started sweating. With this many bodies in close proximity, we were bound to start smelling each other soon.

"It's hot in here," Liam said, removing his jacket as well. "Are you okay, Kenz? Do you need anything?"

Kennedy sat beside Grace, who looked ready to burst any day now. "I'm fine, thanks."

I claimed the chair between Max and Toby. Eugene must have brought some extra seats over today because there wouldn't usually be enough for all of us. As it was, the people near the back of the pub had to stand. The atmosphere was cheerful though, conversation humming around us and the scent of beer inescapable.

A makeshift stage had been set up to the rear of the area used as a dance floor, and Blair stood behind a microphone stand, tuning his guitar.

"Where's Summer?" I asked.

Toby leaned closer. "She's getting ready out back with Bailey."

"Right." Of course she'd want to look her best. Not that Summer ever looked bad. "I might get a drink. You want one?"

He pointed at his half full pint glass. "I'm good, thanks."

I got up and made my way between the bodies separating me from the bar. Both Eugene and Heather were on bartender duty, and I told Heather which beer I wanted, swiped my card, and leaned against the solid wood of the bar top while I waited.

A light touch landed on my arm. "Excuse me?"

I blinked and refocused on the dark, doe like eyes set in an elfin face that had appeared in front of me. "Yeah?"

The woman glanced at the table I'd come from and rubbed her glossy pink lips together. "Is that Kennedy Cox?"

"It is," I said slowly.

Kennedy didn't keep her presence here secret, but I was reluctant to do or say anything that might encourage someone to fangirl all over her.

She stepped closer, her teeth catching on her lower lip. "I would be so grateful if you'd introduce me to her."

I edged along the bar away from her. "You're welcome to introduce yourself. She likes meeting fans."

"Liked" might be an overstatement—*sorry Kennedy*—but I wasn't comfortable with aiding and abetting this woman's quest to rub shoulders with a celebrity.

Her eyebrows furrowed, and she pouted harder. "But I would be so grateful. Wouldn't you love to find out just how grateful?"

Heather passed me my beer, and I took it.

"Sorry, but no," I told the woman and ducked around a big guy in a coat to escape her.

I returned to the table, glancing over my shoulder to make sure I hadn't been chased.

"What did you do to upset the hottie?" Toby asked, raising his glass to his lips.

"She wanted to meet Kennedy," I said.

He gaped. "And you told her no? Are you crazy?"

"I didn't feel like bothering Kennedy for nothing." I gave him a warning look.

He ignored it. "Well, I'm more than happy to make the introductions...provided you don't mind, Kenz?"

Kennedy sighed. "It's fine. Go ahead."

Toby smacked his glass onto the tabletop hard enough that we all cringed and shot to his feet. "Be back in a minute."

"Sorry," I said to Kennedy.

She grimaced. "You know I don't mind meeting fans. I just feel icky that Toby is trying to use me to get a girl."

A few seconds later, Toby was back, dragging the woman behind him by the elbow. She jerked away, patted her silky black hair into place, and offered her hand to Kennedy.

"Hi! I'm Chanele. It's so nice to meet you. I'm a massive fan—especially of your movies with Gray Anderson. You two are so good together."

Liam scowled, and she must have noticed, because she giggled nervously.

"I mean in movies," she said. "I'm sure you and your husband are obviously better for each other in real life."

"Thanks." Kennedy smiled at her kindly. "It's a pleasure to meet you, Chanele. Where are you visiting Destiny Falls from?"

"Wellington. Some friends and I are staying at the Ski

Resort." She looked around as if searching for them but came up empty. She scanned the faces around the table. When her gaze landed on me, she glared.

I glared right back. She was welcome to offer whatever perks she wanted to secure an introduction, but I didn't have to take her up on it just because she was pretty and felt entitled to a man's attention.

Toby sat, and Chanele did another visual sweep of the table, her face falling when she realized there were no unoccupied chairs.

"I'd be happy to sign something for you, if you'd like," Kennedy said.

Chanele brightened. "Yes, please. Can we get a photo too?"

"Of course."

Chanele passed her phone to Toby and circled around to stand beside Kennedy, who rose from the chair. There was no way to avoid having others in the photo since the pub was so crowded, but Chanele didn't seem to care. She beamed at the camera. The flash went off, and a moment later, the overhead lights dimmed.

Kennedy returned to her seat.

"The show must be about to start," Nate said, the obvious implication being that Chanele should go back to her friends.

"Wait. Let me give you my number," Toby said, and entered it into her phone before giving it back to her.

Chanele hovered for a few seconds longer, as if hoping a seat for her would materialize out of nowhere, but then she thanked Kennedy and backed away, bumping into someone as she did so.

"Hey!" they protested.

"Watch it," she snapped back, throwing another little wave over her shoulder as the crowd closed around her.

"Well, that was fun," Nate said. "Don't take this the wrong way, Grace, but I'm glad you write under a pen name and aren't as famous as Kennedy."

Grace chuckled. "So am I."

I snorted to myself. I'd just bet she was. Even as low key as she was, she'd had to deal with a stalker who'd basically wanted to steal her life.

On the makeshift stage, Blair tapped the microphone and began to strum the opening chords of one of his band's songs. The music was cheerful, and a little country. I'd listened to a few of his songs and found the band's sound difficult to categorize. Some of it veered more folksy while other songs almost seemed to pay homage to classic rock.

Bailey emerged from the back, carrying a second microphone stand, which she placed a few yards away from the one in front of Blair. As soon as it was in place, she returned to the door and signaled for Summer to come through.

The instant I caught sight of Summer's long legs in sheer black stockings, heat stirred in my gut. I shifted position, angling to get a better view of her. Her dress was almost blindingly white. The sort of thing that would have looked virginal if not for how short it was. The skirt barely covered her ass.

When she circled around behind the microphone and smiled, I nearly swallowed my tongue. Holy fuck. She looked absolutely divine. Dark eye makeup, cherry red lips, and a beauty spot painted on the left side of her face, just beneath her eye. Her hair fell over her shoulders and down her back like golden silk.

My fingers twitched. I wanted more than anything to wrap my hands in that hair, pull her head back, and suck a mark onto the tanned skin of her throat.

I'd always known Summer was beautiful, but right now, she was fucking sexy.

Even thinking that made me feel like a deviant. She was Liam's baby sister, and—as I knew—off limits, but every part of my body was completely attuned to her. I wanted to devour her, and for everyone to know that no one was allowed to touch her other than me.

If only.

Blair continued to play, and Summer held the microphone and swayed. When she started to sing, I froze in my seat.

I couldn't move. Couldn't think.

Her sultry voice wrapped around me, setting my nerves alight and hardening my cock. Had she always sung like a siren and I'd been immune, or was this a new incarnation of Summer?

One thing was for sure: I certainly wasn't immune anymore.

She held me in her thrall. Her gaze locked on mine, her green eyes made fiercer by the dark circles around them. Blair's voice joined hers, raspy and oddly comforting. Together, they crooned about a lost love, and she stared right at me the whole time.

I couldn't have looked away if I'd tried.

They finished the song, and Summer tore her gaze away to smile at Blair and exchange a few words. My gut burned. Irrational or not, I didn't want her paying any attention to another man when she looked so much like a debauched fairytale princess.

Blair's fingers moved quickly across the strings as he started another song. This one was more upbeat, with the kind of rhythm people could stomp their feet to. And this crowd did. By the end, the floor was vibrating from the force of dozens of feet pounding the wood. The clapping and cheering could probably be heard a block away.

Blair and Summer played three more songs, and I didn't

move from my chair or once take my eyes off Summer. She enthralled me.

When their set finished, Summer stepped down from the makeshift stage and Blair switched off both microphones. Summer caught my eyes briefly, but then gave Bailey a thumbs up and started moving toward the door through to the back rooms. Before she got there, a pair of men intercepted her.

I was on my feet immediately. I didn't recognize either of the men, which meant they were out-of-towners and didn't know anything about Summer other than the fact she looked like sin and could sing like an angel.

"Isn't this when you should be playing overprotective brother?" I asked Toby.

He laughed. "Summer is allowed to get some action if she wants. It's been long enough."

I glanced at Nate, who just stared back.

"You think I'm leaving my incredibly pregnant wife for even a second?" he asked.

I turned to Liam, who raised his hands placatingly. "They're just talking. I know better than to intervene. Unless she looks like she's leaving with them, it's harmless."

Max didn't say a word, just nodded in agreement.

Well, damn.

Summer had four brothers present and none of them seemed to think she needed saving.

I guessed it was up to me.

24

SUMMER

"CAN I BORROW YOU FROM YOUR ADORING FANS?"

I turned away from the men who'd been showering me with compliments and shivered when I caught sight of Asher's dark expression. He looked like he was trying to devour me with his gaze.

He held out his hand, but I hesitated. He'd behaved strangely last time we were here for a party, and I had no idea whether he was leading me away to act on the slumberous promise in his eyes or if he was going to drop snarky comments about why I shouldn't flirt with these men, as he had with Darcy and Blair.

"Who are you?" the shorter of my two companions demanded. I hadn't been told either of their names yet, but it was nice to be flattered without expecting the other shoe to drop like with some people.

A muscle in Asher's jaw twitched as he glanced at the man. "Someone who knows her better than you."

He extended his hand an inch further, urging me to take it.

I placed my hand in his, my eyelids fluttering shut at the exquisite sensation of my palm sliding over his. He clasped my hand, his strong fingers holding me firmly. Butterflies erupted in my stomach. Was this it? Had he finally decided to do something about the connection between us?

He led me to the door I'd been heading to before I was interrupted and ushered me through. Out the back of the pub, he went straight to Dad's office and, when I followed, he closed the door behind us.

"What is it?" I asked, standing in the center of the small space.

One of his hands twitched toward me, but then fell to his side.

"You were incredible," he breathed, emotion burning in his deep brown eyes. "I knew you could sing, but I had no idea how talented you are. You're fucking amazing, Summer."

My heart swelled in my chest, and I smiled so widely my jaw ached.

"Thank you," I whispered, hoping he didn't notice the thickness of my voice.

His gaze flicked down my body and back up. He refocused on my face, and his tongue darted out to wet his lips. Hope twisted almost painfully in my gut. Was that desire in his eyes?

"Why didn't you pursue singing more seriously?" he asked, stepping closer. "Surely, there's a chance you'd be able to do it professionally."

My breath caught. He really believed I was that good?

"It's very competitive," I said, doing my best to answer his question, but it was difficult to keep my thoughts in order with him looking at me like that. "I enjoy singing, but

I don't know if I would have continued to enjoy it if it had become my career."

He frowned, but seemed to understand because he said, "It's something that was only meant to be a hobby for you."

"Exactly." My pulse raced, and I could barely stand still. Everything inside me screamed that we were teetering on the brink of something that could change our lives. "Besides, if I'd taken up singing professionally, I'd probably have to leave Destiny Falls. My family is here. Even when I went away to study, I always intended to come back."

One corner of his mouth hitched up. "You're the glue that holds them together, you know?"

I shook my head. "The family has always been close."

"Perhaps, but you're the one who makes a point to keep in touch, and to help when people need it—even if they don't appreciate your meddling at the time."

"You think I meddle?" I pouted. "That's not very nice, Ash."

He laughed and rolled his eyes. "You'll survive." He was quiet for a moment, but then continued, "I've been feeling upside down when it comes to you recently."

"Oh?" The sound escaped me in a breath of air. Unintentional, and somehow the more powerful for it.

He stepped forward again until only two inches separated us. I could practically feel the heat from his body.

"When you came back from university, I was thrown off by how beautiful you were. I honestly had never thought of you romantically before then, but all of a sudden, there you were, gorgeous and impossible to ignore." He sighed. "I tried to tell you once. Do you remember that?"

The memory appeared, vivid as if it had happened yesterday. "You were drunk. I'd hoped you'd come back later, when you were sober, but you never did."

He grimaced. "I assumed you no longer had feelings for

me. You made a snarky comment—something about how you were a fine wine that had improved with age whereas I was more of a cheese on the verge of turning moldy."

I felt a twinge of guilt. "I'm sorry."

I'd been bitter at the time. Still hurting.

"It's fine. I understood. But after that day, you didn't seem to want anything to do with me, and anytime we talked, we ended up arguing." He cupped my jaw with his strong, warm hands. "I'm tired of fighting with you."

I gazed up into that face I'd admired so many times before. Rawness and vulnerability were carved into every line of his expression. "Then let's not fight."

"I'd like that." His lips curved ever so slightly. "After tonight, there is absolutely no doubt left in my mind that I will never, ever see you as a surrogate sister again. I'm sorry for hurting you all those years ago. I wish I could take it back. I never meant to cause you pain."

"You couldn't know that your perspective would change," I said, even though the voice in the back of my head was shouting that I'd spent endless stretches of time reliving that awful night and shouldn't accept his apology. "The truth is, I thought I was an adult then, but I was still a teenager, and you were in your twenties. I understand why you reacted the way you did."

He released a shuddering breath. "I'll never forget how devastated you looked."

I tilted my face toward him. "Perhaps not, but you can make new memories instead."

Asher dipped his head toward me. His lips hovered, millimeters above mine, for what felt like an eternity before I stretched onto my toes and closed the distance between us. I rested my palms on his chest and shut my eyes, savoring the sensation of his soft mouth against mine.

He exhaled and took hold of my hips. I breathed in his

air, giddy from the knowledge that something which had been inside him seconds ago was now inside me. There was an intimacy to exchanging breath that nothing else could rival.

Or so I thought until he groaned and pulled me flush against his body. My nerve endings danced everywhere we touched, and I could barely think straight as he tilted his head to access my mouth more fully.

A floorboard squeaked behind us, and I leapt out of Asher's arms, scooting backward until we were at least six feet apart. I froze, expecting the door handle to turn any second, but it didn't.

Across from me, Asher was breathing hard, his chest rising and falling rapidly. He didn't pay any attention to the noise outside though. He was completely focused on me.

"Summer—"

"Hold on," I said. "I need to check to make sure no one is listening."

I couldn't deal with someone overhearing our conversation, and I was eighty percent sure someone was lingering just beyond the door. I crossed the room, opened the door and slowly pushed it outward, careful so as not to ram it into anyone who might be on the other side.

The hallway was empty. I looked left and right, and for some ridiculous reason, even glanced up at the roof, but no one was there.

"Weird. I was so sure..." I trailed off.

"Are you okay?" he asked from directly behind me.

I flinched, startled by his proximity. "Fine. I just thought I heard something."

"So did I. But whoever it was is gone. Come back inside. We need to finish this conversation."

I returned to the office and shut the door. I walked as far

from the door as possible, hoping to prevent anyone from listening in.

"What is this?" I asked, gesturing between us. "Are you going to say that kiss was a mistake?"

"No." He rushed over and took my hand. "I would never say that. You could never be a mistake."

I wanted to believe him. I wanted it badly. But I also knew that he could easily change his mind with a little time to think, so by going along with him now, I'd be opening myself up for a world of hurt.

I chose my words carefully. "I'd love for there to be something between us, but you've been very hot and cold with me lately. I need to be sure you're serious before we go any further."

25

———————

ASHER

MY PHONE BUZZED WITH AN INCOMING MESSAGE JUST AS I returned from my last callout of the day. My shift was officially over as of ten minutes ago and I was looking forward to getting home and relaxing. I drew my phone out of my pocket and read the text awaiting me.

Summer: *Can you come to the clinic as soon as you get off work? It's important.*

I frowned, anxious to know what this was about. We'd left the situation a little up in the air the other night. I'd assured her that I would never suggest letting anything happen between us unless I was serious, but I knew she'd need more reassurance than just a few throwaway words, and honestly, so did I. If I couldn't offer enough to make her happy, I'd rather know that now than be hurt later.

I changed into my street clothes and returned my work gear to my locker. I hesitated, glancing at Liam's locker beside mine. Should I wait and tell him about the development between Summer and I before I went to meet her?

I dithered for a moment, torn between loyalty to my best friend, the knowledge there was every chance he'd remind me of all the ways I wasn't what she needed in a man, and the desire to see Summer and make sure everything was okay as soon as possible.

In the end, I opted to leave. I'd have plenty of opportunities to talk to Liam later, when I was feeling strong enough to stomach the concerns he'd no doubt have about my suitability for his sister. Besides, the conversation Summer wanted to have might be relevant in terms of how much I decided to tell Liam.

I drove to the veterinary clinic. Only one car was left in the parking lot, but Summer wasn't inside it, so I went to the front door, which slid open automatically.

"Summer?" I called.

"In here!"

I followed the voice through to an office behind reception. I'd never been in that room before, but it was clearly a space shared by several of the staff as there were three desks positioned against the walls, one of which had a desktop computer at either end.

Dozens of photos adorned the walls, many of animals, but I spotted a few of the Braddocks among them. Summer was working on a laptop at one of the desks. She glanced over her shoulder and gestured for me to join her.

"Pull a chair over," she said. "There's something I need to show you."

So, this wasn't about our relationship?

"What is it?" I asked, grabbing a wheeled chair and dragging it over beside her. I sat and studied her face. Strain lines bracketed her mouth, and her lower lip was red, as if she'd been biting it a lot. "Is everything okay?"

She caught her abused lower lip between her teeth. I wanted to smooth my thumb along it and soothe the soreness, but I didn't dare when things between us were so precarious.

"I have Cookie's blood test results," she said, pointing at the document open on her laptop.

I scanned the screen, but it all looked like tables of gibberish and numbers to me. I understood some basic medical terms from working as a paramedic, but veterinary science was a whole other beast.

"And?" I asked, since she clearly had more to add.

Her face fell. "Cookie had elevated levels of a common household pesticide in her bloodstream."

"Fuck." I'd known something like that was a possibility, but I'd foolishly hoped she'd just eaten a neighbor's chocolate bar. "Do I need to worry about any further damage to her system?"

She waved her fingers back and forth. "Difficult to say. It's unlikely, since she seems to have recovered well. You haven't noticed any unusual behavior, have you?"

"No. Except that she's resting more than usual."

She made a humming noise. "We'll continue to monitor her, but I expect she'll be fine. The pesticide is present, but not at an alarmingly high concentration. I think the treatment we put her through should be enough to have her out of danger."

"Thank God." But my mind was already firing through the connotations of this. "I double checked my garden shed before I took her home, and there's no way she could have gotten into it. She must have been exposed to the pesticide somewhere else. I'll have to talk to my neighbors."

"Yes, do that," she agreed, but looked like she wanted to add something else.

"What?" I asked. "Don't hold back on me."

She pulled a face. "I'm not, exactly. I'm just..." She tugged on the end of her ponytail, visibly agitated. "Do you remember how she was outside the morning after my birthday party?"

I nodded.

She pursed her lips. "I'm worried that this wasn't an accident."

My eyebrows pinched together. "What do you mean?"

"Is there any reason someone might have poisoned Cookie on purpose?"

"Are you serious?" The question came out before I could hold it back. Because of course she was serious. Summer wouldn't joke about something like this. She took animals and their safety very seriously.

But that didn't mean she was right.

"No," I said. "I'm sure someone has just been spraying their garden."

She looked doubtful. "Or putting down bait for rats? This was more that kind of poison than the type you'd use to deal with bugs."

"Plenty of people have rat problems. Especially in winter when it gets cold outside."

"Maybe. But does Cookie go inside anyone else's house? Because I can't imagine most people put bait for rats outside. What would be the point? They're only an issue when they come into the house."

I shrugged. "So she went into someone's home. Stranger things have happened."

That made more sense than an unknown person trying to poison my cat. Who the hell would do that? No one had ever taken a dislike to Cookie, and only a sick bastard would take out their anger at a person on their pet.

No, this must be just a coincidence.

Although...I recalled how poorly I'd felt that morning, and the fact I hadn't thought I'd drunk enough to be so wrecked. If Cookie had been poisoned, was it possible I had been too?

I shook my head. No, I was being paranoid.

"It must have been an accident," I reiterated.

Summer's eyes narrowed, and her chin adopted a familiar stubborn tilt. I almost groaned. Damn, I'd upset her.

"I appreciate you being concerned for me," I added. "Why don't you come and keep me safe in person this weekend? I'm going cycling on Saturday and I'd love to have company."

Her nostrils flared, and her eyes narrowed even further. "I know what you're doing, Asher Heaton, but I'll let you get away with it this once. We'll have to go somewhere tame though because my mountain biking skills are rusty."

I stood and wheeled the chair back to the desk I'd taken it from. "I will. I'll message you the details." I paused, recognizing that I needed to say something else, but uncertain what. "Thank you for caring so much about Cookie. I promise, I'll ask around and I'll be careful with when and where I let her go."

I backed toward the door, still facing her.

"Be careful yourself too," she said. "Take precautions."

I nodded as I turned away. A lump formed in the base of my gut. I wanted to dismiss her words, but I couldn't completely, because as far-fetched as her ideas were, I couldn't deny the fact that something felt off. I just didn't know why.

26

SUMMER

I sat opposite Bailey, shivering as the door opened behind me and another customer entered Taste of Destiny, bringing a chill breeze with them.

"What is it you need to talk about?" Bailey asked, sipping a bright purple smoothie.

I inhaled the delicious savory scent of the warm cheese scone I'd bought for lunch, then glanced at the salad in front of Bailey and felt a stab of guilt. I should probably be eating salad too, but with the morning I'd had—having to euthanize a family's beloved pet—I needed the carbs.

I looked around to make sure no one was listening to her, then leaned across the table and said, "Asher kissed me after my set with Blair the other night."

"What?" she squealed, attracting the eyes of every single person in the cafe.

"Shush," I hissed.

"Sorry." She looked sheepish. "I'm just so excited for you. Was it good?"

I nodded. "It was sweet. Nothing heavy, but that made it feel more real."

Her eyes crinkled at the corners, and she scrunched up her nose. I could tell she was doing her best not to squeal again. "Tell me everything."

I did, starting with when Asher approached me while I was talking to those other men, and ending with his invitation to go cycling with him on Saturday.

"Do you think it's a date?" I asked.

"Definitely."

When I raised my eyebrows, she did it right back.

"What?" she continued. "When was the last time he asked you to go cycling with him?"

I considered this. "Good point. I don't even remember."

"Yet he does it within days of kissing you?" She grinned. "It's totally a date."

"I hope so."

Another blast of cold air whipped through the cafe, and I glanced toward the entrance. At the sight of a familiar face, my heart sank. Dark hair, bright blue eyes, and a trim figure clad in denim and cashmere. The last time I'd seen her, she'd been kissing the man I loved.

Bailey followed my gaze. "What is she doing here?"

"I don't know." I'd heard that Ashley Moore had moved to the North Island to be with her new man. I definitely hadn't seen her for a couple of years. So why was she back in Destiny Falls?

"Don't let her distract you," Bailey said, as if she had a direct line to my spinning thoughts, which had already started whirring about whether Asher would still want me now that the glamorous Ashley was back in town.

After all, he'd dated Ashley before. The other woman didn't have the added complication of being either younger than him or his best friend's sister. She was older than me, arguably more mature, and just all around more convenient.

If I knew why they'd broken up in the first place, her appearance might not worry me, but as it was, I had no idea. One day, they'd been an item, and the next, she'd been leaving Destiny Falls in her rearview mirror.

"I'll try not to." I watched as Ashley stalked to the counter and placed her order. She moved to the side and turned to scan the room. Almost immediately, she spotted me looking at her. I winced. It was too late to look away. Her face lit up, and she headed straight for us.

"Hi," she said, flashing a pearly smile. "I'm surprised to see you two here during the week. I'd have thought you'd both be at work."

"Extended lunch break," I said.

"I make my own hours," Bailey added, her tone verging on smug. Fair enough. She'd worked hard to get to where she was.

"Are you here to visit your parents?" I asked, hoping she'd say yes.

"No." Her smile turned wry. "I'm back to stay."

My stomach dropped. "Oh. Um. Well, welcome back!"

"Thanks." She beamed.

I couldn't bring myself to reply. All that was running through my head was how everyone thought she and Asher were so cute as a couple. Asher and Ashley. Ash squared. How fucking adorable.

"Do you have a job yet?" Bailey asked, picking up my slack.

"No, so if you hear of anything, let me know."

Bailey nodded. "We will."

I had a brief flash of satisfaction. It was easy to think of her as perfectly put together, so it was nice to learn she wasn't. Although it was ugly of me to feel that way when she'd never done anything to earn my dislike.

Ashley's order was called, and she glanced around. "I'd better get going. It was nice to see you."

As she left, Bailey took my hand. "Don't worry about her," she said quietly. "She and Asher are in the past. They broke up for a reason."

"Yeah, but what was the reason?" I asked.

She didn't answer, and the anxiety roiling in my gut only amplified.

My phone buzzed, and I checked it. "Oh, my God."

"What?" Bailey demanded.

I looked up at her, my eyes wide. "Grace has gone into labor."

———

AT 11.13 AM THE NEXT DAY, GRACE AND NATE WELCOMED BABY Finn into the world while the entire Braddock clan, including Grace's Aunt Desdemona and brother, Ezra, filled the waiting room at the Queenstown Maternity Hospital.

We'd been waiting all morning, after having spent the night at a nearby hotel, and finally, a nurse announced that Finn had been delivered and both he and Grace were safe and healthy.

I slumped against Kennedy, weak with relief. I'd known, logically, that there was no reason to think the birth wouldn't be smooth, but I'd also been involved with plenty of difficult births at the veterinary clinic, and I'd seen how quickly things could go sideways.

"Would Nana, Grandpa, and Big Sister like to come through?" she asked.

Mum hesitated. "Is Grace feeling up to visitors?"

The nurse smiled kindly. "Yes, but only a couple at a time. Dad was very firm on that."

I laughed. "I bet he was."

Nate took overprotectiveness to the extreme when it came to Grace. Of course, I could understand why. If I'd discovered someone I loved bleeding out on their kitchen floor, I'd probably be overprotective too.

Mum held Tess's hand, and Dad took up the rear as they followed the nurse out of the waiting room. I got up, stretched, and bought a packet of nuts from the vending machine, then returned to the chair and scrolled through social media.

A while later, Mum and Dad emerged, both grinning widely. Dad's eyes crinkled with joy, which took years off him, and Mum was practically floating on air. They both loved babies. I mean, they'd had six of their own, and that pretty much said it all.

"He's beautiful." Mum sighed. "He has Nate's eyes, and Grace's dark hair."

"How heavy?" Max asked.

"Seven pounds, two ounces," Mum said.

Max nodded approvingly. "A decent weight."

"Can we see them?" Toby asked, bouncing excitedly.

Mum and Dad exchanged a glance.

"Two at a time," Dad said firmly. "Any more than that and you'll overwhelm them. Poor Grace is exhausted, but she's hiding it well and does want to see you all."

It didn't surprise me that Grace would be doing her best not to let on how tired she was. She was an expert at putting on a good face.

"Why don't Summer and I go?" Max suggested.

No one argued, although Toby looked disappointed. But Max was Nate's twin, and he'd always been close to Grace, so it made sense for him to be the next to visit. I wasn't sure why he'd chosen me to accompany him, but I was eager to see them, so I wouldn't question it.

We walked down the hall together, Max's shoes clopping on the vinyl floor. I nudged him with my shoulder.

"It'll be your turn for a wife and baby soon," I said.

His expression was wistful. "I'd like that, but I haven't had much luck at dating."

"You'll find the perfect woman." I considered whether to drop a hint about Bailey but decided not to. She'd asked me not to meddle, and while I desperately wanted to just in case it could make two of my favorite people happy, I respected her wishes. After all, I knew how mortified I'd be if someone did that with Asher.

"Maybe." He sounded resigned, and I itched to hug him, but at that moment, we arrived at Grace's room.

Max knocked and we entered. Grace lay on a surprisingly large bed, her eyes half-closed. Tess sat cross-legged near her feet, and Nate lounged on an armchair, the baby cradled against his chest.

"Hey," I said softly. "How are you doing?"

"All right," Grace murmured.

"She did so well." Nate gazed over at her, awestruck. "She was incredible."

"I'm sure she was." I bent over the bed and kissed Grace's forehead. "Hi, Mama."

A smile curved her lips, weary but content. She'd always wanted to be a mother, and now she'd not only achieved that, but with the man she'd loved secretly for over a decade. No one deserved happiness more than her.

"Any lingering pain?" Max asked her as I moved closer to Nate and leaned over to get a look at my new nephew.

Grace sighed. "I feel like I was hit by a truck, but I don't think it's anything out of the ordinary."

"No, that's not unusual." Max scanned her from head to

toe, even though most of her was hidden by the covers. "A lot of people don't realize how much of a full-body experience giving birth is. Every muscle in your body contributes."

I met Nate's eyes. They were slightly unfocused, as if he couldn't quite believe what was happening.

"Can I meet my nephew?" I asked.

"Come closer," he said.

I did, and he shifted the bundled baby so I could gather him in my arms.

"Be careful with him." He watched like a hawk, so I stayed close, hoping to ease his concern.

I gazed down into a small, red face. Finn's eyes were closed, but he had a little button nose and a thatch of brown hair.

"Hello cutie," I whispered. "I'm your aunt."

He gurgled and blinked open those massive blue eyes. My breath caught. He was so tiny and delicate, his life only just beginning.

I couldn't help but wonder if, one day, I'd be holding my own baby like this. Did I even dare to dream?

27

———

I double checked that Cookie had a full bowl of water and locked the cat flap, so she'd have to stay inside while I was away. I was still reluctant to let her out when I wasn't around.

"Do you think this is a date?" I asked her. "I'm not sure."

She meowed plaintively and snuffled in her empty food bowl.

"You already had breakfast. So, Cookie, date or not?"

Honestly, I don't know which I'd intended it to be when I'd asked. The invitation had been out of my mouth before I'd thought it through, partly because of a desire to distract Summer from her theory about someone having poisoned Cookie and partly because I just wanted to spend more time with her.

But this wasn't a traditionally date-like activity, so I didn't know what to expect. No doubt she was experiencing the same uncertainty. At least I wouldn't be alone in it.

Did I want it to be a date?

Kind of.

But we also needed to take things slow and figure out where this was going before we leapt into the deep end. Particularly when we had Liam to think about. My conscience insisted that it would be best if my best friend knew before I officially started dating his sister—*if* I did—despite the earful he'd no doubt give me about not being the steady, reliable man she deserved.

Cookie wound around my legs, purring. I squatted to pat her, stroking the length of her soft, furry body.

"Thanks for listening," I told her. "I'll see you later."

I locked the back door, checked that the latch was firmly in place, and did the same out front before going to the garage. My cycle was already loaded onto a rack on the back of the car, and I opened the garage door and reversed out.

During the drive to Summer's cottage, I gave myself a pep talk.

"You've got this. It's just cycling. Talk to her, get to know her better as a person rather than as part of the extended Braddock clan. Take it easy. Keep it light."

Unfortunately, I didn't feel any more confident by the time I arrived. I didn't usually have issues with my confidence, but then, the women I dated weren't usually as deeply enmeshed in my life as Summer Braddock was. There were so many ways I could screw this up.

I parked on the side of the road and got out, glancing up at the overcast sky. It was a bit chilly, but we'd warm up as soon as we got moving.

Summer stepped through the front door, and for once, I didn't force myself not to notice how good she looked, or how tightly the cycling shorts clung to her lean thighs and nicely curved ass. She jogged down the stairs, her tank top riding up to reveal a strip of tanned skin above the waistband of her shorts. My mouth went dry.

"Good afternoon," she called, grabbing hold of her bike, which was leaning against the porch, and wheeling it toward the car.

"Hi." My heart thumped when she turned her smile on me at full wattage, and I had to swallow before I was able to talk. "You ready to go?"

"I think so." She patted the bag strap over her shoulder, which I hadn't previously noticed. "I have a sweater in here if I need it, a raincoat, a puncture repair kit, and snacks. Is there anything I've forgotten?"

I glanced at her handlebars, noting the helmet hanging off them. "Water?"

"Got that too."

"Then I'd say we're all good."

She steered her bike to the rear of my car and helped me lift it onto the rack, then moved out of the way so I could secure it in place. Once that was done, I double checked all the ties and locks, and returned to the driver's seat. Summer got in the other side and dropped her bag on the floor between her feet.

"Where are we going?" she asked, pulling the door shut.

I turned the key in the ignition. "Do you know Castle Hill?"

"Not really."

"There's a walking trail down the Castle River Valley, but if you turn off a little before that, there's an easy mountain biking trail that cuts through the forest on the side of the hill." It would be safer for her than any of the trails up Destiny Peak.

She frowned. "I've walked in Castle River Valley. I just didn't realize there was anything else there."

My chest puffed with pride. "I'll be able to introduce you to somewhere new, then."

A few kilometers out of town, I turned onto a gravel

road. We juddered over potholes, and I knew that if we followed the road to the end, we'd arrive at the start of the walk Summer had mentioned doing before. Instead, I turned off onto a road that was hardly more than a dirt path.

I slowed to a crawl. Branches scraped the sides of the car, and I was grateful I drove an older model and wouldn't lose any sleep over a couple of new scratches.

"Are you sure it's all right to drive down here?" Summer asked.

"Yes." I gritted my teeth as I concentrated on the road. The back tires dropped into a slight dip in the earth and the bottom of the car bumped against the edge of the hollow. I put my foot down and got us out of there before we became stuck. Getting stranded in the forest certainly wasn't the right way to make a good impression on Summer.

We shot forward, and I exhaled, the band around my chest loosening as the road widened and the trees gradually moved further from the vehicle.

"Did you know Ashley has moved back to town?" Summer asked.

I glanced at her. "What?"

"Ashley." She looked at me meaningfully. "Your ex."

"Oh." I turned back to the road and fought the urge to groan. "No, I didn't. Where did you hear that?"

"From her. I saw her at Taste of Destiny." Her voice was strained. She felt some way about Ashley being back in town, but I couldn't get a read on her without looking, and I couldn't do that because I needed to focus on getting us to the trail safely.

"Good for her, I guess," I said distractedly.

Hopefully she'd keep her distance from me. I had absolutely no desire to revisit the past with her, but Ashley had never been good at letting go. It was one of the reasons I was glad when she decided to move away. It meant I didn't have to ward off her advances every time she got maudlin and decided that she'd been wrong to end our relationship.

Finally, we reached the small parking area. I parked on one side, out of the way in case anyone else turned up, although I doubted they would.

Summer laughed. "Well, that was a bit of excitement."

I grinned. "It's only just beginning, sweetheart."

We both froze. Slowly, I turned to face her. Her mouth hung open and her pretty eyes were wide, surprise sparkling in their emerald depths. Tension thrummed between us.

I cleared my throat, cutting the tension, then opened the door, and got out. I moved around to the back of the car and started to unload our bikes.

"Ash."

I glanced over at Summer, who'd gotten out too and was watching me warily. "Hmm?"

"It's okay," she said softly.

"I know." My voice broke, so I repeated more firmly, "I know. Let's get these ready to go."

"Okay." She let me off the hook, grabbing her helmet from the car and clicking it into place as I finished with the bikes.

I walked over to her and slid my finger beneath the strap, testing its tightness. The silken skin of her neck was smooth against my hand, and I wished I could linger there, but I was trying to be on my best behavior.

"Looks good," I said huskily. "Have you sunscreened?"

"I did it at home."

I leaned closer, inhaling the subtle tang of sunscreen on the skin at the back of her neck. If I'd been less flustered, I'd already have noticed. I put my own helmet on and waited while she strapped on the small backpack she'd brought with her.

"We'll go up that way." I gestured at a trail that led into the forest, up a slight incline.

"Uphill?" she whined. "Do we have to?"

I laughed. "It's either uphill on the way there and downhill on the way back, or vice versa. I thought you'd prefer to end with the downhill."

"No, you're right." She straddled her bike. "I'm just not sure my legs are up for this."

"We'll take our time. There's no rush." Tongue in cheek, I added, "Don't try to show off. That's a surefire way to end up on your ass."

She huffed. "As if I need to show off. I'm brilliant already."

I gestured toward the trail. "Well, go on then. Lead the way, you big talker."

She pushed off and cycled toward the trail. I waited for a few seconds to give her space and then followed behind. As she'd said, she was a bit unsteady, but she didn't push herself too hard and we made our way along the trail, shaded by trees. My legs began to warm, and I breathed in the familiar earthiness of the forest as I studied her slim form ahead of me.

We reached a fork in the trail, she called over her shoulder for directions, and I told her to turn left. We cycled along the dappled earth path, the weak sun filtering through the treetops to light the way.

Eventually, we reached the small, clear stream at the end of the trail. I got off my bike and perched on a rock near the water. My heart was light, and I couldn't wipe the smile from my face. Spending time with Summer like this, just the two of us having fun, I could imagine our future. A lifetime of weekends spent in the hills with banter and laughter.

I wanted that.

I nodded toward the stream. "You should put your feet in the water."

She gave me a look. "Do you have any idea how freezing that probably is?"

"Yup."

She crossed her arms and arched one eyebrow. "I'll do it if you do it."

I bent to untie my shoelaces. "You're on."

I removed my shoes, set them aside, and tucked my socks inside them, then slowly approached the stream.

"It's not too late to back out," I said, anticipating just how icy the water would be on my warm feet.

"Like hell," she retorted. "It's all right if you need to though. I understand. Your old heart might not be able to take it."

I narrowed my eyes. "Put your money where your mouth is, Braddock." With that, I stepped into the water and immediately gasped, my breath stuttering. "F-fuck, that's cold."

Summer stepped in beside me, and somehow managed not to make a sound. "It's fine," she said. "Totally fine."

I playfully shoved her shoulder. "You're so full of shit."

She lifted one foot above the surface and flicked me with water. "Hey, catch."

"Oh, my God." I lunged for her, and she sprinted out of the stream, shrieking with laughter. I caught her on the stream bank and tickled her sides until she begged for mercy.

We flopped onto the ground side by side, both breathing heavily, and even though the earth was cool and damp, neither of us seemed in a hurry to move.

After a while, we picked ourselves up, dried our feet as best we could, and put on our soggy socks. The ride back was more of a gentle cruise with the occasional peddling than actual exercise. We were both quiet, but the silence between us was comfortable.

We'd nearly reached the parking area when a loud crack startled us both. I stiffened and looked around. A sound like that could have been a branch breaking off a tree, or a distant gunshot, or any number of other things we needed to be wary of.

Unfortunately, while I was distracted, Summer shrieked, and my eyes snapped forward just in time to see her front wheel hit a branch across the trail, throwing her from her bike.

28

Sharp pinpricks of pain burst along my shins, and I cried out.

"Summer!" Asher leapt off his bike and rushed over to me. "Are you okay?"

I lay in the dirt, my hip throbbing where I'd landed on it, and groaned. "I think so."

"Where the hell did that branch come from?" he asked, slipping one of his arms beneath me and helping me into a seated position.

"I don't know. It might have been there from the beginning, but I didn't notice because of whatever that noise was."

"It wasn't there when we arrived," he said, his gaze skimming down my shins. "It must have fallen since then."

I shifted my legs so I could see them better and winced. Several tiny stones were embedded in my skin and a large graze stretched down the center of each one, right along the shin bone. My left knee was bleeding from a small cut, and my other ached from the way I'd landed.

"Can you get up?" Asher asked. "Does anything feel broken?"

I answered his second question first. "I don't think so. Hold on, let me see."

He offered me his hand and pulled as I tried to stand, but pain tore through my left ankle and I hissed between gritted teeth.

"That doesn't sound good." He dropped to his knees and ran his hands over my ankle. "Let me know when it hurts." He pressed around my ankle joint and then around the top of the foot.

"You know, I thought the first time you felt me up would be sexier than this," I said, then grimaced as he touched a tender spot. "There."

He sat back on his haunches. "I think it's sprained. We'll take you home, ice it, and keep it elevated. I'm so sorry, Summer."

I frowned. "What? Why?"

His lips firmed. "Because I told you that you'd be safe with me, and you got hurt."

I fought the urge to roll my eyes. "There's no way you could have known that something would make a sound at just the right time to distract me from a fallen branch."

"Still, I should have been more careful. Other people would have." He shuffled around beside me and wrapped his arm under my left armpit. "I'll help you back to the car. Keep your weight on the other foot. The right ankle is okay, isn't it?"

"Seems so."

Using him for support, I straightened, and together, we limped down the trail toward his car. It took far longer to get there than it ought to, but in the meantime, I had plenty of opportunity to appreciate Asher's strength. I knew he was fit, but he must have been taking half my weight and didn't show any strain at all.

At his car, he walked me around to the driver's door so he could unlock it, and then escorted me back around to the passenger side. He opened the door, guided me onto the seat, and shifted it as far back as it would go, then instructed me to put my foot on the dashboard.

"I'll be back as soon as I can," he said, his eyes serious. "Shout if you need anything. I mean it."

"I will," I promised.

As soon as he was gone, I leaned forward and set to work picking stones out of the scrapes on my shins. Most of them either brushed off or came out without too much fuss, but a couple were embedded more deeply, and I winced as I wriggled them loose.

"What are you doing?"

I squeaked, my hand flying to my chest. Eyes wide, I turned to look out the passenger door. "You scared the shit out of me."

Asher smirked. "Sorry.

I huffed. "You don't look it."

He lowered the bikes—of which he was controlling one with each hand—to the ground. "Maybe because you should have been waiting for me rather than trying to deal with your injuries yourself."

I rolled my eyes. "All I was doing was getting the stones out."

"And yet, I'm a paramedic and you're not. Should have waited for me." He opened the back door and rifled around, returning a moment later with a first aid kit. "Turn toward me."

"I'm a vet," I told him as I pivoted to make it easier for him to see my legs. "I'm perfectly capable of cleaning wounds."

"Do vets practice on humans?" he asked facetiously.

I eyeballed him and curled my lip.

"Because paramedics do," he continued, unzipping the first aid kit and withdrawing a handful of antiseptic wipes.

"I can handle the basics," I said defensively.

To my surprise, he smiled at me. "I know, but you don't have to when I'm here. Let me help you. After all, I'm the one who got you into this mess."

His gently spoken words took the wind out of my sails.

I nodded. "Okay, then. Thank you."

He knelt in front of me, took hold of my uninjured ankle and held it in place as he used an antiseptic wipe to clean the cuts and scrapes on my right leg. I gritted my teeth through the stinging pain and did my best not to let him see how much it hurt. It was ridiculous how painful the smallest abrasions could be. In contrast, the gash on my knee hardly hurt at all.

He discarded the wipe and cleaned my other leg, then ran a wipe over both and dabbed at my knee. The wound there had stopped leaking blood and was beginning to crust. He carefully removed debris, one hand cupped around my calf to hold it in place.

That done, he dug a Band Aid out of the first aid kit and used it to cover the gash, then scanned the other cuts and scrapes up my shins.

"I don't think there's any point in covering them," he said. "Unless you want me to, so we can ensure they're kept clean."

I shook my head. "No, I'll just be careful."

"Okay." He lifted my lower leg to examine the ankle. "I have a compression sock we can put over this for the time being, but we need to ice it as soon as we can. Are you sore anywhere else?"

"My hip."

He set my leg down and searched the first aid kit, presumably for the compression sock. "Is the skin broken?"

"I don't think so. Just bruised." To make sure, I pulled at the waistband of my shorts and looked beneath them. "Nothing is bleeding."

"Good." He withdrew the compression sock. "Would you rather put this on yourself?"

I tried to bend forward, but my hip throbbed. "Can you do it please?"

His expression softened. "Of course."

With brisk, efficient movements, he removed my shoe, peeled off my wet sock, dried my foot with an unused sweat towel, and pulled the compression sock over my toes and around my heel. It came up to mid-calf, and I couldn't help wincing. The pressure wasn't particularly comfortable.

"Too much?" he asked.

"It doesn't hurt. It's just a strange feeling."

"I know. You wouldn't believe how many times I've had to use these things."

I chuckled. "Do you make a habit of injuring yourself?"

"It goes with the sport." His face darkened. "I am really sorry about this. You told me you were rusty, and I promised we'd be fine, and here you are. Hurt."

"Don't blame yourself." I swung around, returning my legs inside the vehicle. "It was an accident. No one could have known it would happen. Like you said, that branch wasn't there earlier, and we were going slow. It was just unlucky timing."

"If we'd been going more slowly, I might have noticed it." He looked frustrated, and even though I didn't blame him at all, I understood why. It was easy to carry guilt, and based on how reluctant he'd been to pursue anything with me, I suspected that guilt weighed more heavily on him than others.

I forced a smile. "Take me home and coddle me and I'll be fine."

He gave a strained smile back. "Sure."

He packed away the first aid kit, loaded the cycles back onto the rack, and got in the driver's side. He started the engine and drove us back along the narrow road we'd taken earlier.

While we were driving, he didn't speak much. He seemed to be brooding. It worried me a little, but his mood eased the further we got from Castle Hill. By the time we reached my place, the strain lines around his mouth had disappeared, even if he still seemed a little off balance.

"Wait here," he instructed, and I watched, mildly amused, as he unloaded my bike and wheeled it to the porch. He opened the vehicle's rear door and slung my bag over his shoulder. Finally, he opened the passenger side door and helped me out.

We hobbled up the path to the front door. I told Asher where to find the key in my bag, and after a brief search, he pulled it out with an exclamation of victory and slotted it into the lock. Once inside, he guided me to the sofa in the living room.

"Sit here," he said, maneuvering me onto the end cushion.

My lips twitched at his bossiness. "Sir, yes, sir."

He ignored me and reached around to pull the lever that raised the leg rest. "I'll be back in a moment."

He hurried into the kitchen and returned less than a minute later with two ice packs and a bag of frozen peas. He positioned one ice pack and the peas around my ankle and passed me the other ice pack, which had been wrapped in a tea towel.

"For your hip," he said.

"Thanks." I pressed it against my side and leaned back

on the sofa, closing my eyes. "I have to say, this isn't how I imagined today going."

He snorted. "Me neither."

I bit my lip, unsure whether he intended to stay. If I wanted clarification about what exactly this was, then now was the time to do it.

"Asher," I said slowly, "is this a date?"

Before he could answer, there was a knock at the front door.

He jumped up. "I'll get it."

He strode out, and I heard voices as he opened the door, then footsteps down the hallway.

"Summer!" Kennedy exclaimed, rushing into the room with Liam behind her. "Asher said you fell off your bike. You're so lucky he saw it happen so he could make sure it was nothing serious. How are you doing?"

I smiled at her weakly. Right, so that's how we were selling the fact he was at my house.

Looked like it would be an afternoon of lies...and not getting answers. Asher would never risk talking to me privately while Liam was here.

29

———

Liam and I strolled down Centennial Street together, huddled beneath an umbrella. Water trickled down the back of my collar and onto my neck, and I shivered. It was one of those wet winter days when I never felt warm no matter how many layers I wore.

"Have you seen Summer since Saturday?" I asked, glancing at the entrance to Taste of Destiny up ahead, where we'd temporarily find shelter.

"No." Liam glanced over at me. "Kennedy checked in on her and said she was doing all right."

I grimaced. "I would have liked to drop by yesterday, but Mum called and asked for help clearing out the garage. By the time we were done, the day was basically over."

"I'm sure she doesn't expect you to hover over her just because you happened to be driving past when she fell," Liam said. "She's not hurt that badly. Max took a look at her ankle and said you were spot on. It's a sprain and should heal by itself in a few weeks."

"She won't like having to take it easy." Summer was always in action. I hardly ever saw her being still. It was my fault she'd have to slow down. I should have taken the lead, rather than sending her ahead of me down the trail. If I'd been in the front, she never would have hit that branch and come off.

I hated that I'd proved to both of us how inadequate I would be as the man in her life. I wanted to prove my fears wrong, not right.

"He told her not to use it too much, but I can't see her paying any attention to that," he agreed.

"Stubborn."

He elbowed me. "Not at all like someone else I know."

He pushed open the cafe door and held it open while I retracted the umbrella and shook the moisture off it. The morning was quiet, so we made our way to the counter and gave Eden the fire house's order. Eight coffees and one herbal tea.

We sat at a small, round table near the counter while we waited. There was a jingle as the door swung inward and a sopping wet woman ran inside.

"It's crazy out there," she exclaimed, automatically scanning the shop's interior.

I stiffened. I'd recognize those bright blue eyes anywhere, even if the rest of her looked like a bedraggled cat. "Hi, Ashley."

Her eyes widened, and then she grinned. "Ash! It's so good to see you!"

She strode toward me, her arms open for a hug, but something in my expression must have warned her off because she stopped before reaching me.

"Oops." Her smile faltered but returned quickly. "I forgot how wet I am."

"You must have been out in the rain for a while," Liam said, eying the dripping ends of her hair.

"Yeah." She scrunched her nose. "It wasn't raining this heavily when I left Mum and Dad's place. I wasn't expecting it to go south so quickly. But Asher, I can't believe I'm just running into you like this. We should get together properly sometime."

"It's nice to see you too," I lied, unsure what to do in the face of her enthusiasm. "I heard you're back for good."

She nodded. "For a while, at least." Her smile turned sly. "Definitely longer if I have a reason to stay."

My chest constricted. I didn't like the way she was looking at me, or the meaningful way she'd said that. "How are your parents? I haven't seen them around for a while."

It was the best thing I could think of to deflate any romantic ideas that might be whirling through her mind. No one could have sexy thoughts while discussing their parents.

"They're fine. Both keeping busy. Dad did a course to renew his first aid certification on the weekend so he can continue being part of the search and rescue team. Speaking of, do you need more hands on deck there? I could take a course as well."

I glanced at Liam, who knew more about those details than I did.

"More hands on deck is always good," he replied. "You're best to talk to Connor though. He's the one who runs the team."

Even while he spoke, her gaze never left me. "Maybe I will."

Thankfully, Eden called over to let us know our drinks were ready.

"We'd better go," I said, standing and pushing the chair in.

"Wait." She touched my arm, stopping me in my tracks. "Let's do something this weekend."

I looked over at Eden, who'd arched an eyebrow as she watched the show. "I'm busy this weekend. Sorry."

Ashley's lips pursed. "I didn't say what time."

"The midwinter dip is on Saturday," Liam said, saving my ass. "And then Ash and I have an all-day hike planned for Sunday."

"Oh." She looked disappointed, but then brightened. "I like hiking."

She stared at me. I glanced down at my hands. Liam shifted awkwardly from one foot to the other. No one said anything even though she was clearly angling for an invitation.

"Maybe I'll see you at the midwinter dip," she said finally.

I tilted my head in acknowledgement and ducked around her. Liam and I carried a tray of drinks each out of Taste of Destiny. Outside, I used the wall to help balance the drinks while I opened the umbrella.

"What was that about?" Liam asked quietly as we began to walk. "You were a bit rude to her."

I groaned. "I'm afraid she wants to get back together. You know how she kept coming around every time she got moody before she left town, saying how sorry she was to have ended it, and that she'd never find anyone better than me. Even though she was the one who told me I worked too much and was never emotionally available to her when she needed me."

He winced. "Yeah, I remember. Our jobs aren't exactly relationship friendly."

"You make it work," I pointed out. Surely, if Liam could manage a healthy relationship with Kennedy, I had a chance at doing the same with someone else. Although he had always been better at balance than me.

"Only because Kennedy matters more to me than anything else." His soft smile took the wind out of my sails. "If you prioritized Ashley…"

I blew out a breath. The problem was that I didn't want to. The only woman I'd been tempted to prioritize over the job was Summer, and I had to admit that being preoccupied with her was already making me careless.

"I just don't have the emotional bandwidth to go through that with her all over again," I told him.

"Fair enough." He was quiet for a moment, then added, "But you are looking to settle down, and she does seem interested. Maybe it's worth giving it another shot? Look what happened when I gave Kennedy a second chance."

I shook my head. "I'm not interested in her."

Liam stopped suddenly. I slowed and looked over my shoulder at him.

"But you *are* interested in someone," he said, as if he'd had an epiphany. "That's why you don't want Ashley. There's someone else. Who?"

I hesitated and considered denying it. After all, hadn't I proved that I was exactly what Summer didn't need? Careless, reckless, irresponsible. But even thinking of keeping my distance from her exhausted me. I wasn't sure how much longer I could do it.

"Yeah, there is," I admitted. "I'm still figuring out where we stand though. I promise, as soon as it's official, you'll be the first to know."

30

———

SUMMER

I ADMIRED THE EXCELLENT VIEW OF ASHER'S BACKSIDE AS I limped behind him up the trail to Destiny Tarn. Tight butt, strong back, broad shoulders, and those lean, muscled legs. I couldn't wait to touch him.

Unfortunately for me, that was unlikely to happen today since we were accompanied by almost the entire Braddock posse. Nate and Tess, Max, Kennedy and Liam, Toby, Bailey, Blair, and Asher's sister Frannie, her husband Dean, and their baby Marcy. Not exactly the kind of company that allowed for a romantic interlude.

That said, Asher had my gear in his backpack—a good sign. He'd insisted on carrying it for me. He'd tried to tell me I couldn't come to the midwinter dip at all, but having grown up with five brothers, I could out-stubborn him any day of the week. Anyway, my ankle felt much better. It was still sore but no longer puffy and inflamed.

"You okay?" Asher called back to me.

"Fine," I said, catching Bailey's eye and grinning. She

walked alongside me, also carrying a bag, although hers was smaller. Asher was carrying our lunch as well as a towel and change of clothes for each of us.

"Has he been like this all week?" Bailey asked.

"Yeah." I peeked up at him, but I didn't think he'd be able to hear us when we were speaking so softly. "I kind of like it."

She smirked. "Of course you do. The man of your dreams is doting on you. If it were me, I'd have him hand feeding me grapes off a platter."

"No, you wouldn't." I laughed. "You're far too nice for that."

She glanced behind us, and I wondered if she was searching for Max. She seemed to have an instinctive awareness of him whenever he was nearby. She rubbed her upper arms, which were exposed by the strappy tank top she wore. "It's a bit cold today, isn't it?"

"The water will be freezing." I supposed the whole point of a midwinter dip into a mountain lake was the fact it would be cold, but I seemed to forget that right up until this point in the midwinter dip every year, always having to convince myself to strip into my swimsuit and jump into the tarn.

"You managing all right, Summer?" Max called up, as if he'd sensed Bailey looking for him and assumed it was me.

"Seriously, I'm fine," I exclaimed. "A little sore, but nothing to worry about."

Bailey pursed her lips. "I'm more concerned about Nate, actually. He looks like he's ready to fall asleep on his feet."

"I'm not surprised," I murmured back. "Babies must be a lot of work. It's a pity Grace couldn't come today."

It would be a while before she was up to much in the way of exercise.

"I think she was looking forward to having a quiet house for a while," Bailey said.

"You're probably right."

My family might have been driving Grace crazy. I knew she loved us all, and that everyone meant well with their visits and offers to help, but it must be a lot for someone who'd never had much family growing up.

We crested the top of the hill and passed out of the forest and onto the tussocks. From here, it wasn't much farther. Sure enough, a few minutes later, we arrived at the tarn. Several picnic blankets had already been laid around the shore, with groups clustered on a few of them and others empty—their occupants presumably exploring the area.

I followed Asher around the side of the tarn. He slid his backpack off his shoulders, unzipped it, and pulled out a fleece blanket, which he laid on the ground. He dropped his bag on one edge.

"How long until the dip?" I asked as the family gathered around.

Nate checked his watch. "Ten minutes. Better get undressed. I'll be doing the safety briefing soon."

He hoisted the foldable chair he'd carried up and took it over to the edge of the water, along with a megaphone. Apparently, using the old-fashioned megaphone was easier than lugging up more expensive modern equipment. Or so he claimed. I suspected he just didn't want to learn new things.

Asher unzipped his backpack and passed me a bottle of sunscreen. I took it and reluctantly stripped off my tank top to reveal the emerald green bikini beneath. I enjoyed the flare of heat in Asher's eyes as I pulled my shorts off over my shoes—no plans to walk around in bare feet. Tussock was prickly.

Bailey dropped her bag beside the blanket and undressed too. She'd opted for a one piece swimsuit that looked demure in the front, but when she turned, the swimsuit plunged to just above the top of her bum, showing off miles of sleek back.

"Looking fierce," I said, high-fiving her.

Sometimes I forgot how much of a fitness fanatic my best friend was. Years as a competitive gymnast had honed her body, and although she no longer competed, she went to the gym most days of the week and her hours of hard work paid off.

"You too." She glanced at Asher behind me and winked. "I reckon you need someone to fix up the sunscreen on your back, right?"

I grinned. "You know what, I think I do." I turned. "Ash, can you give me a hand?"

His eyes widened, and for a moment, he looked like a startled deer. "I'm sure Bailey can—"

But Bailey was already shaking her head. "I haven't sunscreened at all yet, and we're going to get started soon."

Asher glanced between us, then with a wry twist of his lips, took the sunscreen. "Turn around."

I did as he said, fully expecting him to squirt a big blob of cold sunscreen onto my skin to repay me for backing him into a corner, but he didn't. Instead, his strong fingers smoothed along the tops of my shoulders. His thumbs dug into the meat of my upper arms, and I groaned.

"God, that feels good," I murmured.

He worked his way down my back leisurely, massaging between my shoulder blades and along the ridges on either side of my spine. If not for the witnesses, I might have melted into a puddle at his feet. As it was, I struggled not to moan with pleasure.

"Good?" His voice was husky, as if touching me had affected him as much as it had affected me.

I cleared my throat. "Yes, thank you."

I took the sunscreen bottle from him and quickly did my legs, arms, chest, and stomach.

Bailey side-eyed me. "You were so lucky no one was paying attention. I know I set you up for that, but I didn't mean for you to get quite so into it."

I ducked my head sheepishly. "I can't think when he touches me."

She giggled. "That much is obvious." She leaned closer and lowered her voice. "If it helps, he couldn't take his eyes off you."

Heat unfurled in my lower belly.

Good.

I'd known, theoretically, that he wanted me—he must, since he'd kissed me—but having someone else see it somehow made it more real. I wasn't built for secrets, even though I'd carried one for years.

Kennedy and Liam, who'd taken up the rear, arrived just as Nate called everyone to gather at the edge of the tarn. We slowly made our way over, clustering beside the water.

I stood with Bailey on one side and Asher on the other as Nate lectured us all on the importance of being careful, not drowning, not staying in too long, and so on. Finally, he reached the part we were all waiting for: the countdown.

"Ten," he called.

"Nine," we all chorused. "Eight, seven, six..."

I took Bailey's hand, and we smiled at each other.

"Five, four, three..."

Asher's arm brushed mine, lighting me up inside.

"Two, one."

The group lurched forward, into the water. I hobbled behind the mass, splashing into the shallows.

"Ready?" I asked Bailey.

"Never." She gritted her teeth. "Let's do it."

Together, we powered into deeper water, releasing our grasp on each other and diving in. My abdomen quivered from the cold, and I burst through the surface, spraying water all around me as my hair flicked over my shoulders. Bailey emerged a moment later, panting and wiping water from her eyes.

Droplets stung the side of my face, and I spun sideways, glaring at Asher, who was poised to splash me again. I cupped my hand and splashed him back, then splashed Bailey, and Toby, who was just ahead of me. They returned fire, and I giggled and shielded myself.

When it became obvious I had no chance of winning, I trotted back to the shore, favoring my left foot. I headed for the blanket and wasted no time grabbing one of the towels Asher had pulled out of his bag. I dried myself quickly, then wrapped the towel around me and flopped onto the blanket.

A moment later, Kennedy, Liam, and Asher joined me. Asher sat close enough that I could feel the heat from his body. We exchanged a glance, our gazes catching for a long moment.

I tore my eyes away from him and immediately noticed a man staring at me from the next group over. I dropped my gaze for a second, taken aback, but then raised it again.

He was still watching me. I cocked my head, wondering whether I knew him. He was perhaps in his early forties, with a stocky build, brown hair and brown eyes. He was fully dressed, in contrast to most other people here.

I was so preoccupied that when a hand landed on my shoulder, I jumped, my heartbeat ratcheting up a notch.

"Jesus, Blair," I exclaimed. "Warn a girl."

31

ASHER

When Blair distracted Summer, I glanced in the direction she'd been staring. She'd seemed on edge for some reason. When I realized who she'd been looking at, my heart ached.

Robert Warner.

The man who'd lost his wife in a car accident. He was gazing out over the tarn, looking as lost as a little boy. Poor guy. I could still remember the sound of his cries and screams when he'd realized the love of his life was dead.

It broke my heart.

We'd lost too many patients during my years as a paramedic, and seeing their grieving relatives always tore me up inside. I couldn't help feeling like I should have done more.

On the few occasions when I managed not to go down that rabbit hole, I instead found myself wondering who would cry for me if my dangerous job or hobbies ever caught up with me.

My parents and sisters, for sure. My friends too. But if I

was dating someone—like Summer—they'd be the one whose life was most turned upside down.

I watched as Robert sighed, and his shoulders slumped. His picnic blanket was empty except for a single bag. It seemed as though he'd come here alone. The back of my throat tightened. In the past, he must have come with Susan. Now, he'd never have her at his side again.

If something did happen to me, was I willing to leave someone in his shoes?

I forced my attention away from him and dug around in my backpack instead, pulling out a couple bottles of water, a bag of sandwiches, a bar of chocolate, and two muffins from Taste of Destiny. Chocolate for me, and blueberry cinnamon for Summer.

"That looks good."

I glanced up and only just managed not to pull a face. Frannie stood over me, and beside her, wearing a cat-with-the-cream expression, was Ashley Moore.

"Want some chocolate?" I offered Frannie, who'd always had a sweet tooth despite going through health food fad diets at least once a year.

She bit her lip. "I shouldn't."

I tore open the wrapping, broke off a piece and offered it to her. "Go on."

She took it. "Oh, fine. You got me. Thanks." She bit into it and smiled. "So good. So, Ash, you didn't tell me that Ashley is back in town."

"I didn't think to mention it," I replied, and she looked at me as though I'd mooned her.

"But perhaps the old flame could be rekindled," she said, nibbling the edge of her piece of chocolate.

"What do you say?" Ashley winked. "Want to see if the embers can be brought back to life?"

Apparently, I wasn't going to be getting away from her easily. "Ashley..."

"Perhaps we could meet up tomorrow to talk more privately?" she suggested. "After your hike with Liam is done, of course."

"I don't—"

"Unless you're already seeing someone else?" she said, shooting a meaningful look at Summer, who was talking to Blair.

My heart skipped. I narrowed my eyes. How the hell had she guessed what was going on between us? And would she mention anything in front of both our families? I didn't like to think so, but Ashley had always been unpredictable.

"Fine," I said through gritted teeth. "Tomorrow. But it isn't a date."

"Don't be rude," Frannie chastened, her dark eyebrows drawing together.

Ashley just laughed and touched her arm. "Don't worry, Frannie. Asher likes to tease, but I know not to take it seriously."

Maybe you should, I tried to communicate with my eyes, but she either didn't pick up on the unspoken message or she willfully ignored it.

"What's been going on with you lately?" I asked Frannie, purposefully diverting the conversation. "We didn't get a chance to talk much earlier."

She shrugged. "Same as usual. I've just been taking care of Marcy and trying to snatch sleep where I can." She shook her head. "I'm obviously not getting enough of it though, because I keep misplacing things this week, and I could have sworn I heard Dean outside while I was making breakfast this morning, but when I checked, he was still in bed."

My gut twisted. I knew how hard it was to function when you weren't sleeping well. "If you ever need me to babysit for a night or two, just let me know. I'm happy to watch Marcy so you guys can have some time to yourselves and get a good night's sleep."

Frannie smiled tiredly. "Thanks, Ash. I don't think we're quite ready to be away from her yet, but maybe I'll take you up on that in a month or two."

"Whenever you need is fine with me."

A guitar strummed behind us, and I sat back and turned away from Frannie and Ashley. Blair had brought out his guitar, which he'd lugged all the way up here—although God only knew why—and his fingers deftly played the strings, striking up a lighthearted tune.

I offered Summer a sandwich, but she shook her head, and began to sing instead. I closed my eyes, letting her voice wrap around me, but then forced them open again. Much as I loved reveling in the sensuality of her singing, I wanted to watch her too.

Her lips curved upward, and she radiated a type of carefree joy that I didn't often see from her. She sang an upbeat Six60 song about roots and family, and when she reached the chorus, the other Braddocks joined in.

She swayed with the music and grinned at Blair, who smiled back, his shaggy hair flopping over his forehead. For once, I wasn't eaten up by jealousy because of their interaction. Somehow, in my gut, I knew that Summer was mine. I had nothing to worry about when it came to him.

"She's very talented," Ashley murmured, loud enough for only Frannie and I to hear.

Frannie tapped her foot to the beat. "She always has been."

Ashley sent me another knowing look, and then stalked away, back to whichever group she'd arrived with.

Summer and Blair finished their song to enthusiastic applause. Summer gave a little bow and Blair called for requests. Someone yelled out the name of another Six60 song, and he started to play.

I shook my head, amused. He must have done some research between now and last time he'd visited. He hadn't known any of the iconic kiwi band's songs then. I passed around the chocolate and sandwiches, making sure to keep some aside for Summer, along with her muffin.

After a few songs, Summer stopped singing and gratefully accepted a sandwich. She ate while Blair played, and before long, we were one of the last groups remaining by the lake.

When Blair packed away his guitar, I decided I'd better do the same with my gear and began to wrap the food and pack it away. The others followed suit. Toby had left earlier with a group of guys his age, and Nate was dozing on the blanket with Tess sitting cross-legged beside him, reading.

Liam nudged Nate's shoulder to wake him and he blinked sleepily and sat up.

"Time to go?" he asked.

"Pretty much," Liam replied.

Groggily, he sat up and stretched, then got to his feet and stepped off the blanket. I shook off the loose tussock and mud from the blanket and folded it away. Once my bag was packed, I slipped my arms through the straps and waited for Max and Dean to lead the group down the hill.

I waited to take up the rear, where I knew Summer would be, so she didn't strain her sore ankle. Hopefully she hadn't overdone it today. By unspoken agreement, we paused until the rest of the group was far enough ahead that we could speak in private before we trailed after them.

"What was that about with Ashley?" Summer asked.

I grimaced. "She wants to meet up tomorrow."

She pursed her lips and gave me the evil eye. "And you said...?"

"I agreed."

"Ash—"

"Wait," I interrupted. "I agreed because she seems suspicious of you and me, and I didn't want her to say anything about it. I made sure she knows that tomorrow isn't a date."

She scowled. "I don't like it."

Honestly, neither did I.

"I promise, everything is over between her and me," I told her, brushing the back of my hand against hers as we walked. Ashley didn't really want me. She'd made it clear when we broke up that I wasn't giving her the time and attention she needed. She'd just temporarily forgotten that.

Summer huffed. "It'd better be."

32

———————

SUMMER

I SIPPED MY CHAI LATTE AND GLARED AT THE ENTRANCE TO Taste of Destiny as Asher sauntered through, with one hand in his pocket and the other on the door. He paused to survey the cafe for an available table, his gaze flickering slightly as it skimmed over me. He raised his eyebrow, but I met his eyes and didn't look away.

Okay, so maybe it was a little childish of me to stake out the cafe during his not-date with Ashley—something I'm sure a more mature woman wouldn't have done—but if I'd stayed home, I'd only have wondered what was happening between them. Now, I had a front row seat. Or back row, I supposed, since I was tucked into the furthest corner of the room from the entrance.

Asher sat at a table beside the window, which still had someone else's used coffee mugs in the center. A waitress scurried over to clear them away and quickly wipe the table down.

"Are you sure you want to spy on them?" Bailey asked from beside me.

"It's not spying," I told her. "We just happen to be here at the same time."

"Uh-huh." She sounded dubious. "At four o'clock on a Sunday, when we're both usually at home, preparing for the work week."

"Exactly."

She drank more of her smoothie—green, this time.

"Not too fast," I warned her. "We don't want to have to get up to replace our drinks, or Ashley will notice we're here."

She rolled her eyes. "We aren't undercover. She's probably going to see us anyway."

"Shh. Let me have my comforting lies."

God bless Bailey, because she did.

I was lucky to have a friend who supported me even when I was behaving borderline inappropriately.

Ashley arrived right on time, and my hackles immediately went up. She was dressed way too nicely for a casual coffee with a friend. She'd taken the time to do her hair and makeup, her dress was more suited to a Michelin-Starred restaurant, and even from here, I could tell her manicure was flawless.

That wasn't jealousy boiling in my gut.

Not at all.

It was just that it'd be nice to be able to maintain a manicure. Being a vet made it next to impossible. And I'd never look that sophisticated, no matter how hard I tried.

Ashley beelined for Asher and leaned over to kiss his cheek. He dodged, and there was a super awkward moment when neither of them seemed to know what to do next, but then she laughed, tossed her glossy hair over her shoulder, and dropped her bag on the newly cleaned table.

She said something, and they both stood and went to the counter.

A few minutes later, Eden brought over our food. A nutty slice for me and a jar of chia pudding for Bailey.

"What's up with them?" she asked softly, gesturing toward Asher and Ashley, who'd returned to their table.

"They're exes," Bailey whispered, not nearly as subtly as she seemed to think. "She wants him back."

I scowled.

Eden leaned toward me. "Don't worry. I saw his face, and he's definitely not into her."

My eyebrows flew up. "Does literally everyone know?"

"About your crush on him?" She smirked. "Probably most people, other than your brothers."

"Thank God for small mercies," I muttered.

"I think Max does though," Eden added thoughtfully. "He's too clever not to have noticed."

This time, it was Bailey's turn to glare. If we weren't in public, there was every chance she'd have bared her teeth.

Eden laughed. "Don't worry, Max is too old for me. You can have him."

With that, she left. We both stared after her, an unsettled silence between us.

Bailey turned to me, her expression panicked. "Do you think everyone knows about my feelings for Max?"

"Of course not," I soothed, although it seemed like a distinct possibility. "Let's never mention this again, okay?"

She nodded mutely.

"Hey guys, what's up?"

I flinched. Bailey squeaked.

Kennedy's mouth twisted with amusement. "Sorry, I didn't mean to scare you."

"It's fine," I said breathlessly. "Just a bit of a workout for my heart. I've heard that's supposed to be good for you."

Laughing, Kennedy sat on the chair facing Bailey and me, with her back to the rest of the cafe. "So, what are you doing here?"

We exchanged a glance. I bit my lip and darted a look at Asher and Ashley.

Kennedy turned and hummed in understanding. "I got it," she said. "Can you still see them past me?"

"Yes," I said quietly.

"Then continue as you were. I'll just sit here while I wait for my order to be ready." She flushed. "I've been craving banana loaf today. I'm buying enough to keep me going for a few days since my tummy seems to have become quite fussy lately."

"Have you been sick?" I asked, concerned.

She shook her head. "Not really. I've felt a little queasy, but it's more a case of not having an appetite, or of certain smells putting me off eating."

"I'm sorry to hear that," Bailey said, laying her hand on Kennedy's. "Make sure to tell Max if you start to feel worse. I'm sure he can help."

"I will." Kennedy's eyes danced with amusement, and I hid a grin. Okay, so maybe Bailey's hero worship of Max was kind of obvious. I only hoped my feelings for Asher weren't quite so blatant.

I broke off a piece of slice with my fork and crunched on it as I watched Asher and Ashley talk. She was leaning across the table toward him, while he seemed to be trying to get as far from her as possible. Satisfaction rolled through me.

"I've just been to see Grace," Kennedy said.

"How is she?" Bailey asked.

"She's tired, obviously," Kennedy said. "She's loving being a mom though. She and Finn are so sweet together. I can already imagine her with another baby, or maybe a couple more."

"Do you know if she wants more kids?" I asked. Neither Grace nor Nate had spoken to me about their plans in that regard.

Kennedy shrugged. "Maybe, but I'm not sure. As much as she loves it, she's also keen to get back to work. I know she's been sneaking away while Finn naps to work on her latest Viking romance story, and she's still researching to make sure she's fleshed out her Destiny Falls historical romance as well as possible."

I cocked my head. "She's worked on that for much longer than she usually does, hasn't she?"

Kennedy looked uncertain. "You'd know more than me, but maybe because it's based on true events, she wants to make sure to get the facts right."

"Hmm possibly." Grace could be a perfectionist.

"You know how she tracked down Jewel and Rocky's descendants?" Kennedy asked.

Bailey and I nodded.

"She's considering reaching out to them. Perhaps having them read the book to fact-check for her."

"That would be awesome," I exclaimed. "She should do it. I bet their descendants would be honored to see how she's bringing their ancestor's love story to life."

Bailey cleared her throat. "Provided it's a woman, because I can imagine men would get weird about the sexy scenes."

"Good point," I agreed. "Why do some men have to get strange about sex in books? It's just like any other part of life."

"Except hotter," Kennedy added slyly.

I laughed. "True. Next time you see Grace, tell her that Bailey and I think she should do it."

"I will."

I glanced toward the window just in time to see Ashley try to take Asher's hand. He slid his hands under the table to avoid her, presumably resting them on his lap.

My lips twitched. I shouldn't take pleasure in his rejection of her and, honestly, if they were anyone else, I'd feel for her, but it was difficult to be sympathetic when she was trying to take my man. Asher seemed to think she had an inkling about us, which made her putting the moves on him pretty insensitive.

Eden brought them a tray of food. A hot drink each, a sweet chili and cream cheese pinwheel for him and a tiny bowl of salad for her. Asher got up and excused himself to the bathroom. As soon as he was gone, Ashley's gaze shifted directly over to me.

I stiffened. Oops, caught out.

She rose to her feet and stalked across the cafe, circling around the customers and full tables separating us. When she reached us, she folded her arms over her chest.

"You're being clingy and weird," she said flatly.

I frowned. "Excuse me?"

She made a sound of impatience. "Unless you and Asher are exclusively dating, then he can do whatever he likes without being spied on."

My cheeks flamed. The thing was, she had a point.

"At least I'm not trying to force myself on him when he clearly isn't interested," I retorted, immediately ashamed of myself for stooping to her level.

She paled, and her mouth fell open. She blinked a few times.

"Hey, I'm sorry—"

I didn't get to finish my sentence because she stomped away.

"Now you've done it," Kennedy muttered. "What's the bet that she's going to tell tales on you to Asher?"

My stomach sank. "I really hope not."

Asher returned and I watched, eating on autopilot, as they started a stilted conversation. I did notice that Ashley didn't try to touch him again, and that satisfied the petty part of me that I couldn't seem to bury.

I looked away. Ashley was right. I shouldn't be spying on them. If anything long term were to happen between Asher and me, we needed to trust each other. But still, one thing did strike me as odd about her.

I shifted my chair closer to Bailey and gestured for Kennedy to do the same.

"Don't you think it's strange that Ashley turned up in town at the same time as Asher's cat accidentally got poisoned?" I asked.

Bailey sighed. "I say this with love, but you're reading way too much into it and making a connection that isn't there because you're jealous and you want her to be up to no good."

I pressed my lips together. I could see the sense in what she'd said, but something about Ashley still felt...off...to me.

"What do you think?" I directed the question at Kennedy this time.

She grimaced. "Usually, I'd agree with Bailey, but with so many insane things happening in Destiny Falls lately, who knows? Stranger things have happened."

33

ASHER

"A long black and a chai latte, please," I said to Eden as I waited behind the counter at Taste of Destiny on Monday morning.

She grinned. "Funny, that's Summer's favorite drink."

I leveled her with a look. "You're fishing."

Her mischievous smile only widened. "Am I catching anything?"

I rolled my eyes. Nosy women would be the death of me. "Yes, I'm taking a coffee to Summer."

"Good." She sounded smug.

I paid and stood aside while she passed my order to the barista and greeted the person behind me. The line was out the door this morning, but that was hardly surprising when this was the only place to get a decent hot drink in town. The service station offered coffee, but it was out of a basic machine and even I knew enough to realize it was bad.

The barista passed my two coffees in biodegradable takeout cups, and I took them and headed outside. I shivered as I stepped into the cold air. It had frosted this morning; I could see my breath fog in the air. The sidewalk was slippery, so I had to be careful as I made my way toward the veterinary clinic.

I was half a block away when a male figure stepped in front of me. I stopped abruptly, almost spilling my drinks to avoid crashing into him.

"James," I said, startled by his scruffy appearance. He'd never been a snappy dresser, but now his eyes were red-rimmed with dark circles underneath and it didn't look like he'd washed his jacket in several days, during which time he'd spilled plenty of shit down the front of it.

James pointed his finger at me. "You told Tia I was fucking around on her, didn't you?"

I straightened my back. The way he was staring me down was obviously intended to intimidate.

"I haven't seen Tia in weeks," I said truthfully.

"You called her then," he said. "Or messaged her. I know it was you. You and Maia are the only ones we told how it happened, and she had the fucking decency to mind her own business."

I snorted. "Do you really think the other guys there didn't hear what happened? You know as well as me that gossip spreads like wildfire around here. Besides, you *did* fuck around on her."

"You haven't denied it." He squared up to me, drawing himself to his full height—perhaps an inch or so taller than I was.

"Listen," I said quietly, hoping to defuse the situation, "all I did was suggest she look into what happened more closely herself." I stood by the fact Tia needed to know the truth, but I was beginning to think I might have made the wrong judgement call in contacting her myself.

He jabbed his finger forward again, stabbing me in the

chest with the tip. "We would have been fine if she hadn't questioned what I told her."

"Would you have?" I asked. "What's your definition of 'fine'? Because to me, it seems like if you were 'fine', you wouldn't have stuck your dick into someone else."

His face reddened dangerously, and his mouth moved, but no sounds came out. For a moment I feared I'd end up having to use my paramedic training to save this douchebag from a heart attack.

"You just want Tia for yourself," he blustered.

I laughed. Sure, Tia was a lovely woman, but I'd never been the slightest bit interested in her. James didn't like that though. His eyes narrowed, his fist drew back, and before I had the chance to react, his knuckles smashed into my face.

Pain tore through my nose, and my mouth filled with thick blood, the metallic tang overwhelming my senses. I stumbled backward, dropping the coffees. One of them splashed down my leg, scalding me, and I cursed.

I straightened and blinked at James, just in time to see his fist swinging at me again. I lunged to the side, gasping as his hand skimmed past my cheek.

"Fight back, you coward," he growled.

I shook my head, wincing when my brain sloshed around inside my skull. Fuck. I might have a concussion. I spat out a mouthful of blood and circled around, trying to keep my distance from him. I could throw a decent punch if needed, but any fight I engaged in would look bad on my permanent record.

Shit. I'd definitely fucked up by spilling the beans to Tia. I was off my game lately.

"I'm walking away now," I told him, my tongue tripping over the words. "You should do the same."

I started to back away. People had emerged from Taste of

Destiny, and I had to hope their presence would defuse the situation.

"Fuck you."

He charged at me. He was so big, it was impossible to avoid him, so I pivoted so my shoulder was the only thing he struck as he rocketed past me. He turned around and rushed me again. I was tempted to try to trip him, but if he hit the pavement, he might be injured.

If you don't do anything, you might get injured.

"Whoa," a familiar voice exclaimed.

Liam.

James spun toward him. "You," he sneered. "You're probably in on it too."

He lunged at Liam, but Keith and Trev, two of Eugene's friends, grabbed him by the shoulders and restrained him.

"Calm down," Keith said.

James tried to jerk free of their hold. "Let me go. These assholes are the reason Tia left me."

"You did that all by yourself," I told him coolly. Even if I was having second thoughts about the role I'd played in this drama, I wouldn't give him the satisfaction of knowing that.

Sirens shrieked down the block and lights flashed as a pair of police cruisers turned onto the street and parked nearby.

"Who called the cops?" James demanded, his expression beginning to pale.

Fuck, this was such a mess.

34

─────

SUMMER

MY PHONE RANG AS I WAS CHECKING MY CALENDAR OF appointments for the morning. I glanced down at the screen. It was Eden.

I raised the phone to my ear. "Hello?"

"Summer, get out onto the street right now," she hissed.

I frowned. "Why?"

"Just do it. Trust me." She hung up.

Bemused, I strode out of our shared office, past Beverley, waving off her curiosity about where I was going to in such a hurry, and crossed the parking lot, which fronted onto Centennial Street.

As soon as I did, my jaw dropped. Blue and red lights were flashing from a pair of police cars parked about a block away, and a cluster of people were gathered outside Taste of Destiny. I ran down the street, grateful for my sensible work shoes.

When I reached them, I realized why Eden had called.

Standing in the center of the group were Liam and Asher. Blood was streaming down Asher's face, and he was carrying himself stiffly, as if hurt somewhere else too.

My stomach dropped, and I raced across the remaining distance between us. I whipped off my scrub top, grateful for my tank top underneath, balled it up, and offered it to him. He took the top without question and used it to staunch the flow of blood.

"Are you okay?" I asked, scanning him for other injuries. The skin beneath his eyes was beginning to take on a purple tinge. He might have a pair of black eyes later today.

"What the hell is going on here?" Nate demanded.

He and Mehrtens, his most trusted officer, had gotten out of their car and positioned themselves between Asher and another man, who was red-faced and cursing up a storm.

I jolted, caught off guard. It hadn't occurred to me to look for whoever had done this to him. I'd been too focused on helping. It was lucky someone had, because the guy was straining to get free and have another go.

"James attacked me," Asher said, loud enough for everyone to hear. "He tried to tackle Liam too, but these guys stopped him."

"You fucking rat!" the red-faced guy shouted. "You've ruined my life!"

"No," Asher replied calmly. "You did that."

The guy, who was familiar—perhaps someone we'd been to school with—used his shoulder to shove Keith aside. I felt Asher tense, prepared for him to attack again, but the guy just pushed Trev off too and wiped his hands on the front of his shirt.

"I'm going to make you regret this," he said.

What on earth could Asher have done to upset him so

much? And was Liam involved too, or had he just tried to intervene?

"I wouldn't recommend making threats in front of the police," Nate said. "Why don't you tell me, in your own words, what happened?"

I was tempted to listen in, but instead I gave my full attention to Asher and Liam.

"You should come down to the clinic," I told him. "I can patch you up properly there."

The corners of his mouth twitched upward, and his warm brown gaze held mine.

"Thanks," he said gruffly. "We have supplies at the station though."

I wanted to roll my eyes. "Of course you do."

They had supplies intended for actual humans, rather than the animal ones I'd have had to make do with, and Maia had the proper training to deal with his injuries—not that they seemed to be severe.

"How's your head?" I asked.

He tilted it from one side to the other. "A bit sore, but I don't think I've got a concussion. My thoughts aren't foggy now that my brain has stopped sloshing around. I'll have Maia assess me to be sure." He looked down at his pants leg, which was soaked with brown liquid. "I was bringing you a coffee, but I ended up wearing it."

My heart skipped, and my insides lightened. I tore my eyes away from his or else it wouldn't have taken long for me to give everything away to Liam.

A raised voice to the left had me turning that way. I sifted through the faces gathered until I landed on Lionel Lowry.

"Just great," Liam muttered under his breath.

"Leave James alone," Lionel huffed. "I say Asher Heaton deserves what's coming to him."

"Shut it, Lionel," Mehrtens snapped. "Now isn't the time for your petty vendetta."

"There's never a good time, sweetheart," he drawled. "We've just got to make do. Go on, James. Take another shot at the useless asshole. Maybe if he gets a tune up and has to heal himself, he'll finally learn how to do his goddamn job properly."

Something flickered through Asher's eyes that I didn't like at all.

A hint of guilt.

"I hope you don't believe him," I said quietly, aware that Mehrtens was trying to persuade Lionel to stop talking. "What happened to his leg is not your fault. He's the one who wasn't as careful as he should have been around a dangerous piece of machinery."

"What do you know, little girl?" Lionel called, obviously hearing me despite my best efforts to keep my words private. "Have you ever needed help and been messed around by incompetent pricks?"

Asher flinched, and I clenched my jaw. I didn't know why he could be so hotheaded around some people and yet meek when others lashed out, but I wouldn't accept anyone kicking him while he was down.

I marched over to Lionel and stopped two feet in front of him. He wasn't a tall man, although he was taller than me, and he'd grown a beer gut since he'd been out of work on the farm.

I leveled a finger at him. "Listen to me, you old crank. It's time for you to grow up and stop blaming other people for things that aren't their fault. Your leg will never be the same again. It's awful. We know that. But you can't take it out on people who were only trying to help."

His bloodshot eyes glared at me from sunken sockets. "I can do whatever I want, missy. Who's going to stop me?"

Nate cleared his throat. "Everyone involved, down to the station. Quit bitching at each other. We need to take statements and discuss whether anyone is pressing charges."

35

ASHER

We were well and truly late for work by the time Nate dismissed us from the police station—after a stern talking to about not disturbing the town's peace again.

No one had filed charges. I wasn't about to have James charged with anything when this whole thing had started because I'd been a bit too blase about confidentiality.

No matter my personal opinion, I should have kept my mouth shut. That was the job. But I'd let my emotions get the better of me and behaved unprofessionally.

I had to get my head on straight.

"Do you want to get a coffee?" Liam asked, walking alongside me.

I glanced at my watch. "We'd better not. Parks is going to be furious already."

He winced. "I reckon it's your job to tell him what happened."

I groaned but didn't disagree. If I hadn't said anything to

Tia, there's a good chance no one would have, even if they'd secretly wanted to.

"You know there's a possibility someone has already filled him in," I said.

"Yeah." He looked miserable.

"Hey, none of it was on you," I told him. "It was my bad call. It'll be fine."

We arrived at the firehouse and all eyes were on us as we entered the staff room.

Maia winced. "He did a number on your pretty face, Ash."

I tried to smile but couldn't quite manage it. "You mind checking me out?"

"Of course not." She rose and came over. "Let me take you out to the ambo, so we have all the supplies we need."

"I hope the other guy looks worse!" Darcy called after us as Maia led me away.

"He doesn't," I muttered to Maia. "Not a bruise on his ugly mug."

She tutted. "I didn't expect anything else. You're not a violent guy, even if you do have a temper on you."

We entered the garage, and she rounded the ambulance and opened the back door.

"Sit on the bed," she instructed.

I climbed in and perched on the edge of the bed, waiting while she sorted out supplies. With gentle, efficient movements, she cleaned the crusted blood off my face and inspected my nose.

"I don't think it's broken," she said. "You can get an x-ray if you'd like though, just to be sure."

I shook my head. "I don't think it is, either, although it hurt like hell when he did it. Gave my brain a good rattle too."

"Hmm." She shone a flashlight in my eyes and asked me

a few questions. "Pupils reactive, and your memory seems fine. Do you have a headache?"

"Not other than my nose throbbing."

She nodded. "Unlikely you've got a concussion, but you know the precautions to take anyway." She smeared white cream on my nose and then the skin under my eyes. "It's probably too late for an ice pack to do much good, but this should help with the pain and swelling."

"Thanks." I was lucky to have her for a partner.

"Uh, Ash?"

I turned toward Zane, whose face was scrunched into an expression somewhere between sympathy and regret.

"Parks wants to see you in his office," he said.

Oh, damn.

I'd known I'd have to debrief him. He wouldn't be thrilled with my behavior.

"I'll be there in a minute," I told him.

He nodded and left us alone.

"Good luck with him," Maia said, tidying away the wipes and ointment.

"I'll need it." Parks was a good guy. Solid. Dependable. No nonsense. But he also didn't tolerate rule-breaking by members of his team, and I'd blatantly done that, even if I'd tried to be clever about it.

I stepped down from the ambulance and made my way out of the garage and along the corridor to Parks's office. The door was ajar, and Liam was already seated opposite Parks, studying his hands.

Our boss looked at me and arched one dark eyebrow. "You're a mess."

"I know," I replied. "I'll change my pants soon. There's not much I can do about my face."

He harrumphed. "Can't say you don't deserve it."

"I know. I'm sorry, sir." I sat beside Liam and ducked my head apologetically.

Parks inhaled, his broad chest expanding. "Am I to understand that you were in a public fight as a result of sharing confidential information about a callout?"

I gulped. "Yes, sir."

I wanted to defend myself. To tell Parks what an asshole James was, and how Tia deserved to know what kind of man she was with, but that wouldn't help the situation, so I kept my lips firmly shut.

"Is it correct that you broke our confidentiality protocol?" His voice was deceptively soft. I knew better than to think that meant I was out of the woods.

"I didn't outright say anything," I mumbled, forcing myself to raise my eyes to his. "I suggested that someone ask more questions about how a particular situation came to be."

"Uh-huh." He stacked his hands on his desk, on the one small part not covered by paper. "Is that in keeping with the intention behind our code of conduct?"

"No, sir," I ground out.

"I'm glad you recognize that." He studied us, looking more like a disappointed father than anything else. I hated that. "You're lucky I'm in a forgiving mood today. You're both on cooking duty for the week, and Heaton, you're cleaning the engine during your downtime today."

Relief loosened my shoulders. "Yes, sir. Of course, sir." I'd gotten off lightly. I could have been suspended for such a breach of protocol. "Thank you."

"Don't thank me. Just get out of here." He flicked his fingers toward the door, dismissing us.

We bolted out and closed the door behind us. As the door clicked shut, I made a silent promise to do my best to focus on my job while I was at work from now on. No letting anything else distract me.

"He wasn't too hard on you before I got there, was he?" I asked Liam.

"Nah." He shoved his hands into his pockets. "Just asked if I'd known you'd said something to Tia."

"Ugh. Sorry. I didn't mean to drag you into trouble with me."

He shrugged off my apology. "Not your fault. Let's just keep the peace for a while before stirring the pot again."

"Amen to that." With all the messy complications in my job over the past few months, I was fully prepared to lay low.

My phone vibrated in my pocket. I checked it and frowned. Several missed calls, many of which were from Summer.

"Excuse me a minute," I said to Liam, ducking into a storeroom off the corridor. I called Summer back and waited for her to answer.

"Ash," she exclaimed, breathless as though she'd run to the phone. "What happened earlier? Nate didn't arrest you, did he?"

"He didn't," I assured her, the note of concern in her voice warming me all the way through. I briefly explained my confrontation with James, and what had led to it. By the time I finished, she was cursing him more creatively than I would have expected.

"He shouldn't have cheated if he wasn't willing to risk his relationship," she said, followed by a string of grumbling about cheaters, dirtbags, and jerks who gave men a bad name.

"I know." I sighed. "I've got to be on my best behavior now though."

"You did the right thing," she said in consternation. "You shouldn't be punished for it."

"But I did break the rules," I reminded her. "It's fine. Parks will forget eventually."

Someone spoke to her down the other end of the line.

"I've got to go," she said. "I'll see you later."

I smiled. "I'd like that."

I ended the call and left the storeroom. Liam had vanished, so instead of continuing on to the staff room, I backtracked to the garage. If I had to clean the engine, I might as well get started on it now. After all, I could use a distraction, and the manual labor would wear me out enough that it might calm my whirling thoughts.

I debated whether to change my pants but decided there was no point if I was only going to get them dirty and wet again anyway. I backed the engine out of the garage, hooked up a hose, and got to work.

Hours later, my muscles ached, and my fingers were numb, but unfortunately, the workout hadn't cleared my mind as much as I'd hoped it would. The shift was over, having been thankfully uneventful after the drama of the morning, but I knew if I returned home, I wouldn't get any peace.

Instead, I said my goodbyes and went home only long enough to collect my bike. I took it to the trails that began behind Destiny Fibers and cycled until my legs and lungs burned.

Darkness descended, and I switched on the lights attached to the front and rear frame of the bike. I stuck to the main trails as I pedaled, trying and failing to outrun my swirling thoughts.

Was the chaos from my personal life spilling over into my professional life?

Was Lionel Lowry right to call me out? Should I have done more to help him?

I'd done what I could, but what if that wasn't enough?

Sometimes, it didn't matter how hard you tried, only what you accomplished. My best efforts had landed him with a severely injured leg, and he wasn't the only one I hadn't been able to help as much as I'd have liked. There were so many.

Faces flashed through my mind. I pedaled harder, but I couldn't outrun them.

Somehow, I found myself back outside my house. My subconscious had steered me home even though I was nowhere near ready to sleep.

Still, I got off the bike, and was putting it away in the garage when my phone rang. I withdrew it from my pocket.

"Hello?"

"Hey." Summer's voice warmed me inside. "I just wanted to see how you are."

"As good as I can be." It wouldn't do either of us any good if I just dumped my problems on her.

"Have you eaten?" she asked as I closed the garage door and jogged up the front steps.

The porch light came on, driven by its movement sensor, and I froze.

"Holy shit."

"What is it?" she demanded.

I didn't answer immediately, too busy staring at the front window beside the door. It had been smashed, a jagged hole in the center, sharp glass edges ready to cut anyone stupid enough to touch them.

36

SUMMER

"Ash," I urged, needing to know whatever was wrong.

He muttered a string of curse words, too jumbled to make any sense.

"Whoa, slow down. What's the matter?"

"Someone broke my window," he panted.

"Shit." This had to be related to the fight earlier. I stood. "I'll be there in a couple of minutes."

"No," he barked. "Don't come. I don't know if whoever did this is still around."

I stood from the sofa, ignoring him. "That only makes it more important for you not to be alone."

"Summer, seriously. It might not be safe. Stay home."

I slipped a jacket on. "Call Nate."

"Okay." He hesitated. "We can deal with it. No need for you to be here."

I hung up. Like hell was I leaving him to handle this on his own.

I grabbed my keys and my purse and rushed out the

front door, sparing a moment to lock it behind me. The Ute was already unlocked—I needed to stop leaving it that way considering what had happened with both Kennedy and Grace.

I drove to Asher's house and parked on the streetside. He was standing at the end of the path closest to the street, his arms wrapped around himself. I threw my door open, hurried over and hugged him. He stiffened for a second, as if unsure how to react, but then pulled me more tightly into the embrace, burying his face in my hair and breathing me in.

"You shouldn't have come," he whispered.

"You couldn't have stopped me." His shirt was damp, and he smelled of clean, masculine sweat. I pulled back slightly. "Where have you been?"

He glanced to the side. "Out cycling."

"In the dark?" Didn't he have any self-preservation instincts? Or maybe he thought he was too big and tough to worry? Never mind that a strong man could hurt himself alone on a mountain just as easily as a petite woman could.

"I had my lights on," he said. "It was fine."

He released me and stepped back. I regretted asking. He had enough on his mind without me lecturing him on bike safety.

"Aren't you cold?" I asked.

"Yeah, but I don't want to go inside until the police are here. What if whoever broke the window used it to get in and they're still there?"

I shuddered. God, I hoped not.

The breeze stirred my hair, and I suddenly wished I'd thought to grab a hat as well as my jacket before I left. Fortunately, before I could stew in my discomfort, two cars pulled up opposite us.

I peered through the darkness, making out Officer

Patton's face as he exited the driver's side of one of the vehicles. The officer with him wasn't one I recognized. An out-of-towner, perhaps. Nate parked behind him, in his personal vehicle. He got out, pulled on a woolen hat—smart man—and strode toward us.

"Thanks for coming," Asher said, addressing all three of them.

"It's our job," Patton reminded him. Not that Asher seemed to hear him. He was staring down the path at the house.

"Show us the damage," Nate ordered, pausing to frown at me, obviously confused about my presence. "What are you doing here?"

"I called Asher to be nosy about the fight earlier today and I was on the phone with him when he saw the window." Mostly true. Or near enough, at least.

Nate rolled his eyes. "So of course you hurried over without stopping to think it through."

I narrowed my eyes at him, but Asher cleared his throat pointedly, so I just huffed and let it go. It shouldn't bother me that my brothers seemed to think me impulsive and reckless. I was too old to need anyone else's approval. Yet it did frustrate me, nonetheless.

What would they say if they found out I'd kissed Asher? Would they consider that just one more poorly thought out decision?

Slowly, Asher led us up the path. As we neared the porch, the overhead light came on, illuminating the gaping hole in the center of his window. Beyond that, the house was dark.

Nate whistled. "Looks like they threw something through it."

Patton tipped his chin up. "You think it was that rather than punching it out to gain entrance?"

"Based on the location of the hole, I'd guess so. They'd have done it closer to the bottom if they wanted in." He turned on the flashlight app on his phone and shone it through the window. "There's a rock on the floor."

"I'll dust the windowsill for fingerprints," Patton's partner said. "I'm not an expert but it'll be better than nothing. You won't get a crime scene tech out here just because of a little vandalism."

He jogged back to their car.

"Do you think this could be related to the fight earlier today?" I asked. It seemed like too much of a coincidence that Asher would get assaulted in the morning and then randomly have someone else throw a rock through his window in the evening.

"What happened?" Patton asked as his partner came back up the path toward us.

Nate briefly explained. "It's possible this is a continuation of that," he agreed. "I'll check with James Conroy in the morning to see if he can account for his movements tonight."

I bit my lip. "What about Lionel Lowry?"

Asher turned toward me, frowning. "Lionel wouldn't—"

"He's an angry man," I said. "Angry people do stupid things."

Nate stepped aside so Patton's partner could access the window. "Summer is right. We should check, just to be sure. In the meantime, Asher, can you unlock the door so we can have a look inside?"

With shaking hands, Asher withdrew a key from one of his pockets and slotted it into the lock. He turned and pushed the door open. Nate touched his shoulder when he tried to enter.

"Patton will go first," he said. "He's fully kitted out in protective gear."

My stomach lurched. It was the sensible thing to do, but I hated the thought that someone with ill intentions might be hiding inside Asher's home, lying in wait.

"Gee thanks, boss," Patton said wryly, but he drew his Taser, held his flashlight high with his other hand, and stepped inside.

"Stay here," Nate said as he followed him in.

Asher and I exchanged glances. I could tell he was listening as carefully as me, hoping that all would be well. A couple minutes later, Nate stuck his head back out the door and gestured for us to come in.

"The place is empty, other than the cat. She's sleeping peacefully on the bed." He jerked his thumb toward the living room. "You need to see this."

Asher's eyebrows knitted together. "What is it?"

Nate just shook his head and led the way into the living room. Patton was crouched on the floor, shards of glass scattered around him and latex gloves on his hands as he held an oval-shaped rock. Presumably, this was what had done the damage to the window.

"Come closer," he said.

We gathered in a circle, everyone being careful not to stand on any large shards of glass. As I leaned over, I realized that a message was scratched onto the back of the rock in block letters. It read:

WHAT SCARES YOU MOST?

I shivered, a cold tendril of fear sneaking down my spine. "What the hell is that about?"

"We were hoping you might know." Patton glanced at Asher. "Any ideas?"

But Asher seemed as stunned as the rest of us.

"No," he said. "I have no idea why someone would write that on a rock and throw it through my window."

Patton slipped the rock into a plastic bag and sealed it.

"We'll check this for prints back at the station. You don't recognize the handwriting?"

"No. But then, I don't know that I'd recognize anyone's writing, other than maybe Maia's and my parents'."

"Fair enough." Patton stood and pocketed the bag with the rock inside. "I don't see any reason why we can't clean up in here now. Boss?"

Nate nodded. "That's fine. We should board up the window while we're here."

He rubbed his upper arms, and it was only then that I noticed he was wearing a thin sweater rather than a jacket. He must have been at home with Grace and Finn when we called and come immediately.

"Ash, if there's somewhere else you can sleep tonight, you should do that," he said. "Just in case whoever did this comes back."

"You can stay at my place," I offered immediately, then added, "I have a spare bed," when Nate looked at me strangely.

I expected Asher to agree. It was the sensible thing to do. I was already here so he could just go home with me, but he shook his head.

"I'll go to Frannie's," he said, rubbing the back of his neck. "I can use their sofa."

He was choosing to worry his sister rather than come with me. Why did that hurt so much?

I tried to shake it off. Asher hadn't noticed my discomfort, and he was already leaving the room. I turned to Nate. If ever there was a time to share my concerns with him, this was it.

"I'm worried someone is targeting Asher," I whispered, glancing at Patton, who made a show of not listening.

Nate put his hand on his hip and cocked his head. "Why?"

I explained how his cat had mysteriously been outside the morning after my birthday rather than in the house where she should have been and had fallen ill from pesticide poisoning soon after.

Asher returned with a brush and shovel just as I finished speaking. His lips pressed together in a firm line, and he studied my face for a moment.

"You're seeing things that aren't there because of what happened with Grace and Kennedy," he said finally. "I had a shitty day, and I've had a run of bad luck and poor decision-making, that's all. Work has been crazy lately, and it's getting to me."

I turned to Nate. "What do you think?"

Frustratingly, his expression gave nothing away. "It's too soon to tell. It's worth looking into just for peace of mind though, and Asher, if anything else happens, I want to know about it."

Asher narrowed his eyes at me, but then nodded. "Sure."

Gratitude swelled within me. My cynical brother hadn't completely dismissed my concerns. Even if Asher still didn't believe me, that was better than nothing. Nate had the resources to start investigating if he thought it was necessary.

Asher knelt and swept up the glass fragments. Nate disappeared out the back door and returned with a large piece of plywood and Patton's partner, who was carrying a hammer and a container of nails.

Together, the three cops boarded the window, taking directions from Asher to ensure nothing was damaged. When they were done, they left, with Nate reminding Asher not to stay here tonight.

As soon as they were out of earshot, I asked Asher, "Why wouldn't you come to my place?"

37

ASHER

Uh-oh. Based on the stubborn slant of Summer's chin and the pout of her lips, I was going to have to be very careful about how I answered this question. A chill skittered over my skin. It was cold inside, although thankfully there was no longer a breeze blowing through the place.

"I'd love to go with you," I said, monitoring her expression carefully for any indication that I might be upsetting her further. "But I don't think it's wise for us to spend a night together until we've labeled whatever is happening between us and told our friends and family about it."

The lines around her mouth softened. "I understand that, but there's a spare bed. Or the sofa, if you're really worried."

I sighed. "I know, and maybe I'm being overly cautious, but I'm not sure you realize how tempting you are. If I knew you were sleeping just down the hall, I might make decisions I otherwise wouldn't."

Her lips curved into a reluctant smile. "I think you're just trying to butter me up."

I shrugged. "Maybe partly, but that doesn't make it any less true. Let's do this right, Summer."

"Fine." She wrapped her arms around me and rested her cheek against my chest. "Let me soak up the feel of you before you go."

I held her close, loving the fact there was no space between us. When she pulled back, I dipped my head and brushed my lips over hers. The kiss lingered but didn't deepen. This moment wasn't about that. It was about connection.

"Will you at least let me drive you to Frannie's place, so I know you got there safely?" she asked after we separated.

"I'd like that." Perhaps it meant something inside me was fucked up, but it was nice to know she worried over me. "Just let me pack a bag."

She sat on the sofa and waited while I went to my bedroom and put a couple of changes of clothes in a bag, along with my toiletries. I'd need a shower soon or I'd stink out Frannie's place.

Cookie was still asleep on the bed, so I scooped her into my arms and carted her to the pet carrier. She gave a mew of protest at being disturbed but didn't struggle. Frannie and Dean had a cat, so I didn't bother packing food or kitty litter. They'd have plenty of that.

With my duffel bag in one hand and Cookie's carrier in the other, I joined Summer in the living room.

She arched an eyebrow at the sight of the cat. "You're taking her with you?"

"Yeah. She's family. I'm not going to leave her here alone if there's a chance of someone coming back."

I might not show it, but the question that had been scratched on that rock unnerved me. Honestly, I was a little scared, and I doubted I'd be able to sleep unless I knew the people—and cats—I cared most about were safe.

We left the house, and I locked the front door and checked that the board across the window was solid, then we got into Summer's Ute, and she drove me several blocks over, to Frannie's charming 19th century home, complete with white picket fence and a well-maintained front garden.

She parked outside and I looked across the center console at her delicate face in the dark.

"Thanks for coming over," I told her. "I don't like you putting yourself in danger, but I appreciate you wanting to be there for me."

"No problem." She reached across, took my hand, and squeezed it. "How about you don't get into any more excitement today though?"

I gave her a tired smile. "It's a deal."

I opened the passenger door and climbed down, then slung my bag over one shoulder and carefully lifted Cookie's carrier out.

"Good night," she said.

"Night." I tipped my head to her and let myself through the gate onto my sister's property. Summer remained where she was until Dean had opened the door and welcomed me inside. Only then did she leave.

"Come on in," Dean said. "We're watching TV."

I stepped inside, and he glanced down at my bag, frowning.

"You here to stay the night?"

"I had a bit of an incident at home," I told him. "Is it all right if I do?"

I knew they'd say yes, but it was polite to ask. I should have called ahead but hadn't been thinking clearly enough to do so.

"Of course. Frannie," he called as we entered the living

area. Warmth greeted us, along with the comforting scent of baby powder. "Asher is here. He's got something to tell us."

Frannie was sitting cross-legged on the floor while Marcy slept in her arms with a plush blue bear on her lap. Dean reached down to take the baby from her, and I sat beside her on the floor. With as few words as possible, I explained the events of the day.

Frannie grimaced as I described my altercation with James Conroy and gasped as I mentioned the broken window. I left out the message on the rock. There was no point in scaring her unnecessarily. Most likely, it had been a nasty prank by James and wouldn't lead to anything else.

"Seems like it's a day for vandals," she said. "Someone punctured a hole in one of my tires yesterday. I wouldn't have realized it was intentional except that they left a pocketknife sticking out of it."

"Fucking kids," Dean muttered. "Those vacationers come here and think the rules don't apply. The police don't do anything about them either."

"They're doing the best they can," I protested. "It's not like they have much in the way of resources."

He grumbled an acknowledgement.

Frannie rubbed her palms together. "Never mind all that. What you need is a good meal and a beer." She reached behind herself to grab a throw blanket from the sofa. She draped it over my lap and then clambered to her feet. "We have leftover low carb bean burritos from dinner. I'll reheat one for you."

I put my hand on her knee to stop her. "How about I have a shower first? I stink."

"Okay." Her eyes shone with affection. "You know where everything is. I'll shut the doors and let Cookie out of her carrier."

"Thanks, Fran."

I took my bag to the bathroom, stripped off my cold, sweaty clothes, and washed myself until I smelled of nothing but soap. Then I dried and dressed in a pair of pajama pants and a t-shirt.

When I returned to the open plan living area, Frannie handed me a plated burrito, accompanied by a bunch of sauces and salsa, and guided me onto the sofa. Over on the armchair, Marcy was sleeping on Dean's chest, as he gently stroked the back of her head.

"What a crazy week," Frannie said quietly. "All of this, and Ashley is back in town too. How did your date go?"

"It wasn't a date," I said, cutting into the burrito and inhaling the delicious scent of spices and tomato.

Frannie rolled her eyes. "So you said, but there could be something between you again, right? I never really understood why you broke up."

"Because she didn't like how much I work," I said bluntly. "She told me that I wasn't around enough, and when I was, I wasn't fully focused on her. She felt ignored. Since I'm still doing the same job and I don't intend to start half-assing it, then nothing has changed, so there's no reason to think we could be happy together now."

Frannie looked disappointed. Hardly surprising. My entire family wanted me to settle down and start a family. I was the lone holdout. Both of my sisters had children, and both were partnered up. Then there was me. The baby of the family. The eternal bachelor who didn't have the decency to start producing grandbabies.

I chuckled to myself. It wasn't quite that dire, although sometimes it felt like it.

"What are you laughing about?" Dean asked.

I shook my head. "Nothing." Deciding to throw Frannie a bone, I added, "I am interested in someone else, Fran. I just can't say who until we have a few things sorted out."

Her face lit up. "Really?"

"Yes, but keep it quiet for now."

She mimed zipping her lips. "I promise."

No doubt Mum would know by morning. Frannie meant well but she'd never met a secret she could keep. Oh well. I'd known that and still chosen to tell her because I had faith in whatever was developing between Summer and me. I just had to hope she wouldn't come to the same conclusion Ashley had—that what I could offer wasn't enough

As I wolfed down the burrito, I couldn't help mulling over Summer's theory that someone was behind everything that had gone off track in my life recently. It was a ridiculous idea. No one could possibly hate me that much. It was just my own carelessness—and the fact I'd let my temper get the best of me once or twice—that was to blame.

Given the arrests of Kennedy's stalker, Tyler, and Grace's assistant, Alice, both within the past couple of years, I understood Summer's paranoia, but there was no substance to it.

Then why did part of me have the sick feeling that she might be onto something?

38

———

ASHER

My eyes were gritty, and my temples throbbed as I met Liam outside Taste of Destiny the next morning. He stood with his back ramrod straight, his arms crossed, and a scowl plastered across his face.

"How come I had to find out that someone threw a rock through your front window, third hand from Kennedy rather than directly from you?" he demanded.

A grimace twisted my face. "I'm sorry. It was a shit day, and I didn't think about telling anyone other than the police."

He nodded, apparently accepting this. Nate must not have mentioned to Grace that Summer had also been there. Either that, or Grace hadn't passed it along to Kennedy. Knowing her, either option was equally likely.

In a way, the fact he didn't question me somehow worsened my guilt over seeing Summer behind his back. He trusted me. And I wasn't sure I deserved it.

"Let's get our drinks," Liam said, huddling deeper into his jacket. "It's bloody cold out here."

He turned and pushed open the cafe door. I entered behind him but stiffened at the sight of Robert Warner ahead of me in the queue. I pulled myself together after a brief pause and moved to stand behind him, rubbing my hands together to warm them. It was cozy inside Taste of Destiny, but it would take a while for my fingers to thaw.

Robert glanced over his shoulder and his eyes widened when he saw me. An instant later, his face fell, as if just seeing me was enough to remind him of what he'd lost. Deep grooves were etched around his mouth and his complexion was pale, emphasizing the dark splotches beneath his eyes.

"Hello," I said awkwardly. "How are you doing?"

He grimaced. "I've been better, but at least I'm out of bed today."

I nodded. "For what it's worth, I'm very sorry for your loss. I wish there was more we could have done"

"It is what it is," he said, and turned back toward the counter.

Liam bumped my foot with his in silent support. God, he was a good friend, and I was an asshole who was sneaking around behind his back when I knew what he wanted for Summer, and I wasn't it.

"You should be sorry," someone snarled from the other side of the counter.

Fuck. I buried my face in my hands. Couldn't I catch a break?

Lionel Lowry limped toward us. "If you were less useless, this upstanding man would still have his wife." He looked at Robert. "Commiserations. I get it. If this lump were any good at his job, I'd still have a leg that worked properly, and I wouldn't have to live on a disability benefit."

I inhaled slowly and clung to the fraying ends of my temper, reminding myself that Lionel Lowry was a bitter man who found fault in everyone.

"Mind your own business," Liam said to him. "Stop trying to stir shit."

I glanced at Robert, curious whether Lionel's attempt to rile him up had succeeded, but he was still looking away from us, his shoulders tense, his posture practically screaming that he wished he were anywhere else.

A bell rang, and we all turned toward it. Behind the counter, Eden was standing on a chair.

"Excuse me, everyone!" she called.

A hush descended.

"I am now declaring this cafe an official drama free zone. Anyone who doesn't like that can please leave now."

A rush of gratitude surged through me. Eden was young, but she was a good person. I mouthed "thank you" to her, and she waved her hand as if to say, "no worries."

Lionel sniffed indignantly, muttered something about the rudeness of youth, and stomped out of the cafe, one foot hitting the ground more forcefully than the other. The unevenness of his footfalls hit me more powerfully than his words could have. They showed what he'd really lost.

Because despite his unpleasantness, he *had* lost something, and that should be recognized.

Eden got down from the chair and a slow hum of chatter began. She started taking orders again, and within five minutes, we had our coffees and were back in the brisk outside air, on our way to the fire station.

We'd just reached the turn off when Grace's Aunt Desdemona emerged from a shop and smiled at us serenely, her gray hair over her shoulders, one colorful dreadlock hanging down the front.

"Don't worry, everything will be all right soon," she said.

"It will come to a head first though." Then she swept past us down the street, her skirts swishing behind her.

Neither Liam nor I questioned what she'd been talking about. We knew better than that. Either it would make sense down the road, or it wouldn't. Instead, we continued to the fire station. Liam started brewing coffee for the others while I did a quick inventory of the ambulance's contents to make sure it was properly stocked.

I finished just as Maia was arriving, and we walked together to the staff room. Liam was shuffling cards, and I went to the fridge and scanned the interior, trying to work out what to make for lunch since Liam and I were on cooking duty. Considering that it was my fault we'd been assigned to the kitchen in the first place, I'd better take the lead.

"Hey, Ash. Your phone is ringing."

I started at Maia's words. I'd been so out of it that I hadn't noticed. I pulled it out of my pocket and hit the Answer button.

"Asher speaking." I hadn't thought to look at who was calling.

"It's Nate." He sounded oddly distant. Perhaps he was speaking through Bluetooth in his car. "I have good news and bad news."

I drew in a breath. "Tell me."

"The good news is, we found a fingerprint on that rock."

For the first time that day, my mood lifted. "That's great!"

He grunted. "You haven't heard the bad news yet."

"What is it?" I asked, uncertain whether I really wanted to know. Couldn't I just enjoy that slice of good news for a while first?

"We haven't found a match. It's obviously still early, but we've run the prints through the local system and haven't had any hits. We're now running it through the national database."

"Oh." My excitement dissipated. "So, does that mean it wasn't a local?"

He sighed. "Just that if it was, they haven't committed a crime in this jurisdiction. Honestly, I'm not sure if this will lead anywhere. It might, but don't get your hopes up."

39

SUMMER

I BREEZED OUT THROUGH THE SLIDING DOORS AFTER WAVING goodbye to Cal and came to a sudden halt. There, waiting by my Ute, was Asher. I paused for a moment, weighing the feelings that rolled through me at the sight of him. As always, I was glad to see him, but irritation lingered, prickling beneath my skin because he wouldn't even consider the possibility that someone might have it out for him.

I started walking again and called out as I drew near. "I hope you had a quieter day than yesterday."

"Yes, thankfully." He seemed off though. His smile didn't reach his eyes.

"What happened?" I asked.

He frowned. "What do you mean?"

I cocked my hip and leveled him with a look. "Come on, Ash. Do you think I can't tell when something is wrong?"

He sighed. "I had a run in with Lionel Lowry this morning."

"Fucking Lionel," I muttered, pressing the key fob to

unlock the door. I pulled the back side door open and tossed my bag inside. "You know what happened to him wasn't your fault."

"Yeah." But his tortured expression said he didn't fully believe it. Why did I have the misfortune to fall for a stubborn man who excelled at self-blame?

"He knows it too," I told him. "He just takes it out on you because you're an easy target."

He scowled. "Am not."

I arched my eyebrow challengingly. "Are too."

He laughed and ran his hand through his hair. "Anyway, are you free tonight? I'd love to spend some time with you. I could come over to your place if you need to go home."

The words came out quickly, as though he was nervous, and I melted a little inside. After years of pining for him, it was nice not to be the only one affected. That said, we couldn't go on like this, so undefined and uncertain.

"What is this?" I asked, drawing on the courage that had gotten me this far with him.

He frowned. "You mean, you and me?"

"Exactly." My hand twitched toward him, but I kept it at my side. If anyone saw me holding his hand, the cat would be out of the bag. "Are we dating? Is this just some weird kind of friendship? Because I can't do friends with benefits with you."

His lips parted. "No, Summer. I'd never ask that of you." His fists balled at his sides. "I want to date you. I want a future with you. I'm just... I'm worried that I won't be enough for you."

My heart stuttered, "Excuse me?"

He shrugged one shoulder. "Ashley broke up with me because I didn't give her the time and attention she needed."

"Ashley and I are *not* the same person." As should be completely evident to anyone who'd seen the two of us standing side by side. "We're not even remotely similar, except that we're both interested in you."

His jaw clenched. "Maybe not, but how many times have Liam and your brothers gone on about how you deserve to have someone stable and responsible, who'll balance you out? Someone with regular working hours, who'll be available to you when you need. My schedule is all over the place, and you and I are both hot heads. I'm completely the wrong person to fill that role."

I gaped at him. "Since when have I cared what my brothers want for me? *I'm* the one who chooses who I date. *I'm* the one who has to live with my decision."

I couldn't believe I even had to say this.

"And honestly," I continued, on a roll. "I've dated responsible guys with steady jobs before. Accountants. Lawyers. Not one of them interested me enough to keep them around. Bland and boring is not for me. You're the one I want, no matter how hot-tempered you are and how unpredictable your job can be. I work long hours too. Are you going to hold that against me?"

He frowned. "Why would I? You co-own a business. Of course that will take up some of your time."

I cocked my head, holding his gaze. "So, what's the problem?"

He held eye contact for a long moment, but then ducked his head. He murmured something I didn't hear, and I had to ask him to repeat it.

He tipped his face toward me. "My job can be dangerous. Not usually, but sometimes. Accident sites are risky. So are fires, and search and rescue callouts. What if something were to happen to me? I don't want to leave you alone."

"Asher," I whispered, tears springing to my eyes. My heart ached for him. How awful must it be to have to consider something like that when getting close to someone?

"Don't dismiss it," he said. "It happens. In my line of work, I have to see grieving partners and family members all the time. I don't want to cause you pain like that."

I glanced around, then, taking a risk, kissed his cheek. "I understand. But the thing is, I already care about you. If anything happened to you, I'd be devastated. That won't change, whether we're together or not, but I'll be a whole lot happier if we do give this thing between us a real chance. Isn't it better to focus on that than to worry about what might or might not happen down the road?"

He rubbed his lips together, and then a heavy breath gusted out of him. "Yeah. I guess it is." His beautiful eyes searched mine. "How did you get so wise?"

One side of my mouth hitched up. "I've spent a lot of time thinking about you—about us."

His fists unclenched, and he inhaled slowly. "Me too."

"So, we're doing this?"

He nodded. "Yeah. We are."

"Great." My heart lifted.

Finally.

Finally, I'd be able to call Asher mine.

"Your place or mine?" I asked, referring to the question that had started this conversation.

He hesitated. "Is mine all right? I left Cookie there. Figured I'd stay at home tonight rather than Frannie's."

Something in my gut tightened. "Your place it is then. I'm sure Cookie misses you."

Not to mention that if he was going to spend the night there, I wanted the chance to have a look around and make sure he was safe. I didn't trust that whoever had broken his window was done causing trouble.

He smiled. "Do you need to drop by your place first?"

"No, I have everything I need. I can follow you over to your house."

He shifted closer, until only a few inches of space separated us. I was tempted to rock toward him and erase the distance, but I was painfully aware that Cal might be watching from the window, or that anyone across the street could see us. If I touched or kissed Asher now, Liam would hear within an hour, and I might lose all the progress I'd made with Asher.

He grinned. "I'll see you there."

He strode back to his car, and I got into mine and started the engine. I waited for him to lead the way, even though I could probably get myself there with my eyes shut. I parked out the front while he opened the garage and pulled inside, then we met on the path to the front door.

A chill swept through me at the sight of the boarded over window.

"Is someone coming to replace that soon?" I asked.

"On Thursday," he replied.

"Good." I didn't like how vulnerable the damage made him.

He unlocked the door and bent to pat Cookie, who was trying to wind around his feet. He scooped her up and carried her through the house toward the kitchen. I locked the door and followed behind. While he fed her, I started the heat pump to take the chill off the air.

"Do you have blankets anywhere?" I called.

His voice came back strong. "In the linen cupboard in the hallway."

I searched the cupboard and selected a fluffy blanket to snuggle in and a heavier comforter in case we needed the warmth. The heat pump was beginning to do its job, but with the unsealed window, it was fighting a losing battle.

Asher entered the living room wearing a woolen jersey

and sweatpants. "I put frozen pizza in the oven. Does that work for you?"

"Sounds nice. I'm in an 'any meal I don't have to cook is a good one' kind of mood."

He laughed. "I'm not sure if putting something in the oven and turning it on really counts as cooking."

I shrugged. "Close enough. The end result is hot food." I sat on the sofa, tucked my legs beneath myself, and pulled the fluffy blanket over my lap. "Join me?"

He flopped onto the sofa beside me and wriggled under the blanket. Then, taking me by surprise, he wrapped his arm around my waist and maneuvered me around until I was lying against his side, our cheeks nearly touching. He turned his face into my hair and breathed in.

"This is good," he murmured, suddenly sounding weary. The tension eased from his muscles, and he snuggled closer. "Usually, after a day like today, I'd have to cycle twenty kilometers to take the edge off, but somehow, being with you helps too."

My heart lifted, and I angled my face away from him so he wouldn't see my massive grin. "I'm happy to be used for endorphins."

His arms tightened around me. "I'd never use you."

His tone was oddly serious, considering I'd been joking around. He must still be raw from our conversation outside the veterinary clinic.

"I know," I assured him.

His breath stirred my hair. "We're going to have to come clean soon, aren't we?"

I pursed my lips, anxious but ready to put myself on the line for a chance at the future I'd dreamed of. "We are if we want this to lead anywhere."

Asher drew back enough to meet my eyes. "That's that, then. You know, I've spent years looking for a woman to settle down with. I can't believe I never realized she was right in front of me all along."

My stomach flipped over. I'd dreamed of him speaking those words to me, but I'd never believed it would actually happen.

"When should we tell our families?" I asked.

He kissed the tip of my nose. "We can start with Liam. This weekend."

My chest tightened. Right into the deep end. I wanted it, but I couldn't deny I was worried about Liam's reaction too. If he was unhappy, would our relationship be over as soon as it had begun?

40

———

ASHER

I sauntered along Centennial Street toward the veterinary clinic after my shift ended, shrugging deeper inside my jacket in an attempt to get warm. White clouds crowded the sky, and the forecast called for snow.

"Asher!"

I cringed, and sped up, recognizing the voice instantly.

Ashley.

Footsteps tapped along the pavement behind me. I looked ahead. I was almost at the clinic. Perhaps if I power-walked, I'd arrive before she caught up to me. I stayed facing forward, feigning deafness as she called my name again.

Unfortunately, when she grabbed my elbow, I could no longer pretend not to notice her. I turned slowly, wondering what she wanted. When we'd met up for coffee, she'd spent the whole time low key flirting, even when I'd told her I wasn't interested. There didn't seem to be anything else to say.

She twirled her hair around her finger and smiled coyly,

as though she hadn't just sprinted down the sidewalk to catch up to me.

"It's Thirsty Thursday. Want to get a drink at Drunken Destiny?" she asked.

"I have other plans," I said honestly. Seeing Summer was a much more enticing prospect than spending time with a woman who'd already dumped me once before and whose motives I didn't understand.

She ran her hand down my arm. I yanked it away.

She blinked wide eyes at me like a kicked puppy. "Are those plans really better than getting properly reacquainted?"

"Yes." One hundred percent. No hesitation.

She huffed. "I can't believe I have to spell this out for you. I'm offering sex."

"And I said no." I folded my arms over my chest. Perhaps it was my turn to spell things out to her. "I'm not a player. I'm only interested in one woman, and I'm sorry, but that isn't you."

Her face fell, and for a moment, I felt a pang of sympathy for her. After all, I had cared about her once. But it hadn't worked out, and there was a reason for that. Now, I had a woman who accepted how I was, and I wouldn't do anything to risk losing her.

She looked down at her hands, blinking rapidly, her eyes shimmering with unshed tears. "I know you're not a player. That's why I wanted to try again with you. You wouldn't do to me what... Anyway,"—she shook her head, apparently determined not to finish her earlier thought—"we were good together, weren't we? Not perfect, but good. Isn't it worth seeing if we could be like that again?"

The rigidity seeped out of my spine.

"I'm sorry, Ash," I said quietly. "For whatever happened to hurt you. But we weren't truly happy together. You were lonely with me, and it was like nothing I did was good enough."

She looked miserable. "I made a mistake when I ended it with you."

"No, you didn't."

At that moment, Summer wrapped her arm around my waist and rested her head against my shoulder. I hadn't sensed her coming and wondered how much of our conversation she'd overheard.

"You were right to end it," I told Ashley, holding Summer to my side. "You and I weren't well-suited, but Summer and I might be, so please don't do this again."

Ashley raised her chin, her lower lip quivering. "If you two are so serious, then why haven't you told anyone?"

"We will soon," Summer said, more gently than I'd have expected. "We've been building a solid foundation first."

Ashley met my gaze imploringly. "But you and I already have a foundation. We could skip that step and pick up where we left off. I'll be less demanding, and maybe you could drop a few hours, and it would work out."

I bit the inside of my cheek to stop myself from snapping at her. She was in a bad place and making poor choices. She wasn't trying to drive me crazy.

"Maybe we had a solid foundation once," I allowed, "but it's rotted away."

Summer's arm tightened around me. "I'm sorry if you're hurting," she said to Ashley. "I know how it feels to want Asher and see him with someone else. It's awful. I wouldn't wish that on anyone. But you have to accept it and let him go."

Her words, intended to comfort Ashley, sliced through me like a knife. I'd done that to her. I'd caused her pain. She'd had to watch as I dated others because I was too cowardly to man up and be with her. I hated the thought that I'd made her feel even a shred of discomfort, but there was no denying I had.

Now, it was up to me to do better. To be a man she could proudly call her own. Who wasn't afraid to stand by her side, no matter who disapproved. Someone willing to take risks for her.

Ashley nodded at Summer, although her glazed eyes made me think she might not have heard everything she'd said. Then she slunk away.

I turned to Summer and gripped her chin. "I will never hurt you like that again."

I kissed her. Right there, in public. On the side of the street, where anyone could see.

Screw them all.

Out of the corner of my eye, I saw a flash of movement. I closed my eyes and ignored it for now. Soon enough, we'd have to face the consequences of my reckless actions. I could take this one moment with her and savor it. Who knew how long the peace would last?

41

———

ASHER

"What are you looking at?"

I flinched. "Damn, Liam. Don't do that."

He'd snuck up beside me so silently I'd had no idea he was there. Thankfully, he didn't seem to realize I'd been surreptitiously watching his sister as she chatted with Bailey at the bar.

He laughed. "You were so distracted, I didn't even have to tiptoe. Got something on your mind?"

"Yeah, kinda." I waved my hand dismissively. "I'll tell you more about it later."

Summer and I had agreed to talk to him tomorrow, but considering that at least one person had seen us kiss yesterday, I was beginning to think it would be best to do it tonight. I didn't want him to hear it from anyone else. But Drunken Destiny on a busy Friday night wasn't the time or place for the conversation.

Liam smirked. "Intriguing. What do you think has got Ash so distracted?" he asked Zane, who was sitting beside me on a stool at a table on the side of the pub furthest from the door. It was warm in here, but snow was falling softly outside, beginning to settle on the pavement.

Zane glanced up, startled. "Um, what?"

I laughed. "He's too busy daydreaming about Blair Carter to pay attention to anything."

Zane blushed. "Can you blame me? He's all gruff and sexy, but he can dance like magic and the way he sings…" He sighed. "And he was right under my nose. Why didn't I make a proper play for him, guys?"

"I think we need more drinks," I told Liam instead of answering Zane. I was an expert on coming up with reasons not to ask someone out when I was interested in them, so I was the last person who could give him the response he needed. "I'll get them."

I slid off the stool and weaved through the crowded pub toward the bar. Pop music from ten or fifteen years ago played quietly through the speakers, and the room buzzed with anticipation. The skiers were excited for the new snowfall.

I waited while Bailey and Eugene worked their way through the line of customers. When I reached the front, Bailey smiled at me. She'd somehow managed to maintain a conversation with Summer between serving people, and everything in her bearing said this was just another night despite the crowd and the snow.

"Three of the darkest beer on tap," I told Bailey, and waited while she poured the drinks. I glanced at Summer and, finding her looking back, winked. Bailey set the glasses on a tray and slid it over. I took the tray and turned, then stiffened, a frisson of concern zapping through me as I spotted James Conroy pushing his way toward Liam and Zane.

I skirted around people, careful not to upend the drinks

while making my way back to our table as quickly as possible. Whatever James wanted to say to them, it couldn't be good, and the last thing we needed was a fight breaking out in Heather and Eugene's pub.

I arrived just in time to hear James throw me to the wolves.

"Did you know he's fucking your baby sister?" he asked Liam conversationally, smirking at me as I placed the tray on the table and wiped my hands on the front of my jeans.

"Who?" Liam looked around, baffled.

James laughed. "Saint Asher. He acts all self-righteous about other people's choices, but all the while, he's sneaking around with sweet little Summer."

I gaped at him. How the hell did he know? Had Ashley told him, or had word already got around from whomever had seen us kissing outside the veterinary clinic yesterday?

Liam shook his head. "If you're going to spread lies, at least make them believable."

Zane's eyes were wide as he glanced from me to James, and something like understanding dawned on his face

I was so fucked.

"Liam—"

"I saw them kissing with my own two eyes," James interrupted, not giving me the chance to take control of the narrative. He wanted to tell this story his way. A nasty sneer curled his upper lip. "You know, you really can't afford to stick your nose into other people's relationships when you've got your own dirty laundry."

My heart sank. I met Liam's gaze. The trust in it wavered.

"It isn't true, is it?" he asked.

"Summer and I aren't sleeping together," I said.

His face slackened with relief. I tried not to take that too hard. After all, I'd already known he wouldn't consider me suitable for her.

"We did kiss, though," I added reluctantly.

He tensed again. "Excuse me?"

Zane had straightened and was sipping his drink while watching us as if we were the evening's entertainment. I guess we'd at least distracted him from moping about Blair.

I shifted from one foot to the other, fully expecting Liam to hit me at any second. "Summer and I are seeing each other."

Liam's breath hissed out between his teeth. "Why would you do that behind my back?"

"Because he's an asshole, obviously," James said.

"Fuck off," we snapped at the same time.

He backed away, but his smug expression stayed locked in place. He'd succeeded in what he'd come here to do. He'd created a rift between Liam and me.

"You know how she used to feel about you." Liam shook his head, disgusted. "I didn't think you were the kind of guy to take advantage of her crush like that."

"I'm not." I thrust one of the beers at Liam. "No one is taking advantage of anyone. We both care for each other, and we're serious about our relationship. We planned to break the news tomorrow."

He didn't look convinced, and he didn't take the drink. "You can't tell me that you just woke up one day and were suddenly crazy about her after all this time. I don't know what's up with you lately, but don't involve my little sister in your crisis."

Summer appeared beside me, a glass of wine in her hand and a groove between her eyebrows. "What's going on? Is everything okay?"

Liam's jaw clenched as he slowly turned to her. "I've just learned that you're dating Asher."

Her mouth fell open, but she clapped it shut quickly. "I am." Her mossy eyes caught mine. "I didn't think we were telling him until tomorrow."

I winced. "Someone else beat us to it."

"Oh." Her teeth scraped over her lower lip, and she studied Liam as if trying to tell how pissed off he was. I could tell her the answer to that.

Very.

Liam pushed his stool back and jerkily got to his feet. "I need to get out of here."

"Wait," Summer said, reaching for him but stopping short. "Let's talk this out."

"I can't." His voice was strained. "I can't think clearly with you in front of me."

He pushed between two big guys nearby and disappeared into the crowd.

"Damn," I muttered.

We'd lost him.

42

SUMMER

"So..." Zane dragged the word out, loud enough to be heard over the voices around us. "You two are together."

"We are," Asher said, taking my hand.

I almost melted right where I stood.

Zane gestured at the two empty stools. "Why don't you have a seat and explain? Summer, you may as well drink Liam's beer."

I took the drink, feeling oddly disloyal, as if drinking my brother's beer was a step too far, even if dating his best friend wasn't.

I glanced toward the bar, relieved that Dad was only just emerging from the back room, a full bottle of vodka in one hand. It didn't seem like he'd noticed anything amiss, and considering how busy the pub was, I doubted anyone else had overheard our conversation, however heated it might have been.

"Summer and I have been attracted to each other for a while," Asher began. "But things started to change that evening when we both ended up at the ski resort for a date, at tables beside each other."

I was glad he'd begun our story there rather than when I'd humiliated myself after my high school graduation. I listened with one ear while I got out my phone and typed out a message to Liam.

Summer: *I'm really sorry if we hurt you. We intended to tell you, and I'm sorry you found out this way.*

Then I sent another one to Kennedy, explaining what had happened in as few words as possible because I didn't want her to be unprepared when Liam arrived home.

I glanced at the bar again, and my gut tightened. Dad was making his way toward us, visibly concerned.

"Did Liam leave?" he asked as he drew near. "Is Kennedy all right?"

I grimaced. Of course he'd be worried, considering he'd nearly lost both of his daughters-in-law recently. I met Asher's eyes, and he gave me a subtle nod.

"As far as I know, Kennedy is fine," I told him. "Liam left because he's upset that Asher and I are dating."

For a long moment, Dad didn't say anything. I briefly wondered if he hadn't heard me. But then he just smiled, slung his arm around my shoulders and kissed the side of my head. He reached his free hand across to shake Asher's.

"I've always been protective of you as my only baby girl," he told me. "But I couldn't have asked for a better man for you. Congratulations, you two."

Thank God.

The tension bled out of me, and Dad chuckled.

"You were really worried, weren't you?" he asked.

"Liam walked out on us when he found out." Asher's voice was strained, and I hugged Dad, then pulled away from him and embraced Asher as well. He needed comforting more than Dad did.

"To be fair, he was caught off guard," Zane said. "That guy just dropped a bombshell on him."

Dad nodded. "Give him time. He'll come around."

I hoped they were right. Especially when Asher was obviously unhappy with Liam's response. They were more than best friends. They worked together. They couldn't afford to be on the outs.

Although in a selfish part of my mind, I was relieved that Asher hadn't denied anything. Even if it hurt Liam, he'd thought I was worth the trouble. People could say what they liked, but it was their actions that counted.

He wanted me. Not perfectly put-together Ashley with their shared past. Not any of the other beautiful, successful women he'd gone on first dates with.

Me.

"So, what are you going to do to make Liam forgive you?" Zane asked. "I'd rather not have to deal with you two going through a divorce as work husbands. You know you're the team dads. If you're miserable, we all are."

Asher's jaw dropped. "We definitely aren't the team dads. That's Parks's job."

"He does have that vibe," I agreed. "Responsible older man. A little bit stern."

Dad pulled a face. "You know Parks has kids, right? I hope you don't make him act like a father at work as well as at home. I can say for certain that his kids are cuter than the lot of you. He has no reason to tolerate it from you."

Zane stared at him as if he'd just announced that Santa Claus wasn't real. "Excuse you, Eugene, but I am just as cute as any of Parks's little ones."

Dad laughed.

Asher rolled his eyes. "In all seriousness," he said to Dad, "what do you think we should do? I'm sure Liam will tell Kennedy and word will get around soon."

Dad tapped his chin thoughtfully. "How do you feel about announcing it to everyone at a Sunday brunch? Heather and I would be happy to host one this weekend."

I exchanged a glance with Asher and nodded.

"That would be great," he said. "Thank you."

People were inclined to be in a good mood at the Braddock brunches, so perhaps that would ease the way.

"I need to get back to the bar," Dad said. He squeezed my shoulder. "Congratulations again. Don't worry. Most people will be pleased for you."

He left, and Asher and I sat with Zane for a while longer. Eventually, he declared that he was exhausted and ready for bed, so I grabbed my jacket and the three of us walked out together. Zane strolled off toward his place while Asher and I lingered on the sidewalk.

"It feels kind of ridiculous that we have to officially announce our relationship before we've even gotten naked together," I said quietly. "It's a bit Victorian England."

Asher shrugged. "Maybe, but that's just what happens when people who are already closely connected begin dating."

"I suppose so." I hesitated. I wasn't ready to say goodbye to him yet, but maybe I wouldn't have to. After all, the person whose reaction he'd been most worried about already knew the truth. Was there any reason for us not to go all-in now?

"What is it?" he asked, searching my eyes in the dark.

I bit my lip. "Since the cat is already out of the bag, perhaps I could come home with you tonight?"

He gazed at me for a long moment, then smiled wickedly. "Yes. You definitely should."

43

NERVES RIDDLED MY GUT AS WE STOPPED BY MY PLACE FOR ME to grab a change of clothes and some toiletries before continuing on to Asher's house. I couldn't help but wonder what it would mean to spend the night with him.

I didn't know whether to expect sex or just some snuggling. Hell, knowing Ash's misguided chivalry, maybe he'd end up sleeping on the couch, determined not to sully Liam's baby sister until after the announcement of our relationship at brunch.

I parked outside his place and got out of the car, slinging my bag over my shoulder. Asher must have beaten me here by a couple of minutes because his car was dark, but a light shone through the house's front window.

I shivered as I got out of the car and fumbled with the flashlight app on my phone. I needed the light to find my way up the path to his front door. I knocked, and he called for me to come in. I entered and took off my shoes, leaving them beside the door.

Cookie sauntered over to me and stretched, arching her back. I bent and patted her, then scratched behind her ears and rubbed under her chin. She purred loudly and sunk her claws into the carpet.

"I'm in the living room," Asher called.

I walked through. The air inside was a few degrees warmer because he'd started the heat pump and the window was no longer boarded up. The window had been replaced, and I watched as Asher drew the curtains, blocking out the outside world.

I shuddered at the idea that someone out there might otherwise have been able to see in. I was reasonably convinced that someone intended Asher harm, but he didn't want to see the truth. I supposed that if someone hated me enough to want to poison my cat and smash my window, I wouldn't want to believe it either.

Asher took my bag from me. "I'll put this in my bedroom." He hesitated. "Is that okay?"

I nodded, and as he left, I scooped Cookie up, carried her to the sofa, and sat with her on my lap. She pulled away, and I let her go. She leapt to the floor and shot me a disdainful look over her shoulder, as if reminding me that I could only snuggle her when she allowed it.

Fair enough. Consent mattered.

Asher returned a few seconds later and sat beside me, pulling me into his arms. I melted against his strong body and rested my head on his shoulder. My mind wouldn't calm though. It raced, unsure where this night was heading and what I ought to do to prepare.

"You seem nervous," he murmured against my hair.

I sighed, embarrassed to be called on it. "A little."

"Why?"

I closed my eyes, heat rising in my cheeks. "I've wanted

you for so long, and now that I have you, I'm afraid I'll do the wrong thing and lose you."

He stiffened for a moment, but then relaxed again, bit by bit, in a way that had to be deliberate.

"I'm sorry I hurt you." His lips moved against my temple with each word he spoke. His breath ghosted over my skin, somehow warming me and cooling me at the same time. "I wish I could go back and warn myself not to tell you that I'd never want you. I wish I could take that back, but I can't, and I'm afraid it will always be between us."

I burrowed closer to him. "I understand why you rejected me. I was young. You did the right thing. But I guess, even though I know that, subconsciously I still feel vulnerable."

He kissed my forehead. "We can take this as slow as you need in order to believe that it's real. I will never push you for anything."

"Thank you." I turned my face inward, toward the side of his neck. "But maybe I want you to push a little."

"Yeah?" He sounded amused. Not enough to annoy me, but enough to let me know that he wanted to humor me, whatever it took. "For what?"

I drew back far enough that I could look into his eyes. I moistened my lips, my heart in my throat. I'd always prided myself on being brave enough to face difficult situations... except when it came to Asher Heaton.

Now, I had to be courageous, or I'd never get what I wanted.

I was strong. I could do this.

"I want to kiss and let it lead us wherever it leads us, without feeling guilty or paranoid about how everything could go wrong," I confessed.

His pupils dilated, turning his dark eyes almost black. "Then kiss me."

He didn't move toward me or take control. He let me make the first move. I both loved and hated that. I loved that he was letting me lead, but I hated how raw it made me feel to be completely real with him.

I brushed my lips against his. First softly, then more firmly. He returned the pressure, angling his head to get better access to my mouth. He tasted like beer and man. I breathed him in, the scent of the forest with a hint of antiseptic leftover from his shift at work.

I'd dreamed of being this close to him for years. Sometimes, when I'd been with other partners, his face had popped into my mind unbidden—and unwelcome. But finally, I could indulge without guilt or recrimination.

I climbed over him, straddling his lap, and wrapped my legs around his narrow waist. Heat pulsed between my legs, and I rocked against him, chasing the sensation. Inside his jeans, his cock was hard as steel, and he groaned as I rubbed along the length of him.

Our mouths stayed connected the whole time, but we weren't kissing, exactly. More like exchanging gasps and panted breaths.

It wasn't enough.

I wanted more of him. I needed to taste him.

I scrambled off him, pulled his knees apart and knelt between them. I reached for the zipper of his jeans, but paused, meeting his eyes, a question in mine.

"Do it," he hissed.

As I drew down his zipper, he grabbed his jeans by the waistband and yanked them down. Not all the way, but enough to reveal his tented boxer briefs, the hard outline of his cock showing through the soft fabric. I cupped my hand over the wet spot at its head and caressed him, then gripped the sides and eased the briefs down.

"Summer," he breathed, his hands burying themselves

in my hair. "Fuck. Summer."

I couldn't take my eyes off his cock. The head was an angry shade of red, the shaft longer than any I'd seen outside of porn, and thick enough to stretch my mouth. I gripped him by the base and kitten-licked the slit. His hands fisted, tugging on my hair but not painfully. Just so that I knew he was there.

"You don't have to—" He broke off when I sucked the head of his cock into my mouth and swirled my tongue around it.

The skin was silky and salty, with a musk that was entirely masculine and not at all unpleasant. I shifted my face forward, taking him deeper. Tears prickled my eyes, and I exhaled slowly, forcing my throat to relax.

"You're incredible." Asher moaned, releasing my hair and stroking the back of my head, his fingers twitching each time I sucked.

I worked him with my lips, tongue, and throat, unable to drag my eyes from his as I brought him pleasure. I'd feared I'd never see him like this, with his jaw slack, his eyes dark, and his breath ragged. Now that I had him here, I never wanted it to end.

Based on the way he strained not to thrust into my mouth, his jaw clenching as he fought to maintain control of himself, he didn't want it to end either.

"Summer, I..."

I swallowed, and his eyes narrowed to slits.

"I'm gonna..." He tried again. "Fuck, I'm gonna come."

My lips curved as I sucked him harder, using my hands to massage the base of his cock. He shuddered and spilled into my mouth, his dark gaze still locked on mine. I swallowed every drop and, when he was soft, licked him clean.

I straightened, and he grabbed me and hauled me up his body. He kissed me, even though I must have tasted like him. Instead of being repulsed, as one of my exes had been, he groaned and deepened the kiss. I kissed him back, lax against him.

"You liked that?" I asked.

"Liked it?" His eyebrows shot up his forehead. "I fucking loved it."

"Good." I smiled, satisfied on every level. Well, except the physical one. But even that didn't feel urgent. My arousal was more of a pleasant undercurrent than a raging need.

"But—"

"But what?" I stiffened, suddenly worried I'd done something wrong.

He smirked and kissed my cheek. "Nothing bad, baby. Just that you had all the fun, and now it's my turn."

"Oh." I wasn't completely sure what he meant by that until he lifted me and deposited me onto the sofa while he dropped to his knees in front of me.

He rested his hands on my thighs, and I wished more than anything that I wasn't wearing pants. "Before I get carried away, I need to say something."

His hands ran up my legs, distracting me from his words. I shook my head, trying to focus.

"What?" I asked.

He grinned, and there was something predatory about it. "You're amazing, inside and out. I want you to make me a promise."

I cocked my head. "What?"

I'd promise him almost anything. Almost.

Danger gleamed in his eyes. "From now on, your talented mouth is mine, and so is the rest of you."

My core turned molten. "Yes. Yours." That was one promise I was happy to make. After all, I'd always been his. "But you're mine too."

"Only yours," he confirmed.

Just like I'd always wished.

My heart felt so full it might burst, but before I could get too sappy, Asher undid my button. I raised my hips so he could yank my pants off, leaving me bare except for a pair of lacy pink underwear.

"You are so sexy," he breathed, never taking his eyes off me.

I squirmed, feeling myself blush. Fortunately, he didn't seem to notice. He rubbed his thumb along the fabric at the bottom of my panties, teasing me with his barely there touch. He continued the gentle torture until I pushed myself against him more firmly. Then he narrowed his eyes and stopped.

"Come on, Ash. Don't—"

His hot mouth covered my sex, and I cried out, my hips jerking, seeking more pressure. He hummed in the back of his throat, and the vibrations rocketed through my core, making my flesh quiver.

I shoved my panties down and he immediately dipped his tongue into my heat and licked me like an ice cream. His eyelashes fluttered as he gazed up at me from beneath them, and his lips quirked as he licked me again, this time brushing my clit with the tip of his tongue.

"Ungh." My head flopped back against the sofa. Any capacity for rational thought fled. All I could do was cling to the cushion as he brought me to the edge with his clever tongue and fingers, spearing inside me, stroking my channel, murmuring encouragement against my damp skin.

His jeans were still half down, and from my angle, I could just see his cock, hard once again and bobbing with each movement.

"Up here," I pleaded.

He tilted his head in question.

"Get up here," I rasped out.

His brow furrowed, he climbed onto the couch beside me. Immediately, I stood for long enough to shed my pants completely, and then I straddled him, settling my sex over his erection, grinding against him. His mouth fell open, and he gripped my hips as I rode his length. He was slick with precum, and I moved over him easily.

He sucked two of his fingers into his mouth and then pressed them against my clit, relentlessly working the bud of nerves until I couldn't think straight.

"Oh, God." My hips stuttered as pleasure crested within me. I didn't stop moving, even as an orgasm rolled through me, and I sobbed his name.

The tendons in his neck strained as his cock pulsed against me. He was coming again.

I'd made him come twice.

I slowed my movements as we both caught our breath, staring into each other's eyes as though we'd never seen each other before.

"You... I..." I didn't know what to say. I slipped off him and cuddled up to his side, hoping that the experience had been as powerful for him as it had been for me.

"Summer, that—" The ping of my phone cut him off. I'd turned the volume right up so that I'd be able to hear it in the crowded bar. Normally, I would have ignored it, but in case it was Liam, I didn't feel like I could.

"Hold that thought." I stood on shaky legs and fished my phone out of my pants pocket. I sighed with relief. "It's just Bailey."

But as I read the preview of her message, my gut tightened.

Bailey: *Are you okay? Liam seemed upset...*

Damn. Not much could dull the euphoria of the moment, but the memory of Liam storming out earlier sure as hell could.

44

———

ASHER

I clasped Summer's hand as we walked to Eugene and Heather's front door together, our feet crunching on the thin layer of snow that had fallen overnight. We hadn't been apart from each other since Friday evening, and I was riding high from being wrapped up in Summer.

Somehow, that only made me more anxious about what was to come.

The fact we hadn't been inundated with visitors might mean that the Braddocks had been respectfully giving us space, or it might mean that they were all furious and never wanted to see our faces again.

Summer squeezed my hand. "It will be okay."

"I know." I could say as much for her sake, even if I didn't totally believe it. But at least, after today, the big reveal would be done. We'd break the news to my family this afternoon and pray to God they hadn't heard it from anyone else or Mum would complain until my dying day.

If there was gossip to be spread, she needed to be the one spreading it.

I knocked, and then opened the door. We each took our boots off and left them in the foyer but didn't make it any further before Grace and Kennedy appeared from the direction of the kitchen.

They each grabbed one of Summer's arms and whisked her away. I started to follow, but Toby stepped in front of me, his arms folded across his chest. He jerked his chin toward the living room.

"Through there," he said.

So, they were going for a divide and conquer approach.

I turned and headed toward the living room, feeling like a man on the way to his execution. There were reasons Summer hadn't dated much in high school, and her brothers ranked high on that list. Even when I'd counted myself among the men determined to protect her, I'd realized we were a bit over the top.

Now, I just prayed they could keep calm enough to have a rational conversation despite the fact I wasn't what they wanted for their sister.

"Morning, Asher," Heather said as I entered.

I frowned, surprised she wasn't in the kitchen, interrogating Summer. But perhaps she thought I was the more pressing issue.

"Good morning," I replied cautiously, glancing around the room. Toby and Max were sitting on the sofa. Max met my eyes and didn't glare. Off to a good start. Liam and Nate occupied the armchairs, and Connor was leaning against the far wall, his chin lowered, expression unreadable.

Heather's kind face creased in a smile. "Before I go, I just wanted you to know that I'm happy for you."

I was so stunned it took me a moment to respond. "Thank you."

She clasped my shoulder and squeezed. "Don't let these knuckleheads scare you away."

She left the room, and I couldn't help but wish she'd stayed. Now I was alone with the Braddock brothers, and I didn't know whether any of them would support me, even if I could be reasonably confident that Max wouldn't let anyone permanently injure me.

Where was Eugene when I needed him? I'd been counting on his presence.

"What about the rest of you?" I asked, not sitting.

Liam didn't make any move to respond. He didn't look thrilled, but he hadn't punched me or sworn at me, and I was willing to celebrate the small wins.

Toby leaned forward, his forearms on his thighs. "As long as you treat Summer right, you and I won't have a problem."

The band around my chest loosened slightly. "Thanks, Tobes."

He grinned. "No problem. I'm going to have so much ammunition to tease Summer with after this."

Poor Summer.

"Don't fuck it up," Connor said. "I don't care what else is going on in your life, she comes first, no matter what."

I met his dark, steady gaze. "Agreed. I won't fuck it up."

At least, I'd do my best not to.

"Good." The corners of his mouth twitched. "Because if you do—if you let her down—I know all the best places to hide a body."

A prickle of apprehension zapped down my spine. If I didn't know Connor well, that might genuinely frighten me. As it was, I was one of the few lucky enough to have realized that his bark was usually worse than his bite. *Usually.* Connor might grump and growl, but he had the softest heart. Not that anyone would dare say so to his face.

"I'll help dig the hole," Nate warned. "Even I know she used to have a thing for you. If the two of you don't work out, it'll hurt her more than you, so I hope you know what you're doing."

"This isn't temporary. It's the real deal." At least, I desperately wanted it to be. I turned to Max. "Do you have any threats to add?"

He shook his head. "I'm not surprised you're dating. I always thought something might happen between you."

I blinked at him, caught off guard. "You're more perceptive than me then, because I didn't see it coming."

"You are taking this seriously though?" Nate demanded, his eyes narrowed.

"Yes." I tried to hold his gaze without giving the impression I was staring him down. "I told you that, and I meant it. I wouldn't mess with the status quo if I didn't legitimately think our relationship could go somewhere long term. We've been testing the waters, but it's still very new. I can't say it's forever, but there's a possibility it could be."

Nate nodded and stopped glaring. "I did wonder whether something was going on when Summer was at your place after you called about the broken window. I didn't ask though, because I hoped you'd come clean on your own. I don't like the fact you were pushed into it."

"We had plans to speak to Liam this weekend, and we intended to break the news to everyone else after that," I told him. "It wouldn't have been a secret for much longer."

Speaking of Liam, he was the only person present who'd yet to say anything.

I knelt beside him. "Are we okay?"

He scowled. "I don't know yet."

My jaw tightened. "Okay, then. I won't push."

I wanted to. God, how I wanted to tell him to just hit me and get it over with. Or to yell at me about how selfish I was.

If he told me all the reasons he didn't think I was good enough for his sister, at least I'd have the chance to argue. This silence gave me nothing to work with.

Still, if he needed time and space, I'd give it to him as best I could.

"I'm trying to get my head around it," Liam said, giving me more than I'd expected. "I can see how you might be well-matched, but I don't like the fact you kept things secret as they were developing."

I nodded. "I get that."

"Like I said on Friday, I also don't know how to feel about the fact Summer has had a crush on you since high school. It seems like a power imbalance. It makes her more vulnerable than you."

I nodded again. In his shoes, I might have the same concerns. "My feelings for her are newer, but they're intense. This isn't some whim."

Before he could reply, Eugene appeared in the doorway. "Brunch is ready in the dining room. Come on through."

Toby stood and whistled. "Phew. The tension in here is a bit much."

The Braddock men trailed out of the room in single file. I went last but was glad to see that Summer had saved me a seat beside her. I pulled it out and sat.

The table was almost full. There was one chair free because Tess was with her mother this weekend. Grace held baby Finn against her chest, and I was curious how she planned to juggle him and eat.

A breeze swept into the room, carrying the scent of patchouli and weed. Desdemona glided in, a deck of tarot cards clutched in her hands. She smiled serenely at each person in the room.

"Sorry I'm late."

I glanced at Grace, whose eyebrows were raised. Clearly, I wasn't the only one who hadn't expected Desdemona. As I looked around, it seemed everyone else was as startled as me. So if no one had invited her, what had brought her here?

45

———

"THERE'S SPACE OVER HERE FOR YOU," GRACE SAID TO Desdemona, gesturing at the empty seat that Tess would usually occupy.

Desdemona bustled over, but instead of sitting, she picked up the chair and carried it around the table, placing it between me and Kennedy. Heather left and returned with a plate, which she set in front of her unexpected guest.

Desdemona angled herself toward me and beamed. "Felicitations on your new relationship."

"Thank you." I looked at Grace. "You didn't mention you'd told Desdemona."

"She didn't," Desdemona said.

Grace shook her head, silently confirming that. Her eyes were as wide as mine. We both knew Desdemona claimed to have psychic abilities, and maybe we even believed she had a powerful intuition, but surely, she hadn't simply woken up this morning and somehow known that my family were holding a brunch to announce the fact Asher and I were dating.

That was too specific.

Heather gestured for brunch to begin, and we all reached for the bowls and platters stationed along the center of the table. I grabbed a Danish and then ladled fruit salad into a small bowl.

On one side of me, Asher piled bacon and eggs onto his plate, while on the other, Desdemona only poured hot water onto a tea bag that smelled faintly of lemons.

"So, Summer," Desdemona said as she set the kettle back down, "I had a dream last night, and for some reason, I'm called to share it with you."

"Okay." I tore off a piece of Danish and popped the flaky pastry into my mouth. For some, this might seem a strange conversation starter, but I'd heard about many of Desdemona's dreams over the years. "What did you dream about?"

She gazed into the distance somewhere over Grace's shoulder and shivered. "I was surrounded by white, and cold to my bones. The kind of cold where you feel like you'll never get warm again."

I frowned. "Do you know where you were?"

"No." She wrapped her hands around the cup of tea, as if needing to chase away the chill still lingering inside her. "Just that it was white. It could have been a white room, or a cloudy sky, or even somewhere in the mountains. All I know is that it's connected to you."

I shredded the Danish, my fingers moving automatically, acting out a nervous habit. "How?"

She shrugged. "I wish I could say, but I have no idea."

Weird.

"Well, you've passed along the message," I said briskly, hoping to put her at ease even though I was anything but.

Something about this made me anxious. But perhaps I was overreacting because I was already in an emotionally fraught situation.

"I have." She twined her fingers together, not looking any more satisfied than I was. "I'll try to remember more, but it's like there's a wall in my mind, blocking out the details."

I wiped my fingers on a napkin and used a fork to gather up some of the smaller fragments of Danish. "Don't stress yourself out about it. I'm sure if it's important, it'll come to you."

She gazed down at her tea, as if she hoped she'd find answers in the bottom of the cup.

I leaned closer to Asher. "How did it go with my brothers?"

He glanced around, checking whether anyone was listening to us. "Better than I expected."

"That's good, right?"

"Yeah." But he didn't sound certain. "Toby seemed fine with it. Max too. Connor and Nate threatened me, but I expected that."

My lips pressed together. "And Liam?"

"Hard to tell."

"Hmm. For what it's worth, Grace and Kennedy are both happy for us, and they don't seem surprised at all."

"Was Bailey?" he asked.

"No," I admitted. She'd squealed and clapped excitedly when I'd broken the news over the phone yesterday, but I hadn't expected any different. Whether it was temporary or permanent, I had my dream man. I'd squeal just as loudly for her if she ever successfully wooed Max.

We finished our breakfast, fielding questions from Toby and my parents about how we'd gotten together. I'd already spilled the beans to Kennedy and Grace, and I suspected that my other brothers would gladly not know, given the option.

"Desdemona, I've been practicing with the tarot deck you gave me," Kennedy said, loud enough for the whole table to hear. "Will you help me do a reading while you're here?"

"Of course." Desdemona opened her deck of cards, which had been resting beside her elbow on the table, and began to shuffle them. Once done, she passed the deck to Kennedy.

"I need a volunteer," Kennedy said.

"You can use me as your guinea pig," Max said good-naturedly.

"Thanks." She cut the deck once and then handed it to him. "Can you cut this again, and then I want you to place cards out in a cross formation." She explained how she wanted the cards, and in what order, and then dragged her chair over to sit beside him.

One by one, Kennedy turned over cards and flipped through notes on her phone, attempting to interpret them. Every now and then, Desdemona corrected her.

"I think this one means that a change is coming." Kennedy glanced at Desdemona. "Is that right?"

"Partly." Desdemona smiled at her fondly, then gave her attention to Max. "You will face a change that you've been resisting. The only way forward is through."

For his part, Max didn't seem bothered by this.

"Change is just part of life," he said. "It's inevitable."

Desdemona's mouth curled slyly. "That doesn't mean we have to like it."

He chuckled. "I suppose not."

Movement in the corner of my eye caught my attention, and I looked out the window.

"It's snowing again," I exclaimed.

"I'll make hot chocolate," Mum said, getting to her feet.

I stood too. "I'll get the Baileys."

Kennedy winked at me, even though we both knew she wouldn't be having any. Not while pregnant.

Mum and I were quiet while we prepared the drinks. We loaded them onto a tray, but just before we took them out, she wrapped one arm around my shoulders and gave me a quick hug.

"Good job, sweetheart," she murmured. "You got your man."

My cheeks heated. "Hopefully, I'll keep him."

She ruffled my hair. "I have faith in you both."

"Me too," I whispered, emotion stinging my eyes.

Perhaps I was afraid to believe in us. I didn't want to get my hopes up and then shatter them. But I honestly thought we could have something special.

I cleared my throat, and between us, we carried the tray of hot chocolates out, being careful to avoid spillage. We drank while watching the snow fall in fat white flakes. I smiled at Asher, and his eyes crinkled in the corners, warmth swimming in their depths.

When we'd finished our drinks, the men cleared the dishes away while the women relaxed in the living room. By the time the men joined us, Finn was starting to fuss, so we decided it was time for everyone to head home. Those who had jackets donned them and we exited through the front door as a group.

As we drew near to the road, I frowned at a car parked a couple of hundred yards away. The Braddocks lived in the country, so there shouldn't be anyone else in the area. Unless perhaps these were tourists who'd pulled over while they looked up directions.

As I watched, the car tore off the grass and careened up

the road, fishtailing when it passed over an icy patch and nearly taking out a street sign.

"What the hell was that?" I asked.

46

———————

ASHER

As we all stared after the car that had sped into the distance, my phone rang. I pulled it from my pocket and checked the screen. It was Parks. Perhaps there was an emergency at work, or he needed cover for someone else's shift.

"Hey boss," I answered.

"Asher." His voice was strained. "Are you home?"

I frowned. "No, why?"

If he needed extra manpower, I could get there quickly anyway, but I'd prefer to have a few minutes to talk over the morning's events with Summer first.

"We've had reports of a fire at your address."

The word didn't compute. "I'm sorry, what?"

Parks heaved a sigh. "Either someone is pranking you, or your house is on fire."

"Fuck. I'll be there soon."

I hung up and shoved the phone back into my pocket, then, without pausing to explain, raced toward my car. A flurry of movement in my peripheral vision let me know that Summer was only a couple of steps behind me. I pushed a button to unlock my car and threw myself into the driver's seat.

"What is it?" Summer asked as I started the engine and pulled onto the road almost as quickly as the other vehicle had earlier.

"Fire at my place," I said shortly.

I was aware of her making a phone call, but I focused solely on the road. As we turned in the direction of home, I noticed for the first time a plume of smoke rising through the falling snow.

I slowed down a little as we entered the township, but I was still going too fast as I took the roads that would lead me home. A siren wailed behind me, and I pulled over to allow the fire engine to pass, then followed quickly behind. We arrived at the same time.

I leapt out of the car and stared, hardly able to believe my eyes. Flames had engulfed the front porch and were licking at the roof and around the sides of the house. As I watched, the front window, which had only just been repaired, cracked from the heat.

My stomach sank. Somehow, I'd hoped that Parks had been wrong, or that perhaps some of my teammates had been responsible for a prank call—although I should know better than to think them capable of that.

"Asher," Summer breathed. "Oh, my God."

Even from a distance, there was no escaping the heat of the fire. Fortunately, it seemed to be centered around the porch and the front door. I doubted it would spread much further. Especially not when help had arrived so quickly.

The fire crew were already unspooling the hose and directing the water at the house.

Parks strode over to us. "Is anyone inside?"

"No," I said automatically, then froze. "Fuck. Cookie."

"Your cat?" he clarified.

"Yeah. I shut her in this morning before I left, and I locked the cat flap." Fuck, why had I done that? I'd wanted to stop her from going out into the cold, but I should have considered what a safety risk it was to trap her in there.

"We'll see if we can find her," Parks said, giving me what was probably supposed to be a reassuring nod before returning to his crew.

"That's good, right?" Summer said, grabbing my arm. "Why do you look so worried?"

"They won't risk themselves for a cat," I explained. "It's protocol. We're not even supposed to risk ourselves for a person if the situation is dire."

She blanched. "Is this dire?"

"No." I shook my head, not taking my eyes off that burning door. Emotion clogged my throat. "But I don't want to rely on them to save Cookie either."

That fluffy demon meant more to me than I liked to admit, and it was my fault she was in danger. I couldn't lose her like this.

Without pausing to ask Parks's permission, I rushed past the fire engine and snatched up a fire retardant blanket. Someone shouted, but I raced around the side of the house, already fishing in my pocket for the key to the back door.

It briefly crossed my mind that opening the door would create a pressure change that could cause the fire to spread faster—or explode. I stopped. I couldn't do anything that might endanger my friends. But then I heard scratching on the other side of the door. I knelt, and through the translucent plastic, Cookie looked at me with big, frightened eyes.

Damn. I couldn't leave her.

Perhaps a small pressure change would be less dangerous. I didn't have to open the door to get her out. A small hole would be enough for me to pull her free.

I bashed the door, hoping to scare Cookie into backing away a few feet, and then I bunched the flame retardant blanket around my fist, using it to protect my knuckles, and punched the cat flap. My knuckles throbbed on impact, but the cat flap didn't break.

I stood and bashed the door again to keep Cookie at a distance. I swung my foot back and kicked the cat flap. The plastic snapped, creating an opening in the bottom half. Quickly, I dropped to my knees and yanked out the broken shards of plastic.

Once they were gone, I reached through and grabbed Cookie by the scruff of her neck. I dragged her through the opening and into my arms. She meowed plaintively and I buried my face in her fur, trembling all over.

"You're okay, girl," I breathed, nuzzling her. "You're okay."

Thank fucking God.

I carried her around the side of the house. Out the front, Summer hovered halfway up the drive, apparently as close to the fire as she was willing to get.

"You idiot!" she cried as I approached. "You scared the life out of me."

A pang of empathy twisted my gut. If she'd been the one to run toward a burning building, I'd be freaking out too.

"I'm sorry."

Her gaze dropped to Cookie. "She's okay?"

"Seems to be." The cat tried to pull away, but I held her tight. "Stay put. You're not going anywhere until the fire is out."

The door had crumbled, except for its timber frame, and only one corner of the building was still burning. Parks was supervising as two firefighters worked to subdue the flames, but then he turned toward me, and I could've sworn I felt the force of his glare through his helmet.

He stomped over and removed the helmet. Yeah, that was quite a glare. Too bad I was too shaky for it to have its full effect.

"You should have let us get your goddamn cat," he growled, tucking the helmet under his arm. "I don't care if you're used to fires. You're not geared up, and you haven't been trained to handle them. Don't do it again."

I ducked my head, still cuddling Cookie. "I won't."

Parks nodded toward the cat. "I'm glad she's all right."

Two cars skidded to a halt on the road beside my property. Liam spilled from the driver's seat of the front one, and other Braddocks emerged from within. Liam raced over to us, his eyes wide.

"What happened?" he asked, breathless.

I shrugged. "I don't know."

He put his hands on his hips and watched as our colleagues doused the last of the flames. "Did you leave an appliance going? The oven, perhaps?"

"No. Nothing." I was absolutely certain of that. As a result of my job, I was ridiculously conscious of fire safety.

Parks grimaced.

"What?" I asked, noticing the expression.

He sighed and smeared a soot-blackened hand down his face. "I could be wrong, but the burn pattern makes me think an accelerant was used. The fire concentrated in very specific areas."

"Shit." It seemed like Summer was right. Someone was out to get me.

"We'll get an arson investigator in," he said, and looked at someone behind me. I turned and saw Nate striding toward us. "Possible arson. Joint investigation?"

Nate nodded. "You got it. Any casualties?"

"None that we're aware of." Parks's phrasing reminded me that there was always a possibility that whoever had done this had gotten themselves injured in the process.

"Asher?"

I stiffened. That was my mum's voice. I spun around and, sure enough, she and Dad were hurrying along the fence line. Deep lines of worry creased her face, and she moved faster than I'd ever seen, opening her arms and dragging me into an embrace that knocked the air from my lungs.

"My baby!" she cried, releasing me so she could check my body for damage. "Are you hurt?"

"I'm okay." I tried to smile, but my lower lip wobbled. I leaned over and kissed her cheek to cover my distress.

"What happened?" Dad asked, echoing Liam's earlier question.

"That's what Parks and I need to figure out," Nate said, saving me from having to answer.

Mum paled. "Are you saying you don't know what caused the fire?"

"Not yet," I admitted. Summer pressed against my side, and I dipped my head to murmur in her ear. "I'm beginning to think you might be onto something."

47

———

SUMMER

Brenda Heaton turned startled eyes on Asher and me.

"What's going on here?" she asked, waving her hand at us, her brow furrowed.

I stiffened. It hadn't occurred to me before I'd wrapped myself around Asher that we'd yet to tell his family we were together. Hopefully, he wouldn't be mad at me for jumping the gun.

"We're dating," Asher said, staring blankly at the charred front of his home. "We were going to tell you later today."

I shivered. He sounded numb, and now that the adrenaline was beginning to seep from my limbs, I realized just how cold I was too. Despite the acrid smell of smoke in the air, and the dying embers of the fire, snow continued to fall around us. I could hardly feel the tips of my fingers, so I buried them in my palms, hoping to thaw them.

"You...and Summer?" Brenda was stunned. "You two are together? Is that what you're saying?"

"Yes." I forced myself to confirm it, since Asher didn't seem capable of much other than holding Cookie and staring at his house.

"That's wonderful!"

Before I could dodge, I found myself squeezed in a tight hug. Brenda was soft and comforting, and it was all I could do not to bury my face in her shoulder. Mum hugs were the best. She kissed my cheek and let me go, then floundered when she realized she couldn't repeat the process on Asher because he was holding Cookie.

"You're happy?" I asked, pleasantly surprised. It's not that I thought she wouldn't approve, but I hadn't expected a celebration either.

"I'm thrilled for you both." She wrapped her arm around her husband Garth's waist. "We've been waiting for Asher to settle down for years, and I know he wouldn't be dating you unless he thought you were the one."

Her words warmed me, although not enough to dispel the ache from my fingers.

"This is lovely and all," Nate said, looking like he thought it anything but, "but we need to get down to the police station and take statements. Asher and Summer, you'll both need to come. "Parks, I'll catch you later today."

Parks nodded.

"Can we come along and wait for them to be done?" Brenda asked, clutching a handful of Garth's jacket. "I don't want to leave my baby alone during such a stressful time."

"You can come to Mum and Dad's place," Liam said before anyone else could reply. "Invite Frannie too. We'll all wait there together."

Brenda hesitated. "Heather won't mind? I'd hate to put her out."

Nate snorted. "Mum loves guests. Liam is right. You should wait there."

"Okay, then."

Asher snapped to attention and looked at his mother. "Could you take Cookie please?"

Brenda softened. "Of course."

He shifted the cat into her arms, and then he and I followed Nate off the property.

"I'll drive," I told Asher.

"Thanks." He passed me the keys. "I think I'm experiencing symptoms of shock."

I got into the driver's seat—the door was still open—and turned the key in the ignition. He circled the hood and got in the other side.

"Once we're at the police station, I'll get a hot drink and a snack from the vending machine. Hopefully that will be enough."

"Hopefully." I kind of wanted to wrap him in a blanket and coddle him, but I doubted he'd appreciate that. "I'm glad your mum was so happy to hear we're dating."

I waited for Nate to pull out onto the road, and then followed close behind him.

"Me too." He laid his hand on my thigh. "I knew she would be though. She adores you, and if you give her a chance at getting more grandchildren, she'll love you even more."

"Thank God." The last thing we needed was for any other family members to kick up a fuss. "I'm sorry my brothers haven't been as accepting."

He grunted. "I wouldn't expect them to. I knew I wasn't what they wanted for you, and I started dating you anyway, so I have to be prepared to face the consequences. Besides, it's fair enough for Liam to point out the fact that you having a crush on me for years does make it a little imbalanced. But I'm so far gone on you, you never have to worry about me taking advantage of that."

"I know." I felt a pang at the reminder that he hadn't always returned my interest, but I tamped it down and focused on the part I could do something about.

Apparently, my brothers thought I needed a boring, predictable man in my life. That didn't surprise me, considering I'd intentionally used my dating life to aggravate them in the past. I was just so tired of them thinking of me as their baby sister.

I was a grown woman with a thriving business and my own home. If they wanted to talk about what I *needed,* I'd be happy to enlighten them that the only thing I needed was for them to respect my right to make my own decisions.

We parked on the road outside the police station and followed Nate inside. Officer Patton was with him, and we were escorted into an interview room. I couldn't help noticing how clinical it was. Almost like my examination room. A couple of cushions and a padded chair would go a long way to making it more welcoming.

But I supposed "welcoming" wasn't necessarily the vibe they were going for.

Asher and I sat on one side of the table. Patton turned on a wall heater and withdrew a notebook from his shirt pocket while Nate set a recording device in the center of the table.

"You're fine if we record this, right?" Nate asked.

"It's okay with me," I said.

"Yes," Asher agreed

Nate started the recorder and he and Patton sat opposite us. Asher talked them through today's events, and then mentioned the shattered window.

Nate faced me. "You thought someone might have a grudge against Asher. That's seeming more likely with this latest development. Do you have any idea who might resent him that much?"

I glanced from one man to another. "What about Lionel Lowry?"

Asher scoffed. "He's all talk. He wouldn't actually do anything about it."

I bit my lip, less certain of that than he was. "He's been simmering in resentment for months."

But Asher shook his head. "James Conroy is more likely. He punched me, and the rock was thrown through my window that same day."

I scowled. "Surely he can see he's to blame for the situation he's in. If he hadn't cheated, then there never would have been a problem."

Officer Patton jotted a note. "Some people refuse to take responsibility for their own actions."

"Anyone else?" Nate asked. "Anyone who might have felt slighted by you? Someone you dated, or pissed off?"

Ashley's name crossed my mind, but I didn't voice it. She was just hurt by Asher's rejection. She wasn't a violent person. A little mean perhaps, or just not considerate of others. I doubted she'd harm anyone though.

"Anyone at work?" Patton prompted.

Asher looked like he'd had a thought. "No one at work, but Frannie's tire was punctured recently, and she said some things had been missing around her house as well. Could that be related?"

"Perhaps. We'll need to talk to her too. Perhaps we shouldn't be looking at who might want to target you specifically, but who might want to use you to get to Frannie."

"I'll arrange an interview with Frannie," Nate said. "Meanwhile, you keep thinking and let us know if you come up with any other ideas." He reached for the recorder. "Interview concluded at 1:15 p.m." He pressed a button to end the recording and sat back.

"Are we done?" I asked, more than ready to get somewhere with a fireplace I could huddle in front of.

Nate nodded. "For now. Ash, I'm afraid you can't stay at your place tonight. You probably know that. The damage alone would put you at risk until an engineer can assess the structural safety of the building, and until we confirm whether the fire was set intentionally, it's a crime scene."

"You can stay with me," I offered tentatively. "Unless you'd rather stay with Frannie again, or with your parents."

He touched my hand and met my eyes. "I don't want to bring danger to your doorstep."

I bit my lip. I understood, but he had to go somewhere. He couldn't just hide out in the woods. "So far, the attacks have been targeted at you—and maybe Frannie. I doubt whoever is behind it will change their focus to me just because you spend a night at my cottage."

He frowned. "But you could get caught in the crossfire."

"He's not wrong," Nate said, helping no one.

"We'll talk more later," Asher said, getting to his feet. He took my hand and pulled me up.

As we left the interview room, Nate warned us to be careful and stay aware of our surroundings at all times.

"We will," I said, but I didn't hear his reply. Once we were out of the building, I stopped walking, and Asher did the same.

"What is it?" he asked.

I scraped my teeth over my lower lip. I needed to make him aware of the consequences of his actions while not giving him a reason to wallow in self-blame.

"When you ran toward the burning house earlier, I was terrified. Please don't do something so reckless again."

He hesitated for a long moment, but then his jaw firmed. "I can't make that promise. I'll do my best to be sensible, but if someone I care about is in danger, I can't just leave them there."

48

ASHER

I PULLED SUMMER INTO MY ARMS BEFORE SHE COULD RESPOND, unable to deal with her wide eyes or the fear etched in the lines of her face. I held her against me and breathed her in, but instead of her usual scent, I inhaled the sharp tang of smoke and sweat.

"I'm sorry," I told Summer. "I should have believed you earlier. It just seemed so far-fetched that someone might be deliberately screwing with me."

She glanced over at me. "Don't worry about it. Now we know we need to be careful."

Despite everything, I smiled. If we'd been in this situation a couple of months ago, she'd have given me an earful about not listening to her sooner. We were making progress.

I held her hand as we walked to the vehicle, and I was grateful as she took the lead and drove us to her parents' place. I didn't trust myself to concentrate on the road right now. She pulled into the drive and parked right outside the house, where someone had generously left an empty parking space.

As I got out of the car and waited for her to lock the doors, I buried my hands in my pockets and shrugged my collar further up my neck.

The snow had picked up, and an icy wind whipped at Summer's hair as she turned toward me.

"I'm amazed the fire could start at all in this weather," she called between chattering teeth.

"They probably used a shit load of accelerant," I yelled back.

We huddled together and made our way to the doorstep. The door opened before we knocked, and Heather whisked us inside.

"You two must be freezing," she said, fussing over us. "I've laid out a change of clothes for each of you in the bath-room. Have a shower and only come out once you've defrosted and are ready to face everyone. Okay?"

Summer's shoulders slumped with relief. "Thanks, Mum."

Perhaps she was as reluctant to face the inquisition as I was. No doubt our family would have even more questions for us than the police had.

Heather guided Summer and I to the bathroom door, then left as we closed it behind ourselves. I don't know how she'd guessed we might want to shower together after the crapshoot we'd just been through, and nor did I want to think about it too much, but I was grateful to her.

Summer turned the shower on, and I stripped off. My jacket, sweater, T-shirt, and jeans hit the floor, and a puddle began to form around them. Summer undressed and put one of her hands beneath the water, which was already steaming.

"It's fine for me, but you might want to check too," she said.

I tested the temperature, wincing as the heat gave me pins and needles in my too-cold hand. I reduced the temperature slightly. It would hurt either way, but at least the contrast should be less now.

I stepped beneath the spray of water first, wanting to double check the temperature before Summer got in. I hissed as the blood rushed to the surface of my skin everywhere the water touched.

Summer's mouth pinched. "Are you okay?"

"Fine," I muttered. "Just stings a bit."

She joined me, and I shielded her from the stream of water, holding her against my body until she warmed enough that the water might not be so painful. I moved aside, and she sighed with pleasure as it flowed down her arms and legs.

She ducked her head beneath the water and tilted her neck back as it soaked her hair. I gulped, mesmerized by the smooth, golden skin of her throat. She lathered shampoo in her hair, then turned to me.

"Did you burn yourself?" she asked, her teeth peeking out from between her lips. "I should have asked earlier."

"I'm fine. The fire hadn't reached the back of the house yet."

"Are you sure?" Her eyes shone with concern. "Sometimes people don't notice. Just let me check."

I opened my mouth to protest but then shut it again. Who was I to stop her from checking me over? I'd want to do the same to her if the situations were reversed, and besides, I liked the idea of her looking at my naked body.

"Arms out at the sides," she ordered.

I held my arms out and she searched each one for burns or cuts. There was a small nick on my forearm, where a shard of plastic had caught on my skin as I'd reached through the broken cat flap to get Cookie, but that was the worst of the damage.

"Arms down again."

She lifted my hand and studied the knuckles. "You're bruised."

"I tried to punch out the cat flap," I explained.

She huffed. "Men. Seriously. A boot would do the job much better."

I pressed my lips together and didn't mention that I'd had to do just that.

Gently, her hands ventured down my torso. She squatted, checking the fronts of my legs—for what, I didn't know, but her proximity to my cock wasn't helping me keep my thoughts clear.

She straightened. "Turn around."

I did as she said and held still while she examined my backside. I was tempted to clench, a little uncomfortable with her scrutiny, but eventually, she declared me free of injuries.

I turned back, pulled her into my arms, and kissed her. "I told you I was fine."

She smiled weakly. "I needed to check for myself."

I kissed her again, dipping my tongue between her lips, tasting her. She gasped and opened for me.

Bang!

Bang, bang!

"You still both alive in there?" Toby called through the door. "If I don't see you in two minutes, I'm coming in."

Summer groaned and rested her forehead against my clavicle. "I can't believe I'm related to him."

"I thought Nate was supposed to be the overprotective one," I muttered.

She rolled her eyes. "It's a twin thing. He doesn't care

who I date, but if I'm ever hurt or scared, he needs to be close. I'm the same with him."

I supposed that was something I'd get used to. "Let's finish up then. I don't want Toby seeing my naked ass."

She laughed and shifted back under the stream of water to rinse her hair. I soaped up while she conditioned and repeated the process, and then I shuffled out of the shower and dried while she washed herself. By the time she was ready to get out, I was already dressed.

"You're taking your time in there," I teased.

"Shut up," she said without any heat. "I have much more hair than you."

My eyes journeyed down her wet, slender body of their own volition. "On your head, maybe."

Everywhere else, she was smooth and tanned. My eyes narrowed. Why didn't she have a bikini line? Was she sunbathing naked during the summer? Or was her golden skin natural rather than a product of time in the sun?

I waited while she dried herself and dressed. She glanced longingly at the blow drier but left her hair wet around her shoulders instead.

We exited the bathroom, and the cooler air of the hallway made me wish I'd donned the sweater Heather had left for me. Fortunately, the living room was warmer.

"About time," Toby said as we entered. He was sitting on the floor, in front of the fireplace, his feet bare and his worried eyes belying the easy smile plastered on his face. "I hope you were both behaving yourselves."

"Toby." Grace shot him a look, then gestured at the coffee table. "I made hot chocolate. I know you already had some earlier, but I thought under the circumstances..."

"Thank you." Summer reached for a mug and gulped down a mouthful. "Wow. That's good."

I glanced around, noting that Finn wasn't in the room.

Maybe they'd put him down for a nap in a spare bedroom. I knew they kept a cot here. Heather and Eugene had been prepared for more grandchildren ever since Tess was born.

"How bad is the damage to your house?" Max asked from the sofa.

I winced. "The front is pretty bad. I'll need to replace the front wall at least, as well as the carpet in the front rooms."

"You'll have to re-paint too," Liam said, winding his arm around Kennedy, who was sitting on his lap. "We'll all help with that."

Gratitude swelled in my chest. "I appreciate that."

Perhaps, despite everything, I hadn't lost my best friend.

"Us too." Frannie raised her hand, drawing my attention. Her slightly dazed expression mirrored how I felt. Things like this didn't happen to our family.

"Where's Mum?" I asked her.

"She popped by her place to gather some of your old things, since you might not be able to get them from your house for a while."

"That's nice of her," Summer said.

Toby patted the floor beside him, and Summer dropped onto the patch of carpet. He gave her a one-armed hug. Strange, how I'd never noticed before that Toby was protective of her in his own way. He may not bluster the way some of his brothers did, but the protectiveness was still there.

Frannie tugged at the end of her ponytail, visibly hesitant. "Mum said that the police think the fire might have been set intentionally. Who would do an awful thing like that?"

"I don't know," I said. "Has Nate called you? He wanted to talk to you too.

I lowered myself down beside Summer, close enough to feel her presence but not to actually touch.

"Me?" She frowned. "Why?"

"Because of your punctured tire. The police want to make sure it's not related."

Her eyes widened. "They don't think someone will try to set *our* house on fire, do they?"

"You'd have to ask them that." I couldn't tell what Nate considered most likely.

"Could someone want to mess with your family?" Liam asked.

Frannie cocked her head. "Who would want to do that? We don't have any enemies."

"I don't know." He grimaced. "I can think of people who might want to get one over on Asher, but not you. Unless it could be an ex?

She shook her head. "I doubt it, although Dean's ex thinks I'm the devil."

Interesting.

"What about James?" Liam suggested, looking at me.

I sighed. "I wouldn't have thought so, but I couldn't imagine anyone doing this, so what do I know?" James was a cheating asshole, but it was a big jump from there to arsonist.

The others didn't seem dissuaded by this. They bounced back ideas among themselves. The whole thing made me sick to my stomach. Did they really believe that more than one person might genuinely hate me enough to want to burn my house down? I wasn't as likable as Max or Toby, but I was a decent guy. I tried to do the right thing.

Fortunately, the discussion ended when Mum and Dad walked in. Dad had a backpack slung over his shoulder and Mum rushed at me, her arms open for a hug. I pushed myself upright and let her fuss over me much the same as Summer had.

Once she was satisfied that I was fine, Dad passed me

the backpack and Mum went with Heather to get extra seats from the dining room.

"Here. A few changes of clothes. They should still fit. You haven't changed much." Dad studied me closely for a moment, then added, "You're welcome to come and stay with us, but we wanted you to have these in case you decide to go somewhere else."

"Thanks." I caught Summer's eye. "Is your invitation still open?"

She took my hand. "Always."

I turned back to Dad. "I'll be with Summer."

After today, I didn't want to be without her. I was bound to spiral, and I'd rather she see me like that than my parents.

He winked. "She's good for you. Maybe too good for you."

I swatted his arm. "Hey."

He shrugged. "Don't mess it up. That's all I'm saying."

"Don't worry. I don't plan to."

Summer didn't seem to know what to make of this, but she smiled at Dad, nonetheless.

"Grace, I heard you were thinking of getting in touch with the original Destiny Falls couple's descendants for your book," she said, changing the subject with no tact whatsoever. "Have you reached out to them?"

"I have." Grace crossed her legs and leaned back against the armchair. "I made contact with a woman who's their great, great granddaughter, or something along those lines. Her name is Corie. We've been chatting about her family history, and she's interested in reading the book."

"She doesn't mind that it's a romance?" Summer asked.

Grace grinned. "She seems excited by that. I get the feeling Corie is a bit of a romantic." Her smile faded and she turned to me. "By the way, have you worked out what's behind the message on that rock they found in your living room? It just crossed my mind that it could be relevant to the fire."

I dragged my hand through my hair. "I don't know, but if whoever smashed my window is the same person who set the fire, and for some reason they want to scare me, all I can say is that they're going about it right."

49

―――――

I collapsed onto the sofa in my living room, trying to ignore how cold it was compared to the toasty warmth of my parents' place. "Do you want to take the spare bed or share with me?"

Asher stood in the doorway, Cookie's pet carrier in one hand and the backpack from his father over the opposite shoulder. "Either is fine. I'd prefer to be with you, but only if you're comfortable with that."

"I am." Although I wasn't sure if "comfortable" was the right word, exactly. My insides felt like throwing a party. I finally had him.

In my house.

In my bed.

Hopefully, in *me*.

I wished the circumstances were different. I'd never be grateful for him losing his house, but I was pleased he was allowing me to take care of him.

"Come on. I'll show you the room and then we can set up whatever Cookie needs."

I led him into my bedroom, wincing at the unmade bed and the overflowing laundry basket. I kept a reasonably tidy house, but I was far from a neat freak. My place would never feature in a Home & Garden magazine.

"You can unpack your clothes here," I said, tapping the top drawer of my dresser, which was empty from the last time I'd done a massive clear out. "Or you can hang them in the closet or leave them in the bag if you'd prefer."

"Thanks." He lowered the backpack to the ground. "What about Cookie?"

"The windows and doors are all shut, so you can set her free. She can go anywhere in the house, but we'll put her litter box in the laundry." I knew some people preferred to keep them in the bathroom, but I personally liked to smell nothing but candles and essential oils while enjoying a soak in the tub. No kitty litter odor welcome.

"And her food?" he asked.

I shrugged. "In the kitchen maybe? Wherever you'd like. Anywhere is fine with me."

He nodded. "Thanks."

He set the carrier on the ground, dropped to his knees, and opened the door. "Come out, pretty girl." He made that clucking sound with his tongue that people use to attract cats. "It's okay."

Cookie didn't emerge. Considering how many different places she'd been dragged around in the past few days, I wasn't surprised.

"While you do that, I'll get her litter box set up," I told him.

"You don't have to—"

His protest faded out as I left the room. I pulled a jacket on and went outside to the car, where we'd left the stuff we'd bought for Cookie on the way home. All of her usual things were still in Asher's house, out of bounds, so she'd needed more.

I tucked the heavy bag of litter under one arm and stacked the bedding, toys, and food in the shiny new litter box to carry inside. I locked the front door and set up the litter box on a few sheets of newspaper in the laundry before filling a bowl with water on the kitchen floor and adding a few treats to another.

When Asher strolled into the kitchen, there was no sign of the cat. "She wouldn't come out, so I left her in there with the door open. She'll leave eventually."

I grimaced, sympathetic to the cat's situation. "It must be a stressful time for her."

He huffed out a breath. "For all of us."

I opened the fridge. "Want a beer?"

"God, yes."

I usually preferred wine to beer, but some days called for it. I got two bottles out, popped the tops off, and handed him one.

He drank deeply, then let out a sigh. "I needed that."

"I'm not surprised. I'm exhausted, and it wasn't my house that caught fire." I rubbed my belly as it rolled uncomfortably at the memory of how frightened I'd been when he'd bolted toward the burning house. As long as I lived, I'd rather not experience that level of terror again.

"I'll understand if you want to go to bed," I continued. "Even though it's early, you're probably having an adrenaline crash."

But he shook his head. "I don't need a bed, but curling up with a movie on sounds nice."

"Let's do that then." I took my beer to the living room, and he followed close behind. I gestured at the sofa. "Sit."

While he got comfortable, I brought up a comedy film

on Netflix. I didn't think either of us were up to watching an action or thriller movie, and a romance would have felt a little on the nose.

As the opening credits played, I hurried into the hall and searched the cupboards for the biggest, fluffiest blanket I owned. I sat beside Asher, tucked my legs beneath myself, and pulled the blanket over us.

During the first scene, Asher tugged me around until he was spooning me, his strong chest pressed against my back. I relaxed into the embrace, breathing in his masculine scent, appreciating the fact that any trace of smoke had been cleaned away.

When the movie ended, I cooked nachos, and we ate them at the table.

"We've never talked much about the future," Asher said out of nowhere.

"I guess not," I replied. I hadn't thought much beyond securing our relationship.

"What do you want it to look like?" he asked.

"The future?" I frowned, considering. "I suppose we date for a while, and if it goes well, we eventually move in together. I don't mind whether that's at my place, your place, or somewhere else."

I loved my cottage, but it was just a house. People mattered more than places and things.

"Do you want marriage?" He paused for a moment, then quietly added, "Children?"

I smirked. "I think you know my stance on marriage. Did you not see the hearts in my eyes at both Kennedy and Grace's wedding ceremonies?"

He chuckled. "Fair enough. But kids? You've never really said."

"I'd like children," I said slowly. "But they're not make or break for me, and if I do have them, I want to keep my job."

He looked at me like I was crazy. "You own half a business. I wouldn't expect you to just give that up to be a full time mum, unless that was what you wanted."

I scooped beans and meat onto a corn chip and dunked it in sour cream. "Some guys would. I know it's old-fashioned, but small towns tend to attract people with those values."

His jaw firmed. "I'm open to children too, and if I had them, I'd want their mother to live life exactly how she pleased. We could work out the details."

"Good." I watched him load salsa onto a chip and crunch into it. "We have plenty of time anyway."

He licked his fingers clean. "What about pets? Are they something you want? I've often wondered because people expect vets to have a house full of them, but you don't."

I reached for my beer, realized it was empty, and set it back down. "I love animals, but it didn't seem fair to have a pet when I work a lot. Especially when... Well, honestly, I wasn't sure how long I would stay in Destiny Falls."

His spoon clinked loudly against his plate as he dropped it. "What? Why would you leave?"

My heart raced. "I don't plan to anymore." I debated whether to put my cutlery down too, but decided against it. With my luck, my trembling hands would break something. "I just..."

"What?" he urged.

I squeezed my eyes shut. "There were days when I thought I might need to get away from here. I didn't know how I'd be able to find love when you were always around for me to compare men to."

His breath caught. He was silent for a long moment.

I forced my eyes to open. "Ash?"

His face had crumpled. "I'm sorry, Summer. I'm sorry for

hurting you, and for taking so long to see what was right in front of me."

I bit the inside of my cheek and tried to steady my breathing. "Everything happened the way it was meant to. Yeah, it hurt, but I was too young. This is how it was supposed to be."

He ran the backs of his fingers along my cheek, whisper soft. "You're amazing. I love the way your mind works."

"You'd better." I tried to make my tone more cheerful. I needed to change the subject. "Because I'm going to use this brilliant mind to figure out who's been after you. No one hurts my man."

"No." His hand dropped from my cheek. "It's too dangerous. Just let the police deal with it."

"The police are understaffed and under-resourced. We can do this."

"No, Summer." His tone was firm. "I won't risk it."

I lifted my chin. "Fortunately, you don't get to tell me what to do."

50

———

ASHER

I approached Susan Warner's body, only this time, her head turned toward me as I drew near. Her sightless eyes fixed on me and her mouth formed words I couldn't understand.

I jerked away from her, only to find myself face-to-face with Lionel Lowry. His mangled leg hung uselessly, and he was supporting himself with a cane. Blood dripped from his wounds as he limped forward.

I stumbled.

"This is your fault, Asher," he growled.

"Asher."

"Asher!"

"Ash, wake up. You're having a nightmare."

I jerked upright and my eyes snapped open, but my vision was blurry. I blinked gritty eyes.

Damn, I felt like I hadn't slept at all. I'd struggled to shut my mind off last night, and I hadn't been sure I'd sleep at all, but I must have dozed off at some point.

"Ash?" Summer sounded concerned.

I drew in a deep breath and tried to calm my racing heart. Sodden sheets covered my legs. I must have been sweating heavily.

"I'm okay," I said, forcing myself to focus on her gorgeous face. Her hair fell in a mess around her shoulders, but no trace of sleepiness lingered in her expression. "Bad dream."

She frowned. "About the fire?"

"No, actually." Although that would make more sense. I leaned against the headboard. "First I was at the site of that fatal accident on the mountain, and then, for some reason, Lionel Lowry was there, but he hadn't healed yet."

She bit her lip. "I'm sorry. That must have been awful."

"Yeah." I dragged my hands down my face. Guilt still sat heavy in my gut, like an undigested meal.

"You know that you can't blame yourself for what happened to them, right?" she asked. "They were in accidents that had nothing to do with you."

I flopped my head back against the headboard, wincing at the slight thud. "That doesn't stop me from feeling guilty. Like, if I'd tried harder, I could have saved them."

Summer hesitated. "I might be overstepping, but have you considered seeing a therapist?"

I stiffened and swung my legs off the edge of the bed, turning away from her. What was with the women in my life thinking I needed help?

"I'm fine. I just need a good, hard cycle. I'm sorry about your bed. We'll need to wash the sheets."

"That's fine. I have a dryer." She didn't call me out about changing the subject. "Why don't you shower while I get started on the laundry?"

I nodded, grateful for the direction. I always felt lost

after work-related nightmares, and having a task helped ground me in the present.

I showered and dressed in clothes from the bag my parents had packed for me.

Thankfully, one of my paramedic uniforms was at the station, so I'd be able to get changed once I was there.

Summer was already in the kitchen when I entered. She opened the pantry door. "There's bread if you want a sandwich or toast. I've got cereal too, or yogurt and fruit."

I grabbed the loaf of bread and toasted a couple of slices, then slathered them with peanut butter. There was no instant coffee, so I drank chai along with Summer, and we sat beside each other at the table.

"Are you going to take today off?" she asked, scooping yogurt and banana into her mouth.

"Nah, I need the distraction." If I moped around her place all day, I'd go out of my mind. Summer didn't push back on this, but the narrowing of her eyes suggested she didn't approve. "Call me if you need anything. Promise?"

"I will."

We finished breakfast and she drove me to the fire station. Snow was no longer falling, but a crisp blanket of white covered the township and extended into the horizon. No doubt the vacationing skiers would be ecstatic. Meanwhile, we'd be fielding more ice-related calls.

Summer pulled up outside the station and I leaned over to kiss her cheek before getting out of the car. I walked inside, strangely anxious to see Liam. Usually, if anything went wrong in my life, he was my go-to guy to talk it over with, but I wasn't sure if I still had that privilege.

"No," Parks said as he stepped out of his office. "Go home. I've already got someone in to work your shift today."

Frustration simmered in my stomach. "But I didn't call in sick."

Parks scowled. "Your house was on fire yesterday. No one expects you to be here."

I jutted my chin out. "Maybe not, but I need to keep my mind off everything."

He glanced toward the staff room door and grimaced. "Fine, but you're not going out on calls. You can take cooking duty."

I nodded. I'd accept what I could get. "Thanks, sir."

He just grunted. "Get to it. Oh, and Heaton?"

"Yes, sir?"

"I never want to see you behave as recklessly as you did yesterday when we're on a job. Got it?"

I ducked my head. I'd been expecting the rebuke. I'd known he wouldn't want me to take Cookie's safety into my own hands, but I had anyway. "I won't."

"Make sure you don't." A slight smile curved his thin mouth. "How's your cat?"

"She's fine." We'd left her at Summer's place, locked inside with a couple of toys, a bowl of biscuits, and her litter box.

"Glad to hear it." He tipped his head toward me and preceded me into the staff room.

As soon as I entered, the conversation abruptly halted. To my surprise, Liam broke away from a group of men clustered around the kitchen counter and hauled me into a hug.

"How are you doing?" he asked gruffly.

"Still getting my mind around it," I admitted, clapping him on the back and drawing away. We had a lot to talk about, but at least he obviously still gave a shit about me.

"We're so sorry about your house," Zane said, dragging me into another embrace.

"Do you have insurance?" Igor asked, keeping his distance even though his eyes shone with sympathy. He wasn't much of a hugger. To be fair, nor was I.

"I do," I replied. "I suppose I'd better call them today."

I'd intended to make the call yesterday, but I'd been overwhelmed and sought refuge with Summer instead.

My other colleagues gathered around, each one taking the time to offer help if I needed it. My heart warmed. This group meant so much to me.

"Any idea who's behind it?" Maia asked, passing me a coffee.

I sipped the drink. It was delicious, which meant that either Liam or Igor must have made it. "I don't know. I haven't heard anything from Nate or Parks, so I assume they haven't figured it out either."

I liked to think they'd tell me if they knew.

"No leads yet," Parks confirmed from the doorway. "We'll get an arson investigator in though. We're taking this very seriously."

As they should. I couldn't even remember the last case of arson in Destiny Falls, besides a few kids setting bonfires that got out of control, and one woman who'd tried to dramatically burn her ex's belongings only to have her whole garden go up in flames.

Darcy nudged my elbow. When I glanced down at him, he gestured for me to go with him. Frowning, I followed him to the side of the room, far enough away from the others that I doubted they'd be able to hear us.

"I just found out about you and Summer," Darcy said, obviously uncomfortable. "I'm sorry if I stepped on any toes the other day. I didn't realize you guys have something going."

"It's fine." I knew I'd been an ass about the situation. He couldn't have known how I'd felt about Summer because I hadn't said a word. "Just don't hit on her again."

He laughed nervously. "I definitely won't."

"Then we're all good." I offered him my hand, and he pumped it.

The alarm sounded, and I immediately lurched into action, but stopped myself before I bolted out the door. I wasn't on duty today. I just had to stay here and make sure my coworkers would have something to eat and drink when they got back.

I headed to the kitchen and got to work. The station was slammed with one callout after another.

When the team left within a couple of minutes of returning in the afternoon, I decided they deserved a treat. I grabbed my wallet, let Parks know where I was going, and wandered down to Taste of Destiny on foot.

As soon as I stepped inside, I came face-to-face with Ashley and immediately regretted my decision to leave the station. I tensed, uncertain what to expect from her considering how we'd left things between us when Summer and I had told her we were together.

But Ashley didn't look upset. Nor did she have the glint in her eye that meant trouble.

"I'm so sorry about your house," she said.

A tiny bit of my tension released, but I was still wary of her. "Thanks. I called the insurance company at lunch, and they've said that as soon as we're allowed back in, they'll send someone to see what we're dealing with."

"That's really good." She cleared her throat, and glanced down at the table, then back at me. "I want to apologize."

"For what?"

Someone entered behind me, and I shuffled out of the way.

She grimaced. "For making you uncomfortable. It's obvious that Summer has won you over, and I shouldn't have pushed as hard as I did. I just wanted someone decent, and I knew you fit the bill." Her lips twisted slyly. "She better hold onto you tightly."

I stared at her, uncertain how to respond. With her words, she was telling me she'd given up on the idea of us, but her tone suggested she might be clinging onto a shred of hope.

I crossed my fingers I was imagining that.

51

SUMMER

"Does this outfit say, 'daughter-in-law material'?" I asked Asher, pirouetting to show him the dress, tights, and jacket I'd chosen to wear for our dinner with his family at the Destiny Peak Ski Resort restaurant.

His dark gaze burned over me from head to toe. I could swear I felt the heat like a caress.

"You look beautiful," he said. "You always do."

I huffed impatiently. "But I'm not always officially presenting myself to your parents as the person you're dating."

His forehead furrowed as if he didn't quite know what to make of me. "No, but they know who you are. You don't need to put on an act for them."

"I'm not, but I want to be prepared." I sat on the edge of my bed and crossed my legs, my skirt pulling up to just above my knees. Was it too short for an occasion like this? Usually, I wouldn't think so, but I'd been waiting for this for so long that I was overthinking everything.

Asher knelt in front of me and raised the back of my hand to his lips. "Just be you. It will be fine." He stood and tugged me up with him. "Let's get the chains onto your Ute."

We were taking my vehicle up the mountain because the snow hadn't melted and the Ute was better equipped for the steep, winding drive than his car. I grabbed my purse and toed on a pair of warm but pretty black boots, and we headed outside together.

It didn't take long to get the chains on—we were both accustomed to using them—and I drove slowly and carefully through the dark to the beacon near the top of Destiny Peak.

When we arrived, I parked next to Garth's SUV. Asher rounded the car and jogged over to take my arm as I got out. The icy air nipped at the exposed parts of my neck and face, and we bustled across the parking lot and in through the front entrance. Tabitha, the resort's owner, sat behind the front desk, as elegant as ever.

"What are you doing at reception?" I asked, surprised to see her there.

She smiled. "Sally called in sick tonight, and no one else was able to get up the hill. You two are meeting the Heatons for dinner?"

"That's right."

She stood and came out from behind the desk, her slim form clad in a sleek trouser suit. "Let me show you to their table."

She led us down a corridor to the restaurant. I couldn't help glancing at the spot where Asher and I had sat when we'd both been here for separate dates. Fortunately, Tabitha steered us away from there, to a long, rectangular table in front of the window. During the day, I was sure it had a spectacular view, but for now, all we could see through the glass was darkness.

We thanked Tabitha and she excused herself. Asher's family had left a pair of seats side by side next to Brenda. Garth, Frannie, and Dean sat opposite us, with Marcy in a highchair at the end of the table.

"Did you run into any problems on the way up?" Garth asked.

"No, it was fine." I accepted the glass of water Frannie poured for me.

He frowned. "You used your chains, I hope?"

Frannie rolled her eyes. "Of course she did, Dad. Summer knows what she's doing."

I shot her a grateful look. He hadn't meant anything by it, but it could be frustrating when men felt the need to give women advice about things we'd known since we were ten. We had grown up here, after all.

"So..." Brenda cradled a full glass of wine. "How long has this been going on for?"

"This?" Asher asked.

"You know." She gestured between us. "You two."

Asher sipped his water. "A couple of weeks."

Frannie placed her palms on the table and leaned toward us. "You've had feelings for each other for longer though, right?"

The way she was looking at me made me think she knew about my years-long crush.

Damn it.

I squirmed in my seat. "Maybe for a little while, but nothing ever happened."

"We've been interested in each other for years but pursuing anything seemed too complicated." Asher rested his hand on my leg beneath the table and gave it a reassuring squeeze. I was glad he hadn't outed my teenage infatuation with him. Not that I'd expected him to, but the fear was always there.

Brenda beamed. "Well, I think it's wonderful you've decided to go for it anyway."

"Thank you." I could have kissed her. I'd always worried about how our families might react if we did get together—although, admittedly, more mine than his. It was definitely nice to get his mother's explicit approval though.

A server came by to take our orders, and the food arrived soon after. We decided not to order dessert because Marcy was getting fussy and Frannie and Dean wanted to get her home.

"This has been lovely," I said as we stood to leave. Garth had paid the bill, claiming it was a family celebration. Another thing that warmed me inside.

I was cause for celebration.

"It has," Brenda agreed, her smile crinkling the corners of her eyes. "Let's do it again sometime."

"Soon," Frannie added, passing Marcy to Dean, who hefted her onto his hip.

We wandered down the corridor, pausing in the foyer to each don our jackets. It was chilly outside and no one wanted to be exposed to the air for longer than necessary. Frannie pulled a tiny, knitted hat from her pocket and fitted it over Marcy's head. The baby cooed at her.

I waved to Tabitha and promised to pass along her good wishes to Kennedy, whose pregnancy she'd heard about earlier this week. Kennedy and Tabitha were old friends of a sort. I didn't really understand their relationship, but then, I didn't need to.

We clustered together at the base of the steps, beside the drive that led out of the parking lot and down the mountain. Asher and Garth were deep in conversation, and I scanned the parking lot. It was packed. The resort must be at full capacity. Something moved in the shadows, and I frowned. Was that...?

"I think there's a person over there," I said, gesturing toward one of the parked cars, where I'd seen movement. I peered into the darkness. Nothing so much as twitched, but I had the distinct feeling that whoever was there was watching me.

"I don't see anything," Brenda said, adjusting her glasses.

There it was. The slightest hint of movement. As subtle as an indrawn breath.

"Hello?" I called.

Asher and Garth's conversation halted, and they both stared at me. Meanwhile, I didn't take my eyes off the shadow that had broken away from a vehicle and was moving rapidly.

I raised my voice. "Who's there?"

"It's probably nothing," Asher murmured. "Just one of the guests."

I narrowed my eyes at him. After the cat, the rock, and the fire, he was still going to assume the best? When I turned back to the figure, they were gone. A car door slammed and then a pair of headlights illuminated the driveway.

The car shot forward, its engine roaring.

My heart leapt to my throat. It was gunning directly for Frannie, who stood at the side of our group nearest the road.

I grabbed her arm and yanked her forward. She screamed. The car screeched past, only missing her by a matter of inches.

52

———

ASHER

"Are you okay?" I asked Frannie as she steadied herself.

"I'm not hurt." The whites of her eyes gleamed in the darkness.

Given the circumstances, "not hurt" was the best we could expect. She looked shaken, and I had no doubt her pulse was racing. Hell, I wouldn't be surprised if she started to go into shock.

"Let's get back inside," Dad said, ushering Mum and Frannie toward the resort. Dean held Marcy close, and Summer and I took up the rear.

As soon as we entered, Tabitha took one look at us and rushed around the reception desk.

"What happened?" she asked.

"S-someone nearly ran Frannie over," Mum stuttered, tripping over the words.

"I'm calling the police." I drew my cell phone from my pocket and found Nate's number. Perhaps I ought to call the station instead, but Nate knew everything that was going on, and I had no doubt he'd want to be involved.

The call connected.

"It's late," Nate groused.

"A car just tried to run my sister down at the resort," I told him.

"Shit." There were muffled noises as he adjusted the phone. "Did you get their details?"

I winced. "No. Hold on." I lowered the phone and scanned the others. "Anyone get the registration number?"

They all shook their heads.

"No, sorry. It was white though. Midsize."

"That's something, at least." He sighed. "I suppose you'd better come into the station and make a statement."

I glanced at Frannie. "Do you need all of us? Frannie is freaked out and Marcy needs to be put to bed."

Nate paused, considering. "They can go home, but I'll need to speak to Frannie in the morning. Can you let her know?"

"Will do. We'll see you as soon as we're down." I hung up and addressed my family. "Frannie, you guys can head home, but Nate will need a statement from you tomorrow morning."

She nodded, her teeth embedded in her lower lip. "Thanks, Ash. I just want to crawl into bed and pretend it didn't happen."

For tonight, at least, she could. Tomorrow she'd have to face reality.

The events of the past five minutes replayed through my mind on fast-forward. Fuck, there were so many ways the night could have ended so much worse.

"What were you thinking, yelling out at someone like that?" I asked Summer. "You knew that if someone was there, they might be dangerous."

She raised her chin, her expression stubborn. "I was thinking that I'm sick of these stupid games and I want them to end. Whoever this is, they're playing with us, and I hate that."

I grabbed her shoulders and looked into her eyes. "You need to be more careful. You could have been hurt. Or Frannie might have been."

She lowered her gaze for a brief second as the barb sunk in. I immediately regretted it, but she couldn't ignore the risks.

"You know, I don't like the fact that you regularly put yourself in danger to help others," she said, raising her eyes again. "You do it every day as a paramedic. You know it's dangerous, but it's part of who you are, and it would be selfish of me to ask you to stop. Likewise, you can't stop me from doing whatever I can to protect you."

"I..." I didn't know what to say. My gut twisted. She was right, but didn't she realize that I'd be devastated if anything happened to her?

"Let's all take a breath," Mum said, interrupting our conversation. "Let's get down the mountain and tell Nate whatever he needs to know. You can finish this after you've both calmed down."

Dean nodded. "Good call, Brenda. I'd like to get my girls home."

Everyone murmured their agreement.

This time, when we left the resort, we were on edge. Frannie was visibly jumpy as we crossed the parking lot, and Dean stuck close to her side, a silent source of support.

We got into our respective vehicles and Summer drove in front onto the road down the mountain. I expected her to go straight to the police station, but instead, she drove to Frannie's place and pulled over. Dad parked behind us and

Frannie and Dean got out of the car. Dean lifted a sleeping Marcy into his arms and carried her inside.

Once the door had closed behind them, Summer silently pulled back onto the road and headed for the police station. Only a few lights were on inside, but the front door was unlocked and we let ourselves in.

Nate was waiting in one of the interview rooms with a laptop in front of him. To my surprise, he was alone, and the place was completely silent.

"No Mehrtens or Patton?" I asked.

"Nah, no need to get them out here on a cold-ass night when we can handle this ourselves," he said, fiddling with the voice recorder. "Any work they're involved in can wait until morning."

Mum and Dad entered behind us, and we clustered around the table. Nate started the recorder and began asking questions. He typed on his laptop while we spoke, and when we were done, he stopped the recorder.

"I've written up your account of events." He turned the laptop so we could see the screen. "I've sent it to the printer. Can you read through and then sign the printout at the bottom to confirm it's accurate."

"Sure." I read it first, and while it was a bare bones accounting, it was correct, so I slid the laptop across to Summer, who then passed it along again. By the time Nate returned with the printed form, we were all ready to sign.

As we left the station, Mum paused just outside and drew her jacket up around her cheeks.

"Be careful," she warned us. "There's a heavy snow forecast. Will you text and let me know you're safe when you get home and then again tomorrow?"

I slung one arm around her and kissed her cheek. "Of course."

We separated, and Summer still didn't say much. It was unnerving, to be honest.

"Are you okay?" I asked once we were in the Ute.

She scowled. "I'm so freaking sick of this person taking potshots at us."

I leaned across the divider and kissed her. Outside, snow was falling again, soft flakes landing on the windscreen.

"The police will find them," I murmured, drawing away from her. "This will be over soon."

A niggling feeling in my gut said I'd just lied to her. I might sound confident, but I wasn't sure this would be resolved soon.

At least, not before someone got hurt.

53

SUMMER

The piercing tone of a phone call woke me. I rolled over and grabbed for the device, blinking at the screen through blurry eyes, but the call wasn't coming to me.

"Ash." I jostled his shoulder.

"Wha' is 't?" he mumbled, raising his head just enough for me to see his sleepy brown eyes.

"Your phone."

Those eyes narrowed, and he sighed and flopped his arm off the side of the bed to retrieve the device.

He stiffened and dragged himself upright. "It's Liam." He accepted the call. "Hello?"

My brother's voice was quiet and tinny. I couldn't make out what he was saying, but Asher nodded and threw off the blankets. He stood and stretched, showing off his toned abs to full advantage, then hitched up the waistband of his boxers and sauntered out of the room.

I watched wistfully as he left. I'd have been happy to

snuggle, but obviously, he wanted some space to talk to Liam.

I lay back against the pillows and closed my eyes. I was surprisingly well-rested. I'd expected to wake up almost as exhausted as I'd been last night, but I must have slept deeply. In the other room, the cadence of Asher's voice rose and fell. I couldn't identify his tone, but when he returned, the phone hanging from his grip, he looked frustrated.

I patted the bed, and he sat. "What's wrong?"

"Nothing. That's the problem. It's like you said last night: I'm ready for this to be over."

I scooched myself alongside him and wrapped my arms around his waist, burying my face against his warm skin. "It will be soon."

Or not.

I hadn't believed him last night, and I got the impression he didn't either.

I grimaced. Okay, perhaps I wasn't in a very soothing frame of mind, but I could be a killer distraction.

I kissed his back and then his side.

"What are you doing?" he asked.

"Come to bed." I tugged on his waist, and he lay down and slung one of his legs over mine. "Let's pretend we just woke up and start this morning properly."

His hands curved around my hips, and he tugged me up against the firm planes of his body. "How do you propose we do that?"

I rested my forehead against his and smiled, glorying in the desire that burned in the dark depths of his eyes. "Kiss me."

He kissed the tip of my nose. The infuriating man.

"Properly," I insisted.

He arched an eyebrow. "Are you saying that wasn't a proper kiss?"

I rolled my eyes. "Kiss my lips, Ash."

"Like this?"

His lips met mine. Soft. Chaste. Almost painfully gentle.

"Closer," I murmured, the sensitive skin of my lips whispering over his. I cupped the side of his face, and his stubble rasped against my palm. I couldn't wait to feel it elsewhere.

I ran my tongue along the seam of his lips, and when he parted them, I flicked it inside. He tasted of sleepy man with the faintest hint of mint from brushing his teeth last night. He groaned and deepened the kiss. My world shrank to that connection between us. At least until I felt the throb of his erection against me.

I rocked, drawing out a burst of pleasure from the friction between us. He grabbed my ass, his fingers sinking into my flesh as he encouraged me to move against him. He caressed the side of my neck, and my head fell back.

"I can't believe I get to see you like this," he rasped, wondering. "Fuck, you feel good. So goddamn perfect for me."

He nipped the muscle where my neck met my shoulder, and I shuddered in response. He soothed the sting with his tongue and ghosted his lips up my neck and around the edge of my jaw.

Determined to level the playing field, I palmed his cock. It filled my hand, hot and heavy despite the thin satin barrier separating us. I stroked his length and teased the tip. My mouth watered, eager to taste him, but I held off. If I did that, I'd want to make him come, and I'd rather he did that inside me.

Instead, I pinched the fabric of his boxers between my thumb and forefinger and tugged it down, slowly exposing him. I wrapped my fingers around him, our kiss growing sloppier as he panted into my mouth and thrust into my grip.

He slid his hand inside my panties and cupped me, putting delicious pressure on my clit. His fingers slipped into my heat, and he teased me and toyed with me.

By the time he pushed one finger inside me, I'd almost forgotten what I was supposed to be doing to him, too distracted chasing my own pleasure.

He smiled against my lips and circled my clit with his fingertip. A shudder rippled through me. I was too close to the edge.

"Condom," I gasped.

He raised his head, his eyes pitch black, his chest rising and falling rapidly. "Yeah. Where?"

"Um." I squeezed my eyes shut and thought. "There might be some in the dresser."

He got off me and made a beeline for it.

"Bottom drawer," I said.

He knelt and sifted through my neatly folded clothes. He made a sound of victory as he extracted a box, and he checked the expiration date on the back before pulling one out.

"I'm relieved you have these," he said, walking back toward me, his erection jutting out proudly. "But I don't want to know when you last used them."

I smirked, pleased by the hint of jealousy in his voice. I wasn't about to admit that it had been a good long while since I'd needed condoms. I was lucky they were still valid.

He stopped at the foot of the bed to roll the condom on. His hot gaze seared my skin as he studied every inch of me. Based on the way his nostrils flared, he liked what he saw.

I did too.

Asher wasn't just good-looking. He possessed an intensity that made him unlike anyone else I'd ever been with. He touched me as though he might never get another chance, and he looked at me with the same kind of astonishment that I experienced every time I remembered I was allowed to kiss him.

"Part your legs, baby."

Heat shot to my core, and I slowly parted my thighs, letting him gaze at me openly. A sense of power thrummed through me. I was in a vulnerable position. Exposed to him. But his hands twitched at his sides, forming fists for the barest second, and a rumble of approval tore from his chest.

I had him exactly where I wanted him.

He knelt over me and peppered kisses up my torso, over my chest, pausing to flick my nipple with his tongue and then brush his lips against mine. His cock nudged against my entrance, and he reached down with one hand to position it properly.

"Are you ready, baby?" he asked.

"Yes," I whispered, unable to take my eyes from his.

I caught my breath as he pushed inside me, bit by bit, stretching me. He moved forward inexorably, never stopping, until he was seated deep inside me.

"You feel me?" he asked, pulsing hot and hard within my channel.

I wet my lips. "I do."

"Good." His lips curled with satisfaction. "You're mine now."

I bucked my hips, his mere words causing me to clench around him. For so long, I'd wanted him to claim me, and now he was. Tears prickled in my eyes, but I blinked them back.

"I am. And you're mine." My tone was firm. It didn't allow for a denial. "So show me."

He bared his teeth. "With pleasure."

He withdrew, and thrust back into me, filling me completely. I arched into him and cried out.

"That's it, baby." He rolled his hips, creating an exquisite slide between our bodies that had me seeing stars. "Say my name."

"Ash!"

His grin was feral. "Yeah, Summer. My girl."

He drove into me again, starting a rhythm that slowly drove me higher and higher. All I could do was cling to him and take what he gave me.

I kissed him as we moved together. His pace never eased. It wasn't fast, but it was relentless. There was no escape from the sensations pouring through me. My head landed on the pillow, and I stared sightlessly at the ceiling as he filled me over and over again, winding me tighter and tighter.

When his movements became jerky, I knew he was close. I grabbed his ass and tilted my hips. His name spilled from my lips as our gazes locked. His eyes were liquid chocolate. Dark, rich, and intoxicating.

"You gonna come for me?" he asked, dragging his mouth down my throat.

I whimpered, unable to speak.

"Come for me, baby. Let me feel you."

I touched my lips to his and let myself go, meaningless words falling from my mouth as I came. He stiffened and thrust deeper inside me than he'd ever been. Another wave of pleasure crested, and I cried out. His cock twitched as he emptied into the condom. I held him close and shut my eyes, burying my face in the crook of his neck.

We lay together, unwilling to separate, until the shriek of his phone once more broke the silence.

"Damn," he muttered.

I laughed weakly. "You said it."

He reared back and carefully climbed off me, his soft dick slipped from my body. He removed the condom, tied it off, and tossed it in the bin. Then he looked around, grimaced, wiped his hands on his belly before grabbing his phone.

He pushed a button on the screen and raised it to his ear. As he listened, all the color drained from his face.

"We'll be there soon," he said, and ended the call.

He turned to me, ashen. "Marcy is missing."

54

ASHER

"Missing, how?" Summer asked, gaping at me.

I drew in a slow breath and tried to control my rising panic. Losing it wouldn't help anyone. "Frannie left Marcy alone in the kitchen for a few minutes, and when she came back, she was gone."

Summer frowned. "Surely Dean has her."

I shook my head. "Dean was outside shoveling the drive. Frannie has already checked. He doesn't know where Marcy is either."

"She's a baby. She can't have just gotten up and walked away."

My stomach knotted. "Exactly."

That was what I was most scared of. If Frannie had left Marcy in a highchair, as she'd said, and neither of her parents had moved her, then someone else must have done. She couldn't have gotten down by herself.

I held out my hand to Summer and when she took it, I

pulled her to her feet. "I wish we could lie around and have a lazy morning, but I told Frannie we'd drive straight over."

"Of course." Her tone was brisk now, and she pulled her hand away and started opening her drawers and tossing items of clothing on the bed. "Let's get moving. Are you going to feed Cookie first?"

"I fed her earlier, when Liam called. She'll be fine."

I hurried to the kitchen, quickly cleaned myself, and found a set of clothes in the bag my parents had packed. I'd run out of underwear, so I had to go commando. I'd just have to hope nothing sensitive would get caught in the zipper of my jeans.

I grabbed my jacket from where it was slung over the back of the sofa and glanced out the window. Snow was falling heavily. Good thing we'd left the chains on Summer's Ute last night because we'd been too tired by the time we got back to her place to remove them.

Summer appeared in the doorway, a bag slung over her shoulder and the keys in her hands. "Ready?"

"Yeah." I leaned over the sofa to pat Cookie, then followed Summer outside. She was already behind the wheel, and I got in the passenger side. As soon as I shut the door, she took off. She drove as quickly as she could to Frannie's place, but with all the snow, she could only go so fast without endangering us.

Somehow, despite the police car parked out front, Frannie's house was as picturesque as ever, with its white picket fence and snow covering the garden and roof. We followed the footsteps through the snow to the front door and I knocked but opened the door without waiting for anyone to answer.

I went straight to the living room and Summer followed behind. I wasn't sure if she'd been in Frannie's home before, but I didn't think so. Voices came from the living room, along with the sound of a woman crying.

My heart seized. *Frannie.*

I strode through the doorway, immediately taking in the scene. My sister sat on the sofa, her shoulders heaving as she sobbed. Dean was rubbing her back and Mum sat on her other side, looking as though she wanted to hug Frannie but wasn't sure whether she'd welcome it.

Dad stood behind Mum. Nate was squatting in front of Frannie, and Officer Mehrtens hovered to his left. That left an armchair free. I dropped onto it and patted my thigh. Summer glanced at Nate, as if debating whether being affectionate with me would upset him, but then she lowered herself onto my lap.

"Thanks for coming," Dad said.

"There's no sign of her?" I asked, holding tightly to Summer in an attempt to conceal my distress. Frannie didn't need me falling apart on her.

"Not yet," Nate said, turning toward us. "I need to get a full statement from Frannie and Dean so I can coordinate a search properly, but in the meantime, I'd like the rest of you to search the house and property."

"We've already—" Dean started.

"Do it again." Nate cut him off. "Babies are small. Perhaps she slid behind something, and you didn't see her the first time."

"But wouldn't she be crying?" Summer asked.

Nate's nostrils flared. "We don't have any time to waste. Get to it."

Summer nodded and stood. I got up too, and we gestured for Mum and Dad to join us nearer the door so that Nate could continue speaking with Frannie without us interrupting.

"Mum, you go through the bedrooms and the bathroom," I said, automatically taking charge since I was on the local search and rescue team and had more experience with this than they did, even if the searches I was part of were usually in the forest. "Summer, I want you to check the kitchen, living room, and bathroom. Dad and I will search outside."

No one argued. I zipped my jacket up and turned to Dad. "You take the front of the property, and I'll do the back. If you finish before me, come and give me a hand."

We split up. I went out through the back door and instantly doubted that I'd have any luck tracking Marcy. There were no footprints in the snow. In fact, it didn't seem to have been disturbed at all. Still, I had to make sure.

Carefully, I took three steps down to the lawn. Almost the entire backyard was lawn, except for a narrow strip of rose bushes along the fence, which was much taller around here than it was at the front of the property. It would be difficult for someone to climb it, but not impossible.

I paced the perimeter of the fence, checking for anything out of place.

No luck.

I walked back and forth across the lawn, just in case Marcy had somehow gotten out here and become covered by the snow. I was halfway done when Dad opened the gate and pushed hard, dislodging the snow that blocked the way.

"Need help?" he asked.

"I'm just double checking she isn't under here somewhere," I explained.

"I'll do the same thing, and we can meet in the middle."

"She wasn't out the front?"

"No."

"Any sign someone had been there?"

He grimaced as he began matching me step for step,

coming toward me. "Not in the garden, but we've had so many people in and out of the house to know for sure who all the footprints belong to."

My heart sank, even though I hadn't expected anything different. "Did you notice any footprints when you arrived?"

He turned and started back the other way. "Yes, but Dean had been outside so they could have belonged to him."

"Damn."

I had an awful suspicion that Marcy's disappearance was related to everything else that had gone wrong lately, and if that was the case, it would be my fault. Whoever was behind those incidents was targeting me.

When Dad and I reached each other, we returned inside. Nate was no longer speaking to Frannie but was on his phone. Both Summer and Mum were in the room, indicating they must have already completed their searches too.

Nate hung up and pocketed his phone. He faced us, his expression grim. "I don't want to scare anyone needlessly, but the fact Marcy isn't on the property doesn't bode well. I don't see how she could have left on her own, and Frannie and Dean seem sure that no one they know would have come by to collect her for any reason."

Nate's eyes briefly met mine, and I saw in them the same concerns I had. "Because of that, we have to treat this as a possible abduction. Connor is initiating a search of the buildings in the forest surrounding the township in case someone took Marcy to one of the unoccupied huts. Meanwhile, I will coordinate a search within the town boundaries."

Frannie hiccupped, and when I glanced over, tears were streaming down her cheeks, and her eyes were puffy and red.

"We'll do everything we can to find her," Officer

Mehrtens told her gently. "Connor and Nate have run searches like this before. They know what they're doing."

Frannie shook her head but didn't speak.

My phone buzzed in my pocket. No doubt it was Connor, mobilizing the team.

"I'll join Connor's search effort," I said.

Summer moved to my side. "So will I."

I frowned down at her. "You don't have any training."

A challenge glinted in her eyes. "Either you let me come with you, or I'll go out on my own."

I huffed. "You'll have to stick with me at all times and do exactly what I say."

"I can do that," she agreed.

Another day, I might have teased her about compliance not being in her nature, but this wasn't the time for kidding around.

"What can we do?" Dean asked.

"Stay here," Nate said firmly.

Dean scowled. "But we want to help."

"The best way you can do that is by being here if Marcy returns. We can't rule out the fact that whoever has her may not wish her harm, and if she is returned, she'll need her parents."

Dean's lips pressed tightly together but he didn't argue again.

"We'll keep you updated," Nate said, and strode toward the door with Mehrtens on his heels.

When they left, the room fell silent, apart from Frannie's shuddering breaths.

I dropped to my knees in front of her. "I'm so sorry."

She stared at me blankly, as if everything inside her was numb. "I don't care. I just want my baby back."

I flinched, even though I knew she hadn't meant anything by the words. "We'll get her."

"Excuse me."

I spun around. Officer Mehrtens stood behind me, a piece of damp paper extended toward me, pinched between her thumb and forefinger.

"This was on Summer's window," she said.

My gut tightened. It was the same handwriting as what had been on the rock thrown through my window.

DOES THIS SCARE YOU?

55

———

SUMMER

"WHAT THE HELL?" I STRODE TO ASHER'S SIDE AND READ THE note. "This is from the same person as the other one."

Officer Mehrtens nodded. "I suspected as much. But what does it mean?"

I stared at the awful words, wondering what their purpose was. "Both notes mentioned being afraid. Perhaps this person is trying to scare Asher and that's why they took Marcy."

"It's a possibility," Mehrtens agreed. She pulled the note away. "Or perhaps they want to scare Frannie, and Summer's Ute was simply a convenient place to leave the note. I'll get this tested for fingerprints immediately. Meanwhile, you two should meet Connor at the information center. I hear that's where he's giving instructions for the search."

She breezed out of the room, leaving us in a state of shock. I searched Asher's face. His expression was drawn, and the set of his mouth was grim. No doubt he was blaming himself for all of this.

"If someone is doing all of this just to scare me, I'm going to fucking end them," he growled. "She's a baby, not a tool to be used in someone's vendetta. Not to mention it's snowing worse than it has in years. So many things could go wrong."

I took his hand. "Let's find her before they do then."

He allowed me to lead him out of the house and to my Ute. We drove to the information center. A light was on inside and several figures were silhouetted against the window. Cars lined the side of the road, so we parked half a block back and walked to the center.

Asher pulled the door open and held it for me. I entered, getting out of the cold wind, even though it wasn't exactly warm inside. Connor was standing at the far end of the room, his broad shoulders and height making him immediately obvious. He nodded to me and Asher.

"Sorry to hear about Marcy," he said gruffly. "If she's out there, we'll do everything we can to find her."

We waited a few excruciating minutes for the rest of the search team to trickle in. Once we'd all arrived, Connor called the room to order. He shifted from one foot to the other when we looked at him, uncomfortable with the attention.

"We're searching for Marcy Gunn. She's nine months old with dark hair and brown eyes."

A rumble of discontent rippled through the room. No one wanted a baby to be in danger.

"Marcy was last seen at her parent's place on Watson Road. She can't walk, and there was no sign she'd attempted to leave of her own accord. Because of that, we're treating it as a possible kidnapping. If you find her, and she's not alone, please do not approach. Whoever has her may be dangerous. Radio me with the location and I'll advise the police."

Asher sucked in a breath. I grabbed his hand and

squeezed, trying to anchor him in the moment so his mind couldn't run wild with worst case scenarios.

"We'll focus on buildings, since it's unlikely anyone is outdoors in this weather," Connor continued, raising his voice to be heard above the muttering. "I'll assign each of you a search quadrant and I want you to clear all buildings within that quadrant."

Nervously, I raised my hand.

Connor's eyebrow shot up. "What is it, Summer?"

I rubbed my lips together, hoping I wasn't asking something obvious. "If someone local took her, then what's to have stopped them from just taking her home?"

To my relief, Connor nodded. "Good question. There's every possibility that's what happened, but if so, it's a matter for the police, not us. They are in charge of the search of Destiny Falls township, and that includes private homes within it. They aren't legally allowed to enter without a warrant, but if anyone refuses entry, that's suspicious in itself."

"True." I supposed all I could do was tag along with Asher and be glad I was allowed to contribute at all. If not for him, I doubted anyone would let me join the search. I had no training. Sure, I knew the trails around the area well, but that didn't mean I had the skills to search for a baby in a snowstorm.

Connor began to shout assignments and hand out maps. The search and rescue team had an app where they could record places they'd visited so others wouldn't double up, but the maps would be useful for anywhere outside of internet service range.

We were given an area near the Castle Valley trail and assigned three buildings to check: a holiday home that should be empty, a rental studio that was awaiting renovation, and an old hunting cabin.

"Do you mind if we use your Ute?" Asher asked, perusing the map. "I can drive if you'd like."

"I'll be fine." I might not know much about search and rescue, but I was perfectly capable of driving in bad weather.

We waited to make sure we didn't miss any instructions and then headed out. We checked the holiday home first. It was a large glass-walled building set just off the highway. I parked outside and Asher and I made our way to the door together. I rang the doorbell, but it didn't make a sound, so I knocked instead.

There was no response.

"Let's circle around the building and see if there's any sign someone is inside," Asher said. "If they are, don't engage."

"Okay." I pulled my hands inside my jacket sleeves, wishing I'd thought to wear gloves when we'd left my cottage this morning. The air was bitterly cold, and my fingers stung because of the temperature change from the warm car to the frigid outdoors.

I picked my way around the house, testing the ground before putting my foot down for each step. I didn't want to accidentally step over a ledge and fall, or trip over a stair.

Thanks to the massive windows, it was easy to see the house's interior, and it looked uninhabited. The furniture was in place, but it was too bare for anyone to be staying there. Asher must have moved faster than me because I'd only got a third of the way around the building when he met me coming the other way.

He pulled his hood more tightly around his face. "Nothing?"

"No."

He jerked his head toward the Ute. "Next one then."

As I drove to our second stop, the rental studio, Asher

recorded our visit in the app. I scanned our surroundings, keeping an eye out for anything that wasn't where it ought to be.

The rental studio was down a narrow road that came off the highway. I drove slowly, worried we might encounter someone coming toward us. If so, I'd have to reverse all the way out. Fortunately, we reached the unit without issue.

It was a small, black building, dark inside with snow piled around. We checked it the same way we had the holiday home and, not finding anything, we left.

The hunting cabin was the most difficult building on our list to get to. It belonged to a national hunting and fishing organization, and maintenance was undertaken as needed by local members. It stood empty for weeks at a time during winter months.

We carried on down the same sideroad the rental studio was on, then turned onto a gravel road, which ended before we reached the cabin. We'd have to walk the last few hundred meters.

I parked, being careful not to slide into a ditch on the side of the clearing. Asher took the radio Connor had given us and shut the passenger door. I jumped down and locked the car out of habit more than anything else. I doubted anyone would be out here to break into it.

A narrow gap between the trees showed where the trail must be. If not for that, it would be impossible to know for sure. The wind buffeted me, and I hunkered down, doing my best to withstand it. I lifted my feet with each step, hating the way icy liquid seeped through my shoes and socks. I'd need to change my socks soon. I should have brought a pair of waterproof boots but as with the gloves, it hadn't crossed my mind.

A sudden, sharp crack stopped me in my tracks. "What was that?"

I hadn't felt anything break under my foot. Asher stopped too, and all around was silent.

Eerily so.

"I don't think we're alone," I whispered.

56

———

ASHER

"It was probably just an animal." Despite the snow, there must still be some roaming around. Deer, perhaps. Although, surely, most would be safe in their den.

"It sounded like a twig breaking under someone's foot." Summer sounded nervous, and I didn't blame her. We were so isolated out here that our imaginations could easily run wild.

"It would be difficult for anyone to hide out here," I pointed out. Perhaps in warmer months, but for now, it would be almost impossible for someone to sneak up on us. The trees were bare, and any shrubs had already been covered with snow. A person moving between them would stand out against the barren landscape.

She cocked her head, listening for something. "But not impossible."

I jammed my hands into my pockets and wrapped one around the radio. "Whoever took Marcy is surely too busy to be running around out here with us."

Unless they left her alone somewhere. We couldn't rule that out. Anyone willing to kidnap a baby clearly didn't care much about their wellbeing.

"The sooner we get to the cabin, the faster we can go back to the car," I reminded her, taking a few more steps along the trail, grateful when she followed my lead.

We rounded a corner, and the cabin appeared before us. My immediate thought was that it looked abandoned, but some of the snow had been disturbed. I held out my hand to stop Summer.

"Remember what Connor said about not approaching if anything looks out of place. No one should have been here, but it looks like a snowmobile or an ATV was parked out front until recently. Let's radio it in."

She nodded.

We ducked back around the corner. Anyone inside may still be able to see us, but we'd be partially hidden by the trees. I raised the radio to my lips and reported our findings to Connor.

"I'll touch base with Nate." His electronic voice was startlingly loud in the silent forest. "He'll send someone out."

"We need to go," Summer murmured. "This doesn't feel right."

I ended the conversation with Connor, and we hurried up the trail together to the Ute. She unlocked it with trembling hands and climbed in.

"Are you all right to drive?" I asked.

"Yeah." A breath rattled between her lips. "Just give me a minute."

I rounded the hood and got in. She hadn't started the engine yet, so it was almost as cold in the car as it had been outside. Summer slotted the key into the ignition and turned it.

Nothing happened.

She tried again. The engine turned over once and then died.

Nerves gathered in the pit of my gut. As she tried a third time, her hands were shaking.

"It's probably just the cold," I said, despite my misgivings.

She huffed. "I've never had trouble getting it to start in the cold before."

I pulled the radio back out of my pocket. "Connor," I said into the device.

"Report," he barked back.

"Summer's Ute isn't working. We'll need a lift out of here."

"The police will bring you back when they come around to check the building."

"Thanks."

I dropped the radio onto my lap and turned to Summer with a reassurance on the tip of my tongue. Unfortunately, at that moment, a gust of wind buffeted the Ute, throwing us both forward. I caught myself on the dashboard, wincing as a pain shot through one of my wrists.

"Are you okay?" I asked Summer, who'd hit her face against the steering wheel. Blood flowed over her lips and dripped off her chin. "Fuck."

I searched the glove compartment for tissues but found only a wad of unused napkins. I passed them to her, and she balled them up and held them against her nostrils.

"Can I?" I asked, reaching for her.

"Yeah."

I felt along the length of her nose with my thumb and forefinger as gently as I could. "I don't think it's broken. Hopefully the bleeding won't last long."

"I really don't—" Another gust of wind tossed us forward, cutting her off mid-sentence. I clutched the seat and Summer braced herself, taking most of the impact with her shoulder.

"Buckle up," I called over the shrieking wind. "This could get dangerous."

Snow pelted the window, falling so thickly, I couldn't even see the gap through the trees anymore. The world was a wall of white.

She struggled to pull the belt on while keeping the napkins in place, so I helped, looping the belt over her shoulder and beneath her arm. I clicked my own into place just in time for the Ute to rock forward again.

An ear-splitting crack almost stopped my heart. I met Summer's eyes and together, we looked over our shoulders just as a massive tree thumped against the earth only a few feet behind the Ute.

Summer screamed.

My heart raced and I grabbed her hand. I stared in disbelief at the massive trunk. It was half the height of the vehicle and spanned the full width of the road.

Another crack, and I flinched, my gut clenching at the realization it had started a chain reaction. The tree had fallen onto another, which slowly fell sideways into another.

How were we supposed to get out of here now?

Even if the Ute did work, the road was blocked, and the trees, while bare, were too dense to drive between. Assuming we somehow managed to get back out to the road, driving in this wind could be catastrophic.

We couldn't stay here though. Not when there was every chance the next tree might land on us.

"We need to move," I told Summer, thinking quickly. "Somewhere the trees won't hit us."

"There weren't any directly around the cabin," she said, staring rigidly through the windshield, obviously terrified.

"Were the lights on?" I asked.

"Not that I noticed."

"I didn't see any transportation either, and there's no garage. If someone was here, they're probably gone. Let's see if we can shelter on the porch."

I released her hand, and she grabbed her purse. We both unbuckled the seat belts, and I picked up the radio and slid a first aid kit from beneath the front seat.

We glanced at each other, as if silently asking whether we were really going to do this, and then by unspoken agreement, opened the doors and pushed our way out. As soon as I shut the door, the wind whipped at my clothing and nearly took my feet out from under me.

I pocketed the radio and tucked the first aid kit under one arm. Summer met me at the front of the Ute, and we linked arms and lowered our heads, squinting through the snow as we made our way toward the trail. My foot connected with a root or rock, and I stumbled, but she righted me. My eyes stung.

It seemed to take forever for the cabin to come into view. The disturbance in the snow we'd noted earlier was almost invisible now.

"We need to check no one is there first," I shouted, hoping she could hear me.

She allowed me to lead her around the side of the building. There was no sign of a snowmobile, motorcycle, or anything else someone could have used to get here. I exhaled sharply, relief loosening the knots in my back. Since we hadn't come across any vehicles on the way here, we had to assume the place was empty.

Moving carefully, we climbed a small slope to the rear of the cabin and looked in through the window. It was difficult to see much inside, but it certainly appeared to be unoccupied.

We continued around the cabin to the front and huddled beneath the roof that jutted out above the entrance. I fumbled with the radio.

"Connor? A tree has come down behind the Ute," I told him, my fingers frozen where they gripped the handheld device.

"Damn." The transmission cut out for a minute, and then Connor said, "When they get to you, you'll have to leave it there and come back for it when the weather clears. Don't worry, it'll be fine. I have good news."

"What?" Unless someone was already waiting on the other side of that tree with their heater blasting and a thermos full of coffee waiting for us, I wasn't sure I cared.

"The police found Marcy."

My jaw dropped. "Could you repeat that?"

Summer leaned closer to the radio as if she, too, needed confirmation of what he'd said.

"We have Marcy." Connor's words came through loud and clear. "We found her abandoned behind the information center. She's on the way to Frannie right now, and Max is going to check her over."

I slumped against the door. "Thank God."

"Is the cabin unlocked?" Connor asked, moving on to more practical matters.

I looked at Summer, who shrugged. She disentangled herself from me and turned the handle. The door opened.

"Yes, it is," I confirmed.

"Good. Go inside. Someone will come to get you, but it won't be the police since Marcy has already been found. They're diverting all their resources to investigating the area where she was discovered."

"Thanks, Connor."

He signed out.

"Are you sure we should go in?" Summer asked.

I pushed the door open wider. "If we stay out here, we risk getting hypothermia. We need to get warm."

I walked inside, and to my surprise, the cabin didn't smell musty. A bench ran along two walls, with a table in the corner and a fireplace in the center of the space. A kitchen counter took up the third wall. A chill skated down my spine at the sight of several rows of cans and dehydrated meals arranged on top.

They weren't dusty. Someone had been here recently.

I rounded the corner and held up my hand to stop Summer. There, in front of a bunk bed, stood a crib with a familiar, blue plush bear inside.

57

———

ASHER

Summer gasped. "Is that...?"

"Yeah." I wrapped my arms around her, burying her face in my shoulder so she couldn't see the crib anymore. "It doesn't mean the kidnapper was here though."

Assuming there *was* a kidnapper. Connor hadn't said. But he had mentioned the police investigating the scene, which surely meant it had been an abduction. If she'd somehow miraculously gotten out of that highchair and wandered off without leaving a trace, they wouldn't bother collecting evidence.

Besides, if no one had taken her, then how would the bear have gotten here?

Her scoff was muffled by the napkins and my jacket. "Oh yeah?"

"It could be from anyone with a baby," I said, hoping to calm her. After the Ute's engine dying and the fallen trees blocking the road, the last thing she needed was another thing to worry about.

She drew back enough to look me in the eye. "People don't just bring babies to hunting cabins in the middle of winter. Besides, that's Marcy's bear. I've seen it before."

"She got it from Destiny Fibers. I'm sure other people have identical ones." I didn't address her previous comment because, honestly, I couldn't. Based on the disturbance outside, the food stores, and the presence of the bear and the crib, this probably *was* the kidnappers' hideout.

"They aren't here now," I continued. "We checked, remember? The tree on the road will stop anyone from driving up, so we should be able to see them coming if they return, but there's every chance they left town when Marcy was found."

She worried her lip between her teeth, clearly not finding any of this remotely comforting. "I hope you're right."

I went over to the bunk beds and pulled a fleece blanket off one. I had the nasty feeling the kidnapper had used it, but that didn't matter as much as caring for Summer did. I wrapped the blanket around her shoulders and guided her to the edge of the bunk. She looked small and frightened as she dabbed at her bloody nose. The flow seemed to have slowed.

I used the radio to contact Connor again.

"We found a crib in the cabin," I told him. "There's also enough food to supply someone for a couple of weeks if not longer, and a blue bear that looks a lot like Marcy's."

"Shit."

I hesitated. "I don't suppose they arrested anyone?"

I was guessing he'd have said as much earlier if they had, but it paid to be sure.

"No," Connor replied. "Marcy was found alone, left on the hood of a car around the back of the information center. Unfortunately, no one saw who dropped her off, but they must have known the center was being used to coordinate the search so someone would find her before she became ill."

"Damn." I was glad Marcy was fine, but it would have been easier if an arrest had been made.

"Be careful out there." Connor's tone was serious. "Is there anything you can use as a weapon?"

"I'll find something, and I'll let you know if anything changes."

"You do that."

I propped the radio up on the kitchen counter and did a quick sweep of the cabin. There were no guns, but there was a woodshed outside, so presumably there would be something that could be used to cut wood. That might make a good weapon.

I pulled the hood of my jacket back up.

"Where are you going?" Summer asked.

"Just to the woodshed."

She shuffled forward and tossed her wad of napkins into the basket by the fire. "But there's already wood by the fire."

"That's not what I need."

Her eyes widened as understanding dawned. She'd been listening to our conversation and must have realized where my mind had gone.

"Be careful," she said. "I'll keep an eye on you through the back window."

"Thanks."

I braced myself for the cold and slipped out through the door. The icy wind slapped at the bare skin of my face, and I had to lean forward with my full weight to get around the building to the shed. The trees nearby swayed dangerously, and I prayed that the clearing was big enough for none of them to damage the building if they fell.

A shrill whistling made my ears ache, and I gritted my

teeth. Another few steps, and I was at the shed. I didn't bother gathering any wood. There was enough inside to last for hours, and I didn't want to juggle any more weight than needed.

I peered through damp eyelashes until, finally, my vision focused on an axe leaning against the interior wall. I reached inside and took hold of the handle. The wood was cold and rough against my skin. There didn't seem to be a second axe, so I turned and dragged it back to the cabin, moving faster this time, the wind behind me.

Just outside the door, a broom rested against the exterior, having miraculously not blown away. I unscrewed the head of the broom and dropped it, then took the shaft inside with me. It wouldn't be as good a weapon as an axe, but it would at least provide some means of self-defense if needed.

I stumbled forward as the wind released its grip on me but managed not to trip over the broom handle or the axe. I held them up so Summer could see.

"Just in case," I said.

She nodded and didn't question me. I knelt and undid my shoelaces, then peeled off wet socks. My toes were freezing, but hopefully someone would be here soon to get us. I could cover myself with a blanket, or perhaps share one with Summer. Having bare feet had to be better than leaving them in wet socks.

Summer removed her shoes too, and once she was done, and we'd both shed our jackets, I sat beside her and held her close.

"I'm so sorry about this," I murmured against her hair.

"Why?" She angled her face toward me. "It isn't your fault."

"I think it is. Whoever did this, it was to get at me. That makes it my fault."

She sighed and rested her cheek on my shoulder. "Well then, all I have to say is that I'd rather be here with you than out there with someone else."

I chuckled and held her more tightly. She shifted around and burrowed her frozen toes into the gap between my waistband and the bottom of my shirt.

I hissed. "Evil."

She smirked, unrepentant. I pressed my palms against the tops of her feet, doing my best to warm them. Bit by bit, blood flow returned. When her toes were no longer icicles, she maneuvered us around so that my toes were against her belly. She rubbed them vigorously.

The radio made a staticky sound.

I frowned. "What do you think that was?"

It happened again.

"Ash? Summer?" It was Connor.

I removed my feet from Summer's belly and swung them to the floor, then crossed to the kitchen counter to answer. "Yeah?"

"We have a problem. The tree that trapped you in wasn't the only one to come down. The road out to you is fully blocked, and I'm not willing to send people out to attempt to clear the fallen trees in this weather."

I thought quickly. "How close can you get?"

"Not within a few kilometers."

My stomach sank. There was no way we could walk several kilometers in a snowstorm to meet them.

"Will you be okay there until the weather calms?" Connor asked.

I looked around. With the food, the fire, and the bedding, we could theoretically be stranded here for weeks before we ran into problems. Seeing out the storm would be fine. Even if Summer's expression said she wasn't thrilled by the development.

"We'll be okay," I said. "There's no point risking more trouble."

"Yeah." He sounded relieved. "I'll have my radio nearby if you need me for anything. Got it?"

"Actually, if someone could drop by Summer's place and make sure Cookie is fed and has water, I'd appreciate it."

"Sure thing."

I thanked him and put the radio down. Slowly, I turned to Summer. "Seems like we might be stuck here for the night."

She grimaced. "This really isn't how I thought the day would go when we woke up this morning."

"Me neither," I admitted. "I'd hoped for a whole lot more cuddling and sex."

She flashed her teeth, for which I was grateful even if the smile didn't reach her eyes. "Me too." She stood up and let the blanket slide off her shoulders, pooling on the mattress. "Why don't I light the fire while you find something to eat?"

"Sounds good." I appreciated her taking the lead with the fire. While I was by no means mentally scarred by what had happened to my house, I imagined I'd have a hard time actually setting a fire so soon after the experience.

She knelt in front of the fireplace and got to work. Meanwhile, I put aside a couple of cans of pumpkin soup and dug around beneath the counter, emerging victorious with a pan. Hopefully the fire would soon be hot enough to cook the soup. I opened a packet of crackers and a bag of processed cheese slices and prepared a few.

The scent of smoke made me stiffen. One by one, I forced my muscles to relax.

"Having any luck?" My tone wasn't as casual as I'd have liked.

Summer prodded a metal poker into the fireplace, her brows pinched with concentration. "It's starting to take off. I'll close the door in a few seconds."

When she did, I breathed a sigh of relief. Not that I thought she'd burn the cabin down, but the acrid smell brought back unpleasant memories and jitters danced beneath my skin.

I offered her a small stack of crackers and she accepted with a smile and bit one in half.

"These taste way better than they should," she said, her mouth full.

"I know. It's probably the adrenaline making us hungry. What should we do while we wait for the fire to heat up?"

She shrugged. "Nap?"

I glanced around, but honestly, there wasn't much else to do. "Sure. Why not?"

If our rescuers couldn't get here, then it stood to reason that the kidnapper couldn't either. We'd be safe enough.

We polished off the rest of the cheese and crackers I'd prepared and climbed into the bottom bunk. Together, we created a nest of blankets and snuggled up, wrapped around each other as the snowstorm raged outside.

Slowly, the fire began to warm the cabin. I intended to get up and cook the pumpkin soup for lunch, but instead, I dozed off.

A sudden noise woke me sometime later. I lurched upright and hit my head on the underside of the top bunk. Wincing, I looked around for whatever had caused the sound, and realized that someone was speaking through the radio.

I struggled loose of the blankets and stumbled over to the counter.

"I'm here," I said, snatching the radio up.

"Just wanted to let you know." Once again, it was Connor. "Keith went out on his ATV to see if he'd have any chance of getting to you, and he found another set of tire tracks in the snow. One that didn't come from either us or you. Someone else has tried to get to that cabin."

58

———

SUMMER

Something wasn't right. Forcing the last vestiges of sleep from my mind, I pushed myself upright and blinked until my eyes adjusted to the dim lighting in the cabin.

"What's wrong?" I asked Asher, who sat at the table, his shoulders rigid.

The scent of cooking pumpkin filled the room. He must have started heating the soup.

"Everything is fine," he replied a little too quickly. "I'm just watching the snow."

I rubbed the sleep from my eyes. "Has it slowed at all?"

"A little."

I got up and padded across the wooden floor to stand in front of the fireplace. "At least with the weather like this, we can be reasonably sure that no one will try to get out here."

"Yeah." But he frowned.

Okay, something was definitely wrong.

"Seriously, what's the matter?" I asked, holding my hands to the heat to warm them.

He shook his head, but almost didn't seem aware of doing it. "It's just been a hell of a day."

My heart ached for him. First, his niece had vanished—possibly because someone had a vendetta against either him or Frannie—and now we were stuck here. No wonder he didn't feel well. I only felt semi-decent because I'd had a nap. If he'd been stressed, he might not have slept at all.

I knelt and checked the fire, then added another piece of wood. Hopefully the snow would stop by morning. It must be late afternoon now, and I doubted we had any chance of getting home. We had enough wood in the cabin to see us through the night, but tomorrow, we'd have to venture out and collect more.

Asher stood and walked over to check the soup. He grabbed a spoon from the counter, dunked it into the pot, and licked soup from the back of it.

"Good enough," he said. I got out of the way, and he carried the pot to the counter and divided it between two bowls. "There's no bread to go with it."

"That's fine." I hadn't expected there to be. Whoever had brought food to the cabin had focused on non-perishables. Without a freezer, most bread wouldn't last for a week, let alone longer.

We ate together at the table. Neither of us said much. I was warm all the way through thanks to the fire, but the food was nonetheless soothing. There was nothing like sitting inside with a bowl of soup or a hot drink on a cold day. If not for the fact we were stranded here, inside a kidnapper's hideaway, I might even be enjoying myself.

When we finished, we used a little of the stored water to rinse off the plates but didn't wash them properly. It was best to conserve the water in case we needed to drink it.

Determined to take Asher's mind off Marcy and his family, I held his hand and led him to the bed. "Hold me?"

He smiled tenderly. "I'd love to."

We snuggled beneath the blankets. After a while, the warmth from the fire became too much, and I stripped off my shirt and pants. Asher did the same, and I noticed with a smirk that his eyes kept traveling to the exposed parts of my legs and torso.

I slid one of my calves between his, relishing the rasp of his hair against my smooth, sensitive skin. His breath caught, and when I tilted my head to look at him, his pupils had almost swallowed his irises.

Something hard pressed against my thigh, and my eyes widened. "You..."

He grimaced. "Not the time for it, I know, but you're so damn sexy."

I pursed my lips. "Why isn't it a good time? We're stuck here. Connor has already said that no one is coming until the weather clears. It's not like there's anything else to do."

"What if someone is out there?" he asked, his eyes flicking toward the window.

"Whoever has been here is hunkered down, staying safe and dry. I doubt they'll go anywhere until the weather clears."

One side of his mouth began to hitch up. "I don't have a condom."

I grinned. "I do."

I'd taken to carrying one in my purse after we'd decided we were officially together.

A smile spread across his face. "You're smart."

"I like to think so."

I kissed him, slow and deep. His big hand curved around the side of my face, and my insides fluttered excitedly. Even now, I wasn't over the novelty of having Asher Heaton touch me.

Wriggling my hips, I erased any space between us, and

pressed myself against his thigh, rocking gently as lust sizzled through me. Asher reached behind me and undid the clasp of my bra. I slid it down my arms and he tossed it aside. I lifted myself up on my elbow just to double check the bra hadn't landed in the fireplace.

"It's fine," he murmured, dropping kisses on my lips and cheeks.

I encircled his erection with my hand. It was hot, hard, and looked good enough to eat. I scooted down his body and sucked him into my mouth.

"Fuck, Summer." His hands threaded through my hair, but he didn't pull.

I teased his head with my tongue, then took him as deep as I could. He groaned as I swallowed around him. My jaw ached, but I licked along the underside of his cock as I drew back, and then sucked him down again, my cheeks hollowing. His grip tightened in my hair.

"No more, baby," he said. "Not unless you want me to come."

I smiled around him, satisfaction surging within me. I did want that, but I also wanted the release his dark tone promised. I slid back up until I was face to face with him. To my surprise, he gripped the back of my neck and plundered my mouth, twining his tongue with mine.

"I love tasting myself on you," he rasped.

A full-body shiver rolled through me. "I didn't know you were so possessive."

His eyes were almost black as he held my gaze. "Neither did I until you."

His arms wrapped around me, and he ground his cock against my clit. I rocked against him, and he groaned. He sucked one of his fingers into his mouth, his black gaze holding mine, and then he slipped his hand between us and used his finger to toy with me. He teased my clit, stroked down my center, and circled my entrance.

I pressed against his hand, and he cupped my sex and kissed me. I melted into the embrace, almost forgetting about his hand until he pushed his finger inside me and crooked it. My head fell back, and I gasped. His cock throbbed against my hip.

"Want you," I said.

"Not yet."

Another finger joined the first one, stretching me. He licked into my mouth, his eyes burning as he brought me to the edge with his touch.

He slid a third finger inside, and then withdrew them all, leaving me empty.

"Ash," I protested.

"I've got you."

I narrowed my eyes. "Faster."

He chuckled. My eyes narrowed further. If he could laugh, then he wasn't nearly gone enough.

He rolled the condom on, but as soon as he tried to crawl over me, I shuffled out from under him and pushed him down until he was on his back. I positioned his erection beneath me and lowered myself onto it, squeezing my eyes shut as he filled me.

"Oh, god." It was somehow too much and not enough at the same time.

I waited for my channel to adjust to the intrusion, and then rolled my hips. Asher grabbed me by the waist and held on. I lay over him, staying low enough not to bump my head, and rode him with sensual motions that created exquisite friction against my clit.

He pulsed inside me, and I beamed down at him, a burst of confidence arising from the desire plainly written across his face. His lips were parted, his breathing uneven, as he thrust up into me. I continued to move sinuously, tightening the delicious thread of pleasure until I cried out, my inner walls clenching around him as I fell apart.

Asher waited until the last spasm and then rolled me beneath him and pushed into me over and over again, his movements jerky. With a hoarse shout, he stiffened inside me and came.

He lowered himself onto me, careful enough not to squish me. I closed my eyes and basked in the sensations rioting through my body. There was physical satisfaction, yes, but also a bone deep sense of contentment, as if, despite everything, I was exactly where I was supposed to be.

I was vaguely aware of Asher removing the condom and pulling me into his arms, and then the world faded to black.

Until the smell of smoke woke me.

59

———

ASHER

A scream rent the air.

"Fire!"

What?

I fought off the remnants of a dream and raised my head, then blinked, barely able to make sense of what I saw. Smoke filled the cabin, and flames licked along one panel of the back wall. Had a spark found its way clear of the fireplace?

I glanced out the window. It was difficult to tell through the smoke, but the snow didn't seem to be falling as thickly as earlier. The place was silent except for the crackle of the fire, suggesting that the wind had died down.

"Take the blanket and get out," I said to Summer, who'd already clambered off the bed. "I'll try to smother the fire."

This was our only shelter, other than the Ute, and for all we knew, that could have been flattened. We couldn't afford to let the fire consume the cabin, and we might have a chance at stopping it since the flames were concentrated at the end wall.

"I'll help," she said, yanking her shirt over her head.

"No," I snapped, moving quickly now myself. "If I have to worry about you, it will distract me. I know more about fire management than you do."

She huffed but nodded.

I lurched toward the counter and grabbed the four liter bottle of water I'd opened to rinse the dishes earlier. It was awkwardly sized, but all the bottles were the same, so it would have to do.

I unscrewed the lid, carried the water to the burning wall, swung the bottle, and tossed a stream of water onto the flames. They flickered but didn't subside. I tried again and again, until the bottle was empty, but the fire hadn't retreated at all.

Damn.

Water wasn't going to fix this. I needed something else. Out of the corner of my eye, I saw Summer moving. She'd donned her shoes and was running toward the door, carrying her clothes bundled inside one of the blankets.

The blankets.

I rushed over and snatched up the other blankets we'd been using. I dragged it across the cabin and tossed it over the bench attached to the wall. The flames beneath the blanket whumped out. I lifted it again and tried to hit the wall with the broad side of the fabric, but it was difficult to do so on a vertical surface.

I inhaled a lungful of smoke, and coughed, the smoke burning the inside of my throat. Desperately, I looked around the cabin for something that might work. Surely, there was a fire extinguisher somewhere.

But no, this was an old hunting cabin, not one of the more modern huts managed by the government. There was no fire extinguisher, and nothing else that could be used in case of an emergency.

The flames jumped from the wall, catching onto a sachet of freeze dried potato on the counter. The sachet went up in a puff of smoke, and the fire raced across the surface of the counter, using the food packaging as fuel.

Fuck, fuck, fuck.

There was no way to get this fire under control. The best I could do was get to safety. Hopefully the Ute was still standing so we could shelter inside.

Doing my best to keep a clear head, I grabbed the radio and my discarded clothes. I didn't have time to put them all on, but I yanked on my jeans and jammed my feet into my wet shoes. The fabric was sodden and cold, but in the circumstances, that might not be a bad thing.

I sprinted to the exit and shoved the door open. I had to stop on the threshold for a second so my vision could adjust. It was no longer snowing, and the air was still. Because of that, I had a perfect view of Summer where she stood twenty yards away, facing me, clad in only her shirt, underwear, and shoes.

I also had a perfect view of the man holding a gun to her temple.

60

———

SUMMER

WITH THE COLD METAL OF THE GUN PRESSED TO THE SIDE OF my head, I could hardly remember how to breathe. A chill had permeated my body, starting at that tiny point of pressure and radiating outward. Even though it was cold outside, the coolness inside had nothing to do with that.

It was all fear.

The guy had grabbed me as soon as I ran out of the cabin. I hadn't had a chance to see much about him other than the fact he was older than me and had dark hair. Beyond that, he could be anyone.

I drew in a shaky breath, and the chemical scent of gasoline burned my nose hairs. I struggled to remain still as the horrifying realization set in that he'd most likely caused the fire by dousing the end wall with gas and lighting it up. The same way Asher's front porch had been soaked with accelerant and set alight.

A fuzzy, crackling sound came from Asher, or perhaps I was imagining it. Spots danced in front of my eyes, and the pounding of blood in my head was as loud as the ragged breathing of the man behind me.

His free hand—the one not holding the gun—was wrapped around my arm. I was desperate to yank the limb away from him and run for cover, but I couldn't see that ending well.

His grip firmed, and my gut clenched with disgust. I wanted to wash myself until I forgot that he'd ever touched me. Despite the fact he hadn't groped me, I felt violated. He was threatening my life while I was nearly naked. That added insult to injury.

I met Asher's eyes. He looked as scared as me, but there was something other than fear in those brown depths too.

Recognition.

Whoever the man behind me was, Asher knew him.

"What are you doing, Robert?" Asher asked.

The crackling sound happened again, but this time, a few seconds of someone talking burst through. The only word I could make out was "smoke". The noise must be coming from the radio clasped in Asher's hand.

"What I have to." The man—Robert's—voice trembled.

In fact, every part of him seemed to vibrate with barely leashed tension. From my position, I couldn't tell if he was angry, scared, or something else.

"You don't have to do anything," Asher said, oddly calm considering the burning building only a few yards from his back. "Just let her go. You don't have any problem with her. Your problem is with me."

But Robert's grip on the gun didn't waver.

"You..." He broke off, sucked in a breath and started again. "You didn't even try to save Susan. Because of you, I had to live through my worst nightmare. I want you to feel the same pain that I did."

He jammed the gun harder against my temple.

"I want you to be just as scared as I was, trapped in the car, not able to help her. And then when help did arrive— when *you* arrived—you didn't even use the defibrillator on her. You didn't do CPR. You just let her die."

My chest strained, and I forced myself to inhale slowly and evenly. It wouldn't do Asher any good if I fainted. But the pieces of this puzzle were beginning to fit together, and even though my heart ached for what Robert had gone through, fury also burned through my veins because he was wrong to blame Asher.

"I didn't let her die," Asher said levelly. "She was already dead."

"You should have tried!"

I flinched, the shout way too loud this close to my ears.

"People can be brought back," Robert insisted.

Asher shook his head. "Not when they've lost that much blood, or when their brain has been without oxygen for that long."

"You didn't try," Robert repeated, increasingly agitated.

"We had to prioritize. Your wife was gone. You weren't."

"If you'd asked me to choose between us, I'd have chosen her!" He sounded bereft. I couldn't help feeling sorry for him.

"It wouldn't have mattered. You'd already lost her. If we'd focused on her, we might have lost you too."

Robert didn't reply.

"So, why have you been doing all of this?" Asher asked, one of his hands messing with the radio. Robert hadn't noticed yet, and I hoped he wouldn't, or we might be in even more trouble. "To punish me for not saving her? To get revenge?"

Robert sighed. "At first, I just wanted to scare you. That's why I drugged you and poisoned your cat. But it wasn't enough. Why should you get to have people you love when I don't? It isn't fair."

"You wanted to make me feel the same way you did." It wasn't a question.

"Yes." His voice was firm, and some of the tension left him.

My throat tightened. Surely, this wasn't good. If he was calm, didn't that mean he'd come to some kind of decision?

"Is that why you targeted Frannie?" Asher asked. "And why you took Marcy?"

"Yes." Metal knocked against my head, and I almost jolted, not expecting it, but managed to keep myself under control. Robert must have moved his hand. "I couldn't do anything with the baby though. She's innocent in all of this. But your girlfriend is another matter. She knows what you are and chooses to be with you anyway."

I shifted from one foot to the other, beginning to feel the chill of our surroundings, as well as the bone-deep coldness inside me.

I didn't know what to do. Should I drop to the ground and hope Asher could tackle Robert before he got off a shot? Or would it be best for me to stay still?

"Summer is a veterinarian." Asher was still fidgeting with the radio. "She helps animals. She has five brothers, a niece and nephew, and parents who love her. Let her go."

I met Asher's eyes, hoping to read in them what he wanted me to do, but all I saw there was the same terror that was freezing me in place.

"She should have better taste in men," Robert growled. He shifted his stance, pushing the gun against my temple so forcefully that I had to kink my neck to the side. "But I'm a more reasonable person than you, so I'm going to give you the choice you didn't give me. You can save yourself—or save her. Either way, one of you isn't leaving here."

My chest tightened so much that it was difficult to drag enough oxygen into my lungs. If I were the heroine in one of Grace's books, this is the moment when I'd experience a flash of brilliance and somehow take Robert down.

But this was real life, and I had no idea how to take down a grown man who was both taller and heavier than me. Perhaps I should elbow him in the ribs or stomp on his foot. I had to do something. I couldn't just stand here.

"I choose Summer," Asher said, no hesitation. "Hurt me, not her. She doesn't deserve this."

"No," I mouthed at him.

"I'm sorry for getting you into this." He smiled sadly. "I love you."

Robert scoffed, and suddenly the gun was no longer aimed at me, but at Asher. "Why should you get to choose to save your girlfriend when I didn't get to choose to save my wife? You made the choice for me, and you chose wrong."

Oh, shit.

So...what? He was going to kill both of us?

I wasn't prepared to wait around and find out. I drove my elbow backward, feeling it hit something soft. When Robert gasped and curled forward, I shoved his arm, driving the gun away from Asher.

He didn't drop the weapon though.

I grabbed for it, fear pulsing through my veins with each hammer of my heart. If he hadn't intended to shoot us, he sure as hell would now. He wound his leg around mine and tried to trip me. I grabbed onto his shoulders and dragged him down.

We struggled for the gun. He was bigger and stronger, but all I had to do was delay enough for Asher to intervene.

An ear-piercing crack tore between us as the gun fired.

61

———

ASHER

MY WORLD SHATTERED AS I WATCHED SUMMER GO SLACK.

The snap of the gunshot echoed through my mind on repeat.

Had she been shot because of me?

Was she going to die because of me?

My throat constricted. No. It couldn't be allowed. I *wouldn't* allow it.

Summer and I were meant to live a long and beautiful life together, and I wouldn't let this asshole take that from us.

I launched myself at Robert, who was trying to get Summer's limp body off him, and before he had time to respond, I cracked him over the head with the handheld radio. He shouted, and his grip on the gun loosened. I reached for it, but then he rallied and whipped the barrel across my face.

I stumbled backward, but caught myself, ready to attack

again. Only to find myself face-to-face with the muzzle of the gun.

"Don't move," Robert panted, setting his feet apart to adopt a more stable stance. A trickle of blood ran down the side of his face, but he didn't seem concerned. If anything, I'd call the twist of his lips...satisfied. "Now you'll know how it feels to lose someone you love."

I looked down at Summer. She'd slumped on her back, her mossy green eyes barely visible between her eyelashes as she whimpered. Her shirt was dark, but despite that, I could tell that the fabric covering her lower chest and abdomen was soaked with blood. She was bleeding heavily, and who knew what internal damage there might be?

She needed medical help. Urgently.

My fingers twitched. I wanted nothing more than to run to her, drop to my knees at her side and get to work, but I couldn't. Not while he held the gun on me. I couldn't save her if I got myself shot.

"Don't do this," I pleaded. "Look at her. She's in pain. She hasn't done anything to you, and if we don't get her help right now, she might die."

Robert hesitated, but he didn't glance down at Summer. Damn.

"Are you really okay with murdering an innocent woman?" I asked, wondering how the hell to get through to him. I just had to hope that Connor had heard enough through the radio earlier to know how dire the situation was. I could really do with a miracle.

"She's not innocent. She's with you, which makes her complicit."

There was absolutely no reasoning with this man.

Movement in the forest behind Robert caught my attention, but I forced myself not to stare and give it away.

Perhaps if someone was coming, I'd be better off distracting Robert than trying to reason with him.

"You're angry at the wrong person," I said loudly, hoping to cover any noise behind him. Although the hiss and roar of the fire helped with that too. "Be angry at whoever was driving and lost control on the black ice. Or be angry at the universe for putting it there."

If I remembered right, he'd been the one driving, so it was possible he'd been the one to spin out on the black ice. Maybe, deep down, he blamed himself, but he couldn't live with that, so he'd had to find someone else to hold responsible.

Robert stared at me without speaking. So many emotions flickered across his face that I couldn't get a read on him.

Connor appeared from the trees, creeping up behind Robert like a specter from the mist. My stomach lurched. He must have driven to the area and walked over, since I hadn't heard any vehicles. He was carrying something. I didn't dare look close enough to determine what it was, but, fuck, I hoped it could be used as a weapon.

"It's not my fault your wife died," I said loudly, and for the first time, I fully believed it, and any guilt I'd been harboring dissipated. Yes, it was tragic that he'd lost her, but coming after me wasn't the answer. "Would she want this?"

He scowled, and his finger twitched on the trigger. I flinched, but the gun didn't fire.

"Don't pretend you care what Susan would want," he growled.

Connor was only a few yards away now. He raised the object he carried over his head. From here, I could tell it was a branch, although he'd stripped off any leaves and twigs. Perhaps he'd taken it from one of the fallen trees he'd come across on the way.

"I do care," I assured Robert. "Just because I couldn't save her, that doesn't mean I don't know she had value."

His jaw clenched. "Shut up."

"I think—" I cut off when he looked through the scope and adjusted his aim. At the same time, Connor swung.

I lashed out and knocked the muzzle of the gun, so it wasn't aiming straight at me. Connor struck the side of Robert's head with the branch. His knees buckled, his eyes widened, and his finger convulsed against the trigger.

Pain scorched up my arm as he fired, the bullet grazing my flesh and embedding in the building behind me.

I cursed.

Robert crumpled.

Connor knocked the gun from Robert's hands, yanked them behind his back, and pinned him in place. I rushed to Summer's side. She didn't look good. Her skin was pale, her eyes had closed, and her breathing was shallow.

Part of me wanted to panic, but I shoved it into a box in the back of my mind. She didn't need a scared boyfriend. She needed a paramedic.

I could do this.

I could save her.

If I failed this time, I might as well lie down in the snow alongside her.

62

———

ASHER

I peeled Summer's shirt back to expose the bloody mess of her abdomen. The bullet had hit just below her ribs, near the center but slightly to the left. I wanted to check whether it had gone all the way through but was wary of moving her too much.

I considered removing her shirt completely, but she was lying on the ground and would be cold enough without me taking away the only barrier between her and the snow. I glanced around, my mind working furiously, then remembered the blanket she'd carried out.

I raced over to her discarded things and yanked the blanket from under her clothes, then I retrieved her pants and brought both items back to her. Using the pants as padding, I compressed the wound. Hopefully the low temperatures would slow the bleeding, and between that and whatever I could do, I just had to pray she'd survive.

A murmur of voices became audible in the distance. I glanced up, maintaining pressure on the wound. A group of people emerged from the forest. Nate was in the lead, rushing toward us. Several officers accompanied him.

"She's injured," I called to them. "Gunshot wound to the abdomen. Connor is restraining the shooter. She's bleeding heavily. I need a first aid kit and transportation to a hospital. ASAP."

Nate paled, his gaze catching on Summer for a moment, but then, like me, he summoned a mask of professionalism and spoke to the officer nearest to him. The officer turned and ran back the way they'd come.

Another of the officers called for an ambulance and the fire department—although I had my doubts the fire engine would be able to get anywhere near here.

Mehrtens hurried to join Connor, a pair of handcuffs ready to go. Robert didn't struggle as she cuffed him and told him his rights. He just knelt dejectedly, his head low, his shoulders slumped.

"How is she?" Nate asked, hovering beside me. "What can I do?"

I jerked my head toward the wadded up pants. "Maintain compression. I'm going to shift her onto the blanket, so she isn't lying directly on the snow. In this state, it would be easy for her to succumb to hypothermia."

He lowered himself to his knees and took over from me the second I let go of the pants. "Is anyone else here? Any other perps?"

"Not that I know of." I positioned the blanket beside Summer, along the length of her body. At that moment, Officer Patton arrived, clutching a first aid kit and breathing heavily. He must have been the one Nate sent back earlier.

"Put the kit there." I gestured to the side. "Help me lift her. We need to be careful to move her as little as possible."

Patton nodded, his expression grim. He wasn't a trained paramedic, and I'd prefer to have Maia here to help, but we had to make do. I took Summer's upper half and Patton grabbed her legs.

"On the count of three," I said, sliding my hands beneath her to stabilize her. "One, two, three."

Together, we hefted her sideways and onto the blanket, putting her down as gently as we could. Nate shifted around, keeping firm pressure on the gunshot wound. I opened the first aid kit and searched for anything that might be useful. I continued to work, the movements brisk, almost mechanical, as I fought to keep myself calm.

"Fuck." Connor's voice. "She's unconscious?"

"Seems to be." I couldn't let myself dwell on it. "How are you all here?"

"I came back this morning to see whether we'd be able to get through to you," Connor said, watching as I treated his baby sister the best I could. "When I reached the tree that had blocked you in, I noticed it had been cut."

I frowned, momentarily distracted. "Cut?"

"It didn't fall without some help," he explained. "My guess is, your buddy here didn't want you to leave, so he made sure you wouldn't be able to get away quickly. It seemed suspicious, so I radioed Nate for backup, but before he arrived, I noticed the smoke. I was worried because you weren't answering the radio, so I came over on foot."

"Thank you." I meant it wholeheartedly. "Without you, we might both be dead."

Connor glanced up, ignoring my gratitude. But then, emotion always made him uncomfortable. "The paramedics are here. Are you ready to transfer her onto a stretcher?"

Part of me didn't want to leave her care in anyone else's hands, but she needed more than I could give her.

"We've got her," Georgie, one of the paramedics, said as they set down a stretcher beside her. She directed us to each take a corner of the blanket and, with her guidance, we lifted Summer on. Georgie gripped one end, and her partner grabbed the other. They lifted the stretcher and began to walk back toward the road.

I fell into step beside them. "Where will you take her? I want to come."

"An emergency helicopter will be at the medical center shortly," Georgie said. "She'll be flown to Christchurch from there."

Then that's where I'd go too.

"Have you been hurt?" Georgie asked, scanning me, no doubt noticing the blood that streaked my arms and torso.

"A little graze." I held out my forearm to show her.

"That will need to be cleaned and bandaged."

"I know. I can do it myself, as long as I have the supplies." The wound had bled a lot, but it was hardly more than a narrow cut.

"You can do it in the ambulance. That way you're not getting in the way during the flight."

"Thanks." I'd hoped they wouldn't argue against letting me come with them. It was frowned upon to allow loved ones to ride along in case they tried to interfere, but they must trust me not to do that.

When we reached the ambulance, they loaded Summer into the back, and I sat in the passenger seat while Georgie passed me a few supplies and drove us to the medical center. She had to go slower than I'd have liked because of the snow on the road and the fallen trees blocking parts of it.

People must have already been out, getting started clearing the roads because a couple of trees had been sawn into pieces and moved aside, and grit and salt had been laid down to reduce the number of accidents.

I cleaned out my wound, layered gauze over it and taped a bandage on top. Only as we pulled into Destiny Falls did it occur to me that I wasn't wearing a shirt. Biting the inside of my cheek, I reminded myself that my naked torso was nothing any paramedic hadn't seen before.

Georgie pulled into the medical center and drove around the side of the building to the helicopter pad out the back. The helicopter was already there, as was Max, who was leaning inside to speak to the pilot.

I jumped out and strode over to them.

Max turned toward me immediately. "How bad is it?"

"GSW to the gut," I told him. "Possibly a through-and-through, but I'm not certain. She's lost a lot of blood."

He nodded, his brows furrowed, and thrust a bag into my arms. "This has a change of clothes for both of you, as well as a few spare toiletries I had on hand."

I cocked my head. "You're coming with us, right?"

"Yes, but I'll be busy. I need you to take this and update the family. My phone is in the front pocket."

"Got it." Of course, Summer's parents must know by now. Three of their sons were already involved. Surely one of them had called Heather and Eugene. They'd be frantic. I was surprised they weren't here, to be honest.

I hoisted myself into the helicopter and slunk away to the back, where I donned a set of headphones. Georgie and Max loaded Summer in, and then Max jumped in with us and shut the door. The pilot spoke through the headset and performed a few last-minute checks. Less than a minute later, we rose into the air above Destiny Falls.

Max's phone vibrated as we were circling around Destiny Peak. I unzipped the front pocket and pulled it out. Liam was calling. I couldn't answer, but I sent him a quick message to let him know I had the phone.

Liam: *We'll be close behind. Kennedy chartered a helicopter to Christchurch.*

I almost laughed. At this point, Kennedy might as well

buy a helicopter with how much trouble the Braddocks managed to get themselves into.

Asher: *I'll keep you updated.*

The flight was over quickly. I found myself ushered into a hospital waiting room while she was whisked away to surgery. Max went with her to update the surgeon on her condition. I slumped onto a chair beside a vending machine and watched the minutes tick by on the clock on the wall.

The short time it took Max to return seemed to last forever.

"News?" I asked, bolting upright when he trudged wearily into the room.

"Prognosis is good, but gut shots are complicated. We won't know for sure until she's out."

I groaned and dragged my hand down my face. "How long will that be?"

He grimaced. "Anywhere up to two hours would be my guess."

63

SUMMER

I floated in and out of consciousness, dreams catching me and tugging me under, only for a dull throb to bring me back to the present. Sometimes I could hear people around me, but no matter how hard I tried, I couldn't open my eyes.

Finally, the dreams faded, and I woke up in a warm bed. I blinked and started to sit up, but pain shot through my midsection, and I returned my head to the pillow.

Where was I?

The last I could recall, I was lying on the ground, in the snow, while Asher fought Robert for his gun.

Asher.

Was he all right?

He'd said he loved me. Surely, the universe wouldn't be cruel enough to steal him away from me now.

"Easy, Summer."

I smiled. Even as confused as I was, I recognized that voice. "You're okay."

I turned my head. Asher sat on a chair beside the bed.

Some kind of medical equipment was set up beside him, but he didn't seem injured.

"I'm fine," he said, taking my hand and clasping it gently. "But don't ever do that to me again. I was so scared I was going to lose you."

A laugh burst from me, and I winced. "How is this my fault?"

He grimaced. "You're right. I'm so sorry I've caused you so many problems. If I'd just stayed away from you, you'd be safe at home right now."

I tried to squeeze his hand, but I wasn't sure whether it worked or not. "It's not your fault either. That guy, whoever he was, had gone over the edge. No one else can be blamed for what he did. Besides, if you'd stayed away from me, I'd be miserable. We chose each other. No having second thoughts now."

"I'm not." He stroked the back of my hand. "I promise. I'll always want you. I just hate seeing you hurt."

No doubt he worried my family would blame him too.

"Good." I closed my eyes, my entire body weary just from speaking a few sentences, but then forced them open again. "What happened after...?"

Asher pursed his lips and looked as if he was debating how much to tell me.

"I can handle it," I said.

He looked doubtful but nodded. "I wasn't able to take the gun from him. He was holding me at gunpoint when Connor snuck up behind him and bashed him over the head with a tree branch."

I frowned. "Why was Connor there?"

His throat bobbled. "He was worried because he'd seen evidence that someone else had tried to get to the cabin, so he came out as early as he could to check on us. He discovered that the tree that fell across the road had been cut."

My lips parted. Did that mean Robert had been hiding among the trees while we'd checked the cabin? I'd thought I'd heard something, but I'd believed Asher's suggestion that it was an animal. After all, who would linger in the forest during a storm?

But if he'd heard or seen us coming, or somehow known we'd be there, it made sense that he'd have hidden. Or perhaps he'd been coming back from dropping Marcy off behind the information center.

"As soon as Connor realized we'd been trapped there intentionally, he called for help. That's when he noticed the smoke. He walked toward the cabin, and when I didn't respond to his attempts to contact me on the radio, he grabbed a branch to use as a weapon, in case we were in danger." He shook his head. "We were lucky he was there."

"Yeah..." I shuddered to think what might have happened if Connor hadn't been concerned. Asher and I could have ended up both shot and bleeding out together in the snow. "The man... He was arrested?"

Asher nodded. "He's in custody now for attempted murder, along with a list of other things. I'm not sure what will happen to him. He's grieving and he had injuries of his own from the crash that killed his wife. It's possible he suffered a head trauma that triggered him to behave so erratically. All I can tell you is that he's locked up and won't be coming after us again."

"Thank God." I closed my eyes again.

"I love you," Asher murmured. "I don't know if you remember me saying that, but I do, and I want you to know it."

My eyelashes fluttered open, and I gazed over at his gorgeous face, with those dark eyes I'd always loved to feel watching me.

"I love you too," I whispered. "Part of me always has."

He cleared his throat. Emotion gleamed in his eyes. "Robert wanted to scare me, and he succeeded. Losing you would have broken me. I can't imagine my life without you."

I angled myself toward him, cursing the wound that made it impossible for me to roll over. "Luckily, you don't have to, because you saved me."

One corner of his mouth quirked up. "We saved each other. If you hadn't gone for that gun, things might have turned out differently."

"Ah, you're awake."

I glanced toward the doorway, where a man stood in blue scrubs. He was neatly shaven and a little plump.

"Have you had a drink?" he asked.

"Not yet." I was a little thirsty though.

"Hmm. I'll have one of the nurses bring you a glass of water. In the meantime, I just wanted to let you know that the surgery was successful. You should heal completely, other than a bit of scarring."

"Thank you." For some reason, it hadn't even occurred to me to worry that my body might no longer work as it was supposed to, but I was grateful for the confirmation anyway. Suddenly, it struck me that Asher had never said whether he'd been hurt during the struggle. "And Asher?"

The doctor looked confused.

"All I have is a scrape on my forearm," Asher assured me. "It will heal."

"Good."

The doctor left and less than a minute later, a nurse entered with a glass of water. She helped me drink, then passed Asher the glass to hold onto.

"Would you like me to get your family?" she asked.

My eyes widened. "They're here?"

Asher chuckled. "Of course they are. What did you expect?"

"Then yes, please," I told the nurse.

She promised to send them in shortly.

"Brace yourself," Asher warned. "They've been worried sick, and you know how the Braddocks can be en masse."

I grinned. "Can't wait."

I didn't have to.

Toby stormed into the room, his expression frantic, and nudged Asher aside so he could stand beside me.

"This is not okay," he grumbled. "I'm the reckless twin. You're supposed to be responsible and...and...safe."

I almost laughed. Only the recollection of how much it had hurt last time stopped me. "Don't like the tables being turned?"

"Not even a little bit."

I tapped my cheek, and he rolled his eyes but dropped a kiss on it.

The rest of my family was close behind. They gathered around me, and this time, nothing I could do would stop the tears streaming down my cheeks as they fussed over me. I loved this crazy bunch. They were everything to me. And right now, they didn't hesitate to let me know that I meant everything to them too.

My heart was full.

"You two need to be more careful," Liam said gruffly. "Asher—"

"Hey." I cut him off, not willing to take any shit in my current mood. "No more being angry at Asher, okay? I know you guys had this idea of me being with a particular type of man—and the less said about that, the better—but Asher was asked to choose between saving himself and saving me, and he chose me. So, I don't care if you think you know better. No one else could possibly love me more than he does."

The corner of Liam's mouth twitched, and he held his

hands up defensively. "All I was going to say is that you're two of my favorite people, and I expect you to take better care of each other, so we don't have to do this again."

I deflated. "Oh."

Asher laughed, his whole face lighting up. "I love you, Summer."

I smiled at him. "I love you too."

Liam wrapped his arm around Kennedy, who'd appeared at his side. "I had some concerns, but it seems like I was wrong about them. I'm happy for you."

"Thank you." Something settled inside me at his acceptance of our relationship. His disapproval wouldn't have prevented me from being with the man I loved, but I know the discord between them bothered Asher. Hopefully now, they could move on.

"You might be brothers one day," I teased. I turned to Kennedy. "Thank you for flying everyone here."

"Anything for you," she replied, her lips pressed together tightly as if she might cry too. "But only once, all right? I can't keep visiting my best friends in hospitals after they've been shot or stabbed."

I rested my hand on hers. "I'll do my best."

She sniffed. "You'd better. Destiny Falls is supposed to be peaceful."

I snorted. Yeah. So much for that.

64

SUMMER

"So, tell me everything," I said to Grace, who was perched on the side of my bed back home. The overhead light illuminated the room, casting out the shadows. The sun had set within the last hour, and I was grateful she'd dropped by to visit. I didn't feel like being alone in the dark.

Grace tucked her brunette hair behind her ear. "Nate interviewed Robert Warner's family and friends. According to them, he wasn't himself after he was released from the hospital. He became obsessed with Asher because he blamed him for his wife's death."

"But why Asher?" I asked. That had been bothering me, but I hadn't wanted to raise it with him. He was already struggling to move past it without me chasing him around with unanswered questions. "Maia was there too."

Grace shrugged. "I think Asher was the first to approach the Warners' vehicle and speak to Robert, so in his mind, everything that happened after that was Asher's responsibility."

I shook my head. It was nonsensical, but then, everything Robert had done after getting out of the hospital was illogical, so perhaps that just spoke to the frame of mind he'd been in—either that, or an underlying brain trauma.

"He followed Asher around, just to distract himself at first, but then it became more than that."

I nodded, recalling the movement in the shadows I'd thought I'd seen outside Drunken Destiny what felt like a lifetime ago. Perhaps that had been Robert, watching Asher even then.

"So, Robert poisoned Cookie?" I asked.

"Yes. Apparently, that was just a crime of opportunity. He saw the house was empty and he happened to have rat bait in his garden shed. He found the spare key and slipped some of it into her food."

"Who would hurt a sweet animal?" I was disgusted. I'd suspected foul play, but to have it confirmed made me nauseous.

Grace made a sound of disdain. "It doesn't end there. He followed you when the two of you went mountain biking and laid a branch over the track. When he heard you coming, he fired a shot to surprise you, so you wouldn't see the branch until it was too late. Of course, he intended Asher to be the one who hit it, not you."

"Not that that stopped him from coming after me again," I muttered.

Grace grimaced. "Apparently, that's actually what gave him the idea."

I frowned. "How do you mean?"

She shifted position, and I winced as the mattress moved beneath me.

She stopped instantly. "Sorry."

I waved my hand, not wanting her to stop telling her story. "I'm fine."

Her mouth turned downward. "Are you sure?"

"Yeah. I want to hear it all."

"Fair enough." She drew in a deep breath. "Robert saw how worried Asher was about you, and started thinking how it would be proper justice if he had to suffer through a loss like Robert himself had, rather than just being hurt directly."

"But breaking Asher's window was pretty targeted at him," I argued.

She arched an eyebrow. "That seems like a petty scare tactic to me. I don't know, but I'd say it was a spur of the moment thing. The fire was more purposeful, and he set that when Asher wasn't home."

"He was at brunch at Mum and Dad's place," I murmured, suddenly recalling the vehicle that had shot away as we'd left their house that morning.

"They did confirm the fingerprint on the rock was his," Grace said, "and he confessed to setting the fire."

My jaw dropped. "Wait. He's admitted to all of this?"

"Apparently, he's quite a talker once he gets started. Nate thinks he wants to brag, but I believe, deep down, the guilt weighs on him and he sees sharing his story with the police as a way to lessen the load."

"Perhaps." Robert certainly hadn't seemed like a man with much of a conscience when he'd held a gun to my temple, but he had let Marcy go unharmed, so maybe Grace was onto something. Perhaps he simply wasn't mentally healthy when he'd done those awful things, and now, reality was beginning to catch up with him.

"That evening you went to dinner at the resort, he meant to run you down, not Frannie, but there were too many people in the way, and she was the one closest to the road, so she was the easiest target."

"Poor Frannie." She'd been by to visit this morning, and

she'd clearly still been shaken. She'd clung to Marcy the entire time they were here.

"I can't even imagine how scared she must have been." Grace's tone was strained. "If someone kidnapped Finn, I'd lose my mind."

"Speaking of, where is he?" I asked, only now realizing she hadn't arrived with him.

"With Heather. I'll pick him up when I leave here."

"You'll have to bring him by later this week so I can have baby cuddles with my nephew." There was something about holding babies that just made the world seem okay.

"I will." She smiled. "Is there anything else you want to know?"

"No, thanks." I'd pieced together most of it. Robert had taken Marcy to the cabin, where he hadn't thought anyone would look for them, but he'd had regrets and dropped her off where he knew she'd be found. "I'm tired of depressing stuff. What's been going on with you?"

Grace laughed. "Nothing that can rival getting trapped in a cabin and shot."

I rolled my eyes. "You've been stabbed, Grace. You have plenty of your own exciting stories."

She inclined her head in acknowledgement. "I've been talking with Jewel and Rocky's descendant, Corie. She's confirmed a few things for me, corrected a mistake I made, and she even shared a family legend. Want to know what it was?"

A smile slowly spread across my face. This sounded like more fun than dwelling on Robert Warner. "Uh...of course!"

Grace leaned closer. "The family believes that Pearl was left an inheritance by her father."

I scrunched my nose. "But I thought he practically disowned her after she ran away with Rocky?"

"The legend says he came to regret the estrangement,

and he tried to make contact but never found her, so he left her a sizable inheritance in his will. But—and here's the intriguing part—she never claimed the inheritance. Her family believes it's hidden somewhere in Destiny Falls."

"That's fascinating." I struggled to sit upright, and Grace helped me. "Do you think it's true?" Could there be a secret treasure right here in our little town?

"I doubt it." She fluffed my pillows. "It's an interesting story, though."

The latch on the front door clicked, and I flinched instinctively, my heart leaping. I inhaled slowly and released my breath as I mentally counted to six. I'd been jumpy since I'd woken in the hospital, but hopefully, I'd stop jumping at every noise soon.

"Summer?" Asher called.

"In the bedroom!" I didn't know why he'd expect me to be anywhere else. He'd asked me not to leave the bed while he delivered a box of "thank you" baked goods to the fire and police stations, and I'd promised I wouldn't.

He strode in, wearing a peculiar expression.

"What is it?" I asked.

His eyebrows knitted together. "I just had the strangest conversation with Lionel Lowry."

My gut tightened. "Oh?"

If that grumpy old man had been harassing Asher at a time like this, I'd—

"He apologized."

My mouth fell open. "Excuse me?"

He looked as bewildered as I felt. "He asked after you. Told me you were a good girl and that what happened to you wasn't right. He said it had forced him to re-evaluate a few things. He's still angry about what happened but he's going to try to stop taking it out on me."

"Huh." I'd never expected the old farmer to have it in

him to see the error of his ways. "Well, that's good, right?"

"It is." But Asher seemed uncertain.

"You delivered the treats without any problems?" I prompted, in case he needed something to take his mind off Lionel Lowry.

He nodded distractedly. "I also saw Ashley having a coffee with one of the schoolteachers. They looked pretty cozy."

"Hopefully, she won't bother you anymore." If she did, we'd have to have serious words. I understood being hung up on Asher, but that didn't excuse poor behavior.

"Yeah." He visibly pulled himself together and sent Grace a strained smile. "Thanks so much for visiting. Sorry, my head is a bit of a mess at the moment."

"No problem at all." She stood and straightened her designer sweater. "It was lovely to see you both. I'd better go pick up Finn."

She bent to hug me, then touched Asher's arm on the way out of the bedroom. He took her place on the bed, and for a long moment, he and I just looked at each other.

For some reason, I giggled. He barked out a laugh, then covered his mouth. I giggled again. A stream of laughter burst from him, and he curled over, his shoulders shaking.

"Why are we laughing?" I gasped, unable to stop.

"I have no idea." Tears leaked from the corners of his eyes. "Maybe all the craziness has finally gotten to us."

I pressed my lips together and tried to gather myself. Asher did the same, but his forced seriousness only made me start again.

When we finally caught our breath, Asher took my hand and kissed the back of it.

"I love you," he said. "And I'd really, really like to date you. Without any fires, or gunshots, or poisoning, or excitement. Just you, me, and a nice dinner. What do you think?"

Warmth settled deep within me. "I'd love nothing more."

EPILOGUE — FIVE WEEKS LATER

ASHER

I carried the platter of pizza into the living room, breathing in the mouthwatering aroma of tomato and spices. We'd cooked this pizza ourselves, rather than using a frozen pre-packaged version, and I was proud of our efforts. I glanced up and came to an abrupt stop.

Summer sat on the sofa holding out a narrow, rectangular box with a bow tied around it.

"What's this?" I asked, placing the pizza platter on the coffee table.

She passed me the box without answering. It was an exercise watch. Taped to the front in block letters was a note that said:

CHECK THE SPARE ROOM.

A frisson of excitement ran through me, followed quickly by nerves. What the hell was going on?

I went to the spare room. The door was shut. Odd. The doors in Summer's cottage were rarely shut. I opened it and my jaw dropped.

384

"That's a..."

"Is it okay?" she asked anxiously. "I visited the shop in Queenstown and told them I wanted the best they had."

"It's perfect," I breathed, staring at the top-of-the-line indoor exercise bicycle. I turned toward her. "But what's the occasion?"

She nibbled on her lower lip. "I was hoping you might want to move in together, and considering yours was damaged during the fire, it seemed like a good incentive to have one here."

I laughed, drew her into my arms, and kissed her. When I pulled back, I nuzzled her nose.

"I don't need any incentive other than you. I've been thinking about how much I'd like to keep living with you." I'd been staying with her while my house was repaired. "I'm worried it might be too soon though. Doctor Friedman warned me against making any major life decisions right now."

I'd started seeing the therapist the week after Summer was shot. God knew I'd put it off long enough. I was beginning to realize that exercise only cured so much. I couldn't keep ignoring my mental health and hoping everything would work out.

Summer leaned against me, her curves molding to my body. "If it's too soon, we can wait. There's no hurry."

I kissed the end of her nose and paused to consider the possibility. Did it feel too soon? No, not really, considering we'd been sharing her cottage for weeks already.

She rested her cheek against my chest and snuggled closer. "Why don't you talk it over with Dr. Friedman, and if you decide you're ready, we can find a new place together. Somewhere we both feel at home, and which doesn't have any bad memories."

I wrapped my arms around her and kissed the top of her head. "I'd love that."

She smiled impishly. "I love you."

"And I love you too." I closed my eyes and held her close, reveling in the feel of her. I couldn't believe I'd come so close to losing her.

Cookie twined beneath my legs and meowed. I bent and scooped her into our embrace, turning it into a group hug.

My family.

All those years when my family had been urging me to settle down, I hadn't realized just how amazing it could be to have someone to call my own. Now, happiness bubbled inside me every time I so much as thought of Summer.

She was mine, and one day, not too long from now, I'd marry her.

Summer Heaton had a nice ring to it.

I kissed her forehead. Perhaps I hadn't seen it all those years ago, but Summer was my destiny. I'd never let her go.

THE END

EXCERPT FROM THEN THERE WAS YOU

Katarina Hopa glanced at the messy surface of her desk and wished she'd thought to tidy up before meeting with her landlady. She was nervous enough about formally getting together for the first time since she'd rented the property she operated her bed and breakfast from. She didn't need the added worry that the stack of papers on her desk, cupboards, and floor might give Maureen Adler the impression she wasn't the competent businesswoman she pretended to be. She wanted to make a good impression.

Maureen sat opposite her, alternately sipping a latte from Café Oasis and pursing her lips. She looked distressed.

"Is everything okay?" Kat asked tentatively.

Maureen released a heavy sigh. "I'm afraid not, my dear."

Kat's stomach clenched with worry and she instinctively looked at the photograph beside her computer for comfort. Teddy's handsome face smiled out at her. She swallowed hard, pretending he was with her in this moment. He should have been. Running this beachside bed and breakfast had been their shared dream for when she retired from professional rally driving. But now he was gone, and she was on her own, trying to make sense of a world without him in it.

Maureen followed her gaze, and her face fell. Even though Maureen had barely known Teddy, he and Kat had honeymooned at the B&B when Maureen and her husband Andrew had run it, before Andrew had become too ill to continue managing the business.

"I don't know how you go on without him," Maureen said. "I dread the day I lose my Andrew."

Tears prickled the backs of Kat's eyes. "I know you do. Hopefully it doesn't happen anytime soon."

She wished she could tell Maureen that the loss became easier to deal with over time, but in her experience, it didn't. She felt the gaping hole that Teddy had left in her life every day. Even three years on, the ragged edges of her pain hadn't healed.

"About that." Maureen placed her coffee on the desk and folded her hands on her lap. "Andrew has taken a turn for the worse."

Kat felt a pang of sympathy. "I'm so sorry to hear it."

Maureen nodded in acknowledgement. "The thing is, I'm having trouble paying for the care that could give him a few more months—or even years, God willing."

Kat bit her lip. Was Maureen raising rent? Was that what this was about? Kat knew she paid less than the market value, but they had a deal. She'd done a lot of work on the property during the years she'd been managing the B&B. She'd renovated rooms out of her own pocket. Not many other tenants would do that.

"I've received a very generous offer on the property from a developer. He wants to build an exclusive resort in the place where Sanctuary currently stands."

Her words hit Kat with the impact of a sledgehammer. She felt blindsided.

"I didn't know you were planning to sell."

Maureen grimaced. "I've been holding out for as long as possible. You know I'd prefer to wait until you're able to afford to buy us out, but he approached me out of the blue and the money he's offering could make a massive difference in terms of Andrew's treatment."

Kat couldn't swallow past the lump in her throat. She couldn't ask Maureen not to sell when doing so might give her more time with her husband. Kat had ended up in her current financial situation—barely more than broke— because she'd poured all the money she had into trying to save her husband after the traffic crash that had eventually killed him and had left her scarred and emotionally broken.

"Have you already signed the papers?" she asked, her stomach knotted.

"No." Maureen's lips curved slightly upward, giving Kat the faintest trace of hope. "I can't afford to turn him down though. Not unless I get a counteroffer." She leaned forward and reached across the desk to clasp Kat's hand. "I don't care if you offer less than the developer. I'd rather you have the property than him. I told him I'd have an answer for him in two weeks. If you can put together an offer in that time, I'll accept it, as long as it's reasonable."

That trace of hope vanished. She doubted any bank in the country would allow her to take out a mortgage with them based on her current finances and her income history for the years after the accident. But she had to try.

"Thanks, Maureen." She squeezed the other woman's hand. "I appreciate you giving me a chance. I'll make an appointment with the bank to see if they're willing to work with me."

Maureen nodded. "I'm glad to hear it. I hope they do." She released Kat's hand and sipped her drink again. "I wish I didn't have to put you in this situation. It's not fair to you."

Kat sighed. "It's not fair to you either, but you have a chance to spend more time with Andrew. If someone had offered me the same when Teddy was dying, I'd have taken them up on it in an instant."

"I knew you'd understand." A weight seemed to have lifted from Maureen's shoulders. It had settled on Kat's. "Just so you know, the developer is intending to come for a look around on Monday. Apparently, the main reason he wants this property over any of the others along the coast is the access to the sea caves, beach, and the waterfall, so I imagine he wants to make sure he'd be getting his money's worth."

Kat frowned. She'd rather not have to see the man who was planning to take her home—and the future she was supposed to share with Teddy—away from her.

"Don't worry. You won't need to speak with him if you don't want to," Maureen said, reading her expression correctly. "I've given him a map so he can show himself around."

"Good." She might not see him anyway, if she was planning to visit the bank. They didn't have one in Haven Bay, so she'd have to go to a nearby town. She'd just have to cross her fingers that someone at the bank felt sorry enough for her to pull some strings. Otherwise, she was shit out of luck.

Sterling Knightley sank onto the lushly upholstered armchair positioned in front of the window of his high-rise apartment and took a moment to appreciate the view. From here, he could see most of Auckland's central business district, and beyond the buildings stretched the blue-grey of the sea.

He relaxed in the embrace of a chair that cost as much as a month's rent had where he'd grown up and closed his eyes against the flicker of memory of the dark, dank hole he'd been raised in. The place that had stolen his mother from him, thanks to an infection caused by the mold the landlord had refused to remove.

"Never again," he mouthed. The words had become his mantra in the years since. If they could have afforded a place like this—or even basic treatment for the infection—maybe his mum would still be alive today.

His phone rang, and he withdrew it from the pocket of his suit.

"Hello, Eli," he said, opening his eyes to gaze over the skyline again. Eli was his boss. But more than that, he was a friend who'd changed Sterling's life by taking a chance on him when no one else would.

"Hey." Eli's tone was brisk but warm. "How are things with the Haven Bay project?"

"It's coming along as planned," he replied. "I'll be leaving to check out the property in a few minutes, but it seems to be well situated and the owner is eager to sell—other than worrying about the tenant. The owner's husband is unwell and she's struggling with his medical bills." An unexpected benefit to their proposal. He hadn't known the woman was having difficulties when he reached out to her, but considering his own background, he liked the idea of making life easier for the couple and enabling them to get the necessary medical care.

"Sounds like you have everything under control."

"Of course." Sterling always had everything under control. It was in his nature. "Thank you for having faith in my idea."

Perhaps after more than a decade of friendship, he should understand that Eli would always have his back, but he never took his friend for granted. He knew more than most how vital it could be to have someone in his corner when he needed them, and Eli always was. Making this project shine would be Sterling's way of giving back to him and repaying the trust Eli had shown him over the years.

"I'm sure it will be brilliant," Eli said. "I'll check in with you later. Drive safe."

"I will. Bye." They ended the call and Sterling stood. With one final glance out the window, he strode through his apartment and collected his trunk from near the door. He only intended to be gone for the day, but he'd learned that business trips didn't always go according to plan—especially when negotiations were involved. Better to be prepared.

He left the apartment and locked the door. Next stop: Haven Bay.

ALSO BY ALEXA RIVERS

Destiny Falls

Stay With You

Come Back to You

Always Been Yours

Wish You Were Mine

Haven Bay

Then There Was You

Two of a Kind

Safe in His Arms

If Only You Knew

Pretend to Be Yours

Begin Again With You

Let Me Love You

Never Saw You Coming

Little Sky Romance

Accidentally Yours

From Now Until Forever

It Was Always You

Dreaming of You

Little Sky Romance Novellas

Midnight Kisses

Second Chance Christmas

Blue Collar Romance

A Place to Belong

ACKNOWLEDGMENTS

This book has been a long time coming, so thank you for bearing with me!

A massive thank you to everyone involved in creating *Wish You Were Mine*. Thank you to Shannon Passmore for the beautiful covers, and to Lindee Robinson, Megan Cooke and James Cooke for the stunning photograph. I love that it's a real couple on the cover of this book! It makes my heart warm!

Thank you to Kate Studer. Working with you has been invaluable to me—both on this project and all of our other collaborations. You help make my stories shine.

Thank you to Dinah for polishing the manuscript, and to Anne Victory for making sure the book was ready for the world.

Thank you to everyone who has read the Destiny Falls books, loved them, and waited patiently for more. I appreciate you sticking with me. You're the reason I keep writing.

XO

Alexa

ABOUT THE AUTHOR

Alexa Rivers writes about genuine characters living messy, imperfect lives and earning hard-won happily ever afters. Most of her books are set in small towns, and she lives in one of these herself. She shares a house with a neurotic dog and a husband who thinks he's hilarious. When she's not writing, Alexa enjoys travelling, baking cakes, eating said cakes, cuddling fluffy animals, drinking copious amounts of tea, and absorbing herself in fictional worlds.